the
leftovers

CASSANDRA PARKIN

Legend Press Ltd, 51 Gower Street, London, WC1E 6HJ
info@legendpress.co.uk | www.legendpress.co.uk

Contents © Cassandra Parkin 2021
The right of the above author to be identified as the author of this work has
been asserted in accordance with the Copyright, Designs and Patents Act
1988. British Library Cataloguing in Publication Data available.

Print ISBN 978-1-80031-0-087
Ebook ISBN 978-1-80031-0-094
Set in Times. Printing managed by Jellyfish Solutions Ltd
Cover design by Sarah Whittaker | www.whittakerbookdesign.com

Cassandra Parkin grew up in Hull, and now lives in East Yorkshire. Her debut novel *The Summer We All Ran Away* was published by Legend Press in 2013 and was shortlisted for the Amazon Rising Star Award. Her short story collection, *New World Fairy Tales* (Salt Publishing, 2011) was the winner of the 2011 Scott Prize for Short Stories. *The Beach Hut* was published in 2015, *Lily's House* in 2016, *The Winter's Child* in 2017, *Underwater Breathing* in 2018, *The Slaughter Man* in 2019, and *Soldier Boy* in 2020. Cassandra's work has been published in numerous magazines and anthologies.

Visit Cassandra at
cassandraparkin.wordpress.com
or follow her
@cassandrajaneuk

To darling H
Walking in your own time and space

Chapter One

Left

On the evening my brother and father die, I learn a curious lesson about time.

It's a warm, bright evening, and the four of us are sitting in the kitchen. Our bellies are pleasantly full of the takeaway meal we always share on the last night of our two-week shift. Frey had special fried rice, because he always does. Josh and I can have anything we want, but we've both caught Frey's habit of sameness, and it's good to have a favourite. So I had beef chow mein, and Josh had chicken curry and chips, and now everyone's faintly sleepy and reluctant to move.

The kitchen is peaceful and homely. The dishwasher's humming and splashing, and Frey has wiped down every inch of the dining table – top, sides and legs – with his slow, peaceful movements. Josh and I are drinking coffee. Frey has a cup of tea, sweet and milky. The curve of his fingers around his mug, the small murmurs in the back of his throat as he drinks it, tell me I've made it exactly to his liking, and I feel warm. Warmth inside me, from my simple accomplishment. Warmth against my neck from sunlight through glass. Warmth at my feet because Floss, lazy and content, has come to lie there, the shredded silk of her ears soft against my ankles.

It's a moment of unguarded happiness. A treasure I can revisit, like going to a museum to marvel at a way of life once lived. Something's tickling my thigh, rhythmic and regular.

"My phone's ringing," I say in surprise.

We're allowed to take personal phone calls. Linnea understands we have lives to live in the other two weeks when we're not here with her brother. We could probably go further than either of us ever do. We could slack off on our duties and scroll through newsfeeds, buy things we want but don't need, find words or set cartoon characters free or smash fruits to pieces. But we never do. First: while we could easily evade the cameras we know about, we both have an unshakeable conviction that there are other cameras, in other places, there to keep us honest. (We've never found these cameras, never even gone looking, but nonetheless we believe in them. You can't prove a negative, after all.)

The other reason is that we both genuinely love Frey.

I take out my phone, feel it shudder and jump against my palm. *Mother*, it says, six letters blazing a warning. I've often considered deleting her number, maybe even blocking it, but I can never quite make myself do it. I need to know she can't sneak up on me. I need to pretend that if she calls, I might see her name and choose not to answer.

"I have to take this," I say.

"It's okay," Josh says. "We're fine, aren't we, Frey?"

"I'm sorry." What I am is on high alert, terrified but also resentful. She never calls me. We have nothing to say to each other. Our small scraps of contact come only through my brother Noah, who loves her in spite of everything.

Noah. It must be to do with Noah.

"Don't be daft." Josh's smile belongs to the world I'm in now and not the one I'm about to enter. "We're off duty in two hours anyway. Go for it."

"I'll be quick," I say to Frey.

An outsider would look at Frey's face as he traces out the wood's grain with his fingertip and say, "He's not listening,

8

why bother?" Josh and I have learned to read Frey's small signals – the hesitation of a fingertip, the minute pause in the slow rhythm of his breath, the twitch at the corner of his mouth. We know that he's absolutely listening, that it's always worth bothering. Frey lives in a world of his own making. To come into Frey's presence is to share that world with him, and he's aware of everything we do while we're in it.

"Sorry," I say yet again, this time to Floss as I stand up, trying to spill her off my feet without disturbing her. She groans and stretches, claws clicking as she pads over to lean against Frey's leg. His hand creeps down to pet the dome of her head. We're all acutely attuned to Frey's emotional state, but Floss – being a dog, and unconcerned with human distractions – is by far the most skilled. She knows Frey's absorbing this small disruption to our evening, and would appreciate the small kindness of a warm, furry body.

People often resent Frey. "Nice work if you can get it," I heard a man say to his wife once as we guided Frey around the supermarket. They never see the effort Frey makes to make sense of a world that isn't built for him. He's in a constant battle with his own body, with the relentless assault on his senses. He longs for connection, but also finds it overwhelming. Frey is one of the hardest-working people I know. His work's only invisible if you're not looking properly.

I'm thinking about this, and about Floss's sweetness – a dog being kind to a distressed human as he tries to manage his own emotional temperature – as I go into the hall to take the call. I'm delaying the moment when I have to hear what's waiting for me. It will involve Noah, somehow. He's the only person in my life who's both important enough, and disruptive enough, to have prodded my mother into calling. Perhaps he's in hospital again. But then, it ought to be Dad calling – he's Noah's primary carer and his next of kin.

Unless Noah's sneaked away from Dad and gone to see her. It's the sort of thing he might do, especially if he's managed to hide his tablets. Life with Noah is filled with wild elaborations, kinetic energy looking for an outlet. Stealing a car and driving for a few hours would be nothing to him.

I have to speak to my mother. I feel suddenly empty and terrified, despite my full belly. Maybe Noah's hurt Dad somehow (even in the depths of his mania, Noah is still basically a nice person who tries to do no harm, but there's always the possibility of a frantic fight back against restraint, a wild refusal to accept medication). Maybe that's why she's calling. Maybe it's Dad who's in trouble. And if it's Dad, then Noah's on his own...

In the tiny fraction of silence before the words arrive, I think, *At least it's happened right at shift change. But if it's bad, it might take longer than two weeks, I might have to take emergency leave. Damn it...*

"Hello?" I say. "Are you there?" My voice isn't quavering or tentative. I'm firm and confident. I'm braced and ready.

"Could I speak to Callie Taggart, please?"

Not my mother, but a stranger. Not a friend, not a neighbour; they'd sound anxious, maybe a little triumphant. And besides, my mother wouldn't speak to her neighbours, has never had any friends. This woman is calm and professional, someone who's used to dealing with bad news and sharing it compassionately but without hesitation. It's a skill I learned myself. The first few times you have to give bad news, you feel as if you yourself might die of it. After that, it gets easier.

Something's happened to my mother, then.

"Speaking," I say.

"Ms Taggart, my name's PC Sarah Henderson. I'm sorry to say I have some very bad news."

When they say 'very bad news' – no qualifications or modifiers, no 'I'm calling from the hospital but there's no need to panic', not even 'you need to prepare yourself for a bad outcome' – it means death. She's going to tell me my mother is dead.

Death forces you to confront the truth about the way we love. "Love is blind," we say to each other, "love is infinite,

I couldn't possibly love one of you more than the other." The truth is that Death is blind and Death is infinite and Death loves all of us equally. Love is the literal definition of having a favourite. In the moment before the police officer speaks, I find time to be grateful. *Thank you, Death,* I think, *thank you for not coming for Noah or Dad. Thank you for choosing her instead. You can have our mother, that's fine. Thank you for leaving me Noah and Dad.*

"Tell me," I say. "I'm ready."

Then, in the background of the phone call, there's a low sobbing moan that tingles against the back of my neck, as if a dog is licking me there, a dog that's nothing like our lovely, gentle Floss but some sort of awful hellhound. A creature come to steal away something precious. My mother, despairing.

All right, then. All right. If you must, you can take Dad. But leave Noah. If you're going to make me choose then I have to choose Noah. Dad will understand. Please, Death, let it be Dad. I can stand to lose Dad if I've still got Noah. I'll find a way to make it all work. I can't afford to give him what Frey's got but I'll look again at sheltered housing, I'll see what I can do. Just let me keep Noah. Let me keep him.

"It's about your dad," PC Henderson says.

Thank you, Death, thank you thank you thank you. You're a thief and a disruptor, but at least you've spared—

"And your brother Noah."

No, not my brother, he's not well but he's a gentle soul, you can't have him, not my Noah. But what if it was one of those times where he thinks Dad is trying to hurt me what if it's one of those times where he thinks he has to escape what if Dad had to do something to keep him safe and Noah misinterpreted it and Noah, oh Noah, you'd never survive in prison, even if they let you go to a secure hospital that would kill you, what if they try and take you away from me how am I going to make it all work? Please don't take me away from Frey—

"There's been a—"

Then there's a strange, shuffling sound, a squawk of

surprise and a rattle and clatter, a heavy intake of breath and a new voice, which is also a voice I have known all my life, and still hear sometimes in my dreams, a voice that makes me think of being hungry and alone, rasps against my ear.

"They're dead, Callie. They're dead. Both of them. They've been in a car accident and they're both dead."

"No," I say.

"Yes. Yes. There's no mistake. They're dead, they're gone, it's true. It's just us left, Callie. Just me and you. We're the only ones left. Oh God, what am I going to do now? Noah, my darling boy…"

The wail and shudder of my mother's grief scratches sharply at my spine. That old, rotten, childish thought. *Why do you love Noah and not me?*

Another rustle and scrape. My mother's howls grow a little more distant, and then the unhinged sound coming out of her suddenly drops, as if someone has closed a door on a room. Then the police officer begins talking again, with a terrible steadiness, a dreadful honesty. Her kindness, and in the background, my mother's abandoned shrieks.

I make myself hear each word. I make myself say the words that need saying, practical things like "Was there anyone else involved?" and "Are you absolutely sure it's them?" and small courtesies like "Yes, I understand" and even "Thank you", interspersed with moments when I press my hand to my mouth and bite down until I feel the small bones beneath the skin, because I will not, will not scream; I will not, will not hurt Frey.

"I'm so very sorry to have to tell you all this. Is there someone there with you?"

"Yes."

"That's good. Now, you might not feel it yet, but you'll be in shock. Sit down now, maybe have a cup of sweet tea. Can you put me on the phone to whoever's with you?"

"No." My refusal is instinctive, an urge to keep what's just happened to me safely within its own confines. "No, it's all right, you don't need to do it. I'll tell them."

"All right, but make sure they look after you. I'm sure you'll have questions later, when you've had a bit of time to process. I'm a family liaison officer, so it's my job to answer your questions. I've left a card with your mum that has all my details on, and I'll text the same details over to you on this number."

"Thank you," I say. "That's really thoughtful." I sound as if I'm in control, as if there's something for me to do other than simply endure the pain. I sound as if I'm dealing with something that can be fixed. I can hear Josh murmuring to Frey in the kitchen, the silent pauses for Frey's small, occasional gestures of reply.

Oh, God. Dad and Noah. Both of them, gone.

"Hey." Josh is suddenly in the hall beside me, which means Frey is alone, and I want to push Josh away but I can't, I don't have the strength to do anything other than stand here and not fall apart. "Callie. Are you all right?" He's stroking my hair, petting me the way he pets Floss, kind and comforting. "What's happened?"

"My dad," I whisper. "My brother."

"I thought it must be. Is Noah sick again?"

"Yes. No. Sort of. I don't want to – Frey. We can't leave him…"

"He's all right, he's drinking his tea. I told him you needed me, he'll understand, you know he'll understand, he can last for a minute. It's all right, take a minute. Just a minute. I've got you."

So we stand in the hallway and Josh holds me while I shudder and whimper and swallow down and press back and force my grief into a box inside me. And when that minute is done, we go into the kitchen and find Frey still as stone, fingers clutching the edges of the table, eyes closed, but he's holding on, holding on and waiting, trusting that Josh will keep his word and it will be only for a minute that we have left him entirely alone and gone elsewhere, Floss pressed anxiously against his leg and whimpering a little, and when he hears us coming back into the kitchen the tension flows out of him like water and he smiles at the table and lets his fingers resume their slow, steady tracing of the grain of the wood, and oh my God, how can this kitchen still be standing, how can everything be so *normal* when my whole world has just—

No, I think, a blink of something that could be salvation or could be denial. *Half of my world. Only half. I still have Frey. At least Death didn't take Frey.*

"Thanks, Frey," Josh says. "You're a star. Callie's had some bad news, her brother's not well. Okay, time to pick what's going on the TV. Do you want to watch a programme? Or do you want to play *Minecraft*?"

Frey doesn't move, doesn't look at us, certainly doesn't speak, but we can see him considering, the decision taking shape inside the labyrinth of his skull. After a minute, he stands up, moves towards the living room, picks up his game controller and sits in his spot on the sofa. This transition used to take minutes, Frey stopping every few steps to turn slowly around, check we were coming with him, but now he goes with trusting confidence from one room to another, not looking back. This freedom is a gift we've given him. His trust is one he's given us.

I take my place on the sofa, Josh on Frey's left and me to the right, Floss sprawled across Frey's feet. There's a delicate tremor beginning in the core of me, something I'm afraid Frey will feel and be made uneasy by. I force myself to keep still.

Dad and Noah are dead, their bodies pulled from the wreck of their car after it went over the edge of the cliff road in the town where my mother lives. Their deaths are like a drop of ink soaking into soft paper, radiating outwards. There were long hours today when the news was still travelling towards me, but had not yet arrived.

This, then, is the curious truth about time: its flow is not constant. It can be stemmed and diverted. And if you work hard enough, you can make it stand still. Not everywhere, not for everyone, but enough to make a difference, enough to keep you safe. And if I'm careful – if I hold the news still and quiet in my heart – I'll be able to stop time. As long as the ink doesn't touch every part of the paper, there will be two realities: the larger one where Dad and Noah are dead; and this smaller, more intimate world where they are still alive. No one around me knows it, but I've stopped time, and now I can pivot backwards and forwards over the fulcrum of their ending.

This is a story about time. I need you to understand this.

It's hard, it's taking everything I have to keep time frozen in the moment *before,* when they were still alive and waiting for me to come home, but I can do it for a little longer. In two hours, the others will arrive and Josh and I will hand over our care of Frey, get into our cars and leave for two weeks. In two hours, I'll have to choose which house to go to: the one left empty by Dad and Noah, or the one that's bursting at the seams with my mother and her newly fledged grief.

Chapter Two

Reconstruction (1)

I know how this must look, but I swear to you, I'm not going to see my mother. I'm doing what I'm supposed to do on shift-change day, which is to go home to Dad and Noah. And since they're not to be found in the usual place, I'm improvising. Right now, our routes have converged. Maybe if I go fast enough, I'll glimpse their ghosts. Here's how it must have happened:

They've been alone together for two weeks, but going out and enjoying themselves too. They'll definitely have prioritised having a nice time over keeping the house clean, because that's a trade-off they always make, each of them encouraging the other. But they'll also have done their traditional guilty purge of what they consider to be all of the accumulated filth of the last fortnight. (Since I started working for Frey, I've considerably reset my understanding of what 'clean' really looks like. My first job on coming home is always to clean everything up properly, but it's nice to know they will have at least tried.) They'll be loose and happy, ready for a little fun. What time will they set off? I wind everything backwards, back to the night before.

Cocooned by the sedative qualities of his meds, Noah

will have been in bed by ten and barely stirred. Dad will have woken him, with some difficulty, at about nine. After breakfast, they'll have sat for a while, so Noah could gather his strength. (He hates the sleepiness of medicated life, hates the way it steals his energy. He fights it every step of the way, forcing himself into a semblance of the person he describes as 'real' and 'normal', the person his psychiatrist describes as 'dangerously disconnected from reality' and 'prone to impulsive and potentially harmful decisions'.) By eleven o'clock, they'll have started their cleaning. By twelve, they'll have finished it.

Clothes have always been important to Noah, who loves transformations. One of the signs that he's about to enter another period of illness (a sign I've never dared tell him about, in case he stops doing it) is a sudden preoccupation with accessories. He'll come down to breakfast wearing a trilby hat along with his striped pyjamas and Noel Coward dressing gown. He'll shake cornflakes into his bowl and sit down at the table, pretending everything's normal even though he can't hide the glee, the giddiness that's begun with hats and will soon spiral into mad elaborations of talking walls, talking trees, talking animals, talking everything, the messages joyous at first before turning darker, more alarming. He'll join us for lunch with a spurt of excited chatter (he's had a message from the silver birch at the end of the street, apparently the weather's going to be perfect today) and a long stack of slender silver bangles coiling up his left arm. In this reconstruction, I dress Noah in his favourite outfit, topped with the hat bought for him by a friend from his support group: a soft felt bowler with a screw-in light bulb on top. In my vision, the light bulb gleams like a beacon.

I'm drifting across the lanes, losing my sense of where I am. My foot's pressing too hard on the accelerator, taking my speed up towards a hundred. I straighten the car up and lift my foot and force my hands to relax.

So, then. Time for lunch. Noah loves fast food, craves salt and fat even though it makes his weight gain worse, and Dad loves to indulge him. When I'm there, I make them stick to food that's vaguely nutritious, so this is their last chance for two weeks. They get into the car. Noah can drive in the sense that he has the skill set, once took and passed his test, but he can't drive in any way that's legally allowed. So, Dad is driving, as always.

They go to the drive-through, because Noah loves the food but dislikes the bright lights and harsh disinfectant scent. He's never said anything, but I know what it reminds him of. They collect their order, drive to the river so they can sit and watch the water roll by as they eat. Noah has an outsized stack of burgers with everything on them, a glut of over-salted fries, a bucket-sized milkshake. I'm giving him everything he loves because I know this will be his last meal, but they wouldn't have known that, neither of them would. There's a shadow over the day but they can't see it, they're bathed in glorious sunshine. Noah tells Dad a joke, forcing his brain and his mouth to grind out the words even though thinking is hard for him thanks to the chemical sludge. Dad waits patiently, resists the urge to help Noah out when he stutters or loses his thread, laughs at the punchline.

The trip is Noah's idea, but Dad goes along with it. No carer's perfect, and one of Dad's failings is his excessive willingness to fall in with Noah's schemes. When Noah is well, balanced, his plans are masterclasses in bravura improvisation. ("Let's go to the coast," he'll say, one dull April evening, "and buy takeaway junk and eat it on an empty beach." And two hours later, there we'll be, the three of us alone under the stars.) The trick with Noah is to recognise when the balance is starting to tip. Dad would say I'm too cautious, too closed off to joy.

I would say that Dad is too unwary, too prone to missing the danger. I'd give anything to have been wrong.

Dad looks at the clock. He knows I'll be back about nine in the evening. It's now just after one. Three hours to drive to where Noah wants to go, and three hours back. It's a ridiculous ratio, six hours in a car for a two-hour visit, but Noah never thinks like that, doesn't count the cost of anything. Dad smiles and sighs and thinks of the work he's supposed to be getting done (the arrangement is called 'working from home', but everyone at the firm knows this means he's putting in odd hours in early mornings and late evenings, fitting in around the vagaries of Noah's needs).

Maybe he tries to talk Noah out of it, persuade him that it's too late, they should have left after breakfast. Maybe he gives in straight away. Which would make them both the happiest? For Dad to argue a little, I think. Noah always enjoys sparring.

The day is bright and clear but not too hot. No rain on the horizon. Lovely driving weather. Noah winds the window down so he can surf the currents of air with his hand, feel the invisible shape of their passage. Perhaps he's dreaming of a future where he can take the wheel once more, burn through the day without limits or limitations. Does he know it will never happen for him? Does he sense that his hourglass has almost run out?

They have a good run of it. They stop once for petrol, and Noah chooses snacks while Dad fills the car. Noah tries to resist his cravings. Like many psychiatric patients, the hunger and the weight gain are among his most loathed side effects. But today is his last day, and I decide that some kindly angel has whispered in his ear, told him to enjoy it to the full. He buys sweets and crisps, a tall bottle of full-sugar Coke, and the woman who serves him isn't cruel or judgemental, she just smiles and tells him to enjoy the rest of his day. I stop too, so I can fill the nooks and crannies of my bag and coat with chocolate and sugar and salt. I'm not going to see my mother,

I swear I'm not, but just the thought of being near her compels me to stock up on provisions, just in case.

The motorway's clear and empty. Noah told me once that he sometimes dreams of driving. "Just a full tank and an empty road," he said, "that's the whole dream. I know it doesn't sound like much but I'm so happy in this dream, tearing through the air, like flying…" I was holding his hand in a hospital bay, flimsy curtains flapping and twitching, other people's emergencies unfolding behind them. At least Noah will never have to be there again, never have to survive another period where his brain lets him down.

I leave the motorway at the same place they did, drive down dual carriageways and then back roads that the trees are trying to turn into green tunnels. I wind down the window to let in the bloom of salt and pollen. Frey's home is surrounded by rich red hills and grass so green it looks Photoshopped, but on the long, narrow peninsula of land where my mother lives you can never be more than fifteen miles from the sea, and it follows you everywhere. There's a sense of lightness, of flight and floating. Perhaps that's what called to Noah. He once woke me in the dead of night to tell me he'd just realised he could fly, and did I want to see? The serene knowledge in his face made me think of saints, of miracles, and for a moment, I'd really believed he could do it.

I skim the edges of the town. It feels dangerous to come here, as if my mother might be anywhere, anywhere at all, hiding behind trees, crouched between parked cars, ready to leap out at me and accuse me of – actually, what would she accuse me of? She's the one in the wrong. I tried to make her love me, my God, how I tried, but it was never enough. If she'd loved me, then surely I wouldn't have ended up here, cowering at the base of this short hill with a bag full of chocolate and dirty laundry, trying to gather my strength as if it's me and not the car that will have to make the climb. Surely Noah and Dad would still be—

I haven't come to see her. I won't see her. I make time roll back to the moment when Dad and Noah were here too.

They've enjoyed their drive, they're enjoying the music they've put on and the snacks they've eaten and the companionship they've shared. They're not quite ready for the beach yet. So one of them says, "Shall we drive round the cliffs first?" I guide my car around the tight angle of the turn, imagine Dad doing the same a few hours earlier. Maybe there's a small grinding beneath his hands, the first sign that something's not quite right. Maybe he's been noticing it all the way here, nothing too alarming, just the kind of change that makes you hesitate and think, *that's new.* The sort of miniature strangeness you can put down to a difference in the road surface or an unplanned change of speed. Nothing to frighten, nothing to bring you over to the hard shoulder to make a hasty phone call to a recovery service. Just a little sensation of metal moving in a way that's subtly out of alignment.

Perhaps Dad pauses and glances at Noah. Asks him, "Did you feel that? Did that sound right to you?" And Noah, who is always an optimist even when he's well, replies, "Nope, didn't hear anything," or maybe, "You starting to hear things? Is this where I get it from?" or perhaps, "Yeah, a little bit, but it's nothing. Probably just gravel in one of the tyres. Don't worry about it."

Or maybe there's nothing there at all.

If the car gave out some small signal of distress, then Dad's last thoughts would have been of guilt and regret, that he'd been given an opportunity for escape and missed it, that he'd failed them both. I want there to have been nothing, but I can't shake the belief that I'm travelling through time, and this is not a fantasy but a reconstruction.

No. I'm in charge here. There will be no warning; the thought of it is too painful. I run the film again in my mind, imagine the moment when they finally commit.

Dad to Noah: "Still want to drive round the cliff?"

And Noah to Dad: "Yeah, why not?"

And as Dad turns the wheel, there it is again, that small, wrong sound, that small, wrong vibration—

There's no escaping it, then. There is a warning, but they miss it. The best I can hope for is that it's a small incident, something they instantly dismiss. Maybe something distracts them. A dog dashes out in front of them and Dad has to brake to avoid hitting it. Its owner scurries after it, giving them one apologetic glance. Dad, who is kind, smiles understandingly. Later on, the owner will see the report in the newspaper and maybe walk up to look at the place where it happened. Maybe she'll wonder if the car that went over the cliff was driven by the kind man who didn't run over her dog. Whether she makes the connection or not, Dad and Noah are thinking about the dog and not the car as they roar up the short, steep hill to the cliff road. They're thinking about the dog and they're thinking about the sea, and maybe Noah is thinking about going to see our mother afterwards, the look on her face when he surprises her, the smile she saves for him and has never given to me. (I shake this thought off impatiently. I don't want her there for Noah's last moments.)

Under two minutes left. It doesn't take long to drive around the headland. Perhaps I'll stay here, keep them with me a little longer. There's no need to rush. The cliff road is patient; the drop down to the rocks below will wait.

I'd like to linger, but there's a car behind me and I'm in the way. My knees shake as I let the clutch in, and the engine stalls as I bring it up too quickly. I try again, rev the engine far more than it needs, feel the car jump and shudder. The car behind me hangs a courteous ten feet back, even though I'm being annoying. Perhaps the driver thinks I'm still learning. Up the hill. Past the houses. Another minute and I'll be there, at the spot where they—

There's a barrier across the road, a festival of red and blue lights from parked patrol cars, incongruously like a party.

Noah always loved parties. The car behind me is already turning around, a swift, neat three-point turn and a flicker of tail lights as it disappears back the way we came. I don't want Dad and Noah on the news, their stories blazed across the airwaves between the progress of a planned housing development and the highlights from an agricultural show. Another finger of ink spreading outwards, another shrinking of the place where time is stopped. I know the police won't let me through, but I wind down the window anyway.

"Road's closed," the officer says. "Where were you trying to get to?"

"I wanted to drive round the point," I say. They're the first words I've said for hours. I thought my voice might break, but I only sound tired.

"It's going to be closed until at least mid-morning tomorrow, I'm afraid."

I wait for more, strangely eager to hear how Dad and Noah will be reported, but there's no more. There's no gleam of excitement in the man's face; this is just one more night on the job. I want to tell him that I know how it goes, I'm a nurse, I've picked up body parts and mopped up blood too, but that would just sound weird. He doesn't know that I already know. He doesn't know who I am.

"So you need to turn around," the officer says firmly, and I realise I've zoned out again, my foot revving against the accelerator. Fumes billow around his face. "You can find your way across town to the seafront. Follow the signs to the beaches. Mind how you go, now."

I told you I wasn't going to my mother, and that's still true. I'm here for Noah and Dad. But now I can't reach them, and I'm so, so tired, and I don't know where else to go, what else to do.

My mother's house is full of windows. If you stand in the street you can peer straight through her living room and into the bay beyond. If you're inside, you can see straight down the street. This is how she spots me before I've even left the car, how she's standing in the road and waiting for me. It can't be that she was expecting me. I didn't mean to come myself. There's no way she could have known.

She holds her arms out to me and clutches me against her, mumbling against my hair, and I feel all the tension come out of me in a long shudder, and then we're sitting together on the tarmac and I'm sobbing and quivering and letting her hold me because we are still family, after all, there's still something there between us that we can call on when there's nothing else left. But that's all that's happening here; two people making do with whatever's left. Because even as she holds me and pets my hair, I know in my bones that my mother doesn't love me. She never has. My mother would have gladly sent me over the cliff, and saved Noah.

Chapter Three

Frey

How can I show you Frey in a way that does justice to him? I could tell you his diagnosis, but what would that tell you? I read once that the human brain is the most complex structure, bar none, anywhere in the known universe. Our heads hold as many neural connections as the Milky Way has stars. "Typical," we say, "atypical, a classic case, a textbook example, an unusual presentation, a variant form." As if we're not all typical in our difference. As if it's possible to reduce the endless convergences and divergences of our natures to a single phrase.

So, this is Frey:

Frey is an adult man. He is twenty-four years old, but looks younger. He's not a child in a man's body, or an otherworldly elven creature, or a wistful android, or a sweet, misguided alien. He's not a pet or a well-trained animal, except in the sense that we're all animals. It's easy to infantilise difference, especially the different ones who are quiet and good-natured, like Frey. (In the supermarket, Josh and I regularly have to stop people dabbing and stroking at Frey like a dog, speaking to him in a sweet, soft baby voice and telling him how good he is, even though Frey's taller than they are. It's strange that they understand that they can't pet Floss, but not that they also can't pet the man who depends on her.) He's a grown human, no more and certainly no less.

Frey looks like his mother Ana and his sister Linnea, but he has his father Miles's eyes and hairline. He doesn't enjoy haircuts, but tolerates them for the sake of getting it out of his eyes. We've experimented with bobbles and scrunchies and man buns to stretch the time between trims. But Frey dislikes the traction on his scalp, and the fledgling sprout of hair on top of his head made him look like an old lady's lapdog, so we threw the bobbles away and got out the clippers. The lapdog look was my concern, not Frey's. He checks the mirror to make sure he's clean, but as far as I can tell, he has no personal vanity.

He likes loose, comfortable clothes, well-washed and thoroughly softened. New items are laundered at least three times before he'll put them on. He has a library of hoodies, T-shirts, sweatshirts and tracksuit bottoms, spending at least ten minutes each morning choosing the day's clothes. It's hard to say if he has favourites and not-favourites, if he has some rotation schedule in his head, or if he simply enjoys the ritual of peering into his wardrobe, handling the garments he finds in there. Frey can dress himself but because we leave him alone while he's doing so, he rushes through the process, scrabbling socks onto his feet, leaving hoods tucked awkwardly inside the neckline. The first job to be done when Frey opens the door and smiles down at his feet on discovering Josh or me outside, exactly as promised, is to neaten Frey into comfort. We untuck hoods, lay them flat against his shoulder blades. We adjust cuffs and waistbands. We sit him on the bed and straighten his socks.

Frey brings a deep and consuming enjoyment to a small number of foods. He greets each jacket potato with cheese, each trio of sausages, peas and mash, each ham sandwich, each bowl of takeaway special fried rice (his unfailing Saturday night treat) with the profound pleasure of a man meeting an old friend. We have a two-week rotating menu, with one night a fortnight set aside for showing Frey a new food and encouraging him to taste it. So far he's politely declined any of the new choices we've offered him, preferring the fish-finger sandwich and oven chips we make as a backup. The others have apparently had success with a baked salmon fillet. Josh and I have decided not to add this to Frey's menu while we're with him: we asked him about it, and he looked away and down, which we've learned to interpret as a polite 'No, thank you'. Sometimes I worry that we're cheating him of something he'd enjoy. Sometimes I worry that he's only eating the salmon because he doesn't want to hurt the feelings of the others. Sometimes I wonder if their success and our failure is a sign that they have a stronger bond with Frey, or that we do. Sometimes I wonder if I'll ever know the answers.

Frey can make simple meals, such as garlicky buttered pasta, ham rolls, and toasted sandwiches. He's particularly skilled at breakfast, effortlessly co-ordinating the browning of the toast with the boiling of the kettle and the brewing of the tea, so the toaster flings out its slices just as he sets the kettle down after pouring the tea onto the teabag, and the last smear of jam goes on as his drink reaches its ideal strength. Watching Frey make his breakfast is as beautiful and mysterious as watching a tea ceremony.

Frey is independent in his personal care. He can take himself to the toilet, can wash himself from head to toe, is always immaculately clean. He dislikes baths, although there's one in his bathroom and we clean it daily, but he enjoys the shower. To prevent him from becoming too absorbed by the tumble of hot water, Linnea has fitted an egg timer to the shower door. Frey understands the purpose of this egg timer and can be utterly relied upon to turn it over just before getting in, and to get out as soon as the last grain falls.

Frey is always listening. He doesn't look as if he's paying attention, but he is. If Josh checks his phone and says to me, "That Amazon parcel's eight stops away," Frey will continue doing whatever he's doing with no pause or hesitation. But half an hour later, we'll find him standing in the hallway, braced for the knock at the door, the small disturbance in the peace of his house. If I tell Josh that the tap in my bathroom's leaking, Josh will go to the cupboard where the tools are kept (I should learn to change the washer myself, but Josh can do it and I can't, and we can't leave Frey alone while he teaches me, and Frey finds the sight of the sink being taken partially to pieces too horrifying to look at) and find Frey has opened the cupboard, taken out the toolbox and placed it on the floor.

Frey enjoys clocks and calendars. Each room holds at least one calendar, at least two clocks. If a clock loses its place for some reason (a power cut, a failed battery, or – in the case of the Nixie clock Josh bought him for Christmas – just a tendency to lose a couple of minutes from time to time), Frey becomes distressed, unable to settle or concentrate. Josh and I have become experts at spotting which clock is out of line, and resetting them. Afterwards, Frey spends at least half an hour going from room to room, smiling when he finds that the mechanisms of his day are once more in alignment. There are set times for each activity, set days of the week for each milestone event. Frey understands and will tolerate a certain amount of disruption (parcels brought to the door, men and women coming into the house to repair it, post that arrives either earlier or later than usual, or sometimes not at all), but too many of these events in short succession leave him distressed and anxious, unable to eat or touch anything. Living with Frey means accepting the slow, steady rhythm of a monastery.

Here are the things Frey finds difficult:

Frey struggles with disorder, and with dirt as a form of disorder. For Frey, the natural condition of the universe is to be clean and still. When new possessions come into the house, Frey takes some time fitting them into the spot he considers appropriate. Sometimes the placements make sense – groceries in the spaces left by what they're replacing, a new building kit from Linnea in the cupboard with the other kits. Sometimes they seem utterly opaque. Once, his new trainers spent two months at opposite ends of the mantelpiece, like ornaments. The trainers were a gift from Miles, and we wondered if Frey considered them too special to use, or if he disliked them but didn't want to hurt Miles's feelings by not wearing them. Then, after eight weeks on the mantelpiece, they suddenly came down again and entered Frey's library of footwear.

Order and cleanliness are particularly important to him in the kitchen and the bathroom. If any part of the kitchen is unclean in some way – a smear of butter on the edge of the sink, a scatter of crumbs by the side of the breadboard, a tomato stain on a cupboard door – he'll be unable to use anything in it. If he's hungry, he will stay hungry. If he's thirsty, he will stay thirsty. If he needs to use the bathroom and the bathroom has not been cleaned since the last time, he will wet and soil himself. Josh and I haven't personally seen this happen, but Linnea's vivid description of his time in the residential home ensures we always, always go into Frey's bathroom after he's used it and wipe everything down.

Frey has an intense fear of touching certain raw foodstuffs, even if they're part of a meal he loves. Some examples: he will chop garlic, but will not open a tin of tomatoes. He will peel wet ham from the packet and lay it on the bread, but will not grate cheese. He will handle onions with their brown skins on, but not peel or cut them. Josh and I have long since given up trying to unravel the logic behind these prohibitions, which have the holy weight of a religious taboo.

Frey likes to clean, but only once Josh or I have already cleaned everything for him.

Frey lives in quiet and utter terror of abandonment, his own personal legacy from the long months of lockdown. When he came back home, he couldn't be left for an instant, had to have eyes on someone the whole time. Often, he would wet himself in fear. Left alone, he would simply shut down, retreating into some dark, unreachable place in his own head. Now, Frey has reintegrated the notion of privacy in the bathroom and while dressing, but for showers and getting dressed, one of us must wait outside the door and tap on it every thirty seconds, so Frey knows we're still there.

At night, he mostly accepts Floss beside his bed as a substitute for our presence. But sometimes, still, he taps the wall beside his bed and waits, tense and frightened, for a response. At Linnea's instruction, we initially try tapping back. If he taps again, we tap back again, louder and longer. If he taps a third time, whoever is in the bedroom next to Frey's gets out of bed and goes to see him. To begin with, Frey tapped for us every night, almost every hour, and Josh and I alternated rooms. This is one of the reasons why there are two of us.

(The tapping has diminished and diminished over time, so that now, a night when Frey taps out his secret message is a surprise. It's so rare now that Josh and I don't bother swapping any more, and the room next to Frey's has become mine. I know from the logbooks we keep, along with the others, that Frey stopped regularly tapping for us several weeks before he stopped tapping for them. I know you'll think I'm petty for being so pleased about this, but I can't help it.)

Frey, like any of us, has his passions and his pleasures. He adores jigsaws, and his knack for completing them borders on the uncanny. Watching Frey effortlessly resolve a puzzle consisting entirely of – for example – thousands of blueberries tumbled in a heap, or a single sheep in dazzling close-up with the entire image made from the texture of its fleece, is enough to make you believe in witchcraft. Josh and I are no possible help in completing them, but he likes us to pass him the pieces, one by one. He never returns a piece for later; he simply lays it in its spot on the puzzle mat. I've never yet seen him place a piece wrongly.

Frey likes to colour in – the more complex the design, the better. He uses only colouring pencils; the wetness of paint, the waxiness of crayons, the crumbly smoothness of pastels, the squeak of felt tips all repulse him. His work is careful and precise. He uses varied pressure and feathery strokes to create shade and texture, or adds dots and swirls to make quirky, folksy little patterns. He will adorn the designs of others but not draw for himself, no matter how much we encourage him. He is adept at construction kits of all kinds.

Frey likes to make bread, something he only chooses to do with me. The first time he saw me do it (watching from the corners of his eyes while also colouring in a mandala), I didn't realise he was watching, although he greeted the fresh bread at teatime with quiet pleasure. The second time, he stood up and wandered past me to go to the bathroom, then wandered back again, then gave up all pretence of having somewhere to go and simply walked up and down behind me to see the dough being formed. When I invited him to try, he looked down and away, returned to the safety of his colouring. 'No, thank you.' It took me three months to coax him into that first, frightened touch of the dough. Three months after that, and he joins me at the worktop as soon as the dough loses its stickiness, taking over the kneading, knocking it back like a pro before its second proving. Now we make bread every Thursday afternoon. Josh uses bread-making time to take Floss for an extra-long walk over the hills, so everyone gets something out of the new arrangement.

(Here's a pitiful confession for you: for a short, shameful time, I debated not telling the others about this. In the end, I did tell them. Partly because it would be mean and unfair to keep Frey from a potential source of joy. But mostly because Linnea would eventually see us on the cameras and would ask the others why they never tried bread-making with him, and then the whole story would come out. I wonder if they had the same dilemma about the salmon. But the cameras keep us all honest, and as it turns out, Frey doesn't like to make bread with the others.)

Frey plays *Minecraft* with Josh, watching each other in their faint reflections on the screen, the closest Frey comes to eye contact. (It's thrilling to see, but also makes me a tiny bit jealous. I wonder if Josh feels the same about the bread.) Their creations are titanic, almost frightening, like the castle he's building in the side of a rocky mountain, or the underground railway that leads from the grasslands biome to the jungle and takes twenty-three minutes to ride from end to end.

On the evenings when we're not playing *Minecraft*, Frey sometimes chooses to watch television. He enjoys animal-rescue shows (Josh calls this kind of programme '*Wonder Pets* for adults', and Frey seems to know what this means). He likes soothing afternoon-type programming where objects are rescued and restored in some way, or houses are transformed from wrecks into cosy living spaces. He likes episodes one, twenty-five, twenty-six, twenty-eight and thirty of *Breaking Bad*.

Frey doesn't speak, and almost never vocalises. Sometimes I wake in the night to hear a mumble from the other side of the wall, as Frey turns over, rearranges his bedding, then returns to slumber. Awake, he's almost silent. He occasionally murmurs contentedly when he's particularly pleased by his food. Sometimes when watching *Breaking Bad*, he makes a sharp gasp of satisfaction. These are generally connected to Walter and Jesse working in the laboratory, and Josh and I have wondered if this is because he's thinking of his sister Linnea, of her work in Stockholm.

There's no physical, functional reason for Frey's lack of speech. He's simply never spoken a word. As a baby, he cried; as a toddler, he babbled, then fell silent. I sometimes think of the legend about the Borneo orangutans, who can speak but choose not to, in case we put them to work. This is a dangerous line of thinking – Frey's an adult human male, not a pet, not an animal – and I actively make myself stop following it.

Frey fears the outside world. He ventures into it once a week, when we go to the supermarket. This is his only regular contact with the outside, and it takes a lot out of him. When he returns to the house, the weight that falls off his shoulders is so palpable I think I might find it on the floor. On grocery shop days, he goes to bed two hours earlier than usual, and is asleep almost instantly. We do this even though Frey hates it because Linnea insists, because she says there'll be times when he has no choice but to leave the house, and he needs to build up a tolerance to it. Frey has never been into the garden, has never sat beneath the pergola where the honeysuckle pours out its perfume, never wandered to the wall and leaned against warm stone to admire the slow wanderings of faraway cows. His skin is very pale, and we worry about his Vitamin D intake.

(Sometimes I wonder if Frey sees through Linnea's ruse about the groceries. He's aware that clothes and shoes and jigsaws can be delivered to the door. It's not that much of a leap to imagine groceries arriving in the same way. Maybe he's seen other houses in the street getting deliveries. Maybe he's even worked out that Josh or I could go to the supermarket alone, while the other one stays with him. I wonder if Frey goes along with it because he loves Linnea. I try never to assume anything with Frey, who could know much or almost nothing, but who hasn't yet stopped surprising me.)

Generally speaking, Frey favours silence, but he does occasionally play music. He likes most songs by Elvis, an album called *Fisherman's Woman* by an Icelandic singer called Emilíana Torrini, and Rimsky-Korsakov's *Flight of the Bumblebee*. The stereo system's wired into every room in the house, and when Josh and I hear music, we know it's a sign that Frey's feeling particularly happy. In the car, but only in the car, he likes Bach's *Goldberg Variations.* I asked Linnea once if there's any significance to his choices, if they're connected to happy family memories perhaps, but she shook her head and said no, it was just what he liked.

Frey loves Floss the dog, and Floss the dog loves Frey. For Floss, Frey will overcome his disgust at the wet, meaty texture of the dog food, and will fill her bowl and watch her eat. In the supermarket, Frey often supplements our shop with dry-textured dog treats that he can bring himself to handle and hand-feed to her. For Floss, Frey will open the back door so she can bound outside. In return, Floss stays close to Frey at all times when she's wearing her harness and often when she isn't, and sleeps in a basket at the side of his bed. When Floss returns from her afternoon walk, she goes eagerly to Frey, nuzzles against him as he refastens her harness. Sometimes we hear his murmur of contentment as he fondles her ears.

Despite the indoor nature of his life, Frey takes an interest in the turning of the seasons, the changing of the days. Last year on the 21st of September, he surprised us by making breakfast for all three of us. Our coffee and cereal were prepared in the same microsecond-perfect, co-ordinated way as his own meal, orange juice as an extra touch. On the folded piece of kitchen roll he'd laid beside my plate, a late-blooming rose; for Josh, a sprig of leaves. We were moved and mystified, wondered what it meant. Every morning for the rest of our two weeks we offered him orange juice, in case he was trying to tell us that he liked it too, that he wanted it adding to his routine in some way, but each time, he looked down and away in that heartbreakingly polite 'No, thank you'. It wasn't until he did the same thing on the 21st of December that we realised Frey was marking the key moments of the solar year with his own celebration, generously shared with us.

How does he know? Is it something he heard in school? Does he find the information on his collection of calendars? Does he feel the turning of the sun's tides in his blood? And what does it mean to him, to mark these moments? I don't think I'll ever know the answers. What I do know is that, on my improvised napkin, Frey put a rose, and he picked that rose by leaning out of the living-room window to pluck it from the blooms that twine around the front door, their lavish traditional countryside-ness a strange contrast to the sleek, sharp architecture of the cottage itself. To make our breakfast table pretty, Frey put a part of himself out into the outside world.

Frey has opinions about people, and Frey likes me.

Chapter Four

House

My first night on an Earth without Dad and Noah in it. When I was eleven I swore I'd never sleep in this bed again, but when have I ever succeeded in keeping a promise about my mother? I lie stiff and still on the mattress that's gone unused for over a decade. My coat, its pockets reassuringly filled with easy calories, lies on the floor beside me. I'm wearing my T-shirt and knickers because the clothes I've brought with me from Frey's house are all dirty, ready for the washing machine back at home. Perhaps that house misses us. I picture it waiting and watching like an abandoned pet, wondering how much longer the silence can last.

Perhaps I ought to be there and not here. Perhaps when the police officer told me that no, I couldn't go and look at the place where my dad and my brother just died, I should have driven home. Maybe if I'd driven back to that lonely place, I'd have been so tired that I could have ignored the empty silence, crawled into bed and fallen asleep.

But then, I'd wake up tomorrow morning and find myself listening for the small sounds of Noah, struggling out of the near-coma the drugs put him into. For a few seconds I might think, *why isn't Dad awake yet?* That would be worse than lying in a bed that's not mine, in a room that's not mine, in a house that's not mine, and listening to my mother sobbing in her bedroom on the other side of the tiny bathroom. The strangeness reminds me that my life will never be right again. As long as I'm here, I don't have to worry about forgetting.

Oh, Noah. Now you're shut away in a long metal drawer in a cold room, draped in a respectful sheet. How much was even left to find? When cars go over cliffs in movies, the result is always an instant fireball, but you can't trust the movies to tell the truth.

But Noah's not in a drawer, of course he isn't. If a part of us goes on after we die, his spirit left his body the moment the car took flight. Its metal frame would have tumbled and crumpled, his body would have shaken and battered, organs crashing against bones under the terrible kinetic forces of their fall, but Noah himself would have been free, the way he always dreamed of being.

My mother's crying is growing louder, less inhibited. Maybe she's doing it for attention. *Listen to how much pain I'm in, listen to how much more this hurts me than you.* Maybe she's hoping I'll get out of bed and go to comfort her. I'm good at holding people while they grieve. When you work in A & E, you get a lot of practice. I haven't had to do it since I've been looking after Frey instead, but it's a kind of muscle memory.

I can hear my mother, but I can't see her. I don't know if she's in bed or out of it, sitting up or lying down. I could get out of bed right now, go out of my room and into hers, sit down beside her and put my arms around her. I could stroke her hair, pet her shoulders, tell her it's all right, we'll be all right, we'll find a way through this. We could both pretend not to see the ugly truth: of all the conjunctions of loss that could have been inflicted on our family, leaving the two of us alone together is the worst possible outcome. We are both of us nobody's favourites.

This is the first time in almost twenty years that Dad and

Noah have dared to let the two of us spend time alone. I could get out of bed and go to her, right now. I could take the first steps towards connection. Some semblance of closeness that might, with time and nurturing, become something real.

Behind the separating walls, my mother keens and howls. I take a bar of chocolate from my pocket and stare steadily at the ceiling and watch the small cracks and cobwebs writhe and soften beneath my exhausted gaze. I'm afraid of my mother for many reasons, but the most fundamental one is this. When I was young, my mother left me, and however hard I try, I've never found a way to forgive her for it.

When I next take notice of my surroundings, the room is light again and my mother has stopped crying and gone downstairs. I must have slept, because there's a gap in my information, a stretch of time where the universe has rearranged itself. Maybe my mother's crying was a performance, and she stopped when she realised I wasn't falling for it. After a childhood of her pretending to love me and me trying to believe it was true, I'm poor at reading her intentions. The bathroom is clean but freezing, light and fresh air pouring in through the window that's open to the cold stream of wind. My mother's house is tiny. All her money went on the endless view.

It's almost nine o'clock. Probably I should get dressed before going down. What I really want is my dressing gown, but it's in the bag I left downstairs, half-blocking the tiny hallway. I put on my coat instead, which I know looks ridiculous but at least provides a little bit of armour from my mother's gaze.

She's dressed for the day in faded jeans and a tatty blue jumper, sitting at the kitchen table with a mug of tea, holding it but not drinking it. I thought I'd got rid of all my memories of this house, but now I've found one: coming downstairs with Noah on the first morning after our first night here, and seeing our mother doing almost exactly this – sitting but not moving, with food she wasn't eating and a cup of tea she wasn't drinking – and staring out of the window. That day she was watching the road, but this morning it's the sea that holds her attention. I wonder if she remembers I'm here.

"Good morning," she says, without looking. Of course she doesn't need to look to see who it is. There's no doubt any more, and never will be. Or maybe she doesn't want to see my face and be reminded that I'm her daughter and not her son.

"Morning."

"The kettle's just boiled." There's a great formality to her, her spine rigid, her shoulders very square. "There are teabags in the pot on the side. If you prefer coffee, the jar's in the cupboard."

A good hostess would make me sit down, fuss around me a little, ask what I'd prefer and then make that. A good hostess wouldn't let her guest rummage through the kitchen in an old T-shirt and an anorak. How about a good mother? What would a good mother do? I don't know since I've never had one, but I'm pretty sure it's not this. I let the cupboard door bang, a teenager's expression of resentment because that seems like the most natural mode to choose.

"Did you sleep?" my mother asks, as soon as I'm sitting at the table. I'm still waiting for her to look at me.

"A bit."

"That's good."

"How about you?" *Look at me, Mum, take some notice of your daughter.* I thought I was past needing anything from her but I can't help it, it's instinctual. Even when I'm all she has, I still can't get her to look at me.

"Maybe. I don't remember." My mother's hand tightens on her mug. "I could hear you crying."

It sounds like an accusation. I don't know what to reply. Apart from anything else, it isn't true. I want to cry, I ache with the pressure of the tears in my head and chest, but my night was still and tearless, my pillow stubbornly dry.

"I thought about coming in to see you," my mother continues. "I stood on the landing for a while. But you're a grown woman now and I didn't know if you'd want me coming into your—" Her composure is breaking, I can see the tremble in the surface of the mug she's still not taken a single sip from. On the worktop behind us, the kettle clicks as it cools. "Oh, Callie." She sounds so weary. "For God's sake. Don't you have a dressing gown?"

"It's in my bag."

"Go and get it, then."

"I'm fine in my coat."

"You can't wear your coat, you need a dressing gown. Go on," she says when I open my mouth to protest a bit more, "let me take care of you."

How do you answer a woman who thinks taking care of you is giving you orders and expecting them to be followed? The only reply I can muster is obedience. I even carry my bag upstairs and put it on the floor (there's room on the other bed but I won't look towards that side of the room, I'm too afraid of glimpsing Noah's ghost). I hang my coat on the back of the door, wrap my dressing gown around me. It smells of Frey's house, of fresh air and laundry detergent and the faintest breath of Floss's fur. It smells like home. It smells like happiness. It smells like that other world, where time is frozen and Noah and Dad are still alive.

It hurts so much to think about, but I can't cry, no matter how much I want to. Perhaps she heard her own sobs echoing off the walls and thought they were me. Maybe she's just going mad. Madder. I could get dressed now, there'll be something in this bag that's fit to be worn, but Frey has infected me with his conviction that clothes touching your skin, once removed, must not be re-worn until they've been laundered. The dressing gown it will have to be.

"I've made you some toast," my mother says as soon as

I get back downstairs. "I've put butter on it and there's jam and honey in the cupboard. I didn't know which you wanted."

"Thank you." I'm not hungry, I can still taste chocolate in the crevices of my teeth, but I'm with my mother now and turning down food seems like a dangerous enterprise.

"Sit down and eat it."

"How about you? Have you eaten anything?" If we're pretending to care about each other than I can play too. I won't let her claim the high ground.

She's not listening, she's staring out across the steep slope of the houses to the distant bay. I'm facing the street, conscious of the potential for being spied on, by whatever passing entity might glance in. Wherever you sit in this house, you'll always have your back to a window. Frey would hate it. I can picture the shuffle of his feet, the resistance in his body.

"Mother?" The word feels alien on my tongue. Most of the time I try not to call her anything. Most of the time I aim not to talk to her at all.

"Yes?"

"Have you had anything to eat?"

"What? No, I'm fine, I'm not hungry."

"Don't be silly. If I need to eat then so do you."

"I'll have something later."

"You're having something now." I take a deep breath, then cut my toast in half, trying not to wince as the knife scrapes against the china. "Here. We'll share."

"I don't want it."

"Neither do I, but you're making me eat it." I put the plate between us on the table. "Eat."

The toast is clammy and cool. I force it down with cold, milky tea, watch my mother do the same. The silence is even harder to swallow.

"They're coming to talk to us today," my mother says when the plate is empty.

"Who?"

"The police. They'll want to talk to us both."

"How do they know I'm here? I was going home when I got the phone call."

"I told them you'd come here. It's what people do, isn't it? When something like this happens. They all get together."

"They don't know I'd come to you, though." It's a pointless argument but it's better than the silence. "You could have come to ours."

She stands up, takes the plate and drops it in the sink. "They'll be here at ten o'clock. Go and get dressed."

"I can't."

She looks at me in genuine confusion. "You brought a holdall full of clothes."

"They're all dirty."

"What did you do that for?"

"I was at work."

"At the hospital?"

"Not any more." She's waiting for more, but I won't give it to her. "Can I borrow your washing machine?"

"You won't get it dry before the police get here."

"Then I'll wear what I'm wearing now."

"You're in your dressing gown."

"I don't think the police will care."

"But—"

"Mother. My dad and my brother died last night, okay? I am in fucking *mourning*—"

"Don't swear, Callie—"

"And if you think the police give a damn about a dressing gown…" The proper way to end this sentence would be with a collapse into tears, but I can't make them come. I want to cry, it would feel so good to cry, but I can't.

"I've lost someone too," my mother whispers, and the oddness of her phrasing hums in my bones. She loved Noah more than anything, all of her eggs in one beloved basket, nothing left over for Dad or me. There's an asymmetry to our grieving.

"I suppose I'll have to lend you some clothes," my mother

says. The stairs squeak softly as she climbs them. I can feel her movements in the room above my head.

Now I'm on the sofa, holding another cup of tea I won't drink, my back to another window that makes my skin crawl. Or maybe it's my mother's clothes against my skin. I've accepted her T-shirt and jogging bottoms because she's right, I don't want to meet a stranger in my dressing gown, and I feel as if I've been tricked into accepting a dangerous favour, like a character in a fairy tale. The police are two, PC Henderson and DC Harris. They sit side by side on one sofa, forcing my mother and I to take the other, close enough to feel each other's body heat. I resist the urge to pull away, cram myself into a corner. I keep hold of the mug so she can't take my hand.

"So, Callie. You and your brother and your dad all lived together, is that right?"

"Yes." DC Harris is carefully not judging, but I explain anyway. "I help – helped – look after my brother Noah. He's not well, he can't live independently." No. Wrong tense. Getting married must be like this, getting used to your new name. "Wasn't well, I mean. Couldn't."

She doesn't acknowledge my correction, doesn't show she's even noticed it. "That can't have been easy."

"I didn't mind, I've never minded. Dad didn't mind either." I'm looking at DC Harris but my words are for my mother, tense and distant beside me. "We loved Noah."

Her dark-eyed gaze turns to my mother. "And you and Mr Taggart were divorced?"

"Yes. Since Noah was twelve."

And I was nine, I add silently, knowing she won't even be thinking about this. Even now she measures her life's milestones by Noah and not me.

"I see." DC Harris makes a small note on her pad. "Did they visit you often?"

"I don't know what *often* would be." It's a very my-mother answer. She loves to deflect and withhold.

"Well, when was the last time…?"

"Noah came about a month ago," my mother says, and I twitch with surprise because I hadn't known that. I don't remember the last time I knew Noah to keep a secret.

"How did they seem?"

"Noah seemed – happy," my mother says hesitantly, and I know why. 'Happy' is a word to use cautiously when describing Noah. It's too close to the danger zone of 'manic', a possible warning sign of instability. "I mean, he was calm. He seemed peaceful. We had fish and chips."

"Did you talk to Oliver at all?"

"No." My mother's voice is a cracked bell, their entire relationship held within its flat syllable. "He only dropped Noah off."

"So you did see him? How did he seem?"

"I don't know. Fine, I suppose. It was only for a few seconds." Her body language has closed up. She leans slightly forward, arms folded over her chest.

"So neither of them seemed unhappy?"

"No. I mean, I only talked to Noah. Noah seemed completely fine."

"And it was just a routine visit?"

"Yes. No. I mean, it wasn't a regular thing. Noah came when he could."

"Callie," says DC Harris, catching me by surprise. "Would you usually come on these visits?"

"I can't. Couldn't. I work."

"What do you work as?"

I want to say *does it matter?* I want to say, *don't make me tell you in front of my mother, it's none of her business.* "I'm a residential carer."

"You're a nurse," my mother says, as if she might know the shape of my life better than I do.

"I'm still registered but now I do residential care." What is my mother picturing, I wonder. A hospice maybe, or perhaps a large institution, one of those hellish storage tanks where we keep people who aren't as lucky as Noah or Frey. Certainly not the cool walls and deep windows of the cottage, the way it holds you like a shell, the silence that pools in the corners. "I work two weeks on, two weeks off. Last night was the start of my two weeks off."

"You weren't with your dad or Noah for the last two weeks?"

"No, I wasn't." My guilt's irrational but it's eating my heart anyway.

"How did they seem when you last saw them?"

"They were… fine, normal, I'd say. Noah was calm. Contented." I know what they're asking, what they're thinking, but I won't let that thought into the room with us. "They were planning a lot of walking, I think." This isn't true but it sounds good, it sounds plausible and positive.

"Did Noah or your dad ever talk about ending their lives?" They're nominally asking us both, but it's meant for me. My mother's just the host for this awful meeting. She knows nothing of value.

"God, no," I say. "No, they never have. No. Not ever."

"Ever said anything that suggested they were thinking about it? Talked about finding it difficult to keep going? Worried about the future? Anything like that?"

"No," I say, and then, because even I can hear the lie in my voice, "well, Dad worried about getting older. What would happen to Noah. But only as something we had to solve. Not something that…" I want to cry, to rescue myself from the need to speak, but I can't, my voice stays steady, my face doesn't crumple. "Not something that would make suicide a solution."

"And Noah? Not even as part of his illness?"

"No, he never talked about – doing that. He never did." And this is true. Noah's darkness was directed outwards, in wild fantasies that Dad was his gaoler, was trying to hurt me, was somehow a danger he had to save me from.

Noah's manias, though. His dreams of flight...

I'll think about this later, I tell myself.

"He never did," I repeat, and look them full in the face so they'll believe me. I can see instantly that they don't.

"All right," says DC Harris, and gives us both a small, careful smile. "That's everything we need for now. We've recovered the vehicle, and we'll examine it for mechanical failure. We'll let you know when we know anything. Now, because of how they died, their deaths will be reported to the coroner, who will determine if there needs to be an inquest. That means we won't be able to release their bodies for the funeral for a while, I'm afraid, but we'll work as quickly as possible to get it done. Is there anything you'd like to ask us?"

"Where are they?" My mother's words, harsh and barking, take us all by surprise. A small, swift glance passes between the two officers.

"They're in the hospital mortuary," PC Henderson says gently. "You can see them if you want to. But their bodies were quite badly injured. You might find it more comforting to remember them as they were."

It's not my house, so I don't help my mother see the officers out. Instead, I go to the kitchen and take my clothes from the washing machine, bundle them into the tumble dryer. Treating this place as if I'm at home feels like a violation, but letting my mother touch my things feels worse, and wearing her clothes is the worst of all. I can't wait to tear them off me and scrub myself clean. I can hear the front door closing, the scrape of her feet against the floor as she comes into the kitchen.

When I can't fiddle with the washing any longer, I force myself to look up. My mother's staring out of the window again, her gaze fixed on a distant spot somewhere on the edge of the bay. And for the first time, I realise what it is that draws her eye back and back and back, the way a magnet draws iron.

"I saw it," she says, and I don't know if she's telling me

or herself. "I was looking out across the bay and I saw the car go over."

I can see it, now, the faint disturbance of exposed wood and broken barriers where trees and rails have given way. The scrape of new, raw soil, breaking up the green.

"I saw it happen," my mother repeats, and I am so envious, because she was somehow present in Dad and Noah's final moments, that for a minute I think I might kill her. I could do it, right now. I could grab a knife from the block and plunge it between her shoulder blades. I could reach for the iron frying pan that hangs on the wall and smash it across her head.

Chapter Five

Interview

Have you ever noticed that nurses are always being described as angels? It's meant as a compliment, but if you are one, it's annoying. I do believe in angels, but you won't meet them working in hospitals. Instead, they hover at the edges of reality, occasionally sending a touch of grace your way. I truly think an angel left that copy of *Nursing Times* in the break room. I honestly believe some higher power looked over my shoulder to ensure it opened at the right page.

The advertisement said 'quiet country home', but the interview takes place in a tall, thin slice of Georgian crescent. The advertisement said 'cottage-style garden with views of the downs', but all I can see from the window is expensive traffic making discreet journeys. The advertisement said 'one well-behaved dog', but I can't imagine any animal being welcome in such a sleek, immaculate space. The advertisement said 'care of a young man with additional needs', but this house echoes with the emptiness of deserted rooms.

"Have a seat."

There are three pieces of furniture that could be large

armchairs or small sofas, all in shades of cream. I sit down on the nearest one, and hope I've chosen wisely. My interviewer looks nothing like I'd imagined. Maybe I've accidentally replied to an advert looking for someone to join in a complicated live-in sexual role play.

"Thank you for coming," she says. "I'm Ana Malmberg. Call me Ana, please."

"I'm Callie Taggart."

She already knows this, but she's not unkind, she doesn't say anything. She's entirely polite and welcoming in that way that's also a little bit frightening, as if I might do something rude without even knowing it. If someone led an artist to the doorway of this house and said, "Draw me the woman who lives inside," they'd draw someone who looks like Ana. Pale skin, blue eyes, clothes in shades of charcoal and cream, hair a relentlessly maintained blonde. She's taller than me but probably weighs less. I already know she has money, because this house is worth a fortune and the job's pay is generous to the point of absurdity. But even if I'd only seen her crossing the street or walking into the lobby of a theatre, I'd know. She has that high-gloss finish you can only buy in instalments, over decades and maybe even generations of comfortable wealth.

"This is way too good to be true," my friend Chloe tells me as we lean on opposite walls of the break room, gulping coffee and shovelling biscuits. "These are great, by the way. How do you *always* remember to bring snacks?"

"I know, right? It's perfect, everything about it, the same money but two weeks off in four, Dad can cover the two weeks I'm working…" I'm babbling, but I can't stop. I've been granted an unlikely gift by the universe. All I have to do is reach out and take it. It's dizzying, dazzling. This must be how Noah feels when his brain starts to climb and soar. No wonder he hates taking his meds.

"No, I mean it's literally too good to be true. Nobody pays this much for residential carers. Nobody. And two weeks off in four? Not a chance. It'll be some sort of scam."

I hold out the packet of biscuits to Chloe, then cram in another myself. I ought to eat a banana instead, but the lure of the sugar high is irresistible. "What sort of scam, though?"

"I don't know, personal data theft or something."

"How would that even work?"

"Or slavery. Maybe they're kidnappers." Chloe can never take anything seriously for long. "Or maybe they want a sex worker."

"Then why wouldn't they just look for a sex worker? And who pays that much for sex?"

"Who pays that much for anything? My God, think about it. Two-to-one care, so that's double the salary. And then two more for the weeks you're not there. Four full-time salaries."

"How the other half live." We try not to be resentful – nursing is a vocation, we knew when we started we'd never be millionaires – but it's hard sometimes.

"Fuckers," Chloe agrees. "You don't want to work for people like that, do you?"

I lick crumbs from my fingers. We both know it's perfectly possible to work for people you despise.

"*And* the house sounds bloody lovely as well. There's no way that's genuine. No way."

"So, as the advert said, you'd be caring for my son," Ana says.

Ana's voice has a mesmerising hint of cool Nordic glamour that matches her surname, and her beauty, and her house, and her scent (fresh and cottony, dizzyingly expensive, something I'd try at the perfume counter and then walk away from), and her clothes (more or less ditto). People from her world don't qualify as nurses and drive a ten-year-old Ford Focus and apply for the kind of peculiar job she's advertising. They don't show up for interview with foundation applied like a mask to cover up their early shift, their four hours and thirty-six minutes of sleep, and their night looking after their brother. Ana Malmberg looks exactly like the word *privilege*. If she didn't have a severely disabled son who requires constant care, I might find it in me to hate her.

"There'd be two of you at all times. You wouldn't be doing it on your own."

She hasn't asked me anything yet. She must be waiting for me to go first, testing me out to see what I'll choose.

"What's your son's name?" I ask, because I know from Noah how annoying it is to have someone ask, 'What's the matter with him?' – as if his condition is all you need to know to define him.

"Frey."

I hear this as 'Fray', which makes me think of something unravelling. "And what's he like?"

The brief flicker of a frown. "How do you mean?"

My question sounds like a variation of 'What's wrong with him?' – which I'll need to understand at some point, but which I won't ask yet. Damn it. "I mean… um, what does he enjoy doing? Does he like going out? Staying in? What TV shows does he like? I know he has a dog, the advert mentioned a dog…"

"Oh, yes, Floss. She's a good girl. She loves a good walk, you'd get plenty of fresh air. But she's a working dog, she's not just there for fun."

She's tempting me into the trap. *What does Frey need her to do? What's wrong with your son?* She's left it out of the advertisement and now she's leaving it out of the conversation. I need to know so I can figure out what this job actually is, but I can tell this is some sort of test, and even though it's completely unfair (asking 'What's wrong with him?' is a reasonable, sensible question that requires a precise and careful answer), I desperately want to pass.

"And what about Frey?" I ask. "What does he like doing?"

"He loves jigsaws," Ana says, and I can hear the fierce

warmth in her voice, the pride she feels. "He's brilliant at them. He always has been. When he was little, he used to do thousand-piece puzzles in a day or two, all by himself. And building kits. If you give him a model-making kit, my boy is in heaven."

Good fine motor skills. Ability to hyper-focus. Narrow range of interests. Okay, Ana, you're giving me a few clues but I still won't bite. "Does he enjoy going out to places?"

"No."

A single, flat syllable. The silence is painful.

"Um." I'm too tired to think but I'll do it anyway. A core skill for any nurse. "How about the garden? Does he like gardening?"

"He hasn't actually gone into it yet," Ana says, and I wonder if she's warming up to me or if she's just feeling bad about being difficult. "We wanted a garden because of Floss, and for his carers. But Frey is not keen. We hope he may come round to it." She frowns. "Although we won't force him. Not that, not ever."

No gardening, then. Does he leave the house at all? Will it be my job to drag this young man outside against his will?

"How about, um…" I rack my brains. "Cooking? Does he like to cook?"

"Sometimes. He doesn't like to get wet stuff on his hands, he's a very clean person. But he enjoys joining in."

The advert said 'housekeeping duties'. So I'll be doing the cooking, at least some of the time. That's fine. I find it comforting to be in control of the food.

"And," Ana adds, "he enjoys console games. Are you a gamer, Callie?"

"No. Is that a problem?"

"Not necessarily. As long as one of you knows how to work *Minecraft* and *Fallout*, Frey will be happy."

"My friend's little boy loves *Minecraft*. He's building a roller coaster. Apparently. I don't really know how it works."

"No, neither do I. I have tried, but there's so much to learn, so many little details and recipes and so on... but Frey got hooked on it while he was living in the residential home. I think perhaps it was the only thing he liked about it."

"Is he – um – is he living there now?"

For a minute, Ana looks sick. "No. We took him out of there two months ago. He's living at the cottage with my ex-husband Miles. His sister Linnea visits when she can, but she lives in Stockholm. She's in medical research. Not possible to work remotely."

Miles is an English name. That explains, perhaps, what Ana and her son are doing in this country. Her daughter, Linnea, in Stockholm. The family's coming into focus for me, but I can't get a clear picture of its most important member. The heroic amounts of coffee I've drunk has given my hands a faint tremor, and the exhaustion it hasn't quite blotted out sings in my ears like a choir. Ana is watching me again, waiting to hear what I'll say next, and I can't think of a single thing. *I need this job so badly, I would be so perfect for it and I would be so grateful and would stay forever if you'd let me.* Maybe I should just say that, see if a short burst of total honesty gets us into a place where we can at least talk more freely.

Oh God, what if I meet Ana's son and he doesn't like me?

"And anyway, I don't think those T&Cs would be enforceable," Chloe says. It's hours later, but we mostly speak in short scraps: 'and' is a perfectly normal word for us to start a conversation with.

"I'm happy with them."

"That doesn't matter, if it's unreasonable it's not allowed. And a year's notice is ridiculous, who expects a year's notice that you're leaving? I bet the governor of the Bank of England doesn't have a year's notice period. I bet Jeff Bezos doesn't have a year's notice period."

"I bet he does."

"Well, he's getting paid squillions."

"So would I be. Relatively. I mean, it's the same money for half the time. That's sort of squillions. And why would I want to leave?"

"But they can fire you, for any reason, with a week's notice. How is that fair? Why don't you get a year too?"

"Just because Rich works in HR."

"You don't need to work in HR to know that shit isn't right."

Then the red phone rings and we have to prep for a man who's fallen off two storeys of scaffolding, and we don't get to talk again that day but it doesn't matter because I know Chloe's right, but I also know Chloe's wrong. It doesn't matter about the terms. If it's what it takes to get the job then I'll accept them.

"Let's talk about you," Ana says. "Why do you want to leave nursing?"

It's the obvious question, but I don't have a proper answer. I'm applying to be her son's carer. She's never going to hire me if I say I want to make more money and give less of myself in return.

"I don't want to leave it, exactly," I say. "But the job doesn't really work with my personal circumstances. I need to find something else."

"What are the personal circumstances?"

I can feel tears prickling. I've put so much hope into this job, spun out a whole frail future from its single strand of silk, and now I'm making a mess of it. If only Noah hadn't needed me so much last night, I could have got a decent amount of sleep and been fresh and prepared.

"I'm looking for a new challenge," I say. "Getting through the pandemic…" I can't say that it was like hell on earth. I can't say that I don't ever want to live through it again. "It's made me re-evaluate my priorities."

It's as close as I can get to being honest with a stranger.

"Yes," says Ana thoughtfully. "Yes, I understand that, actually."

"But seriously," I say to Chloe when our paths cross for a brief pause in a Saturday afternoon shift (day-drinkers and barbecuers, DIY disasters and people who think they're going to jump the queue at the GP, plus a sprinkling of true emergencies who lie cheerfully on their trolleys, telling us they don't want to be a nuisance as their brains bleed and die or their heartbeats stutter to a halt). "Two weeks at work. Two weeks at home. Dad could do the opposite. Noah would have someone with him twenty-four hours a day."

"And when do you get a break? What kind of a life is that for you?"

Then a woman stumbles in clutching a baby and wailing with the kind of primal cry that tells you something truly dreadful has happened, and we don't speak again until we phone each other on the way home to laugh about the patient who came in with a lightsaber up his bum. I love Chloe, but she'll never understand. What's the point of asking, 'When do I get a break?' It's about as useful as asking, 'What if Noah wasn't here any more?'

"We tried residential care for Frey," Ana says. "We did our research. It took months. We looked around so many."

I don't say anything. I don't have to. You don't interrupt someone when they're confessing.

"Money was not the problem. Miles and I had always planned for long-term care."

I keep my face still. I won't let her see how much that word, 'planned', irritates me, as if the difference between her life and mine was that she and her husband had thought to *make a plan*.

"It had great big gardens," she says, a little dreamy now.

"Lovely rooms. Excellent carer ratios. The food was nice, we ate there a few times. We went sometimes by surprise so they couldn't get prepared for us. It was like a beautiful country hotel, only you could go and live there. We joked that we'd like to live there ourselves."

I don't blame her. A house in the country, all my food cooked by someone else, a room of my own. It sounds like bliss.

"We thought he was settled. They gave us good reports, they all said how lovely he was, what a pleasure he was to spend time with. 'No trouble at all', they said."

I wait for more, but there's only silence.

"But it didn't work out?" I say, when I can't stand it any more. I know it's a mistake as soon as the words are out.

"No," she says, suddenly brisk and efficient. "It didn't work out. And so, now, we do things Frey's way." She stands up. "Thank you for coming."

Shit.

"It was nice to meet you." I make myself hold my spine straight, meet her gaze.

"So when can you come and visit the cottage?" Ana asks.

"Sorry?"

"The cottage," Ana says, a little patient, a little patronising. "If you're interested in taking your application further, that is."

"Are you serious?" Chloe asks. "That's not an interview. That's a, that's a – I don't even know what that was. You still don't know what his condition is?"

"I'm going down next week."

"So all that happened was you went into her house, she asked why you wanted to leave nursing, she told you her son used to live in a lovely residential home, and then she asked you for a second interview?"

"Yep."

"They all sound mental," says Chloe, and then our shiny new junior doctor dashes in, white-faced and frantic, and it's two stabbings and a facial glassing just arrived and we're all very busy indeed for the rest of the shift.

The satnav takes me to a tiny village with a long street where none of the houses have numbers. This includes Frey's 'detached modern-style cottage in idyllic rural setting'.

The shape of the cottage is a crisp, sleek curve like a bird's wing, the walls thick and the windows small. There's a tall hedge, a gravel drive all the way around the front, a thick, high fence bisecting the grounds. The cottage-style garden must be behind. I'd love to own a house like this but I never, ever will, not on the kind of money I can make. The only way I'm getting inside is as the paid help.

I knock at the slate-grey slab of wood that fills the doorway. The handle is long and industrial.

Behind the door is a woman who's about my age, but with nothing else in common with me. My first, instinctive thought is *I don't like you*, because she looks wealthy and beautiful and successful and privileged. My second, rational thought is *I'm going to like you,* because I have to, and she has to like me in return.

"Are you Callie?" She sounds like her mother, that hint of the exotic in her voice. "Nice to meet you. I'm Linnea. Come on in."

The hallway is white and minimal, the floor grey slate. The temperature contrast between out there and in here is blissful.

"You can hang your jacket here." She's pointing to a row of black iron hooks. Each peg has precisely one coat on it; each peg has one pair of shoes beneath, arranged side by side. I think of our hallway, every surface strewn with scarves and hats, shoes and bags, tumbled around as if someone's unpacked a circus by shaking out all the boxes. Our home's messier than average, but I cope by telling myself the pictures in the catalogues aren't real.

I arrange my things as neatly as I can, tucking my bag

inside the folds of my jacket. It looks shabby and out of place. My feet are damp with sweat. I'm afraid I'll leave footprints.

"This way," Linnea says, and leads me to the door at the end of the hall.

Behind the door is a kitchen full of light and air. Enormous windows let in a view of a velvet lawn and flower beds bursting with petals. At the end of the garden is a pergola half-buried in honeysuckle. Beyond that is the promised view of the hills, where fat red cattle stand in profile and crop at the grass. I stare and stare, forgetting myself.

"It's gorgeous, isn't it?" says Linnea, and the tolerant kindness in her voice pulls me back through the windows and into the room. She nods towards the table. "This is my brother, Frey."

At the table, an older man with clipped grey hair sits with a younger, fair-haired man who must surely be his son. Like Ana, like Linnea, they both look rich, which seems impossible when their clothes are almost pyjamas. Maybe it's the clean steel frame of the man's glasses that does it, or the way their T-shirts and jogging bottoms look worn and vintage, rather than scruffy and disreputable. They're doing a jigsaw, their heads close and absorbed.

"Dad," Linnea says. "This is Callie. She's the nurse."

"Hi there." The man looks up, gives me a quick smile. His teeth are ridiculously white and even. He'd be charming if he didn't look so rich. "I'm Miles. Frey, mate, this is Callie. We talked about her, remember? Now, how about this piece?"

The picture on the puzzle box is of a series of painted eggs, layered on top of each other. The piece in Miles's hand seems impossibly tiny. Frey takes it, turns it around in his fingers, and puts it down in a space at the centre. Then he reaches down and pets the spaniel at his feet. The spaniel raises her eyebrows and touches her nose to his hand. Frey looks very pink and white, as if the blazing sunshine has never touched his skin.

"Nice to meet you," I say, then, in case Miles thinks I'm talking to him alone, "Hello, Frey. I'm Callie."

Frey takes another piece from his father's hand, places it

in one corner, close to the edge but not locking on, leaving a perfect negative space. His movements are careful and precise. His gaze remains resolutely downwards. I wonder if he'll speak. I wonder how old he is. I wonder what colour his eyes are.

"It's jigsaw time," Linnea explains.

Frey takes the next piece. Fits it into place. Waits for Miles to hand him another.

"That one looks hard," I say.

"It is," says Miles warmly. "All I can do is hand him the pieces."

I'm watching Frey, the still point around which the whole household revolves. I'm trying to work out if he's listening, or if he's completely locked away in his own jigsaw world.

"Your house is beautiful," I say to Frey, partly to show that I recognise his autonomy, his personhood, but mostly because it really is beautiful.

"It's almost new," Linnea says. "Dad knows the man who built it, don't you?"

"Cost him a fortune," Miles says cheerfully. "Passion project of his. Spent a decade building it, had two years living here, then got promoted to Singapore." He glances at Frey. "Came up just at the right time, didn't it?"

Frey doesn't speak, but there's the faintest suggestion of a smile about the edges of his mouth. He's definitely listening, then, definitely present. I just have to learn how to read what he's got to say. Frey reaches down and pets the dog's head.

"You get on all right with dogs?" Miles asks. I bet he wears red trousers to go to the pub.

"I like all animals," I say. I've never actually owned a pet, but it seems a safe enough answer.

Miles is standing up and offering me his seat. "Want to take over for a bit?"

"If that's okay with you," I say to Frey.

Frey is statue-still, serene. Does that mean he'll let me help him, or that he won't? I slide cautiously into Miles's spot. Reach for a piece of jigsaw. Hold it out to him.

A pause like a held breath. I wonder if I've chosen the wrong piece, done the wrong thing. Then Frey reaches out and takes it from me. Places it into an empty space in the centre of the puzzle. Waits for me to hand him the next one.

"You're really good at this," I tell Frey after six or seven pieces, because it feels rude to sit here in total silence.

Frey doesn't reply, but that's all right.

"I saw one once that was completely blank," I continue. "Just white all over, no picture or anything."

Frey takes another piece from my fingers. A blob of colour in one corner suddenly becomes a tiny jewel of an egg, painted with enamelled violets.

"I don't know if that would be fun or not, really," I say, and pass him another piece. "I mean, you'd be pretty impressed with yourself once you'd finished it. But you wouldn't get to see the picture coming together."

Talking to Frey feels right, the way it feels right to talk to patients even when they're unresponsive, even when they're almost gone. Even if your patient's unconscious, before you put your hands on them, you speak to them. "I'm going to move your left leg now, I'll just clean your arm before I change your line, now I'm going to brush your hair." Sometimes you see some sort of response, a softening of muscles maybe, maybe a flicker of eyelids that says, 'I'm listening, keep talking, I want to feel connected'. Sometimes you see this even when you know it's medically impossible. We're taught to recognise these moments as our brains seeking out meaning in random events. But there's always the hope that you're seeing the first signs of someone's own personal miracle.

There's something moving about at my feet, something warm and breathing. Floss the dog gives a little groan, and lies down. Her tail swishes over my toes, comes to rest around my ankle.

"Hey, down there," I say. "Your dog's a little sweetie, isn't she?"

I hand Frey another piece, and another, and another. His movements are slow and dreamy, but the puzzle comes together quickly, each careful placement revealing a new detail. All the tension in my muscles ebbs away, and my scalp tingles with release.

"This is like meditating," I say to Frey. "Do you do this every day?"

"Sometimes we do colouring." Miles's voice makes me jump. I was starting to forget he and Linnea are here. "It's easier to join in with that one. Or we make kits."

"Do you colour the same picture? Or do you have your own?"

"Everyone has their own." This time it's Linnea answering for Frey. The puzzle's almost finished. Just three pieces left. Then two. Then one.

"That was amazing," I say to Frey. "I've never seen anything like it. I could watch that all day."

Am I imagining the slight tension in Frey's shoulders?

"It's all right, Frey," says Linnea. "Callie doesn't mean you have to do puzzles all day. We're following the schedule, the same as always. Don't worry."

And I'd thought I was doing quite well. How badly have I upset him? Will he forgive me?

"It's time for Floss's walk now. Floss!" Linnea pats her thigh, makes a soft chirping noise. "Come here, sweetie."

The warmth at my feet disappears and Floss tick-tacks across the tile to Linnea, ears pricked, tail eager. The kitchen is so implausibly, ridiculously clean, as if I've wandered onto a movie set. The faint scent of dogginess is reassuring, a reminder that at least one of the creatures here is real.

"Come on, then. Out we go." The back door opens and Floss bounds towards it. "Frey, we'll be out for an hour, the same as always. Callie's coming too."

I'd thought maybe they'd give me longer with Frey, maybe even leave me in charge for a while. Maybe they don't trust me. Maybe I've already messed this up beyond repair.

"And Dad's staying with you," Linnea continues. "Callie, we'll be walking on grass – do you want to borrow trainers? I think we're the same size."

She's being kind, but she's also showing how scarily observant she is (I have no idea how big her feet are, but she's right, we're both a size six and the trainers are perfectly comfortable). I take them gratefully, glad not to have to ruin my suede pumps. Floss tears across the garden, then back, then away again to pause by the gate.

"They'll be rich and weird," Chloe tells me, the day I tell her I've got a second interview.

"They might just be rich."

"Rich people are always weird. They're like a different species. They'll have weird rules and they'll look down on you for not knowing them."

"Hey." Dominika puts her head around the door. "I need a chaperone for Room Three. It's a good one."

Room Three has suctioned her DivaCup to the wall of her vagina. I hold her hand and let her squeeze it while Dominika sets her free as gently as she can. *I'll miss this when I leave,* I think. I'm already assuming I'll get this job, that my time here is almost over.

"Now we can talk," Linnea says once we've left the garden. I make myself look calm, slow down, take notice. There's a wide grassy lane here, smooth and green, pleasant to walk on. Floss bustles about, prospecting into dark places and shoving her nose into patches of cow parsley.

"Does Frey mind being talked about?"

Linnea is looking at me with the straight, sharp gaze of someone who's not concerned with being liked, only with deciding whether she likes me. "Would you mind being talked about?"

"Yes," I say.

"Well, then."

We walk on in strained silence.

"He used to be better," Linnea says, sudden and seemingly contextless. She glances at me, waits to see what I'll say. "Sorry, has anyone told you this already?"

"No, not really. I mean, Mrs Malmberg said he—"

"Ms, not Mrs. Malmberg is her maiden name. I have it too."

"I'm sorry."

"Don't be. Our mother's hopeless at explaining things. Did she tell you much about Frey?"

"Um. Not really."

"I expect she told you how nice the cottage was, though."

"It was in the advert," I say cautiously.

"That's my mother." Linnea sighs. "Floss! Leave that." Floss shuffles around a little, as if this will stop us noticing she's stuck her nose deep in a pile of horse dung. "I said leave it… that's it. Come here now. Good girl."

I wait as patiently as I can.

"Frey's twenty-four," says Linnea. "He was at a special school until he was eighteen. Then that finished. Our parents had a plan, of course, they're not idiots. They tried him living at home with Mum. She really tried to make it work. And it did, for a few years. But then it was too much. It's strange, isn't it? You'd think it would get easier, not harder."

"You get tired," I say, with feeling, and I feel Linnea glance towards me, and then away again.

"Yes. So they found a residential home for him. Well, Mum did. Dad showed up to look at the one she'd picked out, and said he'd pay the bills. He works in the City, you can probably tell."

It's fascinating to me, the scorn she has for her father's wealth when it's clear how much simpler her and Frey's lives have been made by it.

"Of course Mum loved it. Fabulous garden, lots of fresh air. Really nice food, they had all sorts of cuisine, always something new to try. Plenty of enrichment activities, crafts and cooking and workshops where they learned new skills. Lots of outings."

"It sounds lovely," I say, cautious because I know this story doesn't end with 'and then he settled in perfectly and everything was great'.

"Yes. She thought so too. He moved in. They were so happy for him. I wasn't sure, but I thought – I mean, she lived with him, she found the home, I thought she knew best, you know?" She sighs. "And then, just after, there was lockdown."

That single word, covering so many different experiences. For Noah, it was the whittling away of all the little kindnesses making a limited life bearable – no restaurants, no theme parks, no cinemas, no shopping, no road-trips – and the inevitable tumble into the dark. I remember it as a time of plastic, sweaty layers wrapped around me like a shroud, and Noah shut away from me, supposedly safe but utterly unreachable.

"We couldn't visit for months. They have residents who are medically vulnerable, so they shut up like a fortress and pulled up the drawbridge. Mum and Dad phoned every few days. I had a Zoom session with him every now and then. They kept saying he was fine... Floss! No. Leave it. Good girl. All right, now we can play with the ball."

We've reached a wide, tall field, curving upwards towards the horizon. Linnea throws the ball. Floss tears after it.

"Do you get to meet the other person you'll be working with before you start?"

"I don't know. I hadn't really thought about it."

"You have to think about it, you'll be living half your life with them. You can't just move in with two random strangers. Come on, what would you say to me if I was trying to do this?"

"The thing is," says Linnea, "the way they measure *fine* is how much disruption the residents cause. Meltdowns. Screaming.

Smashing things. Trying to run away or hit the carers. You know? Frey didn't do any of those things, and so – *fine*."

She's talking about the sort of things Noah does. Noah, in distress, is the textbook definition of a disruptive patient. When his medication dulls his senses and closes down his thoughts, they say he's improved. I can see it makes him different, but I've never thought of it as Noah getting well. The best they've ever managed is to drug him up and wait for the storm to pass. Floss races back with the ball, sits eager and quivering at Linnea's feet.

"The staff were nice. They didn't push him. They'd try and persuade him to join in the craft and the gardening – they were all shut in so they did a lot of craft, a lot of gardening – but they didn't make him. When he stopped coming downstairs, they let him. It was his *personal choice*."

She's so *angry*, this tall, skinny, pretty, privileged girl, pacing up and down the grass. Floss drops the ball at Linnea's feet and then snaps at a wasp, swallowing it down with apparent pleasure. Maybe it tastes spicy, the doggy equivalent of chillies or wasabi.

"I shouldn't blame them, they were doing their best. And Mum and Dad were doing their best too, probably. But how nobody could have noticed that he…" She pauses. "He was in his room almost all the time. They thought he was happy. I kept sending kits and jigsaws, hoping he'd know I was thinking about him. I'd see him on Zoom and I'd wonder, *is he really all right?* I thought it was because we were talking through screens…"

"It's not easy," I say. The first words I've said for a while. First Ana, and now Linnea, sick and heavy with guilt. I've seen people like this before, talking and talking, purgative and confessional. It doesn't matter what I say, in fact it's better if my words are almost meaningless. All Linnea needs is an audience.

"And then. One of the residents started going into his room. They said how pleased they were. 'Danny and Frey are friends', they said, 'they watch television together'. It all sounds fine, doesn't it? Like a really happy thing. I can see why they didn't realise. They told Mum they'd been 'helping with his personal care', which she would have known what they meant if she'd thought about it, Frey doesn't need help with that normally, but that's my mother for you. She only hears what she wants to hear. She thought it meant helping him pick out his clothes or something. I would have got it, but they weren't about to call me in Stockholm... then finally lockdown ended and I could visit him. I was so happy that day, getting on the plane, driving down the motorway to see my brother."

I'm wondering what's coming. Something dark and awful, possibly sexual. Linnea must see this in my face, because she shakes her head.

"No, it wasn't that. It wasn't Danny's *fault*, it was just who he *was*. He yelps and shouts. Thrashes around, knocks things over. Likes lots of personal contact, holding hands and stroking faces. Touches everything. Gets food all over himself. It doesn't sound like much but it was everything Frey's terrified of. He couldn't go downstairs to eat in case Danny sat next to him and touched his plate. Couldn't do his jigsaws because Danny tried to join in. Couldn't use his bathroom because Danny had been in there and left it dirty. We did everything right, we did all our research and we found him this lovely place with kind people, and it still wasn't enough. He still wasn't safe."

"You could let Noah move out," Chloe says. "Sheltered accommodation's not so bad—"

"And who's going to look after him?"

"They have *staff*, that's the whole point."

"They do their best but their job's impossible, we both know that. And why should Noah have to live with a bunch of strangers where the only thing they've got in common is that they can't live on their own? That's not a home, that's a prison."

"And what about you? Why do you have to be the one who goes to prison?"

I shake my head stubbornly. Then Nathan sticks his head around the door to warn us there's a non-responsive motorbike rider coming in and the conversation's over for another night.

"Frey was so thin, so pale." Linnea swallows fiercely, and waves her hand as if she's warding something away. "I could see the outline of his incontinence pants through his clothes. And he looked at me, straight at me – he never does that, not ever – and he grabbed on to my hand and wouldn't let go…"

I think about the questions Chloe told me to ask. I think about the questions I told myself to ask. I don't speak or move.

"I called Mum and Dad. I said I was bringing him home."

"Did the staff let you?"

"They didn't dare stop me." Linnea's glee is almost frightening. "I took him straight out, left everything of his behind, even his jigsaws. He wouldn't let go of my hand, getting into the car was a nightmare. I took him to Mum's place and I told them both Frey wasn't going back, not ever."

"He's lucky," I say. "To have someone looking out for him."

"He's not lucky. He didn't understand about lockdown, he thought he'd been abandoned. Are you all right?"

"Yes, fine. I just…" I can't say that I know how that feels, that my mother left me too. She'll think I'm insane. "Sorry. Goose walked over my grave."

"It almost broke him. He wouldn't let us out of his sight at first. We had to take it in turns to shower and sleep and use the bathroom. When he went to sleep, one of us had to sleep on the floor beside him."

"That must have been hard."

"It was the least we could do." Linnea's eyes blaze. "All of this is the least we could do."

I'm glad for the return of Floss, who has brought a stick for Linnea to look at.

"So," says Linnea, as sudden and shocking as a slap. "Tell me about Noah."

"But you love this job, Cal. All that training we did. Don't give it up now."

"I don't care." I never cry at work, never ever, it's one of the first things you learn not to do, but I'm close tonight. It's been such a long time since any of us felt safe. "All right, I do care, but that doesn't change anything."

"You're such a good nurse. Way better than me."

"Don't say that, you're great—"

"Please, Callie." Chloe's almost crying too. When the first wave was at its height, we had a special room we could use to do this. I wish it was still there. "I need you."

I haven't mentioned my family. 'Tell me about Noah' ought to be the least reassuring thing Linnea could have said. But I'm off balance, confused by a surfeit of wealth and, damn it, I am tired of pretending. Let's be honest. Why the hell not?

"He's my brother," I say. "He... he needs looking after too. Like Frey."

She doesn't look at all surprised. "Tell me more about him."

"He's... well, first of all, he's funny, he's the funniest person I know. He makes these really strange connections, he imagines things that nobody else would. Like, last week he told me that if people came in the same range of sizes that dogs come in, we could be any size from the size we actually are, to the size of a blue whale. And he said, 'Imagine trying to sell your house! Imagine trying to build an office!'"

"Really? The size of a blue whale?" Linnea blinks. "Well, I suppose... chihuahuas are so tiny, aren't they? And then there's those huge dogs, the ones that look like bears... and yet they are still the same species, aren't they? I'd never thought about it before."

"That's what Noah's best at. Thinking of things no one's ever thought of before. And he loves going out, he loves theme parks and funfairs and concerts. He'd go out every night if he could."

"And?" She's looking at me directly now, and the power of her gaze is shocking. I feel like a fly in one of those blue lights they have in restaurant kitchens. *I didn't ask about your brother, Linnea. Cut me some slack.*

"And," I say, too tired to carry on resisting, "sometimes he can't sleep, for days and days. He starts these impossible projects, trying to knock down walls so he can build us a new bathroom, buying things he thinks he's going to need to get it finished. He bought a mini JCB digger once. I mean, it sounds funny now."

Linnea's watching me the way I watched her as she told me about Frey.

"He hates taking his meds, they slow him down and make him put on weight. So when he's stable, he's always hoping this time he's actually better, like properly better, not just with his symptoms under control, so he tries to skip them. And sometimes they just – don't work." I don't talk to anyone about this, not even Chloe, not even Dad, and now I'm telling this stranger in a fancy house who, I'm now sure, is definitely not going to give me a job. I can tell her with impunity. I'll never see her again.

"He starts to get paranoid," I say. "Not for himself, but for me. He says awful things about Dad, says he's keeping me prisoner. Sometimes when I'm at work he locks Dad out of the house."

"That sounds hard."

"We know what he needs to stay well. He needs his meds, and he needs to keep busy, have lots of stuff going on that he enjoys. We used to do better, but then…"

"Lockdown," says Linnea.

"Yes. And it's better now, but we're more tired now, and it's not the same as it was before, and it'll get worse again this winter, we all know it. All the support groups are gone, and the community projects... and Noah, he knows he's the reason we're both so tired, he hates needing us so much. Noah's caseworker's concerned about all of us. He wants us to consider residential care. And I won't let that happen, I just – I won't. And then I saw your advert, and..."

With some difficulty, I make myself shut up. I feel flayed open, tortured. Linnea's expression is faintly satisfied.

"Shit," Chloe says. "You're going to get this bloody job, aren't you? You're going to swan off to live in your lovely cottage in the country."

"I might not get it."

"Yes, you will, I can feel it in my waters." She puts her arms around me. "You absolute cow."

"Sorry."

"So you should be. Leaving me here on my own to deal with this lot. Who's going to bring me biscuits now?"

"That's why you want this job," Linnea says. "So you can take care of your brother. Because you love him."

"Yes."

"So many people have come here," says Linnea thought-fully, "and told me they want to look after Frey. Told me how sweet he seems. How much they love him already. As if they can tell anything about him from meeting him for half an hour. At least you've been honest."

"At least you'll remember me. The first honest candidate."

"The second, actually. The first one was a man who said his most clearly defined ambition was not to be a farmer."

I'm not sure whether I'm allowed to smile.

"Also," Linnea says, "Frey liked you."

"Did he?"

"If he didn't, he wouldn't have done the jigsaw with you. So, would you like the job?"

"What? I mean, yes, of course I want the job."

"Good. Now, before you decide whether to accept, I need to tell you two things."

"Don't you need to ask me anything?"

"No. I already know all about you. That's the first thing for you to know. I had a private detective do a report on you. He told me about Noah. That's one of the reasons I told Mum to see you."

"A private detective?" I have to swallow my incredulous laughter.

"Yes." Linnea is looking at me intently. "So you don't need to tell me about where you've worked before, or your qualifications, or your salary, or any of that. I already know."

It doesn't matter how she knows, it's all information I would have given her willingly anyway. She's offering me the job.

"And here's the second thing. There are cameras in the cottage, in all the communal areas, so I can watch. Is that a problem?"

Chloe said there'd be a catch, and now here it is. It's a problem because it's intrusive and weird, but it's also not a problem because I understand. Linnea is protecting Frey, and that means she'll never, ever trust me. And that's okay. We understand each other perfectly, and that's better than trust.

"That's all right," I say. "I understand why."

Linnea's face softens. "I thought you might. I've seen a lot of people who don't."

I can imagine she has. But I'll accept constant surveillance if it gets me and Dad what we need to keep Noah safe. *Look at me, Mother,* I think, before I can stop myself. *Look what I'll go through to take care of Noah. Look how much better I am than you at loving someone.*

Chapter Six

Roller coaster

You're probably wondering, *Why do you hate your mother? Why are you so sure she doesn't love you?* It's a good question. None of us wants to admit we might be even vaguely unlikeable, to anyone, even strangers. It's much harder to accept when it's one of your own parents.

The answer is this. I finally believed it the day she left me. I knew it for sure the day I left her. And I had my suspicions almost every day of my childhood. Here's the first time I began to realise:

"Today's going to be awesome," Noah tells me, bounding into my bedroom. It's too early, but it's impossible to stay asleep when he's here. Even if he wasn't my favourite person in the world and someone I don't want to miss out on, he simply won't allow it.

"Where are we going?" I ask, because I still don't really understand.

Noah rolls his eyes. "Paradise Park."

"What's that?"

"It's an amusement park."

"What's an amusement park?" Sometimes it's painful, getting people to tell you things.

"It's got loads of rides. You know like at the church fete? With the teacups?"

Suddenly, I'm excited. The church fete is a key milestone in the year, like Christmas and Easter and birthdays. There's always a bouncy castle, and there's always a hook-a-duck stall, and there's always a teacup ride, and Mummy says I can only go on once but Daddy always lets me on again when Mummy's not looking.

"Will there be teacups?"

"Yes," says Noah. "And roller coasters."

"What's a roller coaster?"

"It's like the teacups, but massive. You go up in the air really fast."

I picture gigantic teacups, bigger than a car, flying into space like balloons. "I don't want to go on a roller coaster."

"Yes, you do."

"No, I don't."

"I'll come with you. Come on, you need to get dressed."

I get out of bed and shut myself in the bathroom. I'm completely sure I'm not going on a roller coaster, with or without Noah, but it doesn't matter. I'm five and my brother is eight and it's the first day of the weekend, and today's going to be a good day because we're going to Park… something… and we'll all be together and nothing's going to spoil it.

The drive there is long. I'd quite like to stare out of the window and look for yellow cars until I fall asleep, but Noah and Daddy are too excited.

"*What Animal Am I*!" Dad declares joyously. "Who's got an animal?"

"I've got one." Noah's always so quick. I'll never catch up. I don't even know half the animals he chooses. Dad smiles at him. He loves Noah's cleverness.

"Okay, I'll go first. Are you furry?"

"Yes."

"Vee?"

Mummy's looking out of the window. Maybe she's looking for yellow cars too.

"Yes?"

"What animal is Noah? Your turn to ask a question."

"Um. Are you fierce?"

Noah frowns, considering.

"I might be. I'm not sure. I've got quite big teeth, but I don't think I'd want to eat you. Um, Dad, do—"

"No, don't ask me or I'll know what you are, you melon." Noah clamps a hand over his mouth. "Shall we say you're bitey, but not attack-y?"

"Yes. I'm bitey, but I'm not attack-y. Callie, your go."

I'm trying to do what Dad always tells me to do, to make a picture of an animal in my mind using the clues they give me, but my mind's a blank. I stare madly out of the window for inspiration.

"Are you a cow?" I ask, because there's a field with cows in it.

Daddy laughs, but kindly. "No, sweetie, cows aren't bitey, they eat grass, remember? And it's too soon to start guessing animals, we need more information. Do you want to ask again?"

"All right." I frown, think hard. "Do you live in a zoo?"

"That's a great question," Daddy says. "Brilliant thinking, sweetie. Vee, did you hear that? Vee? Earth to Vanessa?"

"Hear what?"

"Callie's brilliant question. She asked if Noah's animal lives in a zoo."

"Oh, yes. That's very good. Well done, Callie, you're a clever girl."

Mummy doesn't sound as if she means it, but she gets tired sometimes.

"It's a great question," Noah says, and his praise means the most to me because Noah only says something's good when he really means it. "I do live in a zoo. And you've seen me as well, do you remember the time we went to that zoo and—"

"No, stop, don't give her any more clues," Daddy warns. "Yes or no answers only."

It's nice, being reminded that Noah's not completely perfect.

"Right." Dad looks serious. "So you live in a zoo, you're furry and you're bitey but not attack-y… are you some sort of primate?"

Noah looks confused.

"Like a monkey, or an ape – two arms and two legs and a bit like people."

"Oh!" Noah beams. "Yes."

"Okay. Vee?"

"Do you have a tail?"

"Yes. That's a really good question, Mummy."

Noah's good at cheering Mummy up, but I wish he didn't have to. Other mummies listen to their children without being told to, and they look at their pictures nicely and join in games and don't need cheering up all the time. There's something wrong with my family.

"Thank you, sweetie."

"Callie, your turn. You can guess it now if you want to."

I'm still thinking about cows, still wondering if I might have been right earlier, but when I look at Noah's face, I suddenly know the answer.

"It's that monkey!" I say triumphantly. "The one that stole the banana! No, not a monkey, it's… um, it's got a long stripey tail and it lives with its friends and it's got orange eyes. And little hands! It's the animal with hands! The one that stole the banana from that pushchair!" I can still see it, the leap from its rope, the slender furry arm plunging into the bag and coming out with a banana (and how did it *know*?). The shrieks of surprise, the chaos when its friends saw what it had and came bounding over to ask for their share, the keeper torn between laughter and dismay. We played *Stealing the Banana out of the Pushchair* for weeks.

"Yes! It's called a—"

"No, don't tell me, I want to guess."

"Let her guess, Noah, don't tell her—"

"It's a lemur, Callie! And you guessed it! Clever girl!"

"Well done, Callie." Daddy's driving, or he would reach over and ruffle my hair. "You're a clever girl."

"Can you not shriek so much, please, Callie? I've got a headache."

When Mummy says things like that, there's always a little silence afterwards. It's like when you fall over and, for a second, you think you might not have hurt yourself, and it's going to be okay. Then you look down and see the graze and everything starts to hurt and you can't stop yourself from crying. I can feel this happening to me right now.

"You guessed brilliantly," Daddy says. "Do you remember the keeper? She had to go and get all the other lemurs' lunch before it was time? Because they were so upset about the other one getting a banana?"

I'm glad we have Daddy. I wouldn't like to spend a whole day out with just Mummy. I picture angry words over breakfast, crossness about our clothes, shouting and sighing whenever there's a queue or if I drop something.

I can imagine a day out with just Daddy, though. That would be brilliant.

'Like at the church fete', Noah said, and I've been picturing a bigger version of that, but the amusement park is nothing like it, not at all. At the church fete there's teacups and hook-a-duck and the bouncy castle and the sweet stall and that's it. All I have to decide is which one I'll save for last. Here, everything's loud and giant, millions of people everywhere, all knowing what the rules are, which rides they've got enough money for. Daddy tells us all the rides are free, we've paid at the entrance and we can go on as many things as we want, but that doesn't seem right to me.

"Look at those horses, they're like on that cartoon you watch," Noah says, and I see a big roundabout with horses on gold poles. My heart jumps.

"How much does it cost?" I whisper, wishing I'd kept my mouth shut because I can't bear to hear, 'We don't have enough money'. I've never seen anything better than this, if I'm allowed on this it will be the best thing that's ever happened.

"I told you, sweetie, it's paid for. Go on as many times as you like." Daddy gives me a little push forward. "Look, it's stopping. Jump on."

"She's too little." Mummy is frowning and anxious, and sometimes when she says things like this Daddy agrees with her. "She might fall off."

"I'll go with her," says Noah. "I'll hold her on."

"Oh, would you? You're such a good boy." Mummy has a special smile for when Noah's nice to me. I'll never get to look after Noah and get Mummy's special smile, but at least I'll get to go on the horses, and Daddy lifts me up and Noah climbs on behind me and I've got my hand in the horse's mane and the music's beginning.

"The horse is called Blue," Noah shouts in my ear over the sound of the music, and I wants to tell him the horse is called Fluttershy, but then the ride begins and I can't get the words out. I lean back against the golden pole instead, and pretend this is a real horse that's allowed to sleep in my bedroom and it can talk, but only to me, and I ride it to school every day.

"Did you enjoy that?" Mummy is hovering as soon as the ride slows, ready to lift me off.

"Can I go on it again?" I ask, without any real hope.

"Course you can," says Noah, loud and confident. "We can, can't we?" And Mummy laughs helplessly and agrees, because it's Noah asking and not me.

"Look, Callie, that horse is called Joey, can you see?" Noah points at a collection of shapes on a painted ribbon on the horse's neck. I can just about see they're meant to be letters, but reading them is beyond me. "And this one's called Lucky. Shall we have a ride on Lucky?"

Daddy's watching now, his arm around Mummy's shoulder and his fingers petting the side of her neck, and it's almost perfect, everything's almost just right. Then I see the look on Mummy's face, all tight and clenched, as if Daddy's hurting her, and the colour drains out of the world.

"It's all right." Noah pats my hand, puts it into the thick scrubby mane of the horse. "Mummy's just tired. Hold on tight." And as the music starts I forget about Mummy and Daddy, and we're off again, the two of us whirling and whirling, and when Noah leads the way to Mickey, then John, then Celeste, I know this is the greatest day of my life.

The day goes on and on, lights and noise and ice cream, punctuated by the strange, cool dimness of the toilet block that feels like being plunged into deep water. Noah crams beside me in a car with a metal pole on the back called a dodgem, and we tear around a hot metal arena, crashing into as many other people as possible. The impact's so hard it almost hurts, I almost cry, but I make myself keep smiling, because Noah loves cars and I love Noah, and he rode five horses for me. Between teeth-rattling collisions, I check to see if Mummy's looking, seeing me being so grown-up, doing something nice for Noah. But every time I catch her eye, she turns away. I look and look for the giant teacups that float in the air, but only see the ordinary kind. I ride them, just once, in honour of the days when I didn't know there was anything better. To my astonishment, Mummy joins me, and stretches out her hand and runs it over my hair a few times while I sit, frozen in place, not daring to move.

I can sense what's coming next before anyone says anything. 'Time to leave' is written in the firm square shape of Mummy's face, in the way Daddy's shoulders slump. We still haven't found the roller coaster, and I'm sorry for Noah but glad for myself, because I'd have had to go on it with him and I absolutely don't want to.

Then – as if this has been his plan all along, as if the whole of the rest of the day has only been waiting for this moment – Noah pulls me away into the vast, blind jostle of the crowd.

"Come on," he whispers.

"Where are we going?"

"We're going on the roller coaster."

"We can't go off on our own."

"We'll be quick. Come on, it's going to be brilliant."

I'm frightened. We're not supposed to be doing this, slipping through the crowds without Mummy and Daddy, not ever, but Noah's so happy and sure, so I scramble after him anyway. I'm frightened, but I also feel special, because Noah's bringing me with him. We're going for an adventure together, and he's holding my hand the whole time. We join a line of people queueing for a wooden platform with a row of carriages.

"It's a train," I say, puzzled.

"It's a roller coaster," Noah insists, even though this is nothing like what he said, and we climb on board, behind an older girl with pretty hair clips and a fat man who almost doesn't fit.

"You're a little one," the attendant says as he presses a big metal bar down over our knees. "Are you definitely tall enough for this?"

"She's got long legs," Noah says, with such utter confidence that the man nods and walks away. I wonder why I need to be tall enough for a train.

"Where does it go?" I ask.

"Up in the air," Noah says, and points.

It's so big I haven't even seen it. The track rises off the ground, up into the air, twisting and curving.

"But that's high," I say.

"All the way up to the sky," Noah replies, and points to a

towering metal ring that I've been noticing all afternoon but had thought was some kind of sculpture.

"No, it doesn't."

"Yes, it does. Hold on, it's starting."

And to my horror, the train's moving, and it's taking me with it.

No, I think, too frightened even to scream as it creeps up the first slope. *It's stopping,* I think, as it pauses. Then there's a whoosh that takes the breath out of my lungs, and the train tumbles down and forward and up and around another loop, banking to the side so I'm pressed against Noah.

"I want to get off!" I scream. "I want to get off I want to get off I want to get off—"

"It's all right, we're together." Noah takes my hand. "Ow, don't hold so hard. Don't be scared. It's fun."

I'm slipping all over the seat. Maybe Noah was joking, the train can't possibly get up that high, it can't possibly drop that far...

"Here we go," says Noah. "Hold on, Callie."

The loop's coming. There's no escape.

"It's all right," Noah says. "It'll be like flying. Don't be scared. I wouldn't bring you if it wasn't safe."

He's so serene that I almost stop being scared. Noah wouldn't take me anywhere if it wasn't safe. I'm frightened, but suddenly I've got room for something else, something I'm picking up from Noah. Noah loves this. Noah can't wait for the loop. Noah wants to fly.

"Okay," I say, the only word I can manage because my throat's so dry.

"Get ready," Noah says.

And as the train roars and my tummy turns over and my hair falls away beneath me, it really does feel like flying.

Afterwards we're in trouble, which we both knew we would be. Noah's saying all the right things – he's sorry, he didn't think, he was just so excited to go on the rollercoaster, he thought Mummy and Daddy were behind him, he thought they were waiting in the crowd because they didn't want to queue. I know he's lying, but I don't say anything. My knees are shaky and I'm glad I don't have to eat tea for a while.

"And what the hell were you thinking? Don't just stand there daydreaming! Answer me!"

It's only when Mummy grabs my arm and forces me to look at her that I realise she's talking to me.

"What?"

"Never mind *what*, young lady. Don't you know how dangerous that was? You're both too small for the rollercoaster! You could have fallen out, do you hear me? You could both have fallen out and smashed into little pieces on the ground—"

"Vee, don't. She's five."

"She should have known better. What were you thinking, making your brother take you on there? Well?"

This is so outrageously far from what happened that I can't speak.

"It was my idea." Noah's face is anxious, his voice high. "Not Callie's. And I'm not too small, I measured, and Callie's almost—"

"Don't defend her. She's old enough to know."

"Come on." Now Daddy's on my side too, which ought to feel like enough, so why am I still so upset? "Stop shouting at her. She's little, she doesn't know. And anyway, there's no harm done."

"He could have fallen out!" Mummy's face is wild. "He could have been killed, and it would have been all her fault!"

People are stopping to look now. I want to disappear.

"Vanessa. Stop this now." Daddy's acting like he's in charge, but I can see he's afraid too. There are three of us and only one of her, but we're all still afraid of her.

"Your brother could have been killed." My mother hardly looks like herself. If she doesn't stop looking at me I think

I'm going to wet myself in terror. "And it would all have been your fault."

And that's it; the end of the day. Noah tries to get a game of *What Animal Am I* going, but I shut my eyes and pretend to be asleep. In a few minutes I really am asleep, and I only wake up when we park outside our house.

"And," Noah is saying as they climb out of the car, "I'll have a special horse ride just for Callie, not for anyone else. Do you hear that, Callie?"

"What?"

"I'm going to have an amusement park when I grow up. And I'll have a horse ride just for you."

Mummy and Daddy are smiling at Noah, because he's being sweet and looking after his little sister. They've all moved on from the argument that still feels fresh to me. But they're all acting like they're happy, so I try to act happy too. And for a few minutes, everything's smooth and nice, and when Daddy kisses Mummy on the back of the neck, Mummy smiles at him.

It doesn't last. I always hope it will, and it never does, and this time is no different. I drop my glass of water on the way to the kitchen, and it soaks into the carpet and now the carpet's damp and according to Mummy it will smell for weeks, and it will all be my fault. I say I'm sorry, but Mummy doesn't want to hear about sorry, she wants me to be more careful. Now I'm in bed, tears drying on my cheeks. Yesterday Noah dropped a whole yoghurt, and she smiled and told him not to worry, accidents happen.

She doesn't love me, I think.

Of course she loves me, I think. *She's my mummy, she has to love me.*

The words she said to me. Noah could have been killed, and

it would have been my fault. She didn't care what happened to me. Only Noah.

This thought is too much to stay in bed with. I slip out from the duvet and tiptoe across the floor. Sometimes, if I can't sleep, I sit on the landing, and Noah comes out and sits next to me. If Mummy finds us there, she'll tell me off for not being asleep and keeping Noah awake too, but tonight I don't care. Whatever I do, I'll always be in trouble, because Mummy doesn't—

Noah's already there, wrapped in a fleecy blanket. He holds the blanket open so I can creep underneath it.

"She does love you," he says, before I can even speak.

How does he know what I'm thinking?

"She doesn't," I whisper, hot with shame.

"She does."

"She doesn't. She loves you. But not me."

I want him to keep arguing until I believe he's right and I'm wrong. Instead, he puts his arm around me and gives me a squeeze.

"One day," he whispers, "I'll build a special roller coaster. And the car will fly into the sky. I'm going to be an engineer so I can learn how to build it."

"She doesn't love me," I repeat.

"Shhh." Noah pulls the blanket tighter. "I'm telling you about my roller coaster."

"But she doesn't, Noah, she doesn't, and it's not fair—"

"What colour shall I make the carriages?"

"Purple." Purple's my favourite colour, but Noah hates it.

"Really? All of them?"

"All of them," I say, knowing Noah will agree, because he loves me, and love means doing things you don't really want to just to make the other person happy.

"All right," says Noah. He's not really cross, it's just part of the game. "The carriages can be purple. Just for you. And then it'll be the best roller coaster in the world."

Chapter Seven

Note

Four days since they died. I've taken a wrong turn into a universe where I don't belong, but it's all right, it's all right, I only have to hold on. There's a world where time is frozen and none of this has happened, and soon I'll go back there. I'll tell Josh and Frey the story of what should have happened in these two weeks, and in doing so, the things we never did and the places we never went to will somehow become reality. There'll still be a place where Dad and Noah are alive.

Today, Noah and I were going to Paradise Park to ride the roller coaster. Noah gets priority access because of his illness, which counts as a disability and which he always finds hilarious. Sometimes people glare, because Noah on a good day doesn't look like he has anything wrong with him, other than possibly being far too fat to have as much confidence as he does. ("I'm thin on the inside," he always says as he festoons himself in clothing so flamboyant it's verging on costume. "We both know this is just the meds.") Sometimes he puts on a performance for the crowds, pretending to have conditions he doesn't, and when I tell him off, tell him it's awful and offensive, he laughs and tells me, "I can get away with it because I'm one of them." Once a man said loudly that being a fat bastard wasn't a proper disability. Noah lunged across the barrier and kissed him passionately on the mouth.

"There's a couple of things we need to talk about," DC Harris says, and my mother and I both tense up, ready for whatever new burden's coming our way. I think about Floss, about the way she watches Frey. About the absolute relaxation that fills her when we take her harness off and she's free to be just a dog. Ten more days until I can take my harness off, go back to the world where my life is right.

"All right." My mother and I speak together, as if we're running on the same clockwork. Harris will take this as a sign that we're close. I feel a childish need to tell her that this isn't true, that my mother is not to be trusted.

"It was actually Noah who was driving," Harris says, and I feel my stomach lurch.

"But Noah can't drive."

"Did he know how?"

"He passed his test, but his licence was revoked. He knows—" I stop, breathe through the hurt, make myself continue. "He knew he wasn't allowed to."

"And he never drove after that? He didn't borrow your dad's car while he was at work, for example? Maybe went out on his own?"

"He's never on his own, not any more. One of us is always with him."

"It must be hard to make that work."

"We manage. We both changed our jobs so we work half-time, two weeks on and two weeks off. Dad's an accountant." I pause. Breathe. "Was an accountant."

"Why did you do that? Was Noah needing more support? Was his illness getting worse maybe?"

The year of the pandemic was hard on all of us, hardest of

84

all on Noah. We'd thought we were going to lose him at the last hospitalisation, that if we got him back at all he'd never be as he had been. It frightened us enough to make us change the whole shape of our lives. But was that a one-off episode, or simply the natural tendency of his illness to progress, over time, into deepening chaos?

"We did it to help him get better," I say, defiant and hopeful. "And he did. It worked."

Harris nods. Not giving anything away. I'm supposed to call her by her first name, which is Ellen. I'm supposed to think she's on my side. "Might your dad have let him take the wheel? Maybe as a treat?"

"No. No, he wouldn't. They both knew the rules." And Noah was a rule breaker, his whole life. He was born to climb under fences, creep into abandoned buildings, crash through barriers…

"I see." Harris writes something on her pad. Handwritten notes are growing rarer. One day soon everything will be recorded instead, sound and visuals, and investigations will be about endlessly reviewing video clips, evaluating everyone's actions. After a year of living in Frey's house, I've got used to the idea of constant unseen observers.

"So," says Harris. "We need to visit your house and conduct a search."

"What? Why?"

"Sometimes people leave notes, or they put out important documents. Or sometimes we find diaries or journals. It can help us understand their state of mind."

"My son," says my mother, "would not have killed himself."

"It's something we need to rule out," says Harris.

"My son," my mother repeats, as if repetition will make it truth, "would not have killed himself. It was the car."

She's making it sound as if the car had a will of its own, as if the car took the decision to fly over the edge. It's almost funny. Almost.

"We're examining the car as well. This is just one line of

enquiry. Would you prefer to be there while we conduct the search? Or would you rather we went on our own?"

Our house. The house we shared. The house that will be a tip, because living with Noah invites mess. It's only since I've known Frey that I've realised how clean a home can be when you really put the work in. And now, strangers, roaming around and judging. If I'm there they'll be silent and respectful, moving carefully through the rooms. If I'm not there, they'll relax into it, joke about the things they find, swap anecdotes about 'Other Places We Have Turned Over'.

"I want to be there," my mother says. As if they're asking her. As if she gets to answer.

"Of course. Callie?"

She has no right to be in that house. No right at all.

"I'll be there too."

"All right, then. It'll be this afternoon."

God, so soon, so soon. I don't want to be here, but I don't want to go there either. I want to be back in the universe of *before,* the universe where I belong. I want to be with Josh and Frey. Ten more days. I can do this for ten more days.

"We can arrange transport for you if you don't feel up to driving."

"I'm fine. I can drive." I am fine, I'll be fine in a minute. It's just all these *windows*, wherever I sit there could be someone peering in. You'd think I'd be used to it but I can't bear the thought of seeing their faces, having to look back. I wipe my palms down my trousers. There's a shadow at the window facing the water, something there and then gone, like a plastic bag blowing around. Then a big black bird perches on the sill, tapping the glass with its beak.

"That's Huginn." My mother, all stone and pronouncements, is suddenly animated. The crow waits calmly as she opens the window. "I need to feed him."

We ought to move, to carry on as normal, but we're transfixed. My mother goes to the kitchen, returns with a white enamelled tin. She makes a soft crooning noise as she opens the lid. She shakes a handful of something into her palm, holds it out.

"Huginn," she murmurs, tender and sweet. "Here you go."

The crow hops onto her forearm. Turns its head to one side and then the other, sizing up the strangers. We keep still, held by our astonishment. The crow looks a moment longer, then dips its fat beak to eat from my mother's palm. It's not being gentle; I can see the judder of her palm with each jab.

"Mealworms," my mother murmurs. I'm not sure if she's talking to us or the bird. "There you are, Huginn. No, don't leave any for me, I don't like them. You have them."

It's all right, I tell myself. *You don't need her to feed you. You have food upstairs. You have money in your purse. The shops are three minutes away.*

"What is it?" Harris is clearly appalled and trying to hide it. "Is it a pet?"

"Not a pet. Just a crow. He visits sometimes."

When Noah and I were ten and seven, in the year before she left us, we begged for a dog. It was all we wanted, all we thought about. We took books from the library and studied different breeds, considered large dogs versus small ones, active breeds and lazy ones. We stalked the local animal shelters and checked our family off against their adoption policies to see if we'd qualify. We took plastic bags from under the sink and went out into the streets and hunted down dog turds that we made ourselves pick up as practice. ("It'll be better when it's our own dog," Noah said brightly, when I was sick behind a bus shelter. "I used to help Mum change your nappies and that was all right. You'll see.")

Dad was willing, pleased by the thought of a new family member. And our mother? Our mother said no, the first time we asked and the thirty thousandth. "Dogs are dirty and take too much looking after," she said, over and over and over. She was completely immoveable. And now she's standing in her own house, feeding mealworms to a wild bird, stroking gently at its back with one finger.

"I'm going out later," my mother tells it. "But I'll be back by tomorrow." The crow hops from her wrist to the window ledge in a single strong leap. Another minute, and it's shaken out its wings and vanished.

"Huginn," says Harris, breaking the reverent silence. "Isn't that one of Odin's ravens?"

"Yes. It means 'thought'."

"So is there another one? Muninn, isn't it? Memory?"

My mother turns her face away, shuts the window firmly. Harris must be looking forward to getting back to the station, to share the news of my mother and her weird corvid visitor.

"Just one," she says. "Only thoughts. No memories."

My mother has a car and I have a car, and my ideal solution is that we both drive up in our own vehicles. But I don't know how to ask for that, and when my mother says, "Would you like to go in my car, or yours?" I tell her we'll take my car and I'll drive. The windows of her house watch us as we leave.

"Let me know if you want to stop," I tell her, and put the radio on. Usually, I'd have a music station, but I can't bear the thought of upbeat songs and banal competitions. I choose Radio Four instead, and we cruise the motorway to earnest discussions and plummy dramas and on-the-hour news. The miles stretch out. Thank God for radio.

"We used to always have music," my mother says suddenly.

"What?"

"When you and Noah were little. Your dad put on music and tried to get you to sing along. Don't you remember?"

I remember she used to censor the songs, rejecting anything with the word 'sexy' or 'sex'. I can see the rigidity of her neck and shoulders, glimpsed from my spot in the back seat. Her fingers hovering over the volume dial, ready to turn it down. My dad, laughing.

"I used to say to myself," my mother says thoughtfully, "one day, I'll be able to listen to Radio Four again." She puts out a hand, pats shyly at my leg. My skin crawls. "And now I'm with my daughter and we're listening to it together."

I don't know what to say.

"I do love you, you know," she says.

'I do love you, you know.' As if she's trying to convince herself. As if she knows I know it's not true – or, if it is, she loves me only in that primitive, instinctual way all mammals love their offspring. Whatever she feels wasn't enough to stop her leaving me. 'I do love you, you know.' Just by saying the words, she's contradicted them.

"We should take a break," I say, and flick on the indicator to turn into the services.

We're there before I expect it, the journey mysteriously compressed by the weight of how much I don't want to arrive. I can't believe how unchanged the house looks, as if Dad and Noah have just popped out to the shops. The grass should be long and unkempt, paint peeling from the walls, windows dropping in their frames. The police are already waiting, their clean, modest saloon parked a little way up the road, leaving the prime spot outside the front gate for us. My mother is pale and frightened-looking, and this makes me angry. This is my home, crammed with my memories. For her, it's just a place she left behind.

"Come on, then," I say, rough and faux-jolly, and I fling myself out of the car and up the front path.

The key resists the lock. DC Harris is here, and two officers in uniform, waiting at a respectful distance. I'm picturing a tussock of post blocking the doorway, the way it is when you come back from a holiday, but there's only a small litter of catalogues and a letter from the bank. I keep forgetting how little time has gone by since it happened. The house smells of cooking, and the three of us. It's not even faintly musty. There's perhaps the slightest hint of a rubbish bag that should have gone out by now, but nothing unsettling, nothing to say that the house knows what's happened and is in mourning. My mother pats awkwardly at my shoulder, as if she's heard the act of mothering described by a stranger in a pub. When I turn my head to glare at her, I see she's crying.

"It's all right." DC Harris is calm, supportive but not affectionate. "Take your time." At least she's not trying to touch me.

"It's so strange," my mother says, as if Harris was talking to her. "I haven't been here since..." She wipes her cheeks with the corner of her sleeve. "It smells just the same."

"Take your time," Harris repeats.

"Right," I say. "How do we do this?"

"Is there somewhere we can sit down? Is the living room this way? The other officers will conduct the search."

"Can't I go with them?"

"It's best if we keep out of their way."

I want to sweep ahead of them, opening curtains, straightening cushions, whisking away crumby plates and stained coffee mugs. I know they don't care how clean or dirty it is. But Noah and Dad have been living like bachelors for two weeks and Noah is messy at the best of times, and, with my perception newly adjusted by two weeks with Frey, I can see the flaws in our way of living.

The sofa is covered in Noah's gloves. Long black opera gloves, a pair of leather driving gloves, some medieval-looking gauntlets. I pick them up, resisting the urge to hug them. These might be the last things in this house his hands touched. The chair has four jackets strewn across it. I lay them on the floor so Harris can sit down. My mother hovers by the mantelpiece, staring blankly into space, her arms wrapped tightly around her body, until Harris encourages her to sit down.

Why is Harris concerned for my mother? It's just a house to her. Nobody's going through her possessions. Nobody's exercising their professional non-judgement about socks taken off in the living room and then abandoned with the vague idea that, at some point, they'll migrate to the laundry.

I stroke the gloves between my fingers. I can hear strange footsteps in the kitchen, voices made respectfully low as the things on the worktops are moved, examined, set down again. The footsteps come closer.

"How about a cuppa?" Harris suggests, smooth as silk, and my mother and I are pulled into her wake and now we're all in the kitchen, watching the kettle as if it's a holy relic, while the officers move around the living room. It occurs to me that Harris is staying with us not to support us, but to stop us from hiding anything. The dishwasher has been stacked and run. I'm glad for that at least. I couldn't bear seeing her look with understanding on Dad and Noah's final dirty plates.

"We're moving upstairs," says one of the officers, and I feel a primal spasm of panic.

"Oh," I say, because I can't stop myself, "oh, please… please…"

"It's all right. They'll be very respectful. We're just trying to find out what happened."

"Can I watch, though? Please can I at least be there? Just the bedrooms. Please let me just look in first and see."

A complicated exchange of glances, and then I'm on the upstairs landing, my mother beside me. I try not to cringe away from the warmth of her flesh. I'm standing outside my bedroom while a strange woman opens the door and looks inside, and I crane over her shoulder and see—

"Is that Noah's handwriting?" Harris says.

That untidy sprawl of his, the thick, fat texture of the ink. Noah enjoyed felt tips as a writing tool. He liked to make his mark on the world.

"Yes. Yes, it is, but please. It doesn't mean anything. He often leaves me notes." This is a lie, and it's a stupid lie. Now she's going to ask me—

"Can we see them? Just to compare the handwriting."

"I don't keep them, I never keep them, they're just stupid stuff, jokes he thinks I might like, things he might forget to tell me." The rubbish coming out of my mouth, all because

I'm afraid of what Noah's written. "Let me read it. I'll read it out loud to you."

"No, don't touch it, please." I'm not being held back exactly, but I'm definitely not getting in there without a struggle.

"But he wrote it to me, it's in my room."

"We just need to be careful." One of the officers, blue-gloved, is already unfolding it. Noah has written *Callie* on the envelope. I should at least be the first to read it. They should at least give me that. Blue hands hold the note out towards me.

> *Callie, sweetheart*
>   *You've always looked after me. Now I'm going to look after you, like a proper big brother. Don't worry, it'll all be fine.*
>   *See you soon. Say hi to Josh and Frey and Floss from me.*
>   *All my love, always,*
>   *Noah*

Various stuff happens that I can't quite process. I get downstairs somehow. I'm in the living room, sitting down, holding a cup of tea, sweetened so much it's undrinkable. Harris has an arm around my shoulders and is telling me to take it steady. My mother's shivering like a dog at the vet's, face jiggling, hands shaking, and she's mumbling something that sounds like, "Why didn't he leave a note for me? He loved me, I know he did, so why didn't he leave a note for me?", and the two uniformed officers are flanking her on the sofa, encouraging her to breathe. My body feels as if it's coming apart, but – weirdly – my mind is perfectly calm. I let everyone make a fuss of me even though part of me suspects I'm play-acting, the way my mother so often does. Behaving this way buys me time to sit behind the barrier of my own eyelids and think:

Okay, so the police read it as a suicide note. But it doesn't matter what they think, only what you know. Looking after you, keeping you safe. That's what he says when he's not been taking his meds properly. But he wouldn't hurt anyone, you know he wouldn't. So, Callie Louise Taggart, how are you going to handle this?

Then I'm asleep, which strikes me as weird because who falls asleep after an experience like that? And how did I get from sitting in our living room with my mother and three police officers, to the passenger seat of my own car, my face pressed against the window? Even before I crack open one eyelid to peek, the scent of her soap tells me my mother had something to do with how I got here.

My mother, driving my car, smooth and competent. I'm in the passenger seat of my car, with my mother at the wheel. The world feels very strange.

"We're nearly home," she says when she sees me stirring, which instantly annoys me because her home has never been mine. "You've slept almost all the way."

I don't feel rested so much as dislocated.

"It was dreadful," she says. "Being back there. In that house. But I did it." She glances at me. "I did it for you."

"You didn't need to," I say.

"Yes, I did. You couldn't have dealt with it by yourself. I had to go and help. It was terribly hard, but I did it."

My left cheek is numb where it pressed against the window.

"You didn't need to," I repeat. "I've been fine without you for years."

Chapter Eight

Away

"Frey used to be better," Linnea said to me, that first time we met. I can still hear the regret in her voice, damage done that might never be fixable. We're both carers, Linnea and I, so you'd think I'd be on her side, 'You were doing your best,' I might tell her. 'You can't pour from an empty cup.' But the truth is that I identify much more with Frey. I know how it feels to be abandoned by someone who's supposed to love you. I can't imagine what Linnea and her parents were thinking. I don't know how they ever could.

Here's how it feels:

You're an adult. Your form of adulthood takes a different shape from most, but you're happy enough. You have a sister whom you love fiercely. You take quiet pride in knowing that she's out in the world, doing good, making lives better. Your parents don't live together any more, and you still secretly wish you could change that. But you know it's all right to love them separately, and they both still love you.

You have places you go, people you see, bedrock routines you rely on. You're missing many of the key skills that capitalism values, but the ancient impulse to create runs through you like veins of gold, and expressing it gives meaning to your days. Others like you have made art hanging in galleries, where people wonder at the strange intersection between what they call genius and what they call disability. You don't really identify with either of these words.

Your world is small, and lacks certain things you'd love to have – a lover who sees you exactly as you are, a home of your own – but you've learned to accept that. You accept the limits you're given, because they're imposed by people you love and trust.

You don't pay much attention to the news. It feels too separate and distant from your own small world. Nonetheless, you hear the beginnings of change, a new set of words and places to turn over in your mind. A city in China that you've never heard of. A new virus that seems like nothing, but that will soon come to be everything.

Stuff like this is your sister's area of expertise. So you watch her without her knowing, trying to gauge whether it's time to be afraid. When she talks to your parents, everyone is anxious.

After a while, you work out that they're not worried for themselves, but for you. They're always worried about you. It's a piece of knowledge you never quite get to file away and forget. Some days that burden's easier to carry, but it's never not there at all.

There's a plan that involves you. You hear the phrases 'feel so guilty' and 'for the best' and 'he'll be safe there'. "Facilities," they say. "Activities. Support." You don't like the sound of this, but your life is contracting by the day. There were places you could go, once. Now they're disappearing. You're at home all the time. Everyone's tired and snappy, and it's partly because of you. The knowledge makes a sore place in your head, a tender spot on your soul.

Then there's a day when your belongings are going into a bag and you're being taken somewhere new, and everyone's telling you they'll come and see you really soon, and now you're somewhere else, and on your own.

The new place is confusing and wrong. Some things are familiar – you find clothes you know are yours, a toothbrush that seems to belong to you – but the building is strange, the rooms too brightly lit, too noisy. But your family must have a reason for bringing you here. They love you. They wouldn't do anything to hurt you.

There are two kinds of people here: the ones who take care of you, and the ones like you, who get looked after. You're used to all of that, being told what to do and where to go feels familiar, but you don't know anyone here, there are too many of them to keep track of, and you can't get used to the way they sound and smell and move. They come into your space in sudden jerks, startling you with touches you don't want, gestures that feel like threats. You can never get away from the other residents, their invasions and their endless curiosities. Their voices are harsh and loud. They ask you questions and questions and questions that buzz in your head. You wonder if it's allowed to ask the staff for help, but they don't seem to understand. They see the other residents grabbing at you, and smile.

Mealtimes are hard. Many of the others make a mess while they eat, dribble on themselves, grab at other people with sticky hands. You know you ought not to mind but you can't help yourself. This whole place feels dirty and dangerous. You keep your eyes turned down, decide not to look at anyone in case it draws their attention, and eat what little you can stand from the strange tastes on your plate.

Maybe you're the one in the wrong. Maybe you're supposed to like all of this. And your family are coming soon. They said they'd come soon, and they will.

* * *

There's a garden here, which you're meant to enjoy. You try it just once, because you're tired and hungry and you don't know how to refuse when they grab on to your arm and lead you outside. (Why are they touching you? Why do strangers keep touching you? How is this allowed, why are they all acting like it's normal to take hold of someone you barely know and not let go? You accept it because you're polite, you know it's not okay to yell and flail and push them off, but it makes you shudder. When did they last wash their hands? Who else have they been touching before they got to you?) You used to accept going out, but you're tired and confused and lonely and hungry, and all of these things mean you can't tolerate it today. It's beyond what you can bear.

Just when you think you might die from it, you find an escape you never knew was there. You close your eyes and something happens in your head, and then you're somewhere safe and quiet and peaceful. It's dark and limited, this place, but it's better than the noises and the sights and the wind on your skin and the excited shrieks of others. You stay in this place for a time that could be short or long.

When you come out again, you're back in the room you're supposed to call yours. One of the staff is there with you, murmuring, "You don't need to go outside any more if you don't like it." He seems kind, but you're wary and nervous, and you can't yet be sure.

You remember the dark, safe place in your head. You'd never known it was there before. You might need to go there again.

There aren't enough clocks here. You don't know what time or day it is. Is it soon yet? Has enough time passed for your family to come?

There's a sense of tension now, a feeling that wasn't there when you first arrived. You listen and listen and listen, ravenous for scraps of knowledge, craving it almost as much as you crave food you can actually eat. You remember there was a sickness coming, dark fingers of infection reaching out across the world. Is that what's happened to your family? Are they all sick now? Are they all dead?

A parcel comes with your name on it. It's from your sister. The joy of not being forgotten is deep, but brief. On its heels there's another, darker thought. *If the postman can still come here, why won't they?*

You try not to think about this. You're getting a grasp of time again now. You can find your way through the flow of the days, feel the rhythm you're supposed to live by. The food at breakfast is all right, it's hard to mess up toast, and you're growing used to being hungry in the afternoons and evenings. There are activities you're supposed to join in with – paints, clay, raffia – but you're allowed to refuse, as long as you're not rude about it. You know these refusals upset the staff, they'd prefer you to take part, but you can't, you simply can't. To sit in a room full of noisy strangers, let them be near you, put your hands into textures that repulse you… it's not possible. You long for drawing pencils, colouring books, but you don't have any way to ask.

You retreat to your room instead, and wait for the time to pass. *This will end,* you tell yourself. *They told you they'd see you soon.*

You've been in places like this before, for short, painful periods, but you don't think it's ever gone on for so long. You used to always know instantly what day it was, but in here every day is the same. Only the hours unfold with endless regularity, each dreadful moment marching on into the next.

Another parcel arrives, and then another. Now you have jigsaws and colouring books. You're grateful to know your family's still alive, but it's no substitute for seeing them.

After a while you notice something frightening: *nobody in here has any visitors.* The world's clearly going on beyond the locked front door – there are deliveries, television programmes – but no visitors, ever. You're not the only one who's been—

No. You haven't been abandoned. There must be a chance, still. 'Soon', they told you, and you cling to that promise.

They tell you, all the time, you're safe. They say you don't need to be so anxious, everything's all right, they'll look after you. They tell you all of this, but you can't believe them. Maybe they're keeping your family from you. Maybe they come to the door every day, only to be turned away. That might be it.

You know escape is impossible. Even if you managed to get outside, you wouldn't know what to do next. You need your family, but they don't seem to need you. It's getting harder to believe they're still out there.

Instead, you make a different kind of escape. You stop going to the dining room, even though you're hungry. Instead, you stay quietly in your room, looking at the walls, breathing in and out. The rest of this building is cursed, contaminated, but in here everything's safe and clean. Apart from the times when the staff come in to do the things they do – which is all right, there's a schedule for that, you can manage it – you're alone.

You're afraid the staff will force you downstairs to eat. You're prepared for this, prepared to hide inside your own head if you must. But as it turns out, you don't need to. They bring you food on a tray. Each plate's an unwelcome surprise because now you can't find out in advance what the meal will be and get mentally ready for it, but at least there are no dirty hands or dirty faces. No strangers who smell and make noises and grab for you. One of the staff brings a gaming console and shows you a strange cubic world that you can shape into whatever you want, and you get lost in it for hours. It's like a miracle.

If you can just have this, you'll manage to hold on until 'soon' comes.

One of the staff comes into your room at a time you're not expecting it. They're smiling, carrying a laptop. As you watch in alarm, they set it down on your desk and turn the screen towards you. There's a face on the screen. It's your sister. She's looking at you. She sees you. She smiles. She waves.

It's such a shock that you don't know how to process it. You glance towards the screen, look away, just in case you've made a mistake, projected your own longing into reality. No, she's really there. You know it's just a screen, but still your hand reaches out. Her hand does the same. If you wish hard enough, perhaps in some digital dimension your fingers will meet.

She's talking to you. She's asking you how you are.

You want to ask her 'How do you think I am?' You want to say, 'Are you coming to get me out?' You want to beg, 'Please will you take me home now?'

She asks you questions. The man, smiling in his uniform, answers on your behalf. You're too confused to listen to the words, so you concentrate on their tone. Your sister is anxious, unhappy, as if she doesn't approve of what she's seeing. The man is conciliatory and soothing, smoothing everything over.

Then, too soon, it's over, her face disappears, the laptop closes. The man says he's going to the next room now, because "we need to get around all of you that we can". You wonder if this will ever happen again. You wonder how long you'll have to wait to find out.

Then, the thought that flattens you. *What if this is soon? What if this is what they meant by seeing me? What if I have to stay here forever?*

You're not always easy to live with, you know that. They think you don't notice, but you do. You've seen the looks on their faces when you've needed things to be a certain way, when you've wanted something they didn't or hated something they love. You've heard the muttered conversations, the whispered arguments. You know why your parents aren't married any longer. It's why you try so hard to fit in with the world, even though you know you'll never succeed.

You'd always thought you'd done enough, that *your best* was enough for them to love you. Maybe you're here because they've had enough of you. Maybe they couldn't stand you any longer. You're still trying not to let this thought settle in when the next unbearable thing happens.

You're getting used to how your life is now. You're not happy, but maybe you don't deserve happiness. Maybe all those years when you thought you were all together, all loving each other, were a lie. Maybe they're happier without you being there. That thought – that their love isn't enough for them to accommodate your difference – hurts your heart, but you'll learn to accept it. At least they still send parcels. At least they haven't given up on you completely.

The door opens without a knock. He's in your room before you know it. He's large, bumbling, a bit grubby. You can smell him, a scent of old food and unwashed skin. He's smiling and looking happy, waving at you as if you're pleased to see him. He's making noises, the closest he gets to speech. You can't move for the terror of it. You sit motionless, afraid movement will summon him over, watching from the corner of your eye.

He moves around your room. Touches your things. His hands are soft and pudgy and there's a layer of grime at the wrists. You can picture him in the craft room, hands in the clay, the paint, the glue, lost in the sensory joy of touch. You've never understood how anyone can want to do that, but you're happy enough for them to get on with it, as long as you don't have to join in. Except now you're having to join in, because here he is in your space, leaving traces of himself on everything, and how are you supposed to get him out again?

He stays only a few minutes, but the time seems endless. When he's gone, you look slowly around your sanctuary, wondering how it can ever be cleaned.

He comes back every day, staying longer each time. You hope the staff will save you, but they seem to think it's fine, telling you how nice it is that you've made friends.

More and more places become untouchable. Your television, which he adores, switching it on without asking, smiling and flapping in your direction when something comes on that he particularly likes. Now you can't play your console any more, because he's touched the screen and the controller and left fingermarks. He picks up your duvet, wraps it around himself. You leave it lying on the floor, curled up small on the bare sheet. He pokes at your colouring pencils with curious fingers. You let them lie in their tin, jumbled and out of order. The worst times are when he uses your bathroom. Now you can't go in there any more, and you sit motionless as your body does what it must. The staff murmur in concern when they find you, undress and re-dress you as if you're a baby. The shame is painful, but going in there when *he's* touched everything is impossible.

You can feel yourself withdrawing, shutting down, giving up. You've spent so long trying to fit into the world, and what has that got you? A small room you didn't choose, food you can't eat, a building full of strangers, and a mortal enemy who everyone thinks is your friend. Your family told you this wouldn't be forever, they told you they'd see you really soon, and you believed them, but it's not true. 'Soon' will never come. They've sent you away because you're too hard to live with.

The dark place in your head is calling you. You go there more often now, feeling nothing and seeing nothing. Occasionally you come back into your body to find you're being touched and handled, cleaned and fed and groomed. You accept this because you know it will end, they'll do what they need to and then they'll stop and you'll be alone. They bring the laptop and you see your sister on the screen, and you want to beg her to come and get you, but you don't know how. Easier just to drift, let others care for your body, while you shut yourself down. Sometimes you come briefly back into yourself and find a whole day's gone by.

And then.

There's a stir in the air that even you can feel. Something's happening outside in the courtyard. There's a voice you think you recognise, not exactly shouting but not far off. You think about glancing out of the window, but you don't dare look in case you're wrong.

Someone comes into your room, guides you downstairs. Your body doesn't want to move, your legs are not quite co-operating. It's been a long time since you last came out at all.

Now you're in a room with a big pane of plastic that divides it, floor to ceiling. Where can you get a pane of plastic like that? If you could have a pane like that, you could keep your room secure. You're so busy thinking about this, admiring and longing, that you don't realise for a minute who's on the other side of it.

Your fingers touch the screen. Her fingers meet on the other side. There's still a barrier between you, but it's smaller than it was. She's talking to you, but you're not listening, only looking. She's wearing something over her mouth, and you remember the virus everyone was talking about, in the days before you came here. You'd almost forgotten there was a before. You'd definitely given up on the concept of soon.

Then she's standing up, going away, and you want to go after her, but you can't, there's no way through the screen. The door to your side of the room opens and it's going to be the staff, coming to take you back to your room, and you get ready for that, but it's not the staff, it's your sister, she's come for you, 'soon' has tumbled into 'right now', and you grab on to her hand and don't let go and don't let go and don't let go.

There's quite a lot of shouting. Quite a lot of movement. You endure it because her hand is in yours, you'll accept anything as long as her hand is in yours. Finally, you hear her saying your name, over and over. She's asking you something. She's asking what you want. If you want to stay here. If you want to leave.

You don't like to look into people's eyes directly. The feeling of it jangles in your bones, as if you're touching electricity. But you make yourself do it, you need to speak her language for once. You take a deep breath and look into her eyes.

It hurts, it jangles and it hurts, but it's worth it.

More shouting. She still has hold of your hand. Her hand is the only thing that feels real. Holding it is the only way to be sure she doesn't disappear. You clutch it tightly, determined not to lose this one thing. You don't let go even when she takes you outside. The sunlight's bright and sudden and you have to cover your eyes with your other hand.

Somehow, you're both in her car, and you still haven't let go. When she changes gear, your joined hands move the stick in unison. She's repeating something to herself over and over. After a while, you find the focus to understand what she's saying.

"Never again," she's telling you, "never again, never again. Never again."

You think about 'never again'. You think about 'soon'.

You wonder how much you can trust what's happening to you now, if you'll get dragged back there. Her hand, her presence, is all that stands between you and the dark.

The shape of our brains can change to reflect our lived experiences. Some of these pathways are useful shortcuts – *this is how I roll over, this is where my hands are, this is how to stand, to walk, to speak.* Some of these pathways are maladaptive. There's a track in your head now, leading straight to that dark and shut-down place inside. Now when things are hard, it's an effort to stop yourself going into it. Some of them are like scars. *I thought I was safe, but I'm not. The people I trust can abandon me. Everything I have now can be taken away.*

And after the long imprisonment you've survived, what wouldn't you do to avoid being sent back? What wouldn't you tolerate to escape being locked away again? When you've spent time in hell, mere discomfort seems like a good deal. This is why, in the future you can't imagine yet, your carers will be watched. Your scars will make you needier, more frightened, but they'll also make you more willing to endure.

In the meantime, there's one thing you know you can trust, one thing you know is real: you have your sister's hand in yours. As long as you're holding on to it, you know this is happening. As long as you're holding on to her hand, you know that 'soon' can't be taken back.

Chapter Nine

Wild

Here's an ugly confession for you: I have a deep and terrible need for constant validation. I do know how unattractive this is. If I met myself on a date, I'd think I was too needy, too anxious to please. I cope with this yearning by starving it, not letting myself think too hard about the possibility of being wanted.

Maybe that's where I went wrong. Maybe I repulsed my mother by trying too hard. Maybe that's why she had to leave me. If I chased after you the way I chased my mother, would you enjoy it? Or would you think, *she's too much like hard work, I'm getting out while I can*?

I'm nine years old. I'm sitting on the back doorstep, chilly because today isn't quite how it looks. It's cold, but the sun's shining. It's a school day, but we're not going to school. Mum doesn't live here any more and says she never will again, but Dad insists it's only temporary, and today we're all going out as a family. I'm awake before Noah; the final dollop of strangeness. I sit on the doorstep, pretending the sun's warm enough to bask in, and think: *What if Dad and Noah are both dead? What if I have to go and live with Mum?*

I picture it as if I'm watching a film. I'm going up the stairs, knocking on Noah's door and then on Dad's, peering in to see their bodies lying in their beds. I don't know what dead people look like, so I skip to the next scene, which is me on the stairs, waiting for Mum. The front door swings open.

Mum stands in front of me, tall and frightening. She says, "Well, I suppose you're coming to live with me after all, then." Her arms around me feel like when you've argued with your friends and you're all snotty and upset and the teacher doesn't really want to touch you, but they make themselves do it anyway. I know it's not a proper hug because Dad and Noah hug me too, and theirs are real and warm.

My fantasy continues. We get into her car. She makes me sit in the back. She always asks Noah if he wants to sit in the front (she says he's allowed because he's taller than me), but Noah says he'll get in the back so he can look after me. Now I'm all she's got but she still won't let me get in the front seat, because my mum is really a Wicked Stepmother and now my life's going to be awful. I'm actually making myself cry over this, I'm sitting on the back doorstep and imagining a future where it's just me and Mum, and there's a strange, painful pleasure in it. I'm very cold now and I want my breakfast, but I'm going to keep going, just in case... just in case...

I rewind the film to the beginning, try a different, sweeter version:

Dad and Noah are dead, and now I'm all alone. Mum rushes in and gathers me into her arms, and this time it's true, she really wants to be close to me. She kisses me and pets my head, and it feels wonderful even though Dad and Noah are dead. Except maybe they're not dead, maybe they're just ill and I'm the only one who isn't, so I called Mum and told her we needed help, and she came because she still loves us, after all. And on the way over she realised how much trouble Dad and Noah would have been in if they didn't have me. I'm the reason Dad and Noah are still alive. And finally she sees me properly, and she loves me, after all…

It's dangerous to dream about things you can't really have. I'm saved by Noah thundering down the stairs, 'like a herd of elephants' Mum always says, and I hold on to my daydream a few seconds longer, letting myself relish it now I know it's definitely not true, and then Noah bursts into the kitchen and says, "How are you awake before me? This never happens. This literally never happens."

His energy spills out into the room. He's skinny and lovely and funny and bright, everything I want to be. I get up from the cold concrete step, feeling numbness prickle and tingle in my legs.

"Shall we make pancakes? Let's make pancakes." Noah's already rummaging through the cupboards.

"Do you know how?" Noah's forever producing new skills I didn't know he had.

"We made them at school on Pancake Day. It's flour and eggs and milk and you mix them all up." His voice is muffled by the cupboard. "Get a bowl. And a whisk."

We don't know how much of anything we need, so we drop ingredients into the bowl and stir until it looks about right. There are lumps of flour, but Noah says that won't matter, and there's a lot more batter than we were expecting, but Noah says we'll just have to eat a lot of pancakes. Just as Noah's lighting the ring on the stove, Dad wanders in, and I'm worried he might be cross but he just laughs and says "Why not?" and then the doorbell rings and it's Mum and we're supposed to be ready to go, but there are three of us and only one of her so when Noah begs her to have pancakes with us, she doesn't have a choice.

Mum sits down. Noah and I put out the plates. Dad pets her shoulder, and I try to see only his gentle touch, and not her frown and flinch. Noah smiles to himself, as if he's achieved something much bigger than making breakfast.

Here we all are, eating pancakes together. Noah wanted

that to happen, and it has. Today I'm going to be more like Noah. I know what I want, and I'm going to make it happen. The pancakes taste weird – the whole day feels weird – but I eat them anyway.

The day continues to be weird. It's only been four months, but I've already got used to the idea that, now, Noah and I take it in turns in the front seat. But today Mum is there, and it's like we've gone back in time. Except we're still the present selves we've grown to be and nothing in the past quite fits any more, so we have to shuffle and wriggle and make do. Like finding an old exercise book and thinking, *Was my handwriting ever really like that? Did I really know all of this about the Romans?*

We're going to the wildlife park we visited years ago, when I was small. I loved our day there, still go there sometimes in my dreams. I'm not sure how I feel about going back, and my stomach feels squirmy. I wish I could get back inside the skin of the person I was before and repeat the day we had then.

"Come on then, family!" Dad claps his hands as if we need applauding for getting out of the car. Mum frowns and moves away. At the ticket booth he asks for a family of four without hesitating. The people at the ticket booth are obviously fooled; they sell us the ticket without flinching.

Are we still a family? For all of my life up until four months ago, it's been Dad who has gone to work and Mum who has looked after me and Noah. Now, Mum's left us and has her own house and her own car and a new job. Noah is studiously reading an information panel about painted dogs, and Mum and Dad are having one of those fierce, tense conversations that they always insist isn't an argument.

"Look at this," Noah says, beckoning me over. I join him at the fence. The painted dogs are apparently excellent diggers and like to give birth in dens underground.

"I told you I'd buy my own ticket." Mum said she and Dad would be happier apart, but she always seems to be angry. "You could have got a ticket for yourself and the kids."

"But this way's cheaper! I don't get what the problem is!"

"The problem is you need to stop pretending and accept reality. We're not a family any more."

"Yes, we are. We'll always be a family."

Noah and I are both watching now. Dad puts a hand on Mum's shoulder and strokes her skin, careful and gentle. Mum shakes it off as if he's put a scorpion there.

"It's all right," Noah murmurs. His face is very close to my ear, and his breath tickles.

"Don't talk right next to me like that. It feels weird."

"I don't want them to hear, that's all. It'll be a good day, we'll make it a good day."

Mum's putting on a cardigan, covering up the pale bare skin of her shoulders. She looked quite nice in her little pink vest. The cardigan makes her look old and scruffy.

I think about Noah and the pancakes. If you want something to change, you have to change it yourself. I go up to Mum and take her hand in mine, see her twitch of surprise as she looks down at me.

The meerkats are the first animals you come to. They're busy and clever, scurrying around as if they have a schedule to keep and a long list of jobs to tick off. For a few minutes I forget about my project to make Mum love me. One meerkat dives into a hole and one meerkat comes out of a different one, but are they the same meerkat, or two separate animals? I stare and stare, looking for ways to tell them apart, but I can't find anything. It would be much easier if they wore clothes.

Thinking about meerkats in clothes makes me smile, so it might make Mum smile too. She's standing at the next pen, staring into it with her back to us. I stand beside her and take her hand.

"Mum, wouldn't it be good if the meerkats wore clothes so we could—"

Mum gasps and flinches. It takes a long slow moment for her hand to relax in mine, for her face to look pleased to see me.

"I didn't see you there." Her hand is cold. "What was that about meerkats?"

"Wouldn't it be good if they all wore clothes?" I say. The words sound flat and artificial.

"Yes, it would be lovely, wouldn't it?" She smiles, but it doesn't reach her eyes. "Little waistcoats and long dresses and – hats. They'd look so sweet."

"And prams for the babies," I say. Mum hasn't understood my thinking at all, it was about being able to keep track of which meerkat is which, but at least she's smiling. At least I've got hold of her hand.

"Where's Noah got to?" She takes her hand from mine to wave at him. "Noah! Come and look!"

Noah bounds over, followed by Dad. Noah reads the board out to us. Dad watches Mum. Mum walks away, on towards the next enclosure where something spiny and fat is curled up inside a wooden hut, pretending not to be there.

My chest feels tight, but I'm not sure why. We're here to look at the animals, and that's what Mum's doing. There's no reason to be sad.

The ring-tailed lemurs bask in the sun, limbs spread wide. Mum's walking slightly ahead. I run to catch up with her, grab at her hand where it dangles at her side.

"Oh!" There it is again, that little jump and flinch. "Callie, don't creep up on me like that."

"Look at the lemurs, Mum."

"I can see them."

"They've got really long tails."

"Yes."

"And they're sunbathing." I'm running out of things to say.

"Hey, Callie." Noah is always my saviour. "Which one do you think stole the banana? Mum, do you remember that?"

"Fancy you remembering," Mum says, and there's something different about her voice, something comfortable and real. She lets go of my hand and strokes his hair away from his flawless, suntanned face. "You were so little."

"It was brilliant," Noah says, and the smile Mum gives him is hard to look at. "Wasn't it, Callie? You did a picture of it at school."

"I took it to work," Dad puts in. "It's still on the wall by my desk."

I drew that picture in art. It had been brilliant, the best picture I'd ever done, the first one I felt genuinely proud of. I brought it home and gave it to Mum. I'd hoped it would go on the fridge, but Mum left it on the table and when Dad came home, he said it was superb and could he take it to work? And Noah said what a good drawer I was, and everyone had been so nice about it, everyone except—

Mum's walking away from us again. The exit to the enclosure is two gates, and you can't open the second one until the first is closed. She pulls open the first gate, slips through, lets it fall shut. Now we're in here and she's in a little cage of her own, watching us but separate, as if she likes having a barrier between us.

It happens this way all around the park. I pretend to be excited about something and go to tell Mum. Mum pretends to be interested. Dad and Noah come to help me out while pretending they don't need to. We all pretend we're not hurt when Mum walks away. We're not a proper family any more, but we're pretending to be. I wonder if the other families, the proper ones, can tell what's going on, if they notice the desperate way I follow Mum around.

The gift shop is the last part of the day. It's supposed to be fun, but I'm tired and my legs hurt and, according to my mother, everything I think I might want has something wrong with it. ("Don't choose a pencil, Callie, it'll get lost in five minutes." "Not another stuffed toy, you've got a million already." "Why would you want seven plastic stacking monkeys?") Noah's picked a statue of a polar bear. He's watching me with an expression I don't know how to read.

"Why don't you have a model like mine?" Noah asks at last, and his hand, lightly grimy, reaches up to a shelf I can't see properly and plucks something down. It's a lemur, its glassy eyes bright amber, its tail stretched tall. "What do you think?"

"That's a kind lad," our mother says. "There you are, Callie, that's perfect. Why didn't you pick that yourself?"

She's smiling at Noah again, as if he's solved the problem of me. I want to say to her that it's not my fault, I'm not tall enough, I didn't know that was there. I want to say to her that it's her fault, that she should have shown me. But I can't say these things because that's not how it works, she'll never love me if I argue.

"Oh, don't cry," our mother says, which is, of course, the signal for me to start sobbing, great shuddering wails that shame me to my core. Noah takes the lemur from my hand and passes it to Dad along with the polar bear, then takes me outside.

After that, it's just a long slow anticlimax until bedtime. We arrive back at home. We climb out of the car. Mum hugs Noah, and then me. Her embrace for me is shorter and stiffer. Dad reaches out as if he'd like a cuddle too, but she backs away and climbs into her own car. We watch her leave. We go inside. Dad cooks pasta and meatballs for tea. We eat them. We go to bed.

I can hear Dad's voice downstairs. He's on the phone to someone, sounding nice at first and then arguing. There's only one person that can be. He's still trying too, still running after her, just like me. My belly feels tight and anxious. I think, *I'm hungry. I need a biscuit.* There's a packet hidden underneath my bed. I take it and go outside to the landing.

Noah's already sitting at the top of the stairs. He shuffles over to make room for me, takes the biscuit I offer him without telling me off for eating after I've cleaned my teeth. He's holding the polar bear in his hand, turning it over and over between his fingers.

"It's all right," he says. "Don't worry. Dad's fine."

Dad doesn't sound angry any more, he just sounds heartbroken.

"He wants her to come back," I say.

"You can't make someone love you if they don't." Noah sounds cross and exhausted, and somehow this gives me courage.

"You know when you and Dad went to Cornwall? And Mum and I went to the Lake District?"

Noah sighs. "What about it?"

"I was naughty," I whisper.

"That's all right. You were little."

"Is that why she left? Because I was naughty?"

"What? No, of course not, don't be stupid. It's not you, it's her and Dad."

"But I was naughty. And she left me."

Noah puts his arm around my shoulders.

"She didn't leave you, she left all of us. And she still loves us, it's just Dad she doesn't love."

Noah's usually so good at knowing what's in my mind, but this time he's not seeing it. Maybe this means I'm wrong about her? Noah's older than me, he must know best. Then I think, *no, I know what happened, I'm not wrong. I was naughty, and she left, because she doesn't love me.* I think about deep water, about a pebble tumbling downwards. You can pretend something isn't true as much as you like, but the pebble's still there, waiting.

Downstairs, Dad puts the phone down and turns on the television. I lick sugary mulch off my teeth and press closer to Noah's side so I can feel him breathing.

Chapter Ten

Boutique

Seven days into my time in purgatory. This bedroom's starting to feel like mine, and it's like I'm betraying my younger self. I don't want to feel at home here, in my mother's house, with the sound of her sobbing coming to me through the walls each night. I want the sense of strangeness. I want to know I don't belong.

Home is where your heart is, but without Dad and Noah, the house I grew up in is just a building crammed with stuff that doesn't belong to me. I think of my room at Frey's house. It feels welcoming while I'm in it, but sometimes I sense the ghost of the woman who's there when I'm not, lingering in the corners.

I have three bedrooms, I think, *but I don't have a home.* The thought is as light as a plucked feather. I don't know what to do with it. Perhaps my mother will ask me to leave.

We've formed a routine of sorts. My mother wakes first (or perhaps she doesn't sleep in the first place). I listen to her footsteps crossing the landing, her hand opening the bathroom door and turning on the shower. I lie still and rigid as she washes and dresses and goes downstairs. The click of the kettle in the kitchen below me is my signal to begin my own morning ritual.

I'd like to go down in my dressing gown. But my mother always dresses before breakfast, and even though I tell myself that I don't care about her opinion and don't mind what she thinks, I do still care about her opinion, I do still mind what she thinks. Her forcing me into getting dressed before breakfast is one more way she manages to upset and irritate me. I could fight back against this, wear the dressing gown, be a rebel, but I don't. My heart is tender and heavy with grief and loss, and hating her is a welcome distraction. Without her, I'd never make it out of the shower, I would simply sit on the floor of the cubicle and weep and weep until my body turned to water and I could escape down the drain in a single continuous pouring away. But righteous anger strengthens the bones.

I came here from Frey's house, so my clothes are simple and practical and easy to wash. I have other, prettier clothes for my time with Dad and Noah, but I'm glad I don't have them here with me. I don't want my mother to see the person I was for them. Let her think this is all of me there is to see, my jeans washed, soft and worn, my tops plain and basic, my footwear one pair of trainers and one pair of boots.

Downstairs in the kitchen, it's time for the next part of the ritual. I make breakfast; one slice of toast each. I suspect she'd like more, but I like the feeling that my mother is left a little hungry. We've never talked about it, we never will, but food and drink between us is always fraught with meaning.

I don't need to be afraid of being alone with her. I'm a grown woman, I have money and transport and freedom and autonomy and I don't need to be afraid. I tell myself this every day, sometimes every hour. One day I'll believe it.

I put the bread in the toaster and push down the lever. The first time I used the toaster, I nudged the timer a fraction out of alignment – a tiny movement I could pretend was accidental – so the toast would be a little browner than my mother prefers it. I keep checking to see if she's moved it back, but so far she hasn't. Maybe she hasn't noticed. Maybe I didn't move it enough to make a difference. Or maybe she's doing penance.

"Oh," says my mother, soft and startled, as if I've pleased her.

"What? What?"

"Those are my jeans," she says. "I think."

I look down at myself. I'm not wearing her stuff, of course I'm not.

"Yours are Levi's," my mother says. "Mine are from Marks and Spencer."

"I'm sorry," I say. What I am is repulsed, appalled, if she's come into my bedroom without permission, as if she's been watching me as I sleep.

"They must have got mixed up in the wash. It doesn't matter."

"I'll get changed."

"You can borrow them."

"I'm getting changed."

Upstairs, I tear the jeans off my body. I hadn't noticed we're the same size. I don't want any part of me to belong to her. I don't even like seeing the traces of her in my reflection.

"I'll wash them," I say as soon as I get back into the kitchen.

"Don't be silly. You only wore them about five minutes. They looked nice on you, have them if you like."

"I'm fine, thanks." The jeans looked like jeans, not attractive, not hideous. The whole point of jeans is that they don't look like anything. They're what you wear when you don't want to think about how you look. They're what you wear when you want to disappear.

"Really, they looked lovely. Much nicer than on me."

"We're exactly the same size. They look the same on both of us."

"Callie, don't be so prickly. I'm giving them to you. Let me do something nice for you."

"I don't want anything of yours, ever."

I've never been this honest with her before. The shock of telling her the truth is so great that, for a minute, our eyes meet.

I do laundry every day, even though there's hardly anything to wash, just the small accumulations of two women living empty lives. It's a hangover from living with Noah – who was capable, on a good day, of getting through six changes of clothes, and living enough inside each outfit to mean they genuinely needed cleaning – and then with Frey, who needs it for a completely different reason. Doing the laundry is another unwanted gift for my mother, like the overdone slice of toast, like the coffee she makes me. Like the sandwiches she'll make at lunchtime, which I'll devour even though there'll be too much butter and not enough filling.

I hang our few garments on the line, and my mother feeds Huginn the crow. The bird sits delicately on the edge of her wrist and pecks at the seeds, then turns its head to look at me from one side, and then the other. I have no idea how I confused her jeans with mine. A stupid mistake. I won't make it again.

Unless she hid her jeans in my drawer for some secret reason of her own. Unless she's still trying, stealthily and in the dark, to pretend she loves me.

"Let's go out," my mother says, so abrupt it sounds like a rudely given order.

"What?"

"We should go out somewhere," my mother says. "Hey, you, be gentle."

When she speaks to Huginn, she sounds tender. I don't like seeing her feed him. I also don't want to go out with my mother, but then, I don't want to stay in with her either.

"Where do you want to go?"

"I could take you shopping. If you want."

"What do you want to buy?" She keeps trying to make it sound like the trip is for me, but I won't let her.

"New clothes for you," she says. "You don't have anything nice."

"Thanks."

"You know I didn't mean it like that. But there's nothing pretty. It's all jeans and tops and sensible things."

"That's what I wear for work, that's where I was when they called."

"I could buy you a dress," she continues, doggedly determined. "We could both buy dresses. Something pretty."

"What sort of dress?" What I really want to ask is why, why the hell either of us would want to do this, but I'm afraid of the answer.

"A red dress," my mother says. She looks almost dreamy, her finger stroking gently at Huginn's breast feathers. He lets her do it, sits still and serene. "I want to buy us each a red dress, and... and some silly shoes... and then I'll take you out for lunch somewhere expensive. Get your coat. I'll finish pegging this out."

I don't want to obey, but obedience is ground into me like a stain. I go inside, and press my hand against the wall to steady myself. My mother, who I do not love, and who has never loved me, is taking me shopping for a red dress and some silly shoes, and I'm going to let her do it. One of us is clearly going mad.

Or perhaps we're both going mad together. That sounds like fun. Or at least, it sounds more fun than going for a day out with my mother and pretending we're both sane.

We tussle briefly over who's going to drive. My mother wins, which means my mother loses (the one who concedes to the other has the moral high ground), and I climb into the passenger seat of her car. The car park's ceiling feels low enough to crush us, its spaces far too narrow. It's hard to get the door open without scraping it. I grit my teeth and squeeze out through the barely adequate gap.

(If Dad was here, he would have found two adjacent spaces and parked in the centre. I would have told him off, would have made quite a production of being Very Appalled In Public, but that would have been a front, to disguise the truth that I secretly admired his rule-breaking.)

My mother's walking slightly ahead of me, the way she always did, always trying to escape, to be on her own, while I scurry anxiously after. I don't care any more – I stopped trying to catch her when I was eleven – but my feet are slow learners. Then, something impossible: my mother stops and waits for me.

"I walk too fast," she mutters. "I always have. But we don't have to rush today, do we?"

And now she's at my side, matching her pace to mine. I glance at her profile, looking for clues. She catches me looking and gives me a little smile, anxious and pleading, and I know she's lying about being a fast walker.

Good. We can't afford honesty while we're out in public. God only knows where that will lead.

The town centre is hot and airless, pavements and coffee bars jammed with buggies. The windows of the shops are cluttered with things I don't want. I never understand why anyone's surprised by the death of high-street shopping.

My mother takes me into a fussy courtyard of blond-wood shopfronts and box balls in square planters. It's not ugly, it's the opposite of ugly, but it's definitely not somewhere I feel comfortable. I glimpse my reflection in the clean glass, worn trainers and a worn jeans and worn top and sensible haircut, look at my mother beside me, and think, *we don't belong here.*

"Here," my mother says, and opens a door. The name *Sienna* loops across the glass in golden cursive. I want to pick at it with my fingernails, see if I can damage it. Inside is exactly the sort of shop I dread. Sparse clothes that whisper 'we won't fit and that will be your fault', draped artfully from hangers with a supercilious murmur of 'you can't afford anything here anyway'.

"Good morning, ladies. Having a day out?"

So it's one of those shops, the kind where a chatty owner serves helpful little snippets like canapés. 'That's a lovely piece for casual parties. That's real silk, feels gorgeous to wear. I have that one myself, it's one of my favourites.' What I'll hear is the subtext: *don't touch that, don't get fingermarks on it, don't drop it on the floor, don't try it on and rip the seams. In fact, don't even come in here in the first place, and since you're here now you should turn around and go straight back out again, we both know you won't buy anything. This shop isn't for you.*

"We're looking for something a bit special," says my mother, as easy as anything, and the woman lights up as if she's been given the secret countersign.

"Lovely. Wedding, maybe?"

"Not a wedding. But a special party."

The lie flows out as smooth as satin. There's an odd pleasure in watching my mother do something wrong and succeed so utterly. The woman is smiling, coming out from behind her counter, ready to help us browse her carefully curated rails.

"Did you have a colour scheme in mind? I'm Sienna, by the way, lovely to meet you."

(I like that addition of that word, 'scheme'. There's a world of difference between a colour you chose yourself, and a colour scheme that someone – maybe you, maybe the host – has inflicted on everyone. You can go along with a colour scheme, a pawn in their master plan, or flagrantly defy it like a misfit rebel; but there's no escaping the scheme's clutches.)

"Red," says my mother. "We're looking for red dresses. Shoes to go with them."

"Lovely. I don't carry shoes myself, but my friend Eleni has the shoe boutique opposite. I can pop over while you're trying on and bring you some to try?"

"That would be very kind." My mother sounds queenly. My mother sounds *rich*. I already know I can't afford anything here, even if I had somewhere to wear it. Even if there was any moment in my life when I'd want to.

"Oh," my mother adds, "and as this is my treat…" She leans forward and murmurs in the woman's ear, receives an understanding smile in return.

"So." Sienna looks me up and down, considering my possibilities. I force myself to stand up straight. "I don't carry a lot of red, but I do have something…"

She slips through a pair of saloon doors into another part of the shop, returns with two rivers of red spilling over her arm.

"It must be fate, you walking in this morning," she says, confiding and sweet. "This" – she reverently lays a fragile tumble of scarlet silk across my forearms – "is by a lovely new British designer, Jenny Altringham. Beautiful retro pieces, very Old Hollywood. You're going to love it. And this" – for my mother, a waterfall of crimson, the bodice heavy with lace and beads – "is from Belle Jolie. They're a French label, but I can sometimes get my hands on a few of their pieces. Oh, just a minute." She takes my dress back (I'm already thinking of it as mine, even though I've got no intention of owning it), snips with tiny gold scissors at a thick piece of cardboard hanging from the label, and whisks it away. I realise with incredulity that my mother has asked her to hide the price tag. "Let's go to the dressing rooms."

My room has soft carpet, soft lighting, scarves and necklaces suspended from artful coat hooks. The door is an actual door that you might find in someone's house. I can't believe there's a shop like this in this slightly provincial little town, or that I'm inside it, trying on a dress. I turn away from the mirror so I won't have to watch myself undress. I try not to mind that the label says 'L'. The silk feels like petals.

If this was a fairy story, I'd see myself in the mirror, transformed. Because this is real life, I see what I expected to see. My face, bare of make-up. My hair, under-brushed. My body, acceptable but nothing extraordinary. And over it all, this impossibly lovely dress.

"How are we getting on?" The door opens a crack. "Are we decent? Oh, that looks simply beautiful."

I glance again at my reflection. It's still just me. I can see the potential, but no more. Of course, it's Sienna's job to persuade me to buy.

"Would you like to see your mum in hers?" Without waiting for an answer, she knocks on the door of the second changing room. "Your daughter's looking stunning out here. Why don't we get you two together?"

And here it is, the Disney transformation, but enacted on my mother. She's found a hair clip and swept her hair off her face, exposing the clean lines of bone beneath the faint sagging of her flesh. Her neck is thin and beginning to wrinkle, but her collarbones are immaculate still, and she's slim enough to carry off the bias cut. She looks beautiful, which is completely different from pretty. She looks like a witch. She looks like a queen.

"Oh," she says, looking at me. "Oh, Callie."

I mean, if I had the right hair and make-up and shoes, this dress could work. It's lovely enough to get married in, if you were happy to marry in scarlet. But I'm not getting married and probably never will, I don't go to parties and don't really want to, I don't have any possible use for this dress, it's silly and frivolous and what would I even do with it? I suppose I could wear it to go somewhere with Noah, he'd love that, the two of us insanely dressed up for a day at a theme park—

Oh, God. I can't do this. I can't.

"It's all right." My mother's hands are on me, as firm and capable as if she's touched me every day of our lives. "Don't be embarrassed, it's fine to cry. We'll take the dress, Sienna, thank you. Callie? Do you want to wear it home? Or do you want to get changed?"

What I want is to hit someone. What I want is to smash this shop to pieces and then burn the whole district down.

"Here, I'll help you out of it. You don't want make-up on it."

I'm not wearing make-up, but I let my mother undress me anyway, beyond embarrassment. Then she shuts the door and I'm alone with my crumpled clothes and my sensible trainers and the grief that's hit me like a train.

I turn my back to the mirror and cry. Some time passes.

Eventually, I have to stop. I'm not done crying yet, but I can't stay here. Getting dressed takes all I have. I keep my gaze away from my reflection. I don't want to see the mess my tears have made of me. Sienna gives me a kind smile without meeting my eyes, and hands me a glossy paper bag with thick cord handles.

"I hope it all goes as well as it can do," she says, mysteriously. "Your mother picked you out some shoes from Eleni's."

My mother makes vague noises about coffee and cake, but I'm not having that, I am absolutely done. Somehow, she deduces this from the few words I'm able to produce (or maybe it's my intermittent snotty shudders, maybe she can't stomach sitting opposite me in a café and trying to eat). We drive home in silence. At the bottom of the road where my mother lives, my well of tears finally runs dry.

"That's better." I wonder if she means she's glad I'm feeling better, or glad she doesn't have to listen to me cry. "We're home now."

"How much were they? The dress and the shoes, I mean. I'll pay you back."

She parks the car. "No, you won't, it's my treat."

"Why? What am I meant to do with them? What are you

going to do with yours?" She doesn't speak, doesn't glance at me, just sits holding on to the wheel. "You've never taken me shopping. Why now?"

"Because," my mother says at last, "we need dresses."

"What for?"

"There'll be a funeral."

I breathe in sharply. Hold on to it. Let it go.

No. It's no good.

"You bought me a party dress to wear to a *fucking funeral?* To Noah and Dad's funeral? A fucking party dress, like we're celebrating something?"

"We'll be celebrating Noah's life. He loved nice clothes."

"And what about Dad? He's gone too, it's not just Noah. Do you think he'd want us there in party dresses? What? *What?*"

"I thought you'd understand," my mother mutters. Unbelievably, she's looking hurt, as if I'm the bad person here.

"Understand what? Tell me."

For a minute I think we're going to connect. Just for a minute.

"Oh, forget it," she says wearily. "What's the point anyway? It's not as if—"

She doesn't finish the sentence, so I finish it for her in my head. *It's not as if you're the one I want. It's not as if I actually love you.*

As soon as she lets me in, I run upstairs to the bedroom I once shared with Noah, feeling childish and desperate. I want to go home to Frey's house. But I can't go there for another nine days, so I'll take this instead: a door I can shut, one I can expect to be left alone on the other side of.

Chapter Eleven

Supermarket

Home: it's a slippery concept. How much time does it take to feel at home when you're living with two strange men? The answer is surprisingly little. Even during our first week together, when we're still doing everything for the first time, the cottage feels right.

Tuesday is supermarket day. Our first time taking Frey outside. None of us slept well last night – Frey waking and waking and waking; Josh tirelessly reassuring him we were still there, nothing to worry about, no need to be afraid; me lying silently in bed and willing myself to stay put. In the months to come, Josh and I will make our own small adjustments to the routine Linnea outlined for us, so that in the end I'll always be in the room next to Frey's. For now, we're sticking strictly to protocol.

Protocol dictates that we get up, get dressed and congregate in the kitchen for breakfast. Floss bounds outside to do her business, tears around the lawn five times, then dashes back inside. I catch her in a towel, rub dew from her legs and belly. Josh looks as tired as I feel. Frey lays the table for three in that slow, smooth way of his, dreamy and precise. Beside his plate is something red and folded. At first, I think it's a napkin, but it turns out to be a knitted hat. It's the brightest thing I've seen come out of Frey's wardrobe.

"That's a nice hat," I say to Frey.

"First thing he picked out," Josh says. "It's not going on yet, though, is it, mate? Just carrying it around."

Frey pauses in his progress. Floss leans against his legs, and his hand fondles at her ears. She's a different species to us and her brain is smaller and more limited, but she knows Frey the best of all. I can glean a lot from watching Floss. I wonder if Josh has thought of this too. I ought to mention it. It would make us a more effective team.

The timetable says we have to leave by a quarter to ten. Josh and Floss and I are ready at nine forty, just in case, and there's an awkward pause as we stand in the hall waiting for Frey, not sure what to say, whether to fetch him. As the hand on the hall clock ticks over to the quarter-hour, Frey comes out of his bedroom. He's wearing the red hat.

"That looks good," Josh says. "Red suits you."

Frey does look nice in red. Maybe it's a celebration. Maybe he's longing for more variety, and Josh and I can help him blossom. Already I'm falling under Frey's gentle spell, consumed by the desire to connect. He's so sweet, so gentle. I want to give him things that make him happy. I want to show him the world.

At the front door, Frey pauses. Floss, resplendent in her harness, puts her nose into Frey's hand.

One of the many extravagances of Frey's house is that even though Josh and I both have our own cars, there's also one for Frey's use. Three vehicles for three adults who make one five-mile journey each week. What must the neighbours think? Josh takes the car keys without asking, and I accept it without challenging. Two decades into the twenty-first century, and I still take it for granted that the man should drive. Josh puts on the CD Frey likes, Bach's

Goldberg Variations, and I manage not to make a joke about Hannibal Lecter.

In the car park, I have to stop myself from bouncing out of the car in glee. We're somewhere new and different. We're taking Frey on an adventure.

Except that, for what feels like several hours, Frey can't get out of the car.

It's not his fault, he's trying his best. He wants his legs to swivel and reach; he wants his shoes to touch the tarmac. He's being betrayed by his own body. His feet reach for the ground, wince away again. His arms fold tightly around his torso. Josh pats at Frey's shoulder, offers his arm as a lever. Frey folds up a little tighter. Floss flows in and out of the seat, over and over, modelling the behaviour she knows he's meant to produce, her feathery tail wafting across his hands. Frey pets briefly at her head, but remains rooted. The red hat screams a warning. Red for danger. This isn't a celebration hat, it's a danger hat. Frey is trying to ward himself away from the universe.

"Um," says Josh, looking frantic. "I mean, I suppose one of us could stay with him and the other one could nip in and do the shopping?"

"We're not supposed to. It's not on the plan."

"But look at him, he's terrified. Why are we doing this?"

We both know the reasons – he needs to be able to leave the house when he has to, he needs to build up a tolerance – but it's hard to do something that feels so cruel. Frey's shivering. It's not cold, so it has to be fear. There must be a way to help him root himself in this time, this place. I reach for my phone.

"Frey," I say, and hold it out to him. "Look what time it is."

A slow, gradual uncurling. Slowly, slowly, Frey's gaze rests on the clock.

"It's time to go to the supermarket. See? It's ten o'clock on a Tuesday. Time to go shopping. I know you don't want to, but that's what's on the timetable so we have to do it."

Frey's shoulders drop a fraction. He takes a slow breath.

"That's it," I say, even though he's not actually moving yet. "Let's go."

Floss waits at Josh's side, tail low and wagging, mouth half-open. Frey swivels stiffly in his seat. His feet touch the tarmac. He pulls himself upright. He's done it. He's out of the car. His fingers curl around Floss's harness, Theseus clutching his strand of thread.

"There," I say, a little triumphant, a little shaky. "Now we're going in."

The supermarket is a babble of noises, smells and strangers. Everybody looks at us, not staring exactly but noticing our difference – the unusual composition of our party, the presence of Floss, Frey's uncovered face, his slow, shuffling walk. I hold my head high, and try to greet their glances with a friendly smile from behind the fabric. Josh seems genuinely oblivious.

Once we're inside, Frey becomes animated. There's a shopping list, because of course there is, and Frey seems to know every item on it. The hand that isn't connected to Floss reaches unerringly for apples, broccoli, corn on the cob; he plucks fat tomatoes into a paper bag, chooses six bananas from six different bunches, and leads the way to the chilled cabinets. Floss remains pressed against his side. The hat is pulled down over his ears.

By the cheese cabinet, the flow of movement judders and halts. We're supposed to buy Cheddar, fresh mozzarella, a fat triangle of Parmesan. Everything's there, but Frey's transfixed by something Josh and I can't see or sense. His hand reaches out, falls back, reaches out again.

"You all right, mate? Do you want me to get these for you?"

Frey's hand hovers and flutters like a Victorian lady's. He wants to do the task, he wants to complete the ritual, but something's making it wrong.

"Have they moved the stuff around?" Josh's voice is warm

and kind. "The absolute scumbags. Not to worry, we'll learn the new places. Look, what's first on the list? Cheddar. Look, that's the one we want, in the black packet. We'll remember the new spot, yeah? Top shelf, on the left."

Josh is doing the right things, but he hasn't found the right problem. There's something wrong, something that's stopping Frey from touching the cabinet. What is it? It's hard to think in this place, the lights so bright, the music so loud, and the buzzing of the shelf strip, being gently vibrated by the motor of the freezer, is so annoying...

I rip the shelf strip from its housing. The buzzing stops. Frey glances sideways towards me, a slow grateful slide of eyes that never quite make contact with mine. My heart glows. I lay the strip down on the floor. I don't want the supermarket people to think I'm a vandal.

"God, well done," says Josh. "I wouldn't have thought of that."

If Josh had solved the mystery instead of me, I'd be working hard to swallow my jealousy. Instead, he's simply pleased for Frey. Josh is a much nicer person than I am.

The last stop is the dog-food aisle, a test of Floss's boundaries. We see the quiver in her body, the small longing glances. In the dog-food aisle, it's Frey who touches Floss reassuringly, reminding her that they're in this together and he has her back. It's the first sign of something I'll come to treasure: Frey's kindness. There are no dog treats on the list, but Frey adds a packet to the trolley anyway, letting go of Floss's harness for a moment and stretching out his newly freed hand, as if he's trying to distract us. Another sign of something new. For someone who matters to him, Frey will veer away from the safety of the rules.

Even the till is specified for us. The woman nods to us in greeting.

"Hello, Frey."

Frey, naturally, doesn't reply, but I see the angling of his body towards the till, the softness at the corners of his mouth. He seems pleased at being recognised.

"Nearly done now," she adds. Her hands fly over the scanner. Josh and I scramble to keep up. "You're doing really well."

Frey pets at Floss's head. The red hat's pulled down so low he can hardly see out.

"I'm Julie," she says, to me and Josh this time. "I often work this shift. Frey came with his sister for a while, didn't you, Frey?"

Julie raises her voice when speaking to Frey. It's a habit Josh and I are working hard to resist. He's not deaf, he can hear perfectly well, but still it's tempting.

"Afraid it's just us from now on," says Josh. He's charming and friendly, making small talk where I'd really struggle. Maybe Linnea considered this when choosing who to hire. "Well, and the other two. We take it in turns. Two weeks each."

"How's it going?"

"I think Frey reckons we'll do, don't you, mate?"

Josh packs the heavy things. I'm on fruit and veg. The two of us working in sync like an old married couple.

"There you go." Julie passes the final few items over the scanner. From the droop of Frey's shoulders, he might have run a marathon. I hope we can all sleep tonight. Floss is lying down, her chin on her paws. She looks tired too. I've never lived with an animal before, but I like it. I like her doggy little face, the click and pad of her paws. I like the way she greets me sometimes, when I stand in the doorway of Frey's bedroom and murmur reassurance. A box of chocolates come down the conveyor, taking me by surprise.

"Huh," says Josh. "Are those ours?"

Have they crept in from the next customer's load? The conveyor's empty, even though there are queues of two or three people at the other tills. Frey walks in his own time and space, and other people, instantly spotting his difference, tend to avoid him. I'd like to think it's out of respect for his desire for peace, but it's probably because they're afraid we'll be slow.

"They weren't on the list." As supermarket chocolates go, these look rather nice. A pretty box, gold foil and matte paper. A soft blue ribbon tied around.

"Frey?" Josh looks at Frey, who isn't looking at us and isn't giving any sign at all that he's listening and is instead rather busily picking a small fleck of something out of the soft hair lining Floss's ears. Floss sits very still, letting him do it even though she doesn't look thrilled. "Um, mate, are these yours by any chance?"

Frey nestles his chin against his chest. In a neurotypical person, this gesture would speak of shyness.

"It's fine if they are. We can buy whatever you want."

"I think," says Julie, eyes twinkling, "Frey might have got them as a present. For you both. Is that right, Frey?"

Frey's gaze slides slowly upwards, grazes against the edge of Julie's ear. Perhaps she can feel its warmth. Perhaps she feels cold when he looks away again.

"He does it for Linnea sometimes," Julie explains.

"I didn't see him put them in," I say blankly.

"Yes, he's good at that. Aren't you, Frey? That was very nice of you, pet," Julie adds, enunciating too clearly, speaking too slowly. God, this looks terrible from the outside. I'll have to try even harder not to do it.

"Wow. Thanks, Frey. That's really lovely of you. We'll have them after dinner if you like."

Frey looks down and to the left. 'No, thank you.' His fingers are busy with Floss's ears again, and her eyes are half-closed in discomfort. I wonder how long it took to train her to let Frey do things like this, how they made it so she loves him enough to tolerate it.

"They're just for me and Josh? Are you sure?"

"Thanks so much, Frey, that's lovely. Is that the lot? Right, then." Josh takes out the bank card from his wallet, holding it as if he's doing something faintly wrong. Josh and I are both named on the account, but the money in it is Frey's. Spending this money is part of our job, but I still understand Josh's uneasiness, the slightly performative way he handles it.

"You did brilliantly," Julie says, and there's no mistaking the warmth in her voice. "Both of you. Well done."

"Thanks. That's really nice to hear."

I'm so glad Josh is here. If I was here on my own, I'd have muttered something graceless and run away. I'm not good at taking praise from other women.

"Much better than the other ones," Julie adds, lowering her voice. "Poor Frey was in pieces by the end. See you next week."

Frey climbs into the car like a small animal spotting a place to hide. Josh and I unload the shopping, take off our masks to enjoy a deep, victorious breath. The dog treats and the chocolates sit like medals on top of the last bag.

"There," Josh says. "We made it."

And suddenly I'm happy, because he's right. We've been outside the house and coaxed Frey through the ordeal and made it out, and Frey was pleased enough to want to reward us, and we did it well, much better than the others. I hum along to the *Goldberg Variations* as we leave.

"Do you think," Josh asks, and he sounds fascinated and amused rather than horrified. "Do you think Julie's, like, spying for Linnea?"

"I don't know. She did seem to know a lot about Frey."

"God." Josh laughs. "The CCTV and the hidden cameras and the everything aren't enough. She's even got *spies*. That woman really commits."

"What hidden cameras?"

"There won't just be the ones she showed us, there'll be other ones. Nanny cams. Not in the bedrooms or the bathrooms or anything," he adds, seeing my face. "Just, you know. Around."

"Jesus."

"Eh, it's normal. Well, not *normal*, but it makes sense.

Frey's vulnerable. He can't tell her what's going on. She wants to be sure. Hey there, mate, my right of way, yeah? That's it. Thank you."

Floss has gone to sleep, her head on Frey's lap. I'm glad of the music so we don't have to talk. I'm thinking about hidden cameras, wondering if Josh is right. But it doesn't matter. Let her look. If anyone needs to worry it's the others, who (according to Julie) did a much worse job with the supermarket, and (I'm assuming) didn't get chocolates.

I wonder how Frey got them into the trolley. I saw him add the treats for Floss, one hand fluttering by her head so she was distracted, looking at something else. He must have another set of actions for when he wants to surprise us with something nice.

How strange. How unexpectedly sweet. He must really like us.

Another thing to get used to: the weekly Zoom call with Linnea. It seems so redundant to sit on Frey's sofa – Josh and I at either end, Frey in the middle – and wait for Linnea to let us into her Zoom meeting, when she already has access to our lives whenever she wants anyway.

The television screen fills with the shot we've all grown used to. A frowning, peering face, an unflattering angle, the gradual adjustments to make her expression presentable. I peer greedily at this small glimpse of Linnea's world. A stack of books. A creamy white wall. A painting of a woman in a deep yellow chair. Linnea wears a cloudy-looking jumper, lush and expensive. Her hair tumbles about her face. She must be at home. Maybe we'll glimpse a lover wandering past. It would be so nice to see Linnea a little vulnerable, compensation for all the moments she's glanced in on us.

Frey murmurs beside me, so soft I almost miss it. In the picture that fills half the screen, he's smiling. Not the faint twitch at the corners of his mouth, but an actual, honest-to-God smile. I'd thought we were doing well, Josh and I. Clearly, there's a lot more distance to cover before we get to describe ourselves as 'close'.

"Hey." Linnea's smile, I'm certain, is only for Frey. "How are you all doing?"

"Good, I think?" Josh glances at Frey first, and then at me. "No disasters so far. The weather's lush. How are you? What's it like where you are?"

"How's your week been, Frey?" Frey flicks his eyes shyly over the screen. "I called by your *Minecraft* world yesterday. I like the underground railroad. Where will it go?"

"We're going to the jungle biome to get a cat," Josh says. "You start with an ocelot and feed it fish until it's tame. Then it comes home with you. Sorry, do you know this already?"

Linnea smiles, but doesn't confirm or deny anything. It's the second question she hasn't answered.

"I left a little Easter egg for you," she says. Frey's smile grows broader. "It's in a building in your home area, but I won't tell you any more."

"Cool. Shall we look for that tonight? We can leave one in return. Linnea, will you get a chance to look?"

Linnea laughs. Three questions unanswered. It must be deliberate. A power game. The quickest way to win is not to play.

"Shopping went well," I say.

"Yes, I heard. It's not easy but it is important. Did you enjoy the chocolates?"

Josh and I both jump, like small children raiding the biscuit barrel.

"No, it's fine, it's absolutely fine. Frey, that was really kind." Frey pets at Floss's head. "Remember you don't have to do it every time, though, it's not a rule. It's only when you feel like it." Frey tugs on Floss's ears. "Or if you need a rule, we can say, maybe not more than once every three months. That way it stays special."

Who is Linnea to set limits on Frey's pleasures? No, I

can't think like this, Linnea isn't the enemy. I repeat this very firmly, as if I'm a schoolteacher and my rebellious heart is a fidgety child, while Linnea shuffles papers.

"So as we discussed, I've reviewed the cameras a lot for this first week," she says.

I force my shoulders to relax.

"It's obvious everything's going well. Congratulations. You're doing an excellent job."

"That's so good to know." Josh's pleasure at her praise looks genuine. "Thanks."

"I have a few suggestions to make things even smoother." Is there a hint of theatre in the way she rustles her paper? Is she trying to intimidate us? "First of all, when you let Floss out in the morning, could you remember to tell Frey what's happening? He needs to know Floss will be straight back in as soon as she's done what she needs to."

God, she really has been watching us.

"You won't have noticed the changes because they're subtle, but it causes Frey stress. He was checking the clocks much more often for the rest of the day."

Now she's said it, I remember that too. I'd seen the restlessness, but hadn't understood its meaning. I want to touch Frey in apology, but he wouldn't want to be touched.

"And when Floss comes in from her walk," Linnea continues, "make sure to wipe her paws, even if the weather's dry. She hates it so she'll try to get out of it, but she knows it has to happen. Just be firm."

"Got it. Sorry." Josh's turn to look guilty, Josh's turn to glance towards Frey.

The list goes on, small items forming an avalanche of guilt. I have to accept this. It's what I signed up for. My life, and Dad's, and Noah's, are built around me keeping this job. I nod and smile, and hope my thoughts don't show in my face, because right now I'm thinking, *what does it matter if the handle on the fridge isn't polished?*

Beside me, Frey rubs one hand against another. Then,

Floss pushes her nose into my hand. I pet her head and she sighs a little, leaning into my touch.

Did Frey see I was tense and miserable, send Floss over to comfort me? I'd thought of our relationship as transactional – I do things for Frey, Frey pays me. I've been a nurse for almost a decade and I'm still surprised by the pleasure of 'thank you', by the warmth of a kindness returned.

At first, forgetting the cameras was easy. Half an hour after arriving, my gaze snagged on them and I thought, *shit, I'd forgotten.* Half a day, and they were part of the furniture. So we were being filmed. So what? We had nothing to hide.

Now, I can't let it go. Can't move naturally, can't remember how to walk or sit. Don't want to eat. What if Linnea's looking now? What if she sees me blowing my nose? Adjusting my knickers? Scratching beneath the underwire of my bra? I'm only doing what all humans do. But Linnea can see me and I can't see her, and I can't pretend she's never watching, because now I know she is. It's like discovering that God is real, and infinitely interested in you.

Anxiety makes me clumsy. I drop my colouring pencils, and Frey's twitch of distress resonates through my own body. It shatters the leads, so they need endlessly sharpening and can take only minimal pressure. It's not the pencils I care about – there's plenty of money in the household account – but Linnea, seeing me upsetting Frey. I work on the millefiori tapestry design in the book Frey chose for me, my gaze carefully fixed on the page. It's *colouring pencils,* for God's sake. Nothing worth getting upset over.

Colouring time passes. We cook together, the three of us in a dance that gets smoother with each repetition. Already we've given up trying to parse the seeming illogic of the foodstuffs Frey will and won't touch (why will he chop tomatoes but not tear basil leaves, why will he slice garlic but cringe from the crusher, and why will he eat any of these things when he won't go near them while they're cooking?). Already it seems natural to wipe the surfaces in every spare minute.

Josh and I talk continuously to each other, and to Frey. Nothing important, just a slow inconsequential stream of words whose only real meaning is 'we're here, we're with you, we're not going anywhere'. Filling the air with small observations to stop the silence closing in. ("Hey, look, there's a bird in the garden... Do you know what kind?... No, me neither, I'm rubbish at birds... I know, right?... I mean, I can do flamingos and penguins and peacocks and things, but normal ones are all just little brown jobs to me... Maybe we could get a book or something... I bet Frey knows, though, don't you mate?... You know all sorts of surprising stuff...") You'd think this would drive Frey insane, but – just as Linnea promised – he relaxes into it like a warm bath. If she's watching, she'll be pleased—

The plate slips from my hands. The slate tiles are unforgiving. A white porcelain starburst radiates sharp points.

"Shit," I wail. "Sorry, Frey."

Frey goes to the counter, opening the cupboard where the tinned products live, making minute adjustments to each tin's orientation. He looks as if he hasn't even noticed the plate is broken. He looks like a man at peace.

"I'm so sorry," I repeat, to Frey and to his terrible, terrifying sister.

"Hey." Josh pats my shoulder. "It's only a plate."

Frey touches each can like a bird turning eggs. Do birds know if you take one away? Or do they simply have the binary concept of eggs and no eggs? Frey likes things to come in sets, and for those sets to remain whole. Josh sweeps great splinters of porcelain into the dustpan, thick white splinters like knives.

"I broke it," I say. "I'll sweep up."

"It's fine, I'm here now."

"All right, but let me—" There are fragments everywhere, slipping like water between the bristles. I sweep them with my fingers, feel the sharp prickle of broken skin. "Ow, damn it."

"Now look what you've done." Josh sounds almost amused, as if he's been given a small but complex object to look after and is still figuring out how it works. "Stop helping and wash your fingers and I'll finish this off." My fingertips swell with fat beads of blood. "Then sit down. That must hurt."

Josh's kindness finishes off the last of my resistance. I stand over the sink and rinse blood from my hands and let my tears flow and feel glad I'm not wearing make-up.

The crisis is over in minutes. Josh clears the smashed plate, finds the iPad and orders a replacement, shows the screen to Frey and tells him when the order will arrive. Frey barely glances at the screen, shows no signs of listening, but after a minute he comes out of the cupboard and goes to the cutlery drawer and lays the table. Another three minutes and my fingers have stopped bleeding and my nose is no longer pink and we're sitting down to eat, and the universe settles back into place. If Linnea is watching, I hope she'll approve. She'll be impressed with Josh at least, although maybe not so much with—

My fork tumbles through my clumsy fingers and hits the floor. It's clean enough to eat with, but it will upset Frey if I do. I take it to the dishwasher. Put it into its slot. Take a clean fork from the drawer. Sit back down at the table.

"Dropping everything today," I say.

"That's the three out of the way."

"You what?"

"Things like that come in threes. Now you can relax."

Josh is so laid-back it's almost annoying. At our next Zoom meeting, the litany of mistakes will be entirely mine.

"It'll get better," says Josh.

"What?"

"She won't watch this closely forever. It's like when you get a new teacher and they pick at everyone for the first week, so you know you can't get away with stuff. She's just making sure we know whose side she's on."

That's exactly what it felt like. As if Linnea was on an opposing side.

"She's got to treat us like the enemy because we might be, one day. She's in Frey's corner. Not necessarily in ours."

"But—" I say, and then stop, because saying 'But I'm a nurse' sounds pathetic.

"Have you done residential care before?" Josh asks.

"Never. I worked in A & E."

"Well, some of those places are grim. Not on purpose. Just because there's no money. I mean, you must know what that's like."

"Yep. Great people. Horrible environment."

Josh looks at me sideways. "Was everyone you worked with great, though?"

"What?"

"Didn't you ever get wrong'uns? Because we did. People think if they're earning peanuts and the clients have disabilities, they can get away with anything."

I think about the surgeon, Mr Garamand, who made older patients cry and whose nickname was Mr Grabby-Hands. A porter, Simon someone-or-other, who was caught leaving the morgue with his trousers half-buttoned and who suddenly vanished a week later. A midwife whose mothers regularly came back in a week after birth with sky-high temperatures from infected stitches. We know who the dangerous ones are, but we try not to tell outsiders.

"Anyway," says Josh. "That's why she's picking out all the little things. She's not actually saying 'you need to wipe the fridge handle or make sure you clean under the microwave'. She just wants us to know she's looking."

Frey sits at the end of the table, neat and quiet, eating pasta with small, controlled movements. The lights catch on his very clean hair and his eyelashes cast tiny shadows. The thought of hurting him makes me feel ill. Linnea and I are the same, she chose me because we're the same. How can she even imagine I would…?

"It's not fair," I say, before I can stop myself.

Josh looks like a good-hearted laddish type, but he isn't.

A good-hearted laddish type would be appalled, would stand up and clear the plates. Josh sits still and waits.

"All of this, I mean." I can't tell him that it's not fair, that I thought Linnea liked me and trusted me, but I have room for lots of injustices. I'll tell him something else true instead. "It should be like this for everyone who needs it. Why can't we do better?"

"I know. I'd like this for all the clients I've ever had. Even the pain-in-the-arse ones. We're supposed to be a rich country... Frey, mate, are you finished? Yes? Okay, let's clear up."

I rinse my plate, put it in the dishwasher, wipe the sink clean. I haven't told Josh the entire truth, but I can tell it to myself. My problem isn't with Linnea, but with Frey. I want Frey to trust me the way Noah does. I want him to smile at me the way he smiled at Linnea.

Chapter Twelve

Episode

I have to be careful how I tell you this story. This is a story with a monster in it, but it's possible that monster isn't always my mother. Perhaps, instead, it's Noah's illness. It crept into our lives like a smiling friend, disguised as over-the-top schemes and illicit adventures.

Here's the first time it showed its true face:

I'm ten years old. It's Saturday, so Dad and Noah and I eat tea in front of the television. When our mother was here, we ate at the dining table. We have hot-dog sausages in finger rolls, baked beans and corn on the cob, gingerbread worms for after. Dad eats as if he's afraid he'll get caught and told off.

"I'm not supposed to have these," he says, licking brine off his fingers.

"Why not?" asks Noah.

"Your mum says they're disgusting."

"But they're lovely," I say.

"I think that and you think that and Noah thinks that, but your mum… does not think that." He bites the end off another roll. "She says it makes her sick to see me eating them. Got to make the most of it while I can."

Our mother's always telling me off for saying I don't like things ("Just no thank you is plenty of information, Callie, nobody wants the details"). She's been gone for three months, but Dad still talks as if it's temporary, as if it's fixable. Noah hopes, often and vocally, that Dad's right. I hope he's not, and keep my mouth shut.

"We won't tell," I say instead, playing along.

"You're a good girl." Dad pets my head in the way I don't like but accept because he thinks I do. He doesn't know I hate it, and he'll never know because I'll never tell him. Grown-ups often think kids can't keep secrets. I think that shows how good at keeping secrets we really are.

"Want to have an adventure?" Noah asks, his eyes bright and glittery. I jump guiltily, because it's late and it's a school night and I'm on the landing in my pyjamas, listening in on Dad downstairs.

"We're supposed to be in bed."

"Dad won't notice, he's watching the news. So. Adventure. What do you reckon?"

"I don't know. What is it?"

His face is pale with excitement. "We're going to run away."

"We're going to *what*?"

"Shh, don't be so loud! We're not going forever, only a few days or something. Maybe a week. We'll hide somewhere and stay out of sight. And they'll get really worried and get the police to look for us."

"Won't we be in trouble?"

"No, of course we won't, the police are supposed to help, that's their job."

I'm not sure this is right, but Noah's irresistible; I'm carried along without even trying.

"Then when they find us, we say we're only going home if Mum and Dad agree to stay together."

"What if they say no?"

"They'll say yes, they'll have to. They'll be so glad to get us back they'll do whatever we want. It'll work, Callie, I promise."

Maybe it will. Mum won't come back for Dad, and she probably wouldn't care if she never saw me again. But she might just do it for Noah.

"What about food?"

"I've got some stuff from the cupboards." Noah holds up a rucksack. "And I've got some money, out of Dad's wallet. We can go to McDonald's."

My breath catches. "What if he'd seen you?"

"He didn't see me, did he?"

"Won't we get sick if we only eat McDonald's?"

"It'll be fine for a few days. And they do fruit bags and things. We can't go yet, he's still awake. So you need to stay awake too. And pack that blanket from the end of your bed. And get dressed."

"What if Dad comes in to kiss me goodnight?"

"Get right down under the covers."

"But what if he—"

"Shush. I'll come and get you when it's time."

"Are you sure this'll work?"

"Course I'm sure. I can hear their thoughts sometimes."

Noah says this with such conviction, I almost think he means it.

"Come on, Callie. It'll be fun."

I already know it will be. I already know I'll say yes. Noah is the king of having fun. I've got into all sorts of trouble this way, but I've never once regretted it.

Dad's finally in bed. I'm boiling under the duvet, so I fling it off and lie starfished across the mattress, trying to cool off. Noah appears, opening my door and grinning like a maniac.

"Let's go," he says. "We're going to fix everything."

I've never been downstairs after hours. It's like plunging into a different house, that only faintly looks like ours. I'm so nervous I could cry, but Noah's utterly confident, gliding down the stairs, picking up his own shoes and then mine from the heap in the hallway. He's wearing a coat that used to be Dad's. It's too big on Noah, but not as enormous as it would have been a year ago.

The front door's the worst bit. I'm convinced Dad's secretly awake, waiting to catch us. *We'll be in so much trouble,* I think as the door swings open. *He'll never trust us again.* We pad out over the doorstep. *What if we get sent to prison?* I wonder as the door clicks shut. I follow Noah down the front path, enjoying the concrete chill soaking through my socks. *How are we getting away with this?*

But it's really happening. We're outside, on the bench a few doors down from our house, and Noah's helping me with my shoes. I can tie my own laces, but I let him help because it makes me feel safer.

"Let's start walking," Noah says. "The neighbours might look out of the windows." He puts his index fingers to his forehead as if he's listening. "I think they're all asleep but I'm not sure. Once we're out of our street we'll be safer."

You don't have to make it into a game, I think. *This is exciting enough as it is.* I'm thinking *exciting* to avoid *terrifying.* This doesn't feel like a good idea.

But the front door's closed and we don't have a key. We have to see Noah's plan through.

"Where are we going?" I ask. Noah's striding ahead, confident and energetic. I can hardly keep up.

"There's a place in the park. You know the little shelter where the park-keeper keeps his tools?"

I dredge my memory, come up with a picture of a tiny brick hut with a single window and a back wall that smells of pee.

"It's always locked."

"I've sent a message ahead," says Noah. "They'll leave it unlocked."

"Who will?"

"The people who are helping us, of course," says Noah, kind and tolerant. "I've got everything sorted. Oh, wait a minute…" His fingers are at his forehead again, his eyes closed theatrically. "Okay. Come with me."

We crouch behind a tall bush.

"What are we doing?"

"There's a patrol car coming. Listen."

I peer around the edges of the leaves and watch as a small blue car drives past.

"It wasn't a police car," I say.

"I didn't say a police car, I said a patrol car. They're looking for us. But we'll be all right in the park. We need to hurry, though. Can you run?"

Noah's game is frightening and I don't want to play it. I want to be back in my own bed.

"Don't cry," he says, and puts an arm around me. "There's no need to be scared! I'm with you."

We crawl into the park between two bent railings. Noah looks around as if he's expecting people hiding in the bushes. Maybe he's right, I don't know. Bent railings are for people to get in when they're not supposed to. We might not be the only ones creeping out to hide in the darkness. The door of the hut's locked, and I want to cry. Then I think, *Now Noah will realise this is stupid and we have to go back.*

"Okay." Noah's listening to nothing again. It's a game, but he's acting as if it's real. "I see. Right. Got it. No problem."

"Noah, who are you talking to?"

"I can hear them but you can't." He turns to me and ruffles my hair, the way Dad does when he wants me to feel safe and loved. "A problem with the lock, that's all. It'll be sorted by morning. We'll sleep under a bush."

"Under a *bush*?" My voice is high and squeaky.

"Just for tonight. I'll keep you safe. That one looks good."

Noah's acting as if he's in charge but he's not. No one's in charge and no one's looking after us and we're out in the dark, alone.

"Wait." Noah grabs my arm. "Can you hear that?"

"What? What?"

"That sound…" He cocks his head. "There's a search drone. We need to get under cover."

You're not well, I think, suddenly certain. *Noah, there's something wrong with you. Something's gone wrong inside your head.*

"Come *on,*" Noah insists, pulling restlessly at my arm. "In the bushes! Before we're seen!"

I ought to be taking care of him, but I don't know how. I follow him to the patch of shrubs, squeezing between branches until we're somehow inside, surrounded by tall green plants of varying spikiness.

"Let's eat something." Noah digs excitedly in his rucksack, pulls out a half-empty packet of biscuits and an old squash bottle filled with water. "You'll feel better."

I eat four biscuits without tasting them, and feel more awake but not less terrified. Noah talks and talks and talks, about people he calls 'them' and other people who are also, confusingly, 'them'. One set of these people are good and one set are bad, but beyond that, I'm lost. His original goal of getting Mum and Dad back together is forgotten. Now he's planning a new life, where we'll live by ourselves and he'll work with 'them' to keep us both safe from 'them', and it's going to be amazing, exciting, brilliant. He can hear everyone's thoughts without trying, everyone's asleep and nobody knows we're here. We'll stay here until morning, then they will unlock the hut and did I know it's a portal to a huge underground complex? We'll be there for a while, then they'll move us to their base, as soon as they stop looking for us. We just need to hold on until morning. Just until morning. Noah barely looks like himself, he's been replaced by a stranger, a mad-eyed stranger with a shining face and glittery ideas that he flings like confetti, daring me to catch them.

Abruptly, Noah is asleep, so suddenly I wonder if he's faking it. One minute he's talking and talking, the next he's silent, his face turned into the hood of Dad's old jacket, his breathing slow and even. The biscuit packet slips from his hand. He's asleep, so I have to keep him safe. This is how he feels about me all the time. I wonder if we'll survive until morning.

I love you, I think. *It's not your fault. I'll sort this out.*

I count to a hundred to be sure he's asleep. Then I leave Noah and go to find help. I think about knocking on house doors, but there are too many to choose from. Then I see the shape of a phone box and realise I have another option.

I dial 999, trembling a little because I'm so cold and so tired, and then there's a woman, calm and warm, untangling my jumbled replies and confused half-explanations. By some mysterious miracle she guesses my name, seems to know I've got an older brother called Noah, and I know we're going to be all right.

I ought to wait by the phone box, she tells me to wait there. But I can't leave Noah alone, so I tell her exactly where to find us and then hang up on her protests and go back to him. I stroke his hair a little, glad that he doesn't even stir.

"It's all right," I whisper, needing to say the words out loud, make them true. "They're coming to help us. You need to see a doctor and then you'll be better. Don't be scared. It's going to be fine."

As it turns out, we were already being looked for. Dad must have got up to check on me, found my empty bed. The police are with us in what feels like no time at all.

Chapter Thirteen

Reconstruction (2)

Another sleepless night in this bed. I can count the ones left on one hand now, days peeling away like skin. The police think it was the monster that drove Noah over the edge. I won't accept that, though. They know a lot about accidents and incidents in general, but I know a lot about Noah in particular, so my interpretation is truer.

Here's another version:

Dad and Noah have been alone together for two weeks. They won't have been locked in the house; the lockdown months are behind us. Noah loves going out, and Dad loves indulging him. Noah's been good about taking his meds, been happy and coherent and at peace. He was fine when I left them two weeks ago. He wouldn't have spiralled that quickly.

My first sketch was Noah attempting to repeat a long-ago Fish and Chips Under the Stars scheme, this time with only Dad for company. Now, lying sleepless in my mother's house, I see a darker and simpler solution. Noah to Dad: "Let's go and see Mum."

A guilty secret between the two of them. Noah's idea, but Dad would have agreed, because Dad still loved her, in a strange, lost way he never talked about. Of course, Dad wasn't allowed over her doorstep – the most he got was a glimpse of her outline in the doorway. Still, he would have agreed. Partly because Noah wanted to. But also because Dad was a man in love, and lovers will do anything for a glimpse of the one they worship.

That day was ablaze, that fierce light you get as the solstice approaches, each day longer and lighter than the one before. They died just before the pivot, their lives flaring into nothingness like a burned sacrifice. But they weren't burned, they were crushed and tumbled, organs smashing against bones, brains compressed against the thick plates of their skulls…

But here's the important part. At some point, at the beginning of that day's journey or at some point along the way, Noah must have said, "Hey, can I drive? Just for a little while?"

And Dad, helpless and fond, would have answered, "Sure. Why not?"

Maybe he has to coax Dad a little. Maybe Noah reminds Dad that he passed his driving test first time, was driving quite successfully for the first few months until his relapse rolled over him. "I can still do it," he says, that sweet, irresistible smile quirking over his face. "Just a couple of junctions. Give you a break."

Dad gives in easily. He likes doing things that make us happy. All he's ever wanted is for everyone he loves to be happy, so he can bask like a cat in the sunshine. He was the same when we were small – always buying the ice cream, never warning of carsickness and uneaten dinners. It should have been her, not them. It's not fair—

(In the place where I am now, telling myself this story, I can hear my mother, crying through the walls. She's crying again. She's always crying.)

So, yes. Somehow Noah takes the wheel of the car. There are other possibilities, but I like my one, where it's simply an indulgence Dad grants to his boy, whose life has been emptied of so many indulgences.

Noah pulls out onto the motorway, building up speed. An hour and a half to go before the end. They don't know that, though, that's the one mercy of their ending. They move smoothly through the afternoon, racing the slow movements of the lingering sun.

On and on the road goes, motorway and dual carriageway and A-road and little skinny lanes. Noah's content and confident, lost in the flow of driving.

And Dad, in the passenger seat, watching our beautiful, fragile boy. Noah's my big brother but our roles got swapped around, and now I'm the one filled with fierce protectiveness.

Our mother doesn't know they're coming. Noah always says he likes to surprise her. What he means is he's never sure if he'll be able to get there, if his illness will roar up out of nowhere to claim him once more. Of course, he also likes the spontaneity of simply arriving without warning.

("Don't you ever worry she won't be in?" I asked once, fascinated, and Noah shrugged and said, "She always is." Maybe our mother never goes out when Noah might feasibly visit. Maybe she spends her life by the window, hoping today will be the day. I hope that's true. I like to think of her being the one trapped and waiting.)

Noah is still behind the wheel, Dad still in the passenger seat. They're laughing together. I don't know what about, but it's important to me, their laughter. I want them to be happy.

The car climbs the hill. They reach the tight turn. The moment is here.

Perhaps Noah stamps on the brake. Perhaps he's too mystified by what's happening to respond. Either way it doesn't matter. They have too much momentum. Noah has nothing to blame himself for.

The barrier's meant to stop them, but of course it doesn't. It's a wooden fence, and it yields to moving metal. The car tears through, a runner crossing the finishing line.

Time slows down then, stretching like elastic to accommodate the weight of everything it must contain. Dad and Noah reach out for each other. They're together at least, they'll not finish this journey alone. Perhaps Noah speaks. *I love you. It's all right. Don't worry.*

Yes. Yes. I can imagine Noah saying that. *It's all right. Don't worry.* Noah's always believed in the impossibly successful outcome. He's always believed in flight.

Before gravity seizes them, there's a moment when the car is suspended in space. Noah turns to Dad and smiles. 'We're fine', Noah's smile says. 'This is the moment I was born for.' These are the last few seconds of their lives, and Noah fills them with his smile. He isn't afraid. He knows what's coming. Against all the laws of physics, the car is about to take flight. They'll soar towards the sun, loop down to the water, soar high once more and land back on the road. He's been here a million times in his dreams.

I can't stop time. I can't make the car do anything other than what it does, which is to hesitate, tumble and crash. I can't change the pain, which I hope was a single white flash followed by kindly darkness. I can't change what happens. But I can give them that last moment, when Noah smiled at Dad and, with that smile, told him everything would be all right. This is Noah's gift. For a single golden instant, and in the teeth of all the evidence, Noah can truly make you believe that there's nothing to worry about, that everything is really going to be all right.

Chapter Fourteen

Emergency

Josh and Frey and Floss and I are a family, of sorts. We're connected because we choose it, and because we need each other. I don't know quite when they tipped over the boundary from sort-of boss and very intimate colleague into people who belong to me and who I also belong to. But I can tell you exactly when I knew it had happened, because it was the day I almost let everyone down, and yet somehow, they forgave me.

"It helps that you're a nurse," Linnea said when she offered me the job. "It's good to have someone with a medical qualification." I wondered at the time if she'd have bounced me for a doctor, if a doctor had happened to apply. (I'm pretty sure no doctors did – the pay's good, but it's not that good.) Then we all settled into our roles, each day predictable and peaceful, and I forgot about the entire conversation.

So of course, when Frey needs me to actually be a nurse, it takes me a while to even realise.

The alarm chirrups at seven forty-five, as always. I roll out of bed and drop my feet into a patch of sunlight. *Today will be a good day,* I think, already looking forward to walking Floss this afternoon, while Josh and Frey watch *YouTube*. Frey's found a man who deconstructs and repairs watches, and he and Josh are working through his back catalogue. But first there's the morning, breakfast in the clean, bright kitchen, the slow rituals of dressing and cleaning, the lunch we'll encourage Frey to choose. It sounds boring, but I have chaos and excitement in my two weeks with Noah, and I walk into the flow of each day with a sense of peaceful pleasure.

The first unexpected sign is that Floss isn't in her basket. She's pacing between the half-open door and the bedside, glancing over her shoulder. She comes to me and presses against my legs.

"Hey, missus." I pet her head, only for her to pull away and pace back towards Frey. "Do you need to go out? Josh'll be here in a second, don't worry."

The routine is that Josh and I knock on the door and call Frey's name. Josh emerges, yawning and scruffy in his T-shirt and pyjama bottoms. At first it was odd to share such intimacy, seeing him in a way only a lover or a family member might, but the strangeness passed quickly, and now it makes me smile. Floss whines.

"Hey." Josh tickles under her chin. "You all right, my lovely? It's okay, we're here."

In just the way she did with me, Floss leans against his leg. Unlike the way she did with me, she stays there and allows him to comfort her. Floss is fond of me, but she prefers Josh and saves her gentle heart for Frey. I don't mind Frey being her favourite, but I'm somewhat sad not to even come second. Feeling a little rejected, a little snippy, I knock on Frey's door.

"Frey," I say. "It's Callie and it's morning." And because there's already been a miniscule change to how things normally are: "And Floss is out here with us, aren't you, Floss?"

"Frey." Josh knocks too. "It's Josh and it's morning." Nothing.

"Frey." Josh knocks again. "You all right in there, mate? It's Josh and Callie and it's morning."

Still nothing. We glance at each other, then go inside. Floss pushes ahead of us, swishing her tail. Frey is fast asleep. Looking feels like an invasion.

"Frey." I knock again, even though we're already inside. "Frey, it's Callie and Josh and it's morning."

A slow, syrupy moment, and Frey stirs. Floss pushes her head beneath his hand and sighs. His eyes peel open. He looks bleary and confused.

"Hey there, mate. Sorry to wake you, but it's morning."

("Make sure he gets up at the same time," Linnea told us, in that briefing meeting we'd thought would last maybe an hour and that consumed most of a day. "If he's asleep, you have to wake him, even if he looks tired. He needs everything to happen at the same time or he feels lost.")

That's how Frey looks today, glancing at his room from the corners of his eyes. He looks lost.

But then, I never see Frey as he's waking. Maybe this is how he always is.

Frey gets out of bed on sleep-wobbly legs, and the morning clicks into place. Frey goes to the bathroom. Josh takes Floss to the back door. I stand outside the bathroom, tapping every thirty seconds. The toilet flushes. The taps run. Another moment and he'll be out. Another moment. Any moment now.

"Frey?" I tap on the door. "Are you all right?"

Frey doesn't speak, he never speaks, but his feet slide across the tiles and the door pulls gently from my grasp and then he's in the doorway, gaze turned downwards, hair unkempt. He looks faintly bewildered.

"It's time for breakfast," I tell him.

There are signs, there are so many signs, but I don't see them. Frey is oddly off his breakfast-making game, stumbling a little over each step, the delicate mechanism of his timing coming undone. The toast pops up before his tea is mashed, and the slow turn of his head as he realises what's happened strikes me – the person whose job it is to know him – as funny. I smile. God forgive me.

"It's fine," I say to Frey. "Nobody gets things right every time. Do you want me to sort your tea while you get the toast ready?"

His head turns downwards, his gaze drops to the left. 'No, thank you.'

"Okay, shall I do the toast and you do the tea? Oh, wait, you like your toast hot… we can put the toast back in to rewarm it?"

What Frey really wants is for me to make it so that the toaster has not flung his toast out prematurely. Since he can't have that, he'd like me to stop making suggestions that make everything worse (*Would you like me to alter the fabric of reality, Frey? Would you like me to make everything loud and strange and confusing? Heap more confusion on top?*). He's caught in a moment of panic as profound as if the floor were to melt, or the walls to split open.

Floss comes inside and goes straight to him, leans against his leg. He strokes her head. Gathers his strength. Takes the teabag from the mug and puts it on the saucer by the kettle. Plucks his toast from the toaster, handling it gingerly, as if it might come to life and attack him. Since his schedule's gone awry, anything is now possible. I ought to appreciate the heroism of Frey in this moment.

Instead, I think, *that's good, he's going to eat it,* and take cereal from the cupboard. I pour out Josh's breakfast as well as my own – a small act of kindness he'll reciprocate later by making me a mid-morning coffee with my favourite biscuit. We're like an old married couple, expressing our affection not through sex or even touch, but small gestures that say 'I know you, I care about your well-being'. Josh and I eat our cereal. Frey eats most of his toast. We drink our coffee and our tea. The floor does not melt. The walls do not split.

It's my day to clean the bathroom. There's almost nothing to clean – Frey isn't a great creator of mess, and it's sponged down after every use – but I wipe everything, the way Linnea taught us. ("You must go along every edge, even if it looks fine. Frey can't use it if it's not clean.") I'd been afraid Josh would try to shift this responsibility on to me, had my vulgar retort all ready ("You know I don't scrub the bathroom with my vagina, right?"), but it was never needed. We take our turns equally in every chore, and besides, it's hard to get upset about the work of cleaning an already spotless bathroom.

When I come out, Frey's gazing into his wardrobe. I straighten the duvet on his bed and sit down to watch his slow, peaceful choosing. Hands running down soft fabrics. Fingers caressing well-worn T-shirts. Occasionally, a small sound of pleasure that's almost a word. I love watching this, Frey in his flow state, enjoying the day's rituals. But today, that's not happening. Frey isn't choosing his clothes. He's stuck, staring at the floor.

"Frey?" Josh and I try not to touch Frey too much, with our definition of too much being more than we'd touch any other man of about our age who we happen to work for. ("He's a grown adult, not a child, not a pet. It's really important you remember this.") I stand beside him, not touching or patting, respecting his personal space. "Are you all right?"

Frey turns to me then, and for a second he looks directly at me. Our eyes meet. It's shocking, moving, glorious, as likely as Frey sprouting wings. His eyes are blue, like Linnea's, very bright, very beautiful.

I'd like to say I understand what this means. Frey, in extremis, is trying to speak my language, asking for help in a way he's seen Josh and I use a million mysterious times. ("Frey notices everything. He might not look as if he does, but I promise you he's paying attention.") I'd like to say I go instantly into panic mode, recognising the emergency we're facing.

What do I do instead? I smile at Frey, my lips trembling. I think, *he's made eye contact. How lovely.* I say, ridiculously, "Hey there. It's nice to see you. Now, let's get you dressed, shall we? What about those grey joggers with that nice green T-shirt?"

And when Frey lets me pick out his clothes, I'd like to say that I realise this is a warning. But I don't. Because I'm not paying attention, because I'm stupid and complacent, I leave him to suffer for another two hours.

It's eleven o'clock. I'm taking washing from the machine. Josh and Frey are building a wooden Ferris wheel. Floss by Frey's feet, alert and ready even though she'd normally be dozing. There's a trickling, pattering sound, and I wonder if the spin on the machine is broken and the clothes are still soggy. Then I see the dampness of Frey's jogging bottoms, the pool by his feet.

"Frey," I say, slow and wondering.

Frey puts down the carriage he's holding and lays his head on the table.

"Frey," Josh and I say together, and then we're on either side of him, patting at him, coaxing him to look at us, trying to make contact in the ways that feel instinctively right. His hand is hot and dry.

"He's got a temperature," I say.

"Mate, I'm so sorry." Josh puts his hand on Frey's forehead. "And I was sat there building that kit like an idiot."

"Come on, Frey." I pet his shoulder. "Let's get you cleaned up. Stand up. There we go."

It takes both of us to coax Frey to his bedroom. Once there, he stands still and hopeless, all volition vanished. We ask his permission to help him undress, but Frey stares downwards, giving nothing away. Josh peels his clothes off while Frey stands like a mannequin and I fetch the thermometer. When I come back, Frey's naked and Josh has set the shower running.

"You'll feel better for being clean." Josh turns Frey gently towards the bathroom. "Would you like a hand just for once?"

Nothing. Frey seems lost, remote, wandering.

"Frey," I say. "Frey, I'm going to put this thermometer in your ear. It shouldn't hurt, and it only takes a second. All right?"

Frey shivers. Josh wraps him in a blanket. I slip the thermometer into his ear, braced for him to flinch or even lash out. The display reads 41°C.

"It's high," I say.

"Is it dangerous?"

"Maybe. It depends what other symptoms he has."

"How do we find out?"

"Frey." I take Frey's hand. "Squeeze my hand if you can hear me, all right?"

Nothing. Is this because he's overwhelmed, naked at a time when he shouldn't be naked, with everyone crowded into the room he knows is private and something strange poked inside his ear? Or is he too ill to understand?

"Frey. Does your head hurt? Please squeeze my hand if your head hurts. Squeeze my hand if your head hurts, Frey."

Nothing.

"How about your neck? Does your neck hurt?"

His hand rests limply in mine. I look all over for a rash, find a cluster of ruby pinpricks at his collarbone. When I grab a glass from the nightstand and press against them, they shine through, undaunted.

"Okay, we're going to the hospital. Get him into his pyjamas."

"We haven't showered him. He hates being dirty."

"There's no time. Don't argue," I add, because Josh is looking dubious.

"It's not that, I trust you, if you say it's urgent then we're going, but – shouldn't we call an ambulance?"

Josh never acts the way I think he'll act. He's always nicer and more perceptive than I think he'll be. "Sorry, that's a good point. It's a long way, though. We'll be quicker in the car."

At the doorstep, Frey suddenly comes to life. Whatever illness has its claws in him, it hasn't taken his sense of time or appropriateness. He knows it's not Tuesday, he knows he's wearing slippers and pyjamas. We coax and plead, but Frey stands motionless. When we propel him over the threshold, he collapses to the ground. It's the first time I've seen Frey do this, what Linnea calls 'going inwards', and I wonder miserably if it's a measure of his terror, or of his sickness. Floss barks and flinches and shows the whites of her eyes.

"Frey. Frey. Mate. Come on. It's all right." Josh is firm but not rough, his arms cocooning Frey, his voice coaxing him back. I reach into Josh's jeans and take the keys without embarrassment. Step by careful step, Josh manoeuvres Frey across the driveway, towards the open car.

"In we go. That's it. Well done, fella."

I climb into the back. Floss sprawls across our knees. Josh gets into the driver's seat. Frey's shivering again.

"It's all right," I murmur. I want to hug him, if he was anyone but himself I would hug him, but I can't. ("Frey doesn't like to be touched. Please don't do it unless you have to.") "We're going to the hospital," I tell him, "and it's going to be a lot, but we'll be with you. I promise."

Frey reaches for my hand. Clutches it tightly. 'Stay with me', his hand begs me. 'Don't leave me on my own.'

At the hospital, Josh goes ahead, returning with a wheelchair. We manoeuvre Frey into it as tenderly as we can, and rewrap the blanket. (Does it smell of home? And is that scent reassuring? Or is it simply one more thing that's out of place?)

At the booking desk, Josh and Floss crouch beside Frey while I explain who we are, what's going on, the challenges we're facing. The words 'non-blanching rash' guarantee swift attention, but will they carry on listening long enough to understand that Frey is non-verbal, that he's terrified, that Josh and Floss and I are all that lies between him and the void?

"We have to stay," I say, loudly and firmly, to everyone who comes our way. "Yes, both of us. Yes, and the dog too. No, we're not next of kin, we're his carers. Yes, we're authorised to make medical decisions. Yes, he's listening. He's always listening." Everything made a million times more complicated because we have to tease out the delicate tangle of what's normal for Frey when he's well versus when he's sick, and how much of his behaviour is because he's sick and how much because he's terrified. How do you judge possible mental confusion when everything about your patient's world has become a mysterious nightmare?

They're good, the staff. They do what's needed, and they do their best to adapt to Frey's needs. They do this despite their discreet glances and eye-rolls each time Josh and I insist (quietly and politely, then more loudly and rudely) on being with Frey at all times.

I can understand their point, because Frey, to their eyes, is a model patient. He accepts the blood draw, the IV, the catheter, the strangers, with the weary passivity of someone who knows there's no point fighting. Only his hands remain his own, clinging tightly to us as we tell him over and over, "We're here, we won't leave, this isn't forever, we'll go home in the end."

Relief arrives in a rush of synchronicity. Frey's temperature crawls downwards just as the lab results confirm it doesn't look like meningitis and is probably a nasty viral infection.

Then, Linnea, Ana and Miles burst in, white-faced and crying a little, and everyone's focus switches to the sister and the parents, whose role they can easily make sense of.

The human heart is a wayward organ. Mine has room for relief, but also a fat glob of resentment. They're talking to Linnea. Not me or Josh. But what does she know?

"I'm starving," Josh sighs.

"Here." With my free hand, I rummage a chocolate bar from my pocket. "We'll share."

"How do you always have snacks?" Josh snaps the chocolate, takes a bit. "I'm not complaining. Just impressed."

"Superpower," I say, and look away.

In the bed, Frey opens his eyes, glances around the cubicle. It's his first movement for several hours. Floss sits up and shakes her head until her ears rattle.

"Hey," Josh says, swallowing hastily. "Listen, mate. You're going to be fine. You've got a virus and it's made your temperature very high and given you a rash, but you'll be okay. Hopefully they'll let us go home soon."

Frey turns his head a fraction. His slantwise gaze is like sunlight passing over my skin.

"We're both here," I say. "And Floss. Can you hear her scratching away down there?"

A smile tugs at Frey's lips. He takes a breath, lets it go. Closes his eyes.

"That's it," Josh says. "Have a kip, mate, I would. You'll feel better afterwards."

Frey's fingers curl into a hook and tap at the blanket. Without hesitating, Josh and I tap against his hands. 'We're here. You're not alone.' Frey sighs again, nestles into the pillow. Linnea comes into the cubicle.

"I was visiting Mum," she says. "I was showing her the cameras. You took him into his bedroom. Then he was wearing pyjamas and you went to the front door. It was the pyjamas I noticed first. That's how I knew."

She's narrating what I already know, but I still feel like

I'm getting new information. After a minute it comes to me. There really are no cameras in the bedrooms. If there were, she'd have seen us helping Frey to undress. She'd have known before the pyjamas. Josh was right, after all.

Frey's body sinks into rest, and I think, *We kept you safe. We're the ones you trust to stay here with you while you sleep.* And then, *I'm so glad it was Josh and me. Not the others. Not Linnea. We got you through this and I'm glad.* It's a dark, possessive feeling, a strange and greedy thought. I'd feel guilty for having it, but when Josh and I make eye contact across the bed, I see that he's thinking it too.

Chapter Fifteen

Visit

Forty-eight hours. One weekend in two. Four nights a month. Fifty-two nights a year. One month and three weeks. Aged eleven, I work these figures over and over, wrestling them into a manageable size. I could concentrate it into a single stretch, like a prison sentence. A month with our mother in the summer, three more weeks in the winter, and the rest of the year free of that constant dread at the end of each two-week block. I'm always conscious of those two days waiting to pounce. I should write to someone and suggest this as a way of making prison worse.

It's been over two years, and I still don't really understand how she did it. An entire life for herself without us in it – even a job. I'm eleven now, learning about qualifications and interviews and experience, and as far as I can tell, finding a good job is like finding a unicorn. And yet my mother did it. Another mystery I can't fathom: the house she's bought. We're going to see our mother, in a house that's only hers.

Our packed bags are waiting. Mine's half-empty. Noah's is bursting at the seams. Noah always takes more than he needs, always leaves a few things behind. I take only and entirely what I need, refusing even the new toothbrush she bought for me that sits, unused, in the glass in the bathroom. Noah's is replaced periodically. Mine remains untouched. After ten months of visits, it's grown a coat of dust.

Forty-eight hours. One weekend in two. Four nights a month. Fifty-two nights a year. One month and three weeks. At school, we'll talk about the weekend. I wonder what would happen if I said that I spent two days with a woman who doesn't love me.

Noah's happy on the drive, trying to make me happy too. Dad's trying not to show his sadness. He hates being without us, hates our mother not being his. But Noah sings along to the radio as we drive, and soon we're both infected by his happiness. We sing together, making up filler when needed ("The love thing the something, I don't know the words, the words, the words...").

Noah and I are together in the back seat. He always sits with me when we go to our mother's. He's trying to shore me up for the weekend. He thinks I don't notice, but I do.

Something else he thinks I don't know: lately, he's been struggling to sleep. Sometimes he talks in his room to people who aren't there. He's not loud, but still I can't sleep when I hear it. Instead, I stare at the ceiling and will him to stop, until my skin burns and I can hardly stand to stay in my bed. I think he might be going away from me again, and I'm so afraid.

"Looking forward to it?" Dad, trying to keep the mood upbeat.

"Yeah," says Noah. "But I'll miss you. I mean, I don't mind—"

"Don't tie yourself in knots," Dad says, and smiles through the rear-view mirror. "You're allowed to love your mother."

Noah leans forward and pats Dad on the shoulder. He's

good at cuddles and affection, much better than I am. I can spend long minutes debating whether it's okay, and by the time I've decided, it's too late anyway.

The endless ribbon of the crash barriers unspools beside us. I think, *forty-eight hours. I can do this.* Then I think, *why do I even have to?*

My mother's house has frightened me since I first saw it. It perches on a high, treeless street, peering down as if it's deciding whether to jump, two rooms wide and one room deep, with windows on every wall so you can look straight through and out to sea.

Our mother waits in the doorway. I think she watches for us from her bedroom. I don't like knowing she can see me when I can't look back. It's like being spied on, like being judged.

My eyes slip over her face. The first time we came here, she'd brimmed with wild energy, eyes bright, skin flushed. Even her hair seemed alive, crackling with electricity. For the first time, I could see why Dad fell in love with her. But that was months ago, and now she looks old and ugly and used up.

"Hey." Dad leans in to kiss her. She shudders stagily and pulls away. "How are you?"

"Pick them up at the usual time. Hello, Callie." And then, as Noah gets out of the car, "Noah, darling! How was the drive?"

She always asks Noah, never me. If I challenged her on this, she'd say she was asking us both, and I was being prickly and looking for a fight.

"Come here." She holds her arms out to Noah. He goes willingly, eagerly. She holds him tightly, lets go, turns to me. "You too," she says. Her hug for me is short and awkward, her body reluctant. I try not to mind, but I always, always do.

"So how's everything?" Dad, talking to her as if he's going to get anywhere. "Work going well?"

She takes Noah's bag. Mine stays where it is, hanging from my arm, pulling my T-shirt askew. If I challenged her on this, she'd say it was because Noah's bag is clearly much heavier. "Pick them up at the usual time."

"Have you got much planned?"

"Pick them up at the usual time."

"Vee." I hate him using her pet name. He sounds so needy. "I'm trying to be nice."

My mother's face is rigid. I think I can actually hear her teeth pressing together. Maybe they'll crumble and fall out, leave her toothless.

"Pick them up," she repeats, "at the usual time."

"Can't I see their bedrooms? They're my kids too."

"Pick them up," my mother repeats, "at the usual—"

"All right, all right, I'm going. See you on Sunday. Have a nice time. I love you."

Sometimes I imagine Dad saying he can't do without me, and won't I come home with him? And my reply, 'Yes, of course. She doesn't want me here anyway'. I mentally review the snacks I've packed. A box of cereal bars. A multipack of crisps. A stack of foil-wrapped sandwiches.

"See you on Sunday." Dad strokes my hair, not quite ready to leave yet. "Callie – no, I'm being silly."

"What?"

"Keep an eye on Noah, will you?"

I'm torn between wonder and terror.

"He's probably fine," Dad says. "But – just – you know."

After he's gone, there's a moment when we stand on the pavement, my mother holding Noah's bag and staring blankly at the tarmac, as if we've all forgotten what comes next. It's only when Noah touches our mother's arm that she gives a little jump and smiles at him.

"Come inside," she says. "Let's get fish and chips from down the road and eat them out of the paper."

She always says this, making it sound like some mysterious treat. I don't even like fish and chips, I hate the thought of food from the depths of the ocean. If I said this, she'd say I was being difficult, trying to annoy her. She'd say that we always have fish and chips when we come down. It's our tradition. I go into the living room and sit down on the floor.

"Sit on the sofa," my mother says at once. I've been here for under a minute and I'm already doing the wrong thing.

"Why?" I perch on the sofa, my back straight with dislike. "There. Is that all right?"

"Don't be so prickly. Noah, do you two want a drink?"

"I'll make them."

"You're a good boy." She smiles at his back, and I swallow hard.

"Why can't I sit on the floor?" I ask, unable to stop myself. "Noah always does it."

"He's not doing it now, is he? He's in the kitchen getting your drink. Don't argue," she says before I can even try. "This is supposed to be a nice time for everyone."

So many things I could say. I could point out that she started it, picking at me for sitting somewhere she's decided is wrong for some bloody reason (and she'd tell me off for swearing). I could tell her I didn't have a chance to offer to make the drinks (and she'd say I could have gone to help instead of leaving Noah to do it). I could point out that 'everyone' ought to include Dad as well, he's still part of the family (and she'd tell me off for not considering her feelings). I could ask her why she left me, and she would say…

She would say…

"Do you still like pineapple squash?" I don't like her being nice. It only makes me apprehensive for when it's going to stop. "I got some specially."

"Thanks."

"Sit on the floor if you want. I want you to be happy."

My shoulders tense up. What if she really means it? She left me, but we're still here together. That must mean something, surely.

I can't relax here. The rooms are full of the outside, pressing at the glass, trying to get in. I imagine the house's clawed toes clinging to the earth, wide eyes staring out across the dark.

"Are you ready for dinner?" my mother asks Noah.

"I don't know, she might be," Noah replies, his words directed over my shoulder as if there's someone else in the room with us and he's talking to them, then looks as shocked as if he'd accidentally sworn. "I mean, yeah. Yes, please."

"Take your bags upstairs. I'll fetch the fish and chips."

The worst thing about visiting our mother is that we have to share a bedroom. We're too old to share, it makes us both cringe, but by the time we realised, the house was a done deal, so we've had to live with it.

"What about the searchlights?" Noah says, and rubs his earlobe.

"What?"

"The searchlights… in the harbour…" He looks confused, and my stomach feels cold and tight. "Didn't we talk about that? The searchlights? They get in through the curtains and keep you awake."

"No. I don't think so." I know we haven't, not at any point. *Noah,* I think desperately, *please be normal, please. Stay with me. Be well. I need you.*

"That's all right, I can wear a helmet," Noah says. His smile is bright and brilliant. I don't know how to respond. I don't know if he's joking or serious, if he's talking to me or those other people, those ones who nobody else can hear. I ought to tell Dad about this. I ought to have told him as soon as I noticed. But it feels like a betrayal, to share what Noah's keeping secret. And besides, it might all be a mistake.

* * *

My mother serves the fish and chips still in their paper, because apparently this is more fun. I don't see how eating food from a cardboard box is *fun*, but there's no point saying so. Noah eats with enthusiasm. I swirl the contents around, forcing myself to eat what I can, and wait for our mother to notice that my meal has consisted of a small bite of batter and five chips.

She doesn't notice. She's occupied with her own deception, folding her own barely touched portion hastily away. She's getting thin, which is usually a compliment, but not for her. She looks ancient and ugly and raggedy. I cram the wrappers into the bin, half-expecting to be told I've done it wrong. Instead, my mother watches me with what feels like tenderness.

This is what she does, what makes her so clever. Every now and then, she contorts herself into the shape of a normal mother, and I'm fooled every time. Before I can stop myself, I put my arms around her waist and hold on.

There's a moment of stiffness, as if she has to overcome a primal reluctance to touch me. Around the curve of her arm, Noah mutters to himself. For the first time I can remember, I'm the one who pulls away first.

"It's noisy," Noah says, shaking his head as if he has bees in his ears.

The street outside is carless and quiet. The windows are closed too tightly for any sound of water to reach us.

"But it's all right," Noah adds, as if he can see how worried I am. "I don't mind."

"Right," my mother says, as soon as the clock ticks over to eight o'clock. There's something mechanical about her, like she's reading from a script she hasn't quite learned yet. "Off you go for your bath, Callie. And don't take ages, Noah needs to get to bed too."

At home we stay up until ten at the weekend. But Noah won't say anything because he loves her, and I won't say anything because she never listens. In the chilly bathroom, I run a few grudging inches of water. I don't want a bath, I want a shower so I can wash my hair, but if my mother hears it running she'll tell me off for not doing as I was told. I can't imagine why she even cares, I've always thought showers were cheaper, but there's no reasoning with her. My hair feels lank and greasy. I shrug into my pyjamas and go downstairs.

"The bathroom's free," I tell Noah.

"Night, Callie." My mother's smile is small and mean and unreal. The smile I return is its twin. I kiss the top of her head, my lips barely touching her hair.

And now here we are, shut away in this tiny little room. Noah fizzes with energy, trying to keep still but not quite managing it. If he was on his own, he'd be pacing up and down, muttering and laughing.

"One day," Noah says, "we'll get time properly organised. So if you've got a spare bit like this evening, you'll be able to save it up for later, when you want something to go on for longer."

"How would that work? Would you keep it in bottles or something?"

"Electronic storage," Noah says, deadly serious. "They're nearly there with the technology. Just give it a few years and you'll see." He's scrabbling through his bag. "Do you want a book? I've brought loads."

Noah has brought what looks like half his bookshelf. I sift through the collection. He's mostly into science fiction, which I'm not usually bothered about but which will probably be better than lying on my back, staring at the ceiling, trying not to think about the sea and waiting for the time to pass. I pick up a battered paperback with a blue-eyed man wearing a hood.

"That one's brilliant," Noah says. "Seriously, read that, it's excellent."

"All right. Do you want a sandwich?"

"Why do you always bring so much food?" He hesitates. "Have you got crisps?"

I throw a pack across to him, and flick on my torch. Another sign of our mother's impulse towards petty control; once we've gone upstairs to bed, she won't let us have the light on.

There's nowhere to sit but our beds, so we climb beneath the covers and lie down, turning away from each other. It's impossible not to be aware of the other one's presence, the other one's body. I try to lose myself in my book, but I can't do it. So I put off my torch and lie still and quiet and watch the darkness creep in around the curtains.

"Noah," I say when I can't stand it any longer.

"Here."

"Are you all right?"

This is a question I can only ask in the dark. I can feel his surprise, his embarrassment.

"I'm fine."

"Are you sure?"

"Why wouldn't I be?"

"I'm just checking."

His dim shape turns around beneath the duvet. Now I can see his face, the angles unfamiliar in the darkness. "I don't actually think there are scientists working on electronic storage for time, you know."

Noah almost always hears the words behind the ones you actually say.

"And how about you?" he asks.

"Me?"

"You look sad."

"It's this house," I say. What I want to say is that I'm scared about those people I hear him talking to sometimes. "I don't like it." I want to ask him if they're here now. "I wish we were at home."

The television chatters to us through the floor. I lie in bed and listen to Noah, also not sleeping, and occasionally whispering to a presence that could be one person or many, standing beside his bed and muttering warnings only he can interpret.

Time passes, somehow. We do the things we always do. We watch television, the same channel on from morning until night, and our mother sits beside Noah and strokes his head and arm, as if he's a pet or a cuddly toy. We shop for two of the five meals my mother likes to serve us, and Noah and I watch as our mother cooks. Once the shops are safely shut, we go for our prescribed walk around town, looking in windows at things we'll never buy, breaking a single slice of bread into pieces for the harbour swans.

"Will we go somewhere tomorrow?" I whisper to Noah. I know the answer, but I don't like the oily darkness of the water and the bread has run out.

"She doesn't have enough money," Noah says. "It's not her fault."

Our mother doesn't buy nice food. She doesn't buy new clothes. After an initial frenzy of painting and furnishing, she hasn't bought things for the house. She doesn't spend money on anything. There's definitely a shortage in my mother's life, but it's not money she's lacking, it's joy.

Noah doesn't sleep that night either.

The next day goes on and on. Noah, sleepless and gritty-eyed, grows wilder and more peculiar. He begins a project in the yard based around cardboard and packing crates and pieces of wood collected from who knows where, and our mother lets him do it, because she's lost in her own world, not paying attention. The hours tick down. Five, then three, then two. Then one. We're into a time I can measure in minutes.

"Come and look," Noah says, and drags me outside.

His face is white and exhausted, but his eyes glitter. He's built a sturdy wooden frame like a tepee, cardboard layers interlocking like scales. There's a small gap for us to crawl inside, and more cardboard as a floor.

"We can stay here until the fuss dies down," he explains. "Then she won't have to lie about where we are because she won't know. I can stop them from seeing it for long enough for him to go away again. Then we can come out."

"All right…"

"He'll be here soon." He puts a finger in his ear. "Yep – I can hear him, he's just turning up the—"

"Noah. Callie." Our mother is at the back door. "I can see your dad's car."

This is the disconcerting thing about Noah. Sometimes it really seems as if he can see things that he can't possibly see.

"Shit." Noah is wild-eyed. "He's here and we're not ready."

"Yes, you are, your bags are in the hall. Come on inside now."

Noah lets our mother shepherd him inside, but his gaze is quick and darting. When the front door opens, he explodes out like a cork, flailing wildly.

"Noah! It's fine, it's just Dad!" I'm after him as quickly as I can move, grabbing his arm, stroking and patting at him, trying to keep him with me. Dad stops the car in the middle of the road and leaps out.

"Noah! Noah. What the hell, mate? It's all right. It's all right." Noah's trying to get away, but Dad holds him in place and keeps him still, looking round for our mother, who's nowhere to be seen. She only appears when he bellows her name, once and then again. And even as she stands in the doorway, answering his anger with her own, and as they trade insults like caresses, I can see she's not really present at all. Isn't listening to a word. Dad points out how tired we both look, how grubby we are, how Noah's clearly upset (at this point I stop listening, because I don't want to think about Noah's behaviour, about what it means). She's safe in that house Dad isn't allowed to come into. She could disappear inside, an octopus squeezing under a rock, and Dad could never dig her out again.

Noah struggles as we get him into the car, but when we set off he goes limp. By the time we get to the motorway he's asleep, lulled by the hum of the engine. Or maybe it's being away from our mother that's doing it. Something about her seems to invite breakage.

"Has he been... upset... all weekend?" Dad asks. As if we're both adults and Noah is our child.

"Not all the time," I say. The word 'upset' is comforting. 'Upset' sounds temporary, brought on by circumstances. "But he didn't sleep much. He was awake reading both nights."

"Just reading? Nothing – nothing else?"

If Dad asks me specifically about the voices, I'll say something. I will.

"Sorry," Dad says then. "I don't know how I'm expecting you to know, you're in a different room."

"No, we have to share a room," I say, without really thinking.

"You what?"

Two days later, we're taken out of school and shown into an office where a woman in a strict grey suit talks to us across a wide desk.

"I'm Isobel." She holds out a cool hand for us to shake. I hope I'm doing it right. "I'm a solicitor, I've been instructed by your dad. You're not in trouble. We just need to clear something up."

"It's all right," Dad says. He's trying to smile, trying to seem normal. "Just some paperwork stuff."

"So, this is to do with your visits to your mum." Isobel has a notepad with our names written at the top. *Oliver Taggart vs Vanessa Taggart. Children: Noah Taggart, Caroline Taggart. Visitation dispute.* The word *dispute* fills me with a strange, mean hope.

"We go every other weekend," Noah says cautiously.

"Where do you sleep when you're there?"

The tingle in my limbs becomes a throb of expectation.

"Um. In a bedroom. In a bed." Noah's spotted where we're going too. He's looking for a way out, a way to protect our mother.

"Do you and Caroline—"

"Callie," we all say in unison.

"Apologies. Do you and Callie share a bedroom at your mum's?"

Noah hesitates.

"Yes," I say into the silence.

"I see. And you're fourteen and eleven?"

"We don't mind," says Noah. "Do we, Callie?"

It's my turn to hesitate. I do mind, I hate it, and so does Noah. The difference is that he'll tolerate it, because he loves our mother.

"It doesn't matter whether you mind or not, so don't feel guilty," says Isobel. "It's about what's appropriate. You're opposite-sex siblings over the age of nine, so you need your own sleeping spaces. Does your mother have a bedroom?"

"Yes," says Noah.

"All right. So, your mother could give up her bedroom for the weekend, and sleep downstairs. Or she could share the second bedroom with you, Callie." I shiver. "You might not even need to miss a weekend."

"She won't let me inside," says Dad. "How am I supposed to trust her?"

"She lets the children in, though, presumably," says Isobel. "You can tell your dad if you're not happy with the sleeping arrangements, can't you?"

"And I'm not happy about how she takes care of them. I don't think she's fit."

"Maybe we shouldn't have this conversation in front of the children."

"How can I get her blocked from seeing them?"

Isobel frowns. "The bar for removing access is quite rightly very, very high. Children do better with both parents in their lives. Remember, children have rights and parents have—"

"Responsibilities, I know, I know. But don't I have a responsibility to make sure they're safe with her?"

"Which is what you're doing right now. So. I'll draft a letter so she can make changes before their next visit."

"Can I insist on seeing inside?"

"That's… problematic. I really wouldn't advise—"

"What if she doesn't make the changes and they're scared to say? What happens then?"

"What if…" I say, and then stop. Dad doesn't hear me; Noah's staring out of the window, white and anxious. But Isobel – the first person to tell me that I have rights, that I can have a say – holds up her hand for silence.

"Go on, Callie."

"What if I don't go any more?" I say.

I don't dare look at any of their faces.

"What do you mean?" Isobel asks.

"I don't want to go any more," I say.

"Callie," says Noah, wretched.

"I mean it. I don't want to see her, she doesn't want to see me." It feels liberating and painful to say it aloud. "Noah can have our bedroom and she can stay in her bedroom and I'll stay with Dad. And that solves everything."

"Callie, darling." Dad reaches for my hand, pets it gently. "Of course she – of course she wants to see you. What makes you think she doesn't?"

"I don't want to go any more," I repeat stubbornly.

"Noah?" Isobel's voice is very gentle. "What's your take on this?"

Noah looks at me. Looks at Isobel. Looks at Dad. "Mum isn't always great with Callie," he whispers at last.

"What does she do?" Dad is enormous with rage, filling the room. "What's she been doing?"

"Nothing! Nothing, I swear! I wouldn't let her hurt Callie!" Poor Noah, miserable and frightened, trying to do the right thing. I almost wish I'd kept my mouth shut, except I don't. "But – they don't really get on. Callie doesn't have a nice time." He swallows, shoots me a guilty look. "I do. But Callie doesn't. She only goes because we have to."

"Do I have to?"

"No." Isobel sounds reluctant. "You're old enough to choose. But I wouldn't—"

"Then I don't want to go," I say.

Dad is sitting very still.

"All right," he says. "Then that's what we'll say in the letter."

"That's quite a big step." Isobel is talking to me, not to Dad. The sense of power is dizzying. "Maybe take it week by week. Make a decision at each visit."

"But I can say no forever, if I want to?"

Isobel sighs. "It's normal to fall out with your mum sometimes. That doesn't mean you shouldn't see her. Take it week by week."

"But I can still go?" Noah sounds like a very little boy when he says this.

"Of course," says Isobel.

"As long as you still want to," says Dad.

"I want to," says Noah, and I hear the tears he's trying to hold in.

I sit as still as I can. My mother left me. Now I've left her in return. I've done something huge, and I can't tell yet if it's brilliant or terrible, and until I can work out which one it is, I'm not sure if I dare to move.

Chapter Sixteen

Ink

"What do you do when you're not here?" I ask Josh one afternoon.

We don't usually discuss our other lives, but today is a day for small changes to protocol. By now, Josh should have taken Floss far out over the downs. But the heat has come, pressing relentlessly down on us until we're squeezed and flat and helpless. Today even Floss, indefatigable Floss, lies limp against the cool tiles of the kitchen, and when Josh looked in her direction, she turned her face away and crawled further into the shadow of the cabinet.

We thought about Josh taking Floss for a drive instead, just to keep to Frey's routine, but while we stood in the hallway and murmured about how we could manage it, Frey did something astonishing. He went to the cupboard where the colouring things live. He took down three books, three packs of pencils. Then he laid them out on the table and stood next to the chair that's his. 'It's too hot for Floss. We're doing something different. This is the different thing we're doing.' The concession was astounding, and Josh and I took our seats in wonder.

Josh is shading a tropical bird in tints of orange and red. He looks at me in surprise, maybe even pleasure.

"Ignore me," I say, already embarrassed. "I'm being nosey."

"I don't mind." His blush is shy and sweet. Josh looks like a handsome meathead, but he keeps not being the person I thought he might be. "Right now it's mostly surfing."

"I've never tried surfing."

"Once you get the hang of it there's nothing better. Frey, mate, do you want that pencil sharpening?"

Frey curves his lips into his faint, barely-there smile. He's been sitting still, waiting for Josh to notice. He has the manual dexterity to sharpen his own pencils, but something about the process – the disconcerting movements of the shavings as they tumble from the pencil, or perhaps the sharp, woody smell – upsets him. We've seen him do it, shoulders braced and rigid, head turned away, and once we realised how much he hated it, we took over. Possibly, this isn't in the spirit of what Linnea wants (taking a task away from Frey, lessening his small amounts of independence), but if she's ever seen us on the cameras, she's never said anything. Besides, we both love Frey, and don't we all want to do things for the people we love?

"I bet it's like skiing, though," I say to Josh.

He laughs. "It's a warm-weather hobby and it's in water, liquid. It's literally the opposite of skiing."

"No, I mean before you can do it properly, you have to spend a whole holiday learning. Like going on holiday to learn how to drive."

"Yeah, I suppose. There you go, mate." Josh sits back down, picks up his orange pencil.

"And that's it, is it? Just wall-to-wall surfing? For two weeks straight?"

Josh looks wary. I don't blame him. I do sound a bit mad, a bit nosey. Living so intimately with each other, shut up in the same few rooms for fourteen days straight, small courtesies and small intrusions take on a greater weight.

"Sorry," I say. "Ignore me. Really. I'm just chatting."

Josh feathers delicate strokes of colour onto the bird's wing, feathers within feathers. He's much better at this than I am, almost as good as Frey, although I'm getting better. I wonder if I've offended him, if we're about to have our first row. Just as I'm opening my mouth to say that I'm sorry again, Josh begins to speak.

"My mum and dad have a dairy farm," he says. "I don't know if you know anything about farming? What it's like, I mean."

I've never really thought about it. I picture reports on the news about milk prices, wool prices, meat prices; the occasional horror show of diseased animals; Sunday-evening clips of glossy cows and golden fields of wheat and barley.

"I went to a farm once on a school trip," I offer, and then feel stupid, but Josh doesn't laugh.

"So the thing about farming is, it's the ultimate family business. Like, you grow up where your mum and dad work. You get involved from when you're little. All my earliest memories are about the cows and the dogs and that."

"That sounds lovely."

"Well, if you want to be a farmer it's lovely. And there's this expectation... d'you remember teachers asking what you want to be when you grow up? Everyone saying they want to be a vet, or a nurse, or a fireman, or a lorry driver? Because those are the jobs everyone does on kids' TV programmes, so those were the jobs we knew about?"

"That's true, actually. Where are the kids' programmes about people who process insurance claims?"

Josh smiles. "Anyway. I'd say I wanted to be a farmer. And the teachers used to look at me a bit differently. Took me bloody years to realise that was because they knew I probably *was* going to be a farmer. Like, my whole life was laid out from birth."

"Don't you want to?" It's perfectly obvious Josh doesn't want to – why else would he be here, at this kitchen table, colouring in a picture of a bird? But I want him to keep talking.

"I don't. I stopped wanting to when I was about twelve. Well, apparently most people stop wanting to about then. They have this whole organisation to keep you interested – the Young Farmers thing, you heard of that? My parents used to make me go, every single bloody event. Tried to tell them I wasn't bothered when I was fifteen. They looked like I'd gone for them with a kitchen knife. Felt so guilty I did a BTEC in agriculture, then went to uni to do a degree in it. They were thrilled. Couldn't bring myself to tell them it was so I'd have three more years where I wouldn't have to commit."

"Did you graduate?"

"Nah. Dropped out at the end of the second year. Mum cried for days. Dad tried not to show how angry he was, but I knew." He sighs. "They asked what I wanted to do instead and I didn't have a clue. All I'd got was *not a farmer*. Got a store job at Tesco, nothing wrong with that but it's not a career, is it? Got into caring work, thought it sounded more fulfilling. And it is, I love it, made me happy for the first time in my life, but the pay… and everyone was like, 'Why don't you join the family business? You've got it made.'"

"I'm sorry."

Josh shrugs. "First World problems. Anyway, my life wasn't really going anywhere, I was barely making enough to get by on my own. Mum and Dad wanted me to move back home, but that would only have got their hopes up. It was all looking a bit desperate to be honest. Then I got this job. Couldn't believe my luck."

"I know how you feel."

"Yeah, I know you do." He smiles at me. "Anyway. Now I get two weeks a month to be *not a farmer*. So I surf. And I sit on the beach and look at the sky. And I wonder what'll happen when Mum and Dad are too old to manage the farm, and I wonder if one day I'll wake up and wish I'd done everything differently, and I wonder if they'll ever forgive me. So, yeah. That's me. Two weeks of hard work, two weeks of pointless emotional labour."

"Oh my God," I say, with a sense of revelation. "You're the bloke whose ambition was not to be a farmer."

"What?"

"Something Linnea said when she interviewed me. She said… she said I was the second person who'd been honest with her about why they wanted the job. And the first one was someone who didn't want to be a farmer. And that was you! I was picturing some middle-aged bloke with a red face."

"Give me a chance, I'll get there."

"You're fine as you are," I say, surprised when Josh blushes. He must know he's good-looking. Pretty people always know.

"So what were you honest about?" Josh asks.

"Oh." I'm startled; I thought he must already know somehow, that Linnea must have told him if nothing else. But then, she told me nothing about Josh either. "Um. I have an older brother. Noah."

"Cool name."

Noah is so vibrant that just by saying his name, I feel as if I've summoned him. "He's a very cool person. He's also living with serious mental health issues. He can't live on his own. Can't even be left alone, not really."

"Like Frey?"

We glance over at Frey, who sits so still and absorbed it's easy to forget he's there. Only the pencil moving over an intricate sugar skull shows he's a person and not a mannequin. I think about skiing and surfing, the same materials deployed in radically different ways. "The literal opposite of Frey."

I wait to see if Josh will ask what's wrong with him. Josh takes a blue pencil and shades another feather.

"I was a nurse," I say.

"Yeah, Linnea said. That was a relief. Someone who knows what they're doing."

"I worked in A & E, I loved it, it was great. And I love Noah, he's great too. Our dad's an accountant. A partner in a firm."

I wait to see if he'll ask about my mother. The pencil keeps moving.

"Noah needs looking after. He… he sees things, he gets ideas. And if you're not around to stop him, he'll try and actually do them. Stuff like, I don't know, going skinny-dipping in an outdoor pool at night. Climbing on the roof and crossing town without touching the ground."

"That sounds almost fun, in a weird way."

"Right? You can see why he wants to do them. If he tries to talk us into coming with him we can stop him, but sometimes he tries by himself. And sometimes…"

I don't think I've ever talked about this outside of a psychiatrist's consultation room.

"Sometimes he gets these other ideas. He thinks I'm in danger. Like, Dad and I aren't at work, but Dad's taken me away somewhere and he's got to save me. Sometimes he tries to hurt Dad. Never me, just Dad. There's extra medications that help, but the ones he's on already are bad enough. He hates them and we hate them. It's no kind of life."

"You really love him, don't you?"

"I do. Of course I do! He's my brother. So anyway, we were like you really. Dad and me, I mean. We needed to be *not a nurse* and *not an accountant.* And then I saw this job advertised. So now Dad works two weeks and I work two weeks and, in our weeks off, we're responsible for looking after Noah."

"Do you get time for yourself? Like, ever?"

It's the same question Chloe asked, and it makes me feel as if spines are protruding from my skin. Don't touch. Don't get too close.

"I love Noah. I want to take care of him."

"But when do you get to just be you?"

"I'm me all the time. Josh—"

"Sorry. I'll shut up. Tell me what you like to do for fun."

"Theme parks. Noah loves them. Great big roller coasters."

"Really?" Josh grins. "They make me feel sick."

"Me too, but…" I spot the trap the second after I put my foot in it. "But I like the slower rides. We go on those too."

"That's cool."

"And swimming. The beach. That's always good." That's not really true, deep water makes me afraid, but Noah loves it, and when I'm with Noah, I do what Noah wants. "And shopping, we love shopping." Noah loves dressing me up like a doll, picking out clothes I'd never choose myself.

"Christ," says Josh. "I feel ashamed."

"Why?"

"I go home to mope by the ocean because I don't want the family business handed to me on a platter. You go home and look after your dad and your brother."

"Not Dad. Just Noah."

"Yeah, right. Who does the cleaning, you or him? And the shopping? And the tidying up?"

"I don't mind, I like doing it."

"Do you, though? Or do you just like that they like you doing it?"

It's a painfully astute question, a dangerously intimate enquiry. Josh sees me, and it feels like someone rubbing sandpaper over my skin, like being woken up when I want to sleep, like having someone tugging on my arm. Anger's beginning to rumble in my gut, building the way the heat's building outside. Across the valley, a fat black cloud cuts a sharp divide across the sky. Soon there'll be a thunderstorm.

"I need to keep my mouth shut," Josh says, not to me but to Frey. "How are you doing with those pencils, mate? Any need sharpening?"

Frey glances down and to the left. 'No, thank you.' Then, changing his mind, he picks out three pencils from his store, lays them shyly in front of Josh. They look fine to me, barely touched, but Josh takes them gratefully. Now there's some distance between the two of us, and I can breathe again. Did Frey ask Josh to sharpen them so we'd have a moment to recover ourselves? Frey's face is smooth and closed, absorbed in his colouring. I improvise two fat red spots on the wings of my butterfly. I'm neat enough, but I'm not an artist. Not like Frey.

"I might get a tattoo," I say to Josh's back. I've never even considered this before, but it sounds cool and spontaneous. Something you do just for yourself.

"Sweet. What are you going for?"

Noah will love this plan, will adore everything about it. If I give him even a hint he'll get lost in Pinterest and Instagram, trawling the virtual world to find the perfect design. He'll come with me to the tattoo shop, plead for admission, tell me I should go bigger, go bolder, cover my entire arm. "Haven't decided."

"Something everyone can see? Or will it be a secret one?"

"On my wrist," I say, at random.

"I love tattoos on girls," Josh says, and then, surprisingly, blushes. "I mean. It's not essential or anything. I like girls without tattoos too."

"Equal opportunities."

"That's me."

"Or just not fussy."

"That's not me."

"You're fussy?"

"I'm discerning. I like girls that I like. Tell me about your tattoo."

"I just fancy having one," I say vaguely, realising with some surprise that this is true. "Have you got any?"

"A few." Josh sits back at the table, passes the pencils over to Frey, rolls up the sleeve of his T-shirt to show me a stylised tribal sun.

"That's lovely."

"It's a memorial piece… this bloke I knew. Kai. He was a client, but he was a friend too. About our age. We went surfing once. Well, I mean, it was sort of surfing. Mostly he just thrashed around like a dying shark. But it was brilliant. He said it was the best day ever." Josh swallows. "Two months after, he had a massive fit and died."

"I'm sorry."

"Yeah, me too. Anyway. The day we went surfing, he bought himself this T-shirt from the shop at the top of the beach, it had that design on. And so…"

"That's lovely." Maybe I should get something like that, something to bring Noah with me even when I'm here. Something just in case… No, I won't even think that. Noah's healthy and young. He'll live a long time. I'll always have him. Josh is looking at me again in that very open way, making me feel seen in a way I'm not comfortable with. The air presses down on us, hot and thick. Please God let the storm break soon. We need the relief of rain.

"Flowers are always nice," Josh says. "If you want something pretty, I mean. Or a little phrase that means something to you. But not a quote from a crap TV show. I'll properly judge you if you get a line from *Killing Eve* or something."

"Who put you in charge of my tattoo?"

"Or a butterfly. Or a parrot."

"Stop just saying things you can see."

"Or my face."

"Only if you get mine on your arse."

"Deal. But you first. Floss? You all right, sweetheart?" Floss has finally left the cool of the shadowed tiles and is pacing towards the back door. "You need to go out? Okay, lovely. Here we go."

The other side of the valley is hazy with the downpour. A pink-white flash lights up the sky, and I hold my breath and count slowly, reaching seven before the sound strikes my ears.

"It's raining over there," I tell Frey. "Hopefully it's coming our way." Frey smiles a little. "I know, I'm too hot as well. But a good storm will fix everything."

Frey wanders off to the bathroom. When he's returned and I've cleaned it, it will be time to make dinner. Today is Wednesday, so we're having buttered, garlicky pasta with miniature cubes of chorizo stirred into it, plus a separate plate each for broccoli, because Frey gets upset by the sight of the pasta touching the broccoli. At first I was afraid I'd be bored stiff after the first few rotations, each moment mapped out with dreadful regularity. As it turns out, I sort of love it. So much of adult life is consumed with small decisions – what to eat, what to wear, go out or to stay in, watch this programme or that. Frey has chosen to automate all of these choices, and in doing so, he's created an abundance of mental space that I still haven't tired of.

In the garden, Josh and Floss tear about like mad creatures, dancing in the strange, hot light. They look possessed, hair and fur leaping, mouths hanging open, the same expression on the man and the dog. The rain comes just as Frey returns, fat drops like pebbles, so heavy and sudden that Josh and Floss brace themselves against the onslaught. Frey looks directly at them for once instead of from the corners of his eyes, something he normally only does with his laptop or the television. Perhaps it's the protection of the window that sets him free; or that he can see there's no danger of them looking back. Or maybe he's simply forgotten to be afraid.

He glances at me. Looks away again. If Josh did this, it would be a shy reaching-out, a micro-expression of a deeper interest. This can't be what Frey means, but I get that tingle anyway, that little frisson that says, 'There's something significant here. Pay attention to what you do next.'

I'm going to clean the bathroom, but I make a small deviation to pause by Frey's side. The thirsty ground soaks up the rain as fast as the sky pours it out. Josh is dripping with rain, laughing forgetfully as he holds his palms out to the sky. Floss will stink, no matter how well we dry her. She's a clean creature, as clean as an animal can be, but she can't change her nature.

I risk a quick glance at Frey. His expression's rapt, the way he looks when he watches nature documentaries. If I'd had to guess his tastes, I'd choose programmes with families of mammals going about their daily business, or perhaps solitary ocean-dwellers. But Frey is in love with the insect world, and he stares at honeybees and social wasps and leafcutter ants as if they hold the mysteries of the universe.

"Do you want to go outside?" I ask. "We can if you want."

It's absurd to ask. Frey never wants to go outside. It's absurd to read anything into the pause before his response. He always takes the time to think about it. Sometimes when I'm away from him, I think about that pause, the possibilities it holds. For as long as the pause endures, Frey's response remains suspended in paradox, both known and unknown.

I know what I'll see, but I'm still unreasonably disappointed. The glance sideways and downwards: 'No, thank you.' The turning away. The return to the table, where his pencils have slipped out of alignment and must be rearranged. Josh and Floss come inside, laughing and dripping water. Josh wraps Floss in a towel before she gives in to her urge to shake.

"I'm going to clean the bathroom," I say. "Frey, when I come back we'll start making dinner, all right?"

The spell of difference is broken; our afternoon clicks smoothly back into its groove. I freshen the bathroom, wiping down surfaces that are already spotless, pouring cleaner and flushing it away, whisking away the few water-spots. If I stopped to think about it, I could drive myself mad questioning why Frey needs this to be done each time. I could drive myself mad wondering how he even knows. I've lived intimately with him for so many weeks, but I still know him so little.

Back in the kitchen, everyone is in their places. Frey and Josh at the table. Floss – dried off but still smelling faintly of her kind – at Frey's feet. Frey's head is bent over his work. A man at peace. I hate to disturb him, but it would be more disturbing to him to let the moment continue.

"Time to cook," I say, and Frey, as I knew he would, begins slotting his pencils back into the tin. Linnea always buys him artist-quality materials. And why not? He's an artist. I reach for the colouring book that's been designated mine.

Something's been added to the page. Down in the corner, in the margin, someone has drawn a bumblebee. I can see the veins of its wings, the feathery strokes of its body-fur. I have never known Frey to draw anything before. I stare and stare.

"You all right, missus?" Josh, holding pasta and a saucepan, is watching me.

"Sorry. Stuck in a boot cycle."

"No worries. Frey, do you want to get the chorizo out?"

Frey is aware of me; I can sense his interest, his attention, even though he's not looking at me at all. I have that feeling again, that feeling all human beings know. *There's something significant here. Pay attention to what you do next.* With my heart in my mouth, I tear the corner from the page of the colouring book, slip the drawing of the bee into my pocket.

Tattoo artists are capricious and slippery. The good ones are booked up months in advance, and even the not-so-good ones don't want to slavishly recreate someone else's artwork. In the end, I give in and tell the last woman I speak to my shameless sob story: the artwork was created by someone I care for, he doesn't speak but he communicates through his drawings, I can't get it in any other format because this is the only one he can work with. It's the truth, but I feel as if I'm lying, reducing the wondrous complexity of Frey into a sickly tale of selfless carer and sweetly impaired client. But she swallows my mawkishness whole, comments appreciatively on the quality of the drawing, and – while Noah prowls the shop and makes elaborate plans for his own sleeve of ink, and I thank God that this woman has a waiting list for anything larger than a couple of inches – astounds me by scratching a perfect replica of Frey's bee into the delicate skin of my wrist.

The itching of the healing wound is intense and hard to ignore. I calm my skin by pressing my fingers firmly against it and thinking, *soon I'll be able to show him.*

Chapter Seventeen

Lake

My mother left me. You know this, I've told you already. It's just that I haven't… told you.

Those four words. My mother left me. And she did, but maybe not quite how you think. I've dropped hints, the way I did with Noah, hoping you'd somehow guess the truth. But I've been afraid of telling you the whole ugly story. If I tell you, you might think, *there's no way that happened. Someone would have noticed. You'd be more damaged.* Honestly, I've had this thought too.

Also, I'm ashamed. Does that seem strange to you? It seems strange to me, but it's the truth. I'm ashamed of what my mother did, because it's possible I deserved it.

One final reason: I can't be entirely confident it's real. Or rather, while I know some elements are correct, I'm not sure it happened exactly how I remember. I think I must be partly right – I don't like thinking my brain could make such a massive error – but one thing I've learned from Noah is that, sometimes, the things you know aren't the things that are true.

There was a period of my life, less than all the years since it happened, but still more than weeks or months, when I was fixated on solving the mystery. I'd separate the parts I was confident of (Dad and Noah went on a boys' adventure; my mother and I went to a cottage in the Lake District; she went out on the first night to buy groceries; I spent time alone in my bedroom) from the fragments I wasn't quite sure of (maybe-memories that came suddenly, like a plunge into cold water). I made lists, drew diagrams, wrote notes. It's amazing how many different versions of 'possible' you can conjure with the same limited pieces.

But it matters, it really does. Because the crux of it is, am I right to hate my mother as much as I do, or am I wrong? She was a bad mother in a lot of ways, but many parents are. She had a favourite and that favourite wasn't me, but lots of women prefer their son to their daughter. I remember dozens of small wounds where she hurt me with her indifference (bedtime stories unread, kisses ungiven, embraces rejected, achievements undervalued, small mistakes and misdemeanours punished with a primal anger that was never turned on Noah). But is all of that enough to justify the way we are now? There has to be something else, and I think there is, I think the memories I have of fear and hunger and aloneness are true. I think they are. Why else would I be so afraid of her? How else could I be so confident that she means me harm, that she'd delete me from the universe if she could?

But then, Noah used to trust what he found inside his own skull too.

I'm not ill the way Noah is. That's one thing I can hold on to. And because my brain is healthy, I can entertain the possibility of nuance. Maybe somewhere between what I remember, and what seems likely, I'll find reality.

And something must have happened that made Dad uneasy, because this unique configuration of Dad-and-Noah and my-mother-and-me, two and two, was never repeated. I know how much they loved every second of their special fortnight away together. I remember the sunburned tumble of their bodies when they returned, their broad smiles and their easy laughter, the way they greeted us as if they'd had the best time of their lives. But Dad never left me alone with her again.

I'll start with what exists in the memories of others too. Noah's confirmed the bare details of that fortnight. Dad borrowed a camper van from a friend, crammed it to bursting, took his son and headed off into the endless summer days to chase the horizon. Noah remembers leaving: the slide and scrape of the van door, the sputter and smell of the engine, remembers a moment of regret as they drove away. He remembers that he was eleven and I was eight.

When I ask Dad about it, he always says how magical it was. Salt and sunshine and food cooked outside and a different sleeping spot each evening. One gloriously illicit night of wild camping on Bodmin Moor, lying awake until dawn to watch the wheeling of the Milky Way. I remember the way he and Noah looked as they described their holiday over the dinner table that night, the spill of their chatter a painful counterpoint to the deep silence that shrouded their listeners.

Something else I know: Noah doesn't like talking about that holiday. He'll acknowledge that it happened, but when I prod him to reminisce, he looks at me uneasily, as if I'm trying to excavate something that belongs in the darkness. But then, that could be guilt because he and Dad had such a lovely two weeks together, whereas we'd clearly been simply marking time until they came back to us.

But really it doesn't matter what Dad and Noah know, or think they know. They weren't there, and I never told them about the room or the hours or the hunger or the fear. I don't know if it would matter if I had. I was right there, those days are a part of my life, and I'm still not sure I've got it right.

You can see the problem here. It's painful, going over the same events in your mind and getting nowhere.

* * *

So, back to what I know for sure. Noah's eleven; I'm eight. Noah's growing up into that sudden beauty that sometimes comes to almost-adolescent boys. He's perfect, to the point where people actually comment on it in front of him, the way you compliment someone walking a beautiful dog. "Isn't your son good-looking?" older women sometimes tell my mother in the supermarket, and my mother lights up like a torch and runs her hand over Noah's thick hair, Noah's golden skin. Noah himself turns his long-lashed eyes downwards, wraps his arms around his slender body as if he's trying to hide. This is the summer I realise that Dad is good-looking too, this is where Noah gets it from, and possibly, one day, I might experience a similar transformation.

"Have you ever thought about having him become a model?" That's the other thing people say in front of Noah, more than once. Noah always hoots with laughter and says he'd rather be a binman. I can't believe how casually he accepts his own attractiveness, how naturally he receives the gift of being admired. I'd love for someone to stop our mother in the supermarket and say, "Isn't your daughter good-looking?" I'd give anything to have an old lady take hold of her arm and say, "Have you ever thought about having her become a model?"

Dad and Noah, then, off on their boys' adventure like something out of a wholesome children's book, heading into the wilds for campfires and bacon, starlight and washing in streams. Meanwhile, my mother and I will have an adventure of our own.

Dad and Noah plan their trip together. I see them crouched over maps and sheets of paper and wonder if my mother and I will do the same. 'Where would you like to go, Callie?' It's hard to imagine these words in my mother's voice. I hope she won't ask, because my mind is as smooth and blank as cream. The thought of choosing paralyses me. It's a relief when my mother simply announces, "We're going to a cottage in the Lake District, Callie. Won't that be nice?"

I don't know where the Lake District is and it sounds boring, but I reply, "That sounds great. I can't wait!"

And my mother flinches as if I've shouted too loudly.

With Noah and Dad gone, the house is quiet. I go into my room and stay there, feeling as if I'm hiding. My mother rattles around, going up and down the stairs, slamming doors. I wonder if she's looking for me, and for a minute I pretend I'm being hunted, a game where I'm not safe, but it makes me feel nervous so I stop again and try to calm the thump of my heart. When I peek out of the window, my mother's loading the car. I hope she won't glance up and see me, because I know without being told that she won't like me watching. I see two suitcases, one for each of us. I see a box of food. It holds bread, margarine, jam, cornflakes, teabags, milk. Dull, everyday foods for dull, everyday breakfasts.

(My memory tells me I took notice of this food box, that I even thought, *she hasn't put any sugar in so I won't have cornflakes, I'll have toast*, but this is one area where I'm confident I can't trust my memory. I wouldn't have been looking at the food. I'd have been focused on my mother, watching her the way a rabbit watches a stoat. I wouldn't have dared look at anything but her.)

She's cross when she comes to get me, says I should have helped. I would have helped if she'd asked, but having to ask wasn't what she wanted, waiting to be asked wasn't what a good girl would have done. A good girl would have seen she was busy and offered without prompting. Another moment of doubt; I'm not sure if she said this out loud, or if I simply heard it anyway.

This is a detail, the way the box of food is a detail. But maybe what matters is that at some point, in this moment or in some future moment, I had to pay attention. Maybe what matters is that I remember a painful focus on food, a painful awareness that my mother thought I was a bad girl.

I was eight. That's not grown up, but it's not a baby. It's old enough to have some confidence in my recall. I think.

I remember the journey as slow and dull and eerily silent, not even the radio murmuring to fill up the empty spaces between us. I remember stopping at a place called Scotch Corner that I now know is moderately famous in the service-station world. The kind of place you can mention and everyone nods and says, "Oh, yes, I know Scotch Corner", the way you talk about a provincial cathedral or a mid-range department store. We must have spoken as we got out of the car, crossed the car park, used the toilets, got back into the car again. We must have. We can't have done the whole journey in silence.

(I like critiquing my own powers of recall. It makes me feel I can be trusted to evaluate my own thoughts. I like to think I'm quite a good judge of which bits of my memory are likely, and which aren't. I can recognise where I've added doom-laden details to suggest I knew what was coming, so I must be able to rely on myself a little bit.)

So. We make the journey, in silence or not. We don't crash the car. We don't lose each other at the services. We reach the cottage unscathed.

The cottage is small, and the mountain behind it is huge, which makes the proportions feel wrong. You could see this two-week home as either 'nestling', or 'cowering', depending on how dramatic you're feeling.

What am I feeling? Excited, because I'm somewhere new and I want to see where I'm sleeping. Disappointed, because the Lake District seems big and empty with a lot of bare-looking hills and mountains, and boring. Lonely, because I miss Dad and Noah. Nervous, because I'm alone with my mother, and will be for days. There's no way I feel dread. That's ridiculous.

I've never been back to the Lake District. I don't even like hearing its name. I don't make a big deal out of this, it's not like people with a phobia who will shriek and run. But if the Lake District gets mentioned, I'll find a way to escape. Sometimes I think it's the idea of all that deep water, all those towering mountains. Sometimes I think it's evidence that my memory's correct. In my memory, my toe scuffs against a round grey pebble, and because I'm eight years old and this is what eight-year-olds do, I put it in my pocket.

It's a hot summer but the cottage radiators are all on for some reason, and a thin dry heat fills every room, every corner. My mother tuts and sighs, and in my memory I cringe a little because I know that now she'll find something to tell me off for, even though it's not my fault, because I'm the only one here to take the brunt of her irritation. I remember this, but I might be wrong. It seems like quite an adult insight to me.

I do have one piece of definite evidence for what happened in that cottage: the exercise book our teacher asked us to use as a holiday diary. Mine has just three entries. The first begins *It's the first day of the holidays!* then laboriously details just how excited I am to have so many school-free days ahead of me. The second, a day later, describes my set of felt-tipped pens, and mostly consists of rainbow stripes with the colour names written next to them. The third is a single, unfinished sentence:

We are at our special cottage and I can't wate to

In the desiccating heat of a tiny bedroom, my eight-year-old self sits on the bed and begins writing. I'm being a good girl, doing schoolwork even though I don't need to. If I write every day, maybe my mother will read it. Maybe she'll smile and kiss the top of my head. Maybe—

My mother's voice, sharp and tired, calls up the stairs, demanding to know where I am, why I'm not helping her unload the car. The sentence remains unfinished.

It's teatime, but we don't have anything for tea. We've unpacked our suitcases, looked at the views from each window. Now my mother sits on the living-room sofa, staring emptily into space. Dad or Noah would be bustling around, herding us into the car, suggesting restaurants, takeaways, disposable barbecues. Without them, we've run out of steam. I remember watching my mother, worried by her utter stillness. She looks like a clockwork machine whose mechanism has run down. These words are from my adult self, laid onto an eight-year-old's memory. There's no way I was clever enough to think of this image and apply it to my mother's rigid, unmoving shape.

I remember thinking, *we've got bread, we can have bread and jam for tea and cornflakes for breakfast.* I remember thinking, *there's some sugar in those little packets by the kettle.* I remember thinking, *maybe she's just tired.*

My mother explodes into life so quickly, I can still feel the surprise of it. Suddenly, she's on her feet, reaching for her coat, sweeping her car keys from the table.

"Right," she says, as if we've been talking about something, as if we've been doing something together. "This isn't getting tea sorted, is it? I'm going to the shops. I'll be back in a while."

"I want to come with you," I say.

"No, Callie. I can't be doing with you trailing around after me and asking for things when I'm trying to concentrate."

"I won't, I promise, I won't ask for anything…" As an adult, I can hear the whine my eight-year-old self isn't aware of. It must have been awful. I'm being as fair as I can, trying to recognise that even though what comes next still makes my palms sweat, I wasn't some sort of childish saint. My mother was entitled to find me irritating.

"I said no," my mother says.

I was used to her moods. I should have recognised I was over the line.

"Please," I say. "Please, please, don't leave me on my own, I don't want to be here on my own, I don't like it, I want to come with you—"

"I said *no.*" My mother's rage rises like milk in a pan.

"But please, Mummy, please, please, I don't want to stay here, let me come with you, I'll be good, I promise promise

198

promise I'll be good." My nose is starting to run. My mother hates it when I cry.

"Callie. Will you please. Just for once. Listen!" She's almost shaking with rage, and I think, wonderingly, *she's going to hit me.* She's never done that before. The thought is so strange, it's almost peaceful.

"But Mummy, please please please…" It's like I think she might actually change her mind, like she might be moved by my distress. I'm behaving as if she loves me.

"No." Her voice is low and menacing. "I am not taking you with me. Little brats don't get taken anywhere. Little brats sit in their rooms and wait for their mothers to come back and they don't come out until they're told they can! Do you understand? Now go to your room!"

Still I resist. I reach out for her with one pleading hand. I haven't washed yet, we've been travelling all day and now I'm crying, my upper lip glazed in mucus. I must look disgusting.

"Upstairs," she repeats, implacable.

And because it's my mother, I do as I'm told. I go upstairs to my room. I shut the door behind me. I listen to her angry movements as she sweeps through the front door. Slams it shut. Opens the car door. Closes the car door. Starts the engine. Drives away. Leaves me alone.

I'm confident all of this happened. I can recall each moment of that argument, see it from my side and my mother's. That bit's got to be real. It's the part that comes next where things begin to break down.

I know she was gone for what seemed like a long time. I remember seeing the sun sink behind the mountain, that strange lingering half-light as I waited, and waited, and waited, and played with the pebble in my pocket because I was afraid of getting out any books or games, afraid of making a mess and being told off again. I remember the transition from shadow to darkness.

I remember being bored. The fear didn't come until later.

How do you measure time when you have no watch, no clock, no one to talk to? I've tried experimenting with this, shutting myself away in a room with nothing to do, with the goal of seeing how this affects my sense of duration. The experiment never lasts longer than five minutes before I catch myself clawing open the door, racing downstairs to ensure there's still food in the kitchen, still company in the living room. (The last time I tried, I saw Noah – home and stable, but so drugged he could hardly speak – looking at me strangely, as if he was afraid for me. I haven't dared try it since.) My mother was gone for longer than she should have been. But how long?

I remember desperately needing the toilet, bent over and squirming with it, while also being terrified of leaving my room. In the end, unable to hold on, I scrabbled to the bathroom, praying she wouldn't come back while I was in there. I remember the euphoria of letting go, the even deeper relief of not being caught. I remember running back to my room, sitting on the bed, and – finally, blissfully freed of that unmanageable need – being able to think about the rest of my body. I remember thinking, *I'm really hungry. I'm really thirsty too.*

It was August. We'd left after lunch, arrived around four o'clock. I remember the sunlight disappearing. I remember the darkness falling, being in the dark, being afraid of getting into trouble for putting on a light. So she must have been gone for, at least, four and a half hours.

The knowledge that she isn't coming back any time soon creeps in with the darkness and expresses itself in my next actions. I go to the bathroom. I drink deeply from the tap. I pile my dirty clothes in the corner. I think about running a bath, decide not to in case I somehow flood the house. I put on my pyjamas and get into bed, holding my pebble because it's begun to feel like a talisman. I'm hollow and aching with hunger, but I will myself into sleep anyway, telling myself, *she'll be pleased to see I've put myself to bed. It'll be all right in the morning.*

But when I wake the next morning, my mouth dry with the endless, relentless heat—

This is where I have to stop and think about possibilities, probabilities.

I'm not trying to embellish, I swear. It's already bad enough that my mother left me, alone and hungry and frightened, in a strange house, while she went off for long hours without a word. That's already enough reason for how I feel. And from here on in, my grasp of time gets shaky. I can't give a perfect account of how long all this went on for, or how I filled the time.

But in my memory, here's how it goes:

I wake on the morning of the first day and know, instantly and without looking, that my mother isn't here. Humans are good at sensing when they're alone in a house. I'm so hungry I feel shaky and sick.

In the kitchen is the food from home. Bread. Margarine. Jam. Milk. Cornflakes. Yesterday I'd thought this food was dull. Today I cram bread and jam into my face and think, *this is the best thing I've ever eaten.* I don't think about rationing it. Why would I? I'm eight years old. The idea of my mother not coming back is so huge I can't process it. I simply dwell in its shadow, hoping for a glimpse of sunlight soon. I've eaten five slices by the time I feel satisfied.

I go upstairs. I clean my teeth. I get dressed. I fold my pyjamas beneath my pillow. I sit on my bed and wait, turning the pebble in my hand.

The less there is to do, the less there is to remember. I can only summon small fragments, jumbled up like shells in a box that's been given a hard shake. I remember at least two more nights, at least two more wakings, plus fragments that might be different days or might only be reworkings of these two. I remember the last slice of bread. The last cornflakes. The last faint taste of jam on my finger. The globs of margarine that I swallowed, then vomited up. I remember eating toothpaste, drinking water. I remember feeling hollow and transparent, as if I was made of glass. I remember thinking, *nobody knows I'm here. Nobody's looking for me. Nobody will find me.* I remember feeling strangely distant from this thought, as if I was reading about it in a book. I remember wondering about going outside, but then, what would I do next? The cottage was alone beneath the mountain.

Also, I was afraid to leave the house. If I hadn't been hungry and thirsty and needing the toilet, I wouldn't even have left my room. I thought that if she came back and I wasn't where I was supposed to be, I'd be in trouble. I thought if I did what she'd told me – if I passed this test – then maybe she'd finally love me.

In my memory, I think this period lasted for five days.

And then.

The sun is setting. I'm in my room. I'm in my pyjamas, holding my pebble. I'm so hungry I almost don't feel it. And I hear the sound of a miracle. The crunch of tyres on the road outside. The front door opening.

I remember the feeling of everything shifting around me, the nightmare finishing, reality returning. I remember thinking, *can I go downstairs?* I remember thinking, *no. She told me to stay in my room.*

I hear bags rustling, heavy things on a table. Footsteps, slow and tired. My mother coming in to see me, surprised and a little bit cross that I'm awake.

"You're still up," she says, frowning.

I remember thinking, *was I asleep? Is it still just that first day?* I remember thinking, *I must have imagined it. She can't have left me so long, or she'd be sorry when she came back.*

"I'm in my pyjamas," I whisper. "We haven't had dinner."

"I suppose we haven't. All right, come downstairs and I'll make you some soup. You should have something warming."

There's an endless wait as she stands at the stove, the complex, savoury taste of the soup filling my mouth and my belly. I wait for my mother to say something, to make sense of everything. But she carries on as if everything's normal and I think, *I must have dreamed it. It can't have happened.* She runs me a bath, and afterwards I feel clean, much cleaner than usual, cleaner than I can ever remember being.

Five days alone. Is that likely?

But then – I'm sure I'm remembering this right – there's no bread to go with the soup. At breakfast the next morning, there's no milk, and no cornflakes. And my mother glances at me, but stays silent.

After that, everything becomes weirdly normal, a conventional slide show of holiday memories. My mother and I, going obediently about the area as if we've been set it as homework, looking up at famous mountains, looking down into famous lakes. We take a trip on a ferry and my mother stands beside me and smiles, and her smile's almost believable. The time when she left me feels like a dream, vivid for a few moments, then fading quickly. Flashes come back to me at unexpected moments, and they feel almost funny. *I had a dream that you left me on my own for five days, and I was—*

In my pocket is a pebble. I tell myself that it's nothing special, this pebble, just something I found outside. I didn't spend five days holding it tight. My mother didn't leave me on my own. That's not what happened at all.

I drop the pebble over the side of the ferry. Watch it tumble through the clean water. *It didn't happen,* I tell myself. *And if it did, it's all over now.*

* * *

At the end of the two weeks, we load our things into the car and drive home. Dad and Noah get back later than they'd planned, full of stories and laughter. By contrast, our return is earlier, and silent.

"Did you have a good time?" Dad asks at last, when he's finished talking and talking about everything he and Noah have done.

This is the moment to say something. But I must have got confused, she can't have done that. So I reply, obediently, "Yes, a very good time," and glance at my mother to make sure she's happy with this. She's not listening, she's watching Noah as if she's been starved for the sight of him. I might as well not be here.

I don't think about this often. It's bizarre and frightening, something that feels outside of the rest of the flow of time, as if I was accidentally sucked into some sort of repeating loop for a while and then, inexplicably, set free again. Nonetheless, its presence is constant. My eight-year-old self stands on the ferry and watches her pebble fall, tells herself she's also thrown away the memory. As an adult, I know that the pebble is still there, will always be there. It sits below the surface of my life, and whether I choose to look at it or not, it changes the shape of everything above.

And my mother. When she left me, where did she go? Did she think about me at all? When she came back, was she hoping I was still alive? Or did she pray that I'd be dead? I could ask her this, but there's no point because I probably wouldn't believe her answer.

I sometimes think I'll be wondering about this until I die.

Chapter Eighteen

Garden

Enough of all this sadness and trauma, loneliness and terror.
I'll show you something beautiful instead.

It's the middle of the afternoon, and the air feels like the word
'siesta'. Outside is sweet with the scent of growing things
shaking out their leaves and petals. Inside is cool and dim,
thick walls holding the heat at bay.

It's the second Thursday of our shift, so Josh cleans the
kitchen while Frey and I do a jigsaw. He's chosen a picture
of a small cottage in a huge garden. The cottage is brown and
rough, windows glowing with light despite the sunshine that
falls like rain. It's a fantasy of English country living, painted
by someone who's presumably never been here, and it makes
my teeth itch. I pass the pieces to Frey, hypnotised by the
smooth, sure movements of his fingers. Josh stops to watch.

"How do you do that, mate?" he murmurs. "I wish I
understood."

Frey takes the next piece from me, turns it over between
his fingers, glances slantwise at the patches of colour, lays
it down.

"Apparently, jigsaw makers use the same dies to cut loads of different puzzles," Josh says. "Do you think that's how he's doing it? He's learned the cutting patterns? So the picture's irrelevant?"

"Maybe." I think of a trick I've seen Frey do sometimes in the days when Linnea's next shipment of puzzles is due, where he turns the pieces over and completes them upside down. When it's finished, he pushes his chair back and watches as Josh carefully lays a second puzzle mat over the top and flips it to reveal the completed image. His small smile is the Frey equivalent of a 'ta-da'. "That would explain the upside-down puzzle trick."

"You could be a *YouTube* star if you wanted, mate," Josh says. "People would love watching you." Frey's hand, reaching for the next puzzle piece, pauses, stutters. Beneath the table, Floss raises her head. "Oh, no, I didn't mean you have to! Sorry. It's just a way of saying how good you are at it, that's all."

Frey smooths one hand over the dome of Floss's skull. She lays her head confidingly against his knee, gives herself up to the pleasure of being touched. Frey takes the next piece, adds it to the crazy paving of the bridge. I choose another piece, hold it out.

"Hey, look, you got that tattoo," says Josh. His fingers, firm and brotherly like Noah's, move my sleeve aside. "Wow. That's lush. Does it still itch?"

"Yes."

"Who's the artist? It's brilliant. Frey, have you seen this, mate? Callie got a tattoo."

Frey's absorbed in his jigsaw, his fingers stroking over its surface. Floss comes out from beneath the table, stretches effortlessly up onto her hind legs and props her chin and front paws on the table.

"Hey there." Josh ruffles Floss's head. "Is it time for your walk?" Floss, who I don't think was asking for her walk, who I think was simply trying to join in, nevertheless pricks her ears and hops eagerly down. "Come on, then. Frey, we'll be two hours like always, okay? Twenty minutes to drive out, a good long walk and then twenty minutes to drive back. And then it'll be time to start dinner. All okay? Frey?"

Frey, incredibly, isn't listening. His gaze, usually so tentative, so provisional, is anchored to a single spot. The spot on my wrist where his drawing has become part of my flesh.

"It's all right," Josh says. "It's just a picture. A picture on her skin."

I know what it is. Frey doesn't speak, Frey never speaks, but I can hear him as clearly as if he had. His face has a new expression: the faint ghost of a tolerant smile.

"Okay. So, I'm taking Floss out, we'll be two hours, we'll start dinner when I get back."

"Have a good time," I say.

"You too. Frey, if you finish that puzzle before I get back, can you leave it out? I want to see it before it goes away."

We've done this puzzle many times; for some reason it's one of Frey's favourites. Josh is a good person and I like him very much, but he has absolutely no memory for jigsaws. Then Floss and Josh are gone, the car crunches across gravel on the drive, and we're alone.

"I hope you don't mind," I say. "About me using your picture."

I already know he doesn't mind. He drew the bee for me, a glimpse into a part of him I've never seen or suspected. But I have to say something. The sweetness of our silence sings in my ears, but I make myself break it anyway, holding the next puzzle piece out to him.

Am I imagining a slight hesitation in Frey's movements? Am I inventing the flicker of movement that says he'd like to touch the inside of my wrist? The piece I've given him has a fat blob of light pushing out between leaded windowpanes. Frey lays it down in its spot.

"You're so good at that," I tell Frey, and pass him another piece. "It's like a superpower."

One piece of ill-defined floral bloom fits into another one, and now a clump of blue flowers blossom by the slow-moving stream. His hair tumbles over his forehead when he leans forward. If he was a child, I would sweep it back, take advantage of the licence that comes with caring for the young. Frey isn't a child, but my fingers still itch to touch. His hair's soft and fine, washed daily. He's always so clean. I pick another piece, pass it to him, watch the dexterous slide of his fingertips.

There is danger here, I know there is. Dangerous even to let myself look at it clearly, to give it the power of a name. I make myself think of Josh and Floss, striding across the grass and looking back to the place where our house is. In winter, Josh told me, he can glimpse the white walls through the bare trees. From spring to autumn it's serially shrouded in foamy white hawthorn, purple spikes of fireweed, and the slow rot of dead leaves caught in the bushes. But he always looks, he told me once, just in case he can see it, and then laughed at himself for being so invested in glimpsing it.

Josh and Floss are both fast walkers. They might already have climbed the hill and be looking out for our cottage. He's not here, but he could still be watching. Of course, we're always being watched. Linnea could be looking right now. Every time I reach for another puzzle piece, my sleeve slips back, exposing my tattoo.

"I was reading about jigsaw-puzzle enthusiasts," I say as Frey takes another piece. "You know what Josh was saying earlier? About how they use the same cutting tools for different jigsaws? Apparently, some puzzlers find puzzles with matching cut patterns. Then they take pieces from one jigsaw and put them into another." Frey's fingers stumble. "No, it's all right, we won't do it. I just thought it was interesting."

Frey thinks it's appalling, I know he does. I knew he would before I even said the words. He's a puzzle himself, an endless intrigue, and it's tempting to poke around a bit sometimes. Frey continues work on his flat fantasy of outdoors.

It's time to make bread. At the counter, I mix flour and yeast and salt and butter and water, stir until it comes together. I wish we could go outside, stand together in the sunlight. breathing in what the garden breathes out.

"The dough's ready for you," I say to Frey, who's hovering behind me, waiting for the moment.

I'm floury up to my elbows. I wash at the sink, picking sticky clots from beneath my fingernails. Frey's hands are almost as white as the dough. The warm scent of yeast rises into the air. Usually, I enjoy it. Today all I can think is how much I crave fresh air. Cleaned, I stand at Frey's shoulder and watch the dough grow smooth and pliable.

When it's ready to prove, we put it in a bowl with cling film over the top. I clean the surface, again, watch Frey clean it yet again. We have an hour to wait. We're supposed to spend it on the jigsaw.

"We could go outside," I say to Frey. Frey looks down and to one side. 'No, thank you.' "I'm serious, you'd love it if you gave it a try."

Frey's shoulders are tense. If Floss was here, she'd press against his legs, nudging at his hand. Still, I press on. There's an opportunity here, to make Frey's world a little larger, a little richer. To add one more item to the curated menu of his pleasures.

"You know how much you love this jigsaw? An actual garden's even better."

He's frightened, I can tell. But beneath the fear, there's a longing. I know it in the same unfathomable way I knew he was amused by Josh earlier. He's yearning for me to keep going. Linnea was very clear: "You're not here to bring Frey into our world, but to live with him in his." If I upset him, I could lose my job. I reach for another puzzle piece, an offering, a sign that we can stop this frightening conversation now and move on.

Frey's fingers reach out to take it. Hesitate. Brush gently my newly inked wrist. I hold my breath.

And there it is again, as clear as a church bell at midnight. *All right. I'll try it.*

I stand up. Go to the kitchen door. Throw it open. Outside pours in like water. I take a deep breath, savouring. Frey wears soft socks and trainers, as always, and I think about soft grass beneath his feet, but maybe that's too much for him today. I remove my own trainers, though, the slow peel of socks like taking off a layer of skin. My feet are pink, creased, slightly damp. Frey accepts Floss's paws, but human skin touching the floors makes him anxious.

"Deep breath," I say to Frey. "We can go really slow." I'm already giddy with success, getting Frey this close to the open back door. I cross the threshold, feel gravel prick at my toes. Frey stands in the doorway, his gaze straight down.

"It's all right," I say, crunching my toes into the gravel even though it hurts a little. "One step at a time."

His hand reaches down for Floss, but she's away on the tops of the hills. He'll not make it outside, not on his first attempt, not without Floss.

And then. One hand outstretched, reaching for my hand.

I move as slowly as I can, afraid I've misinterpreted, but there's no mistaking the firmness in his grip. His fingers close around my wrist, pressing against the tattoo. He trusts me to keep him safe and I will, I will, I will. He stumbles, grabs the door frame, then slowly lets go again. One foot on the gravel. Both feet. We're outside.

"There," I say. "Well done. That's the hardest bit. Now…"

We take it very slowly, very cautiously, as if Frey is a hundred years old. His shoes creep over the gravel, fumble onto the grass.

"This is a viburnum," I say, holding out a long spray of pale pink flowers. "The bees love it. And this is a rose. Sorry, do you know all this already?"

Frey's gaze slides up from the ground, hovering around my chin. *Keep talking.* I think about children reading books that frighten them, the power of naming what terrifies you.

Slowly, slowly, we creep through the garden. I announce the plants I know – "these are lupins, these are snapdragons, all of these are roses too" – and hope Frey won't mind about the rest. It's hot, we're both getting sweaty, but his fingers never leave my wrist.

I ought to take him back inside. We've done enough for one day. But we're so close to the little covered bench, half-drowned in greenery, so generously deep it's like half a summer house. I can't shake my vision of Frey, at peace in the shade, part of the life of the garden but also detached from it. If I can get him there, he'll feel safe, he'll want to do this again.

"Let's sit on the bench," I say. "It's nice there, nice and cool. That's honeysuckle growing all over it, it smells lovely. Especially in the evening."

I sink down, glad of the shade. Frey must be hot too, but he stands still and rigid in the blazing sun until I tug gently on his hand to bring him beside me. There's a tremble in his flesh, the shock of the new ringing in his bones. His skin is flushed. I think of the Vitamin D his body's making, and sigh contentedly. The house, seen from a new angle, looks unfamiliar; it takes me a minute to assign rooms to each window. This first view will never come to either of us again. A magical thing. Frey and I, working magic together. I suspect that even if Frey could speak, he'd choose silence now, to listen to the small, unpredictable sounds of birds and insects. His fingers tighten against my wrist.

"What is it? Oh." A magpie, glossy and handsome, claims the lawn on strong, hopping leaps while a cloud of sparrows and a pair of blackbirds chatter and mob. I can see why Frey's disturbed. Their sudden movements, unmediated by the safety of windows or television screens, are menacing. "That's a magpie. They're trying to chase it off."

The magpie resists for a while, jabbing its beak towards its opponents, but after a few minutes, it gives up. Frey's grip eases. He breathes a little more slowly.

He's relaxing into it, I think, *maybe even getting to like it.* This will become part of our routine, a small amendment to the schedule. If he does want to do it again, I'll have to tell the others. My heart clenches, cold and jealous. I don't want this magic downgraded into something everyday. I don't want to share.

The cottage is so full of clocks that my natural sense of time has withered away. We could have been here for minutes, or hours. I'm adrift at sea, no way of knowing when I'll find myself on the clock-bound land again. A bumblebee the size of a thumb bustles into the honeysuckle.

"There's a bee. Different to the one you drew me, though." I glance at Frey to see if he's looking, but his gaze is fixed on the place where our bodies are joined.

I could lie, I think. *Even if Linnea saw us leave the house, I could tell her we went for a walk instead. That way I could keep the garden for me and Frey. Even Josh wouldn't know. And Frey would never tell.*

The thought of Josh prods at my sense of time. The clocks are still ticking even though we're not there to watch them. I don't want Josh and Floss bounding down the garden to greet us. I don't want Frey to let go of my wrist and reach for Floss instead, don't want Josh helping him back inside. I'll have to share eventually, but I can keep this a little longer.

"Shall we go back inside?"

The way back's much quicker – Frey's already gaining confidence. He keeps hold of me, his fingers against my pulse point. My tattoo still itches, and I'm grateful for the pressure, soothing the urge to scratch and pick at my flesh. I pause on the doorstep. This has been perfect. Now it's almost over.

"Frey," I say.

There's a gentle pressure on my arm now. Frey, impatient in a way I've never known, is trying to draw me inside. I resist a minute longer, desperate to say what I don't know how to put into words.

"Oh, Frey. Thank you for trying this. It's been the best afternoon… you can't imagine…"

I come inside, close the door. Frey releases my wrist. He's held it for so long, I can feel the ghosts of his fingers. We go back to the table, sit down at the half-finished jigsaw. I glance at the clock, feel another fragment of magic drop away. We've been outside for just under forty minutes. Another ten minutes, and it will be time to knock the dough back.

I hold a jigsaw piece out to Frey. "Want to finish this?"

He reaches out, but it slips through his fingers. Frey's only clumsy when he's exhausted.

"Don't worry," I say. "It's tiring. Doing something new. Next time will be easier."

And then, one more astounding moment in this day of astonishment, Frey raises his head and looks into my eyes, and I see what I should have seen all along. While I luxuriated in sunshine, breathed in flowers, Frey was terrified. He was terrified from the second his feet crossed the threshold. He went outside, not because he was curious, but because he wanted to please me.

There's something here that touches a dark, hungry place inside me. It feels so astonishingly good I can hardly bear to look. Instead, I creep around the edges, touching for a second then wincing away.

Frey made himself do something he hated, because he…

Frey came outside and held my hand, because he…

Chapter Nineteen

High

It's not always easy to see a change coming. We're good at spotting small, repeating routines, less good at recognising the seismic moments that disrupt and shatter. When it first begins to bite, we don't see the true horrifying scale – how could we? – but only the small alterations for the worse. When I turn off the main road just before noon to drive into our estate, the two or three houses with their front gates open chime a faint warning. When I round the corner and see virtuously distanced clumps of people standing and gawping, I know what they're looking at. But I don't think, *this is it, this is the one that tips us over.* Instead, I think, *please God, please Noah, please not now, please not again.*

After a while you lose count of the episodes. The first one stayed with me because of its shocking novelty. The second – worse in many ways because it implied a permanent state rather than a one-off crisis – I remember that one too. After that, it depends what you're counting. The times when Noah's been ill, but we've got him through it? Or the times when we've had to call for help?

I'll remember this one, though, because of the background. A new vocabulary taking shape, all of us suddenly experts on epidemics. Everything shutting up, shutting down, closing off. Dad's office firmly in denial, determined not to send everyone home, thousands of management hours consumed by how seriously they need to take it, how bad it's going to get, what the least worst response might be. Long shifts sweating in PPE like a dead second skin. And Noah, trapped at home, just him and his demons. There's the slow drowning choke of the virus, and there's the destruction it's bringing in its wake. You can see something coming and still have absolutely no power to stop it.

Dad's outside on the front lawn. At least he's dressed this time, at least Noah hasn't shut him out all night so he's had to stay out in the shed in his dressing gown. Someone must have called him at work. We shouldn't have left Noah on his own. We can't devote ourselves to Noah because we need to work; we can't work properly because we need to care for Noah. And we're both drowning, because we don't have time for ourselves.

"Callie." Dad greets me without embarrassment. We're long past caring what the neighbours think. "It's all right, he's not hurt. He's just having a bit of a moment."

Up on our roof, by the attic Velux window, Noah sits astride the ridge pole and watches us.

"He's been up and down from there since at least ten o'clock this morning." It's the woman whose name I can never remember, because Noah once nicknamed her 'Mrs Curtain-Twitcher' and now I can't think of her as anything else. "I saw him from my front room, and I know the time because I always go in there at ten o'clock to—"

"Thanks, that's good to know. Dad, did he lock you out?"

"I've got my keys, but, you know…" Dad smiles, but I can see the hurt.

"Is it the usual?"

"Think so."

I can sense the electric surge of interest that passes between our neighbours, their excitement at a possible insight into the mind of a madman. *Tough luck,* I think. Dad and I aren't embarrassed by Noah's behaviour, but the specific content of his delusions are his private property.

"Right. I'm going in." I wave up at Noah, who waves back, shake my keys to let him know what I'm going to do. He nods approvingly. Then his gaze falls on Dad. Even from his position in the sky, I can sense his rage.

Noah, in the fullest flush of his essential nature, is a tornado. Spirals of clothing laid out across the carpets could almost pass as installation art. The kitchen cupboards are empty, contents regrouped by size across the floor (glasses and cups and tins in one heap, plates and saucepan lids strewn together, the saucepans an unsolved puzzle in the middle of the floor), as if they're part of a display. Chairs are stacked on top of other chairs like mating animals. Every light bulb has a single sock fitted carefully over it. The attic ladder's still in place, but I have to blow out the tea lights placed on every step, two more added to each row to form an inverted triangle of light. That's the part of Noah's illness that always catches me by the throat: the way it sometimes, improbably, leads to utter beauty. Snuffing out the lights feels like sacrilege.

"Noah?" I know he can hear me coming. He hears everything. "Noah, it's just me. I'm on my own."

"It's all right. I can see him. He hasn't moved." Noah sounds far too relaxed for someone who's straddling the steep pitch of a rooftop. "You shouldn't have come in, though, not until they get here to take him away."

"No one's coming to take Dad away." Sometimes, if I catch him at the right moment, I can make him understand that this is his illness talking. "He hasn't done anything wrong. You know that really."

Noah doesn't answer. I stand on the stool below the window, so I can poke my head up and see him. He's smiling tolerantly to himself.

"Noah."

"Yes?"

"You need to come inside. It's dangerous there."

"I'll come in when they've got him. They're taking him to the centre, it's all arranged."

"But why would anyone want to take Dad away?"

The look Noah turns on me chills my bones.

"I keep telling you but you don't listen. If you didn't take those tablets he gives you, you'd remember. He tries to do it to me too. He's reprogramming your brain so he can keep hold of you. But I won't let him. I promised I'd keep you safe and I will."

"Have you been hiding your meds again?" The black, bleak stare disappears, and in its place is the mischievous older brother who can make anything into an adventure. "For God's *sake*, Noah, how do you do it? How? We stand over you while you take them, you show us afterwards—"

"Pocket dimension." He flourishes his fingertips like a magician. "I don't do it for you, only for him. I open it up and drop them in. That's why he never finds them. Oi!" He turns his attention to the crowd on the lawn, points a finger at Dad. "Don't even think about coming inside. You know what I know."

I take a deep breath, brace my hands against the window frame, and wriggle precariously out. It's terrifying and I can hear the gasps and murmurs from below, but Noah grabs my arm, holding me and helping me, until I'm pressed against the dubious protection of the chimney stack, and the two of us are facing each other.

"It's all right," Noah says, as if I'm the one who needs looking after. "I've got you."

My heart races. My palms are clammy. I wipe them against my hip. What a picture we must make, my brother in his frock coat and patchwork trousers, and me in T-shirt and joggers.

"And I was kidding about the pocket dimension," he adds. "I'm mad, but I'm not that mad."

"So you remember you're not well?"

His fingers rattle restlessly against the ridge pole. "It's not that simple, though, is it? I mean, I know you think I'm mad—"

"Unwell."

"Mad," Noah insists with a gleam in his eye, "and I know Mr Mad-Wrangler at the hospital thinks I'm mad, and I know everyone at the support group thinks I'm mad – well, some of them don't, but they're the batshit insane ones so I'm not supposed to trust their opinion…" He slaps the tiles hard. "But I can be mad and still know things that are true. And I'm not wrong about Dad, I know I'm not. You think one thing and I think another, and who knows what's true, really?"

"Do you know we love you?"

"I know you love me."

"And Dad does too."

"Dad…" Noah shakes his head. "He's not who you think he is. I wish you'd listen to me."

"I wish *you'd* listen to *me*."

"You're my little sister. I'm not supposed to listen to anything you say. You're lucky I even let you sit on the roof with me."

I shouldn't laugh, but I do. Maybe madness is catching. I must be a little bit broken, to be sitting up here with Noah, laughing even as I try to assess the strength of his delusions, whether I can talk him down.

"Look at them," says Noah. "Like ants."

The people below don't look anything like ants, they're not nearly far away enough for that.

"Not the size," he adds. "The organisation. The structure. There's worker ants, like Her Indoors and Mr Her Indoors."

"They're both retired."

"They pressure wash the front path every single day, I've seen them do it, it's amazing. And there's soldier ants, like Mrs Curtain-Twitcher. They protect the colony. And then there's the breeding ones, those three women with the babies—"

"I don't know them."

"They go past in the mornings. I think they go to the park. Their babies are like grubs. All white and wriggly."

I thought the queen laid the eggs, but I don't want to interrupt. While he's thinking about ants, he's not wandering dangerously around the rooftop.

"And they all take orders from the queen."

"Who's the queen?"

"Me." Noah doesn't look pleased about this. He looks defeated. "Everything revolves around me. They're standing there because I made them stand there. If I go inside, they'll go away. And if I come back out, within three minutes they'll be right back there again."

I don't like the subtext here, which is that Noah might believe he's commanding the neighbourhood with the power of his thoughts. On the other hand, here Noah is on the roof, and there they all are on the path, all because of him. He's right and he's not right, and I don't know what to do.

"It works on you too," Noah says. "I got on the roof, and you came up too. Even though you hate it. Don't you?"

"I… yes, all right, I do. I don't feel safe. Let's go inside. Please, Noah."

His smile is weary. "All right."

He holds on to me as I scramble inside. I think I've won, I think I'm making progress, but then he lets my hand go, and when I reach for him, he shakes his head.

"I'm staying out here a bit longer."

It's my job to make the phone call; it always is. Dad says it's because I'm a nurse and they'll listen to me, but the truth is he hasn't got the heart. Left to himself he'd keep Noah with him through the whole crisis, sacrifice sleep and food and safety, purge the house of ways for Noah to hurt either of them, clean and dress him with his own hands. It wouldn't work, of course. If love and sacrifice could fix someone then Noah would have been well years ago. He needs medication and twenty-four-hour supervision and the care of professionals who can go home at the end of their shift. I know this, but I still feel like Judas. Noah's shuffles and scrabbles, the sudden frightening fall of a single tile, form the background to the short, kind, hurtful conversation. When I go back to the window he's sitting on the ridge pole, staring into the sky.

"Noah," I say.

His smile is so brave it hurts my heart.

"I know. You've called the crisis team."

"Are you cross?"

"Of course not. You're only trying to look after me." He wraps his arms around himself and shivers. "It'll be all right, I think. They'll find me in there and take me out again. Won't they?"

"It'll be fine," I say, feeling wretched.

"But, Callie." He's looking at Dad on the lawn again, his fists opening and closing. "Fuck, shit, he's still out there. No, I can't go to hospital. Who'll look after you?"

"I'm grown up, remember? I can take care of myself."

Noah tears at his nails with his teeth. "Go and stay with Mum."

"I can't. I have to work."

"This is more important. I mean it, Callie. I'll go with the crisis team if you go to Mum's."

Some people say you should just tell them what they want to hear. Make it easier on everyone. "Noah, you have to go with the team or you'll never get better. But I can't go to her house, you know I can't."

"But you can't be alone with him! Don't let him in the house with you until – I mean, I suppose I could call someone and get them to take you too, but then you'll be alone until they – no, I can't risk it. Callie, you're going to Mum's and that's the end of it."

"Okay. I'll do it."

"You don't mean that."

"Do you want a cup of tea before they get here?"

Noah sighs. "Do you know what I really want? I want two Big Macs with extra-large fries. And a full-fat Coke in a cup the size of a bucket. And a milkshake."

"Vanilla or chocolate?"

"Chocolate. But we haven't got time. And if we go out, *he* might come in while we're gone and then it'll be all that with the hidden cameras again and it'll take ages to find them, he puts them in the walls sometimes and you have to dig them out. Look, if you're not going to Mum's place then you have to sleep in the car until they've been over the place, right? Or outside, it's pretty warm for March, even though they told me the weather balloons aren't working right now..." He slams his fist into the ridge pole. "God, this would be so much easier if you'd just do as I say!"

"Noah."

"It's all right, I'm not angry with you. I'm never angry with you. You're lovely. I remember you being born. She does love you."

No, she doesn't, I think. But there's no point saying this out loud. Noah wasn't there when the Lake District happened, so he's never understood.

It ends the way we knew it had to, with a bed that isn't Noah's and a ward filled with strangers and a series of locked doors. Dad, as always, marvels at the seamless ease of it, and mutters happily about how people don't realise how well-run the NHS is. He still hasn't worked out that this is simply a measure of Noah's illness. Even as the world ends, we find a way through for our very sickest patients. Dad tries to hug Noah when we leave him, but Noah looks at him and he lets his arms fall.

"I'll drive," Dad says in the car park.

We've come in my car, but I give him the keys. It's his way of reasserting control over an unbearable situation. Also, I'm exhausted, not fit to be behind the wheel.

I'm supposed to be back at work in four hours, but I can't. I absolutely can't, I am done. I'll have to call in sick. I've failed Noah. Now I'm failing my team. I'm so ashamed I could weep.

"We'll get through this," Dad mutters, and then stops the car so he can beat his fists against the steering wheel. "Fuck, fuck, fuck! It's all my fault. Sorry."

"Of course it's not your fault."

"Yes, it is. You're on nights, so I'm in charge. He must have been dodging his meds again, mustn't he? How does he do it? I check every time, but he's so clever..." He smooths his hands over the wheel. "He's always been so clever."

"You can't stop it happening, no one can. If he had epilepsy, you wouldn't feel guilty, would you? Everyone's stressed, everything's awful, it's not a surprise Noah's relapsed. Dad, don't cry, please don't cry, you'll make me cry as well."

"I hate leaving him," he whispers, shuddering against my shoulder. "I feel like I've left him in prison."

"It's the best place for him," I say, as steadily as I can. I hate leaving Noah there too.

I manage one visit before they close the ward to outsiders. They've made it as nice as they can in here, but it's a locked ward, and there are limits. Noah's movements are slow and clumsy, and he struggles to focus.

"How are you feeling?"

It's painful to watch the slow assemblage of his drugged response. My brilliant, quicksilver brother.

"Sticky," he says.

"If you need help in the shower you can ask them to—"

He raises a hand, imperious and slow.

"Not sticky. Something else."

I wait. Two patients play air hockey nearby, giggling because neither of them is sticking to the rules.

"Stuck," Noah says at last. "I feel. Stuck. Want to get out."

"I'm sorry. If you're angry with me I'll understand."

"S'all right. You had to. Just hate. Leaving you there. With him."

It's always Dad at the centre of these delusions. Sometimes he's watching me in the bathroom with invisible cameras. Sometimes I'm a domestic slave. Sometimes even I can't work out what's going on in Noah's head.

"He's not hurting me, I promise. Don't you trust me?"

"Trust you. Not him." A long strand of drool lets itself down from Noah's bottom lip. I take comfort from the fact that he notices it, that he manages to wipe it away with his hand. "You're not safe. Wish you'd. Go and stay. With Mum."

"She doesn't want me."

"She does." He frowns at his hand, wipes the wetness laboriously on his T-shirt. "Course she does."

There are so many things I could say in reply, so much evidence I could reach for. But if evidence could change Noah's mind, he wouldn't be ill in the first place.

"Callie." Noah reaches out towards me, takes my hand in his. It's always hot in here, and his hand feels dehydrated and dry. "Please. Get me. Out of here."

"I can't. I wish I could."

"Not safe. Bloody drugs. Take me out."

"Please don't ask that, please. I want to bring you home but it's not allowed, you're not well yet. The nurses are helping you. They want you to get well."

"No!" Noah shakes his head in frustration. "Not for me. For you. Got to look after you." Something grotesque is happening to his face. After a long, painful moment it resolves into a smile. "For all the. All the good. Mad as a box of frogs. What'm I going to do?"

"But you remember you're ill?" This is a key step in the process, a key part of getting Noah back.

"Course." When he's well, Noah's hand gestures are extravagant. Our mother used to tease him about having Italian blood. Today, it just looks like he's trying to swat at a fly. "I always know. Always. Don't ever forget. It's my brain. Um."

Don't interrupt, Callie, don't don't don't. Sit with him. Be present. Give him time.

"Not working right," Noah says at last.

"That's the one."

"So s'not real, is it?"

"What's not real?"

"Any of it." His face contorts with effort. "People coming in room. Doing stuff. Nurses, I mean. Taking their clothes off. Feeling me up. Stealing stuff." Another gurning attempt at a smile. "I see it. Know it's not. Not real. Still see it. Fucked up."

"Don't swear."

The grin grows slowly wider. "Can't. Fucking. Stop me. 'Sides. I'm mad. S'allowed."

"Well, don't do it in front of—" I stop myself just in time.

"You c'n say 'Dad'."

"I was thinking of the nurses," I lie. "They don't deserve to get sworn at, do they?"

Noah looks as if he's thinking of arguing, but then visibly gives up. He looks exhausted.

"Are you tired? I'll leave you in peace."

"Sleep too much in here. Can't stop myself. Bloody knackered." His face splits into a giant yawn. Another silvery string of drool escapes. He doesn't notice this time.

"It'll help you get better." His eyes are falling shut, his muscles slackening. "Okay, I'd better go."

"Callie." He grabs clumsily for my arm, misses, grabs again and connects this time. "Don't go."

"I have to." I want to tell him that I'll come back soon, but the world's getting worse by the day. This could be the last time they'll let me in.

"No. I mean. Don't go. Um. Home. Not while he's there."

"Noah…"

"I know. I always know!" The despair in his face is huge

and heartbreaking. "I know my brain's not working. See stuff that's not real. All the time. So nobody listens. Don't blame you. But what if. What if I see stuff and it's real? What if I'm right?"

"How was he?" Dad has the door open before I've even got out of the car, comes out to greet me in his boxer shorts and dressing gown, no slippers. Mrs Curtain-Twitcher will be in raptures behind her voiles. She loves it when Noah has a crisis.

"He knows he's ill, so that's something. Oh, and he says the nurses are coming in his room at night and taking their clothes off and interfering with him sexually and stealing his stuff, but he knows that's not real so we don't have to worry."

Dad's laughter blends seamlessly into sobs of despair, and that's it, that's all it takes to set me off too. We stand in the hall and sob on each other's shoulders, the front door half-open. Sometimes it feels like we're all three going mad, forgetting how to be human.

"Okay." Dad unravels us, wipes his face and then mine. "Okay. That'll do for now, won't it?"

"I'll make tea."

Dad looks dubious. "I'm not that hungry."

"You will be when you see your tea."

"You'll make someone a lovely wife one day," Dad calls after me, and I laugh and give him the finger without turning around. I add pasta to boiling water, find a jar of sauce, stir everything together as soon as it's ready and slice thick slabs of cheese on top, pop it under the grill for a few minutes to toast. Stodge and carbohydrates, to anchor us to the earth. We eat on the sofa, glad of the warmth of each other's bodies. It's only half past eight but I go upstairs to put on my pyjamas.

Noah's toothbrush is still in the glass. For the times when he has to leave us, he has a special collection of clothes and toiletries in a bag hidden in my wardrobe, the Just In Case bag

I always hope we'll never need again. It's one of the ways we make the separation between Noah when he's sick, and Noah when he's well. Back downstairs, Dad has put out two glasses of milk and a packet of zopiclone.

"I'm going to," he says. "Want one as well?"

"You're not supposed to share medications."

"I know. Want one anyway?"

"Yeah."

He pops out a round blue tablet into my hand. Sleeping tablets work better when they're blue; antidepressants are more effective when they're yellow. One of the many mysteries of the human brain.

"I should go upstairs," I say.

"Stay a bit longer. It takes a while to work."

"If I stay much longer, I'll fall asleep on the sofa."

"I'll carry you upstairs," Dad declares.

"Dad, that's insane, I'm a grown woman. You'll do your back in."

"You're my little girl. I don't mind."

I ought to move, but I'm so warm and comfortable here. Just another few minutes. Just to rest my eyes.

"It's my fault he's ill again," Dad says.

"No, it's not."

"Yes, it is. He's lost all his support structures. All he has is me. He needed me and I wasn't there... God, when will things be normal again?"

I don't know the answer. We could be living like this for months. We could be living like it for years. Once Noah's stabilised and they let him come home, how long will we have until he's back in again? My shoulders and jaw are tight and aching. But the sleeping pill will take everything away.

"How is it at the hospital?" Dad asks softly. He's stroking my hair, the way he used to when I was small. I don't like it, I never liked it, but I let him do it because he needs the comfort of knowing one of his children is safe.

"Awful. But we'll manage. We have to."

"You're amazing," Dad says reverently. "Going into that place when it's so dangerous."

"We have PPE."

"Do you have enough, though? I keep seeing on the news—"

"We're managing. Just about. Don't worry."

"It's never going back to normal, though, is it?"

"It will. I think. In the end."

"I mean Noah," Dad says, very softly. "I always hoped – but he won't, will he? This is how our lives are now." He pets at my hair, over and over on the same spot. My scalp feels overstimulated, but I keep still. "And she won't – she's not – not ever…"

I don't know what to say.

"I'm sorry," he says. "I'm tired. Not making any sense. But we can't keep going like this, Cal. When all this is over, we have to make a change."

I'm falling asleep already. I ought to go upstairs and get into bed, but it's so comfortable here. I shut my eyes, telling myself I'll just rest for a few moments, but the tide of sleep's dragging at me, pulling me under.

Shortly after that, I'm vaguely aware of Dad carrying me up the stairs, laying me gently on my bed, tucking me in. I'm a grown woman, far too old for this. But it's so lovely to be treated like a pampered little princess.

I can sense him standing there, watching over me, loving and warm, and it takes me back to my earliest memories. So many times I'd half-wake in the night to realise Dad had crept in to check on me, tucking the duvet closer around me, murmuring that it was all right, he was just making sure I was warm. In this time when everything else is wrong, it's a pleasure to return to the small comforts of childhood, to pretend we've slipped back to a long-ago moment when I am small and Dad is a kindly giant and nothing bad can happen as long as he stands watch over me.

Chapter Twenty

Morgue

It's thirteen days since they died. It's the day you have to go with your mother to see them. It's one day to changeover day. These three facts crash against the wall of my skull as I wake. I keep my eyes shut as I decide what I'm supposed to do with them.

It's thirteen days since they died evokes the relentless flash of anguish. *It's the day you have to go with your mother to see them.* That's a different pain, a sick dread of what we'll see. I know how bad a traffic accident can look, the infinite damage that can be wreaked on human flesh. But at least I'll know the truth, at least I'll be able to settle on a single set of horrors. Besides, my mother is adamant that she's doing this, and I don't want Noah and Dad thinking I didn't care enough to come.

It's the day before changeover day. That last one is sweet against my tongue. Maybe it's the prospect of leaving this awful house and my awful, awful mother. I can think of only one place worse to be than here, and that's the empty rooms where Noah and Dad will never walk again. But my body remembers a different place. A house with a gravel drive and clean white walls. Slate and wooden floors throughout, because the owner can't bear the sensation of carpet beneath his feet. A room that is, at best, only half-mine, but that I can pretend belongs to me. A man who taps on the wall sometimes to check that I'm still there, still listening. A place where Dad and Noah are—

You're kidding yourself, the more rational part of my brain whispers. *You can't stop time. They're dead there just as much as everywhere else. It's going to catch up with you soon. It's all going to catch up with you soon. You'll have to go back there and tell Josh and Frey that your dad and brother are—*

I get out of bed before I can finish this thought.

Instead of her usual position (hunched at the table, staring vacantly into space), my mother's standing over the stove, stirring a pot with a wooden spoon.

"I'm making breakfast," she says, by way of greeting.

"Okay." I'm instantly on the alert, anxious at the prospect of my mother being in charge of my food. I hate, hate, hate that she still has the power to do this to me.

"It's porridge."

"Righto."

"It's going to be a hell of a day."

"I suppose."

"I thought you should have something warming."

The words take me back to a kitchen that wasn't ours, to a bowl of soup, served without bread and without comment. I try not to shiver. My mother slops lumpy goop into a bowl and passes it to me. Lined up like sentries are a pot of long-life cream, a basin of sugar, a tin of golden syrup, a shaker of salt. She sees me looking at the salt.

"The Scots like salt on their porridge," she says.

"I'm not Scottish."

"No, I know that, thank you, Callie."

That feels better, I can breathe now. I can cope with her sharpness much better than her fitful attempts at kindness, knowing her real self will soon resurface. It's easier to provoke her and get it over with. Now she's sitting down beside me, her hand is reaching towards me, her fingers touching mine. Their movements are stealthy, as if she's trying to trap a spider in a glass.

"I'm sorry," she says. "I didn't mean to snap."

"It's fine."

"No, it's not. Callie, love, it's going to be awful, but we'll get through it together, won't we?"

The unexpected endearment is as shocking as a swear word. I'm grateful for the rattle and flutter of wings, for the tap on the window and the bad-tempered glare of the crow.

"Oh, there you are." My mother's voice is soft and indulgent, pleased because her pet has come to her for something it wants. I want to warn it to be careful, that it's dangerous to rely on this woman for food. I also want to wring its neck. A creature stupid enough to trust my mother doesn't deserve to live. I make myself eat a spoonful of porridge instead, trying not to gag at the glutinous texture that fills every corner of my mouth.

Huginn is balanced on my mother's wrist, his body dipping and lifting as he pecks seeds from her palm. Her finger pets gently at the feathers of his breast. I wonder if he enjoys her touch, or if he simply endures it for the sake of the seeds. I think of her fingers on the back of my hand, the price of the bowl of porridge I'm eating.

"There," my mother croons. "Do you like that? Eat them up." It's sickening, watching her coo over a wild bird when her own daughter sits unnoticed. But then, she did try to notice me. And I didn't like it. I cringed away.

I can do this. Today will be dreadful, but it will end. In fewer than thirty-six hours, I will be elsewhere, and my mother won't know where to find me. I'll be in a house with cool walls and clean floors, set well back from the road, and high hedges so no one can surprise us by glancing in. Josh and I will meet at the lay-by outside the village and drive in one behind the other, timing our arrival so that we arrive, together, at exactly seven o'clock. Floss will nose at our hands before padding back to Frey. There will be a brief and jarring half hour for the handover. And then the others will be gone. They'll be gone, and for two weeks I'll be with—

I force myself to remember the other two milestones that today represents. It's thirteen days since the accident. I'll see them for the first time since it happened.

The place where the hospital cares for the dead is clean, quiet, and hidden away. Parking is tight, everywhere bursting at the seams, and we have to park in a not terribly nearby residential street and walk for an inconvenient distance. I wonder how people manage who are weak with pain or nauseous with drugs, who find it hard or impossible to walk. They can't save the spaces for people who really need them, because we all really need them. Nobody comes here for fun.

We pass the Children's A & E department, painted cartoon animals doing their best to soften the blow. I used to work somewhere like this, I used to be a part of the rush and bustle. As always when you look back on past lives, I'm baffled by my own memories. Did I really walk in through doors like this at the start of each shift, move from cubicle to cubicle, assessing and documenting and reassuring and administering? It seems unreal. Only my mother is real today, so close I can smell the soap she's scrubbed her face with until it's hot and shiny.

The entranceway is clean and calm, the reception empty. There are no emergencies here, no hope or chaos to be managed. The worst has been and gone. All that's left is the admin. Chloe told me once about a new manager who came into A & E on a Saturday night and asked why everything was so disorganised. He'd just been over in Bereavement Services, he said, and everything there ran like a dream… probably this incident never happened, but it gave us a good laugh.

The receptionist is kind and understanding. She's clearly

used to people coming to her in all sorts of states and conditions, from soggy, weeping messes to frozen copers and everything between. A doctor introduces herself and shakes our hands. She's kind too. Everyone here is kind, which you'd think you could count on in a hospital but which isn't always a given. I've worked with a few consultants who could have benefited no end from a stint in Bereavement Services.

There's a walk down a corridor. A room with curtains, as if we're going to see a special exhibit. Which I suppose we are. The doctor's talking to us, explaining what we're going to see, warning us about the injuries that they suffered, the changes that come post-mortem. We think of death as stasis, but it's the beginning of a process, and a freezer can only hold things over for so long. I want her to stop talking, I need silence to get my head together. I don't want to be here, but I won't let Noah think I didn't love him enough to come. I won't leave my father alone with my mother.

The room's cold, but the walls are a soft magnolia, the lighting ordinary and undramatic. They're side by side, one table each, sheets covering them to just below their shoulders. I'd thought I'd be afraid, but how could I be? It's just them. Just my dad and my big brother.

I start with Noah. He's in a state, I can see why it wasn't survivable, but he doesn't look as bad as I'd thought. His face is battered and his neck a little misaligned, thanks to the break that killed him. There are folds of fat around his chin, the pudge bulging out from his armpit. At least he'll never have to take those drugs again. If there's an afterlife, I hope he has his pre-medicated body back, so he can be his old quicksilver self.

I'm crying, but there's a kind of peace in this room. Noah is smoothed out, not struggling any more. He'll never have to struggle any more. I love him and I'll never stop loving him, I miss him and I'll never stop missing him, but at least I know he's finally at peace. If it had to be one of us left over, I'd prefer it to be me. I can't bear to think of Noah going through a day like this.

And besides, a sweetly treacherous voice whispers, *I'll be all right, in the end, one day far from now, because I still have—*

No. I won't think about that here. I picture a freight train, brakes screeching and wheels juddering as it heaves to a shuddery stop. There's something lying on the tracks in front of it, precious and vulnerable, but I won't let it come to harm. This time is for Noah and Dad, and I will be present in this moment, be with them as much as I can, say my last goodbyes to their dear faces. Beside me, my mother is quaking apart, all shuddering flesh and volcano bellows. It's undignified. It's hypocritical. She lost one person she loved. I lost two.

But, the voice whispers, *you're better off than her, because you still have—*

Noah's hand feels like clay. I take it anyway, holding it carefully because I don't want to hurt his broken arm any more than it's already been hurt. My mother's still making that appalling noise. Her face must be a wreck, but I don't look at her. I'd rather look at Dad and Noah. The ugly nakedness of her grief, when I'm doing such a good and disciplined job of keeping my own sorrow inside, makes me angry. Why should I comfort her, when she would never—

Out of nowhere, a sense memory comes to me: my mother, on the day we went to our old house for the search. We're in my car, but I'm in the passenger seat. Her fingers are gentle as they dab at my face with a soft tissue, her gestures alarmingly close to tenderness.

Did she really do that? Should I do the same for her? There are tissues in here. There are tissues everywhere in this place. I could take one out and wipe the mess from her skin. I could rest my fingertips against her temples. I could give her back the words my brain insists she gave to me:

'It's all right. I'll look after you. I love you.'

My mother's touching Noah too now, stroking his forehead, smoothing his hair. I don't like it. Noah is mine, not hers. He loved her, but he loved me more. He could have lived with her, but he stayed with me instead. He stayed with me and Dad.

Oh, Dad. I leave Noah and go to the second table.

Dad's injuries are harder to look at, and I have to take a deep breath before I can face him fully. They've done their best, but there's no disguising the altered shape of his skull or the crushed wreck of his ribcage, barely contained by his skin. I breathe deeply and remind myself that this utter devastation is the last and truest mercy. There would have been no lingering here.

His hand has the same yielding texture as Noah's. I pet at the back of it, remembering the years when it seemed so huge and powerful. These hands bathed and dried me when I was small, held me close when I was sad, applauded me in all my small achievements. When I remember being happy as a child, these hands are what come back to me. The dry texture of their palms. The wiry hair sprinkled over the wrists. I held those hands a lot as a child, because my mother was always holding on to Noah. That's the way our family was, two and two. Dad and me; our mother and Noah. And now, she and I stand side by side in this little room, terrible in its very lack of terribleness, a place where endings are finally faced.

That's it. I've seen all there is to see, done my duty to the dead. I've seen their faces, said my goodbyes, wept over their dear, dead flesh. By the time of the funeral they'll be public property, safely sealed in their caskets. I'm glad I've seen for myself what has happened. I'm grateful it wasn't worse. If they can possibly get away with it, police officers always prefer to say that it would have been very quick, that they wouldn't have suffered, but I know now this must have been true. I want to leave, but I can't, because my mother isn't done. Her examination of Noah is over. She's coming to join me beside Dad. Why does she want to look at him? She pushed him away years ago.

The eruption of her grief has subsided. Now she's calm, shivering a little with the aftershocks, but a human being once more. She gazes down at his face, at his closed eyes, sunken in their sockets because the freezer can't stop all the changes. He looks old and vulnerable. I don't like her looking at him when he can't look back. It feels like spying.

She reaches towards his face, then stops. Her hand flutters as if she can't control it. If I was a better daughter, I would take that wandering hand and hold it, remind her she isn't alone. But for me to be a better daughter, she would have to be a better mother.

"I can't believe you're gone," my mother says, and there's genuine heartbreak in her voice. As if she loved him. As if she'd never left him. "I can't believe you're really gone."

Dad doesn't move, doesn't speak. Of course he doesn't. He's not really here, not in any meaningful way. Still, it feels as if he might be listening. He never stopped loving her, never stopped wanting her back. She could have come to him any time, God knows he would have welcomed her, and everything would have been different. If she'd come back to him, maybe Noah would have been well, or at least less ill. If she'd come back to him, there would have been no reason for them to be in that car, on that road. I'm being ridiculous, I can't blame my mother, but without the counterweight of love, it's easy to tip into cruelty.

"I still wake up in the night sometimes and look for you," my mother says. "Do you know that? Even now. I thought it would stop eventually but it never has. You did that to me. I think I might find you next to me again. Sometimes I even see you, reaching out for me. But you're never there."

This isn't fair. Dad ought to be able to put his side of the story. If the doctor's listening, she'll think it was my dad who left.

I want to find that doctor and tell her what an amazing man Dad was. How he took charge of Noah and me. How he loved us when our mother walked away. How he did all the hard work of parenting, while she shut herself up in her new house by the sea. How I stopped seeing my mother and she just let me do it, never pleaded with me to come back. I want to tell the doctor that my mother is a liar.

"I went out with other men sometimes." Her voice is low, confidential, but I can hear every word. "I even tried having sex with them. Some of them were nice. Much nicer than you. They wanted to make me happy, I wanted to let them. But it was just like you said. I couldn't forget you. I couldn't fall asleep next to another man. You were always right there in the bed with me. You ruined me for everyone else."

This is almost over. One more night and one more day, and I'll be free. If I close my eyes I can imagine I'm already there. I can feel cool slate under my feet, can hear Josh's soft breathing and the slow click of jigsaw pieces, smell the scent of Floss. This place where I am now is one reality, that most people would recognise as the true one. But in the small sanctuary of Frey's cottage, time is frozen. When I get back there, Noah and Dad will still be alive, and I'll be happy again. I'll be happy, because I'll be with—

My mother's still speaking, but she'll run out of words soon. There's only so much you can say to the dead.

"You bastard," my mother says, and for a wild moment I think she might be talking to me.

"I am going to dance on your grave," my mother hisses, her mouth almost touching Dad's ear. "Do you hear me? I'm going to put on my new red dress, and I am going to dance on your bastard grave."

And while I'm still choking on the shock of that, she leans over and spits, a perfect sticky globule of it. It hangs from her lips and then drops onto his cheek, slides down it like a slug's trail.

Chapter Twenty-One

Night

The morgue is a terrible place to be. Let me take you somewhere else instead, back in time to somewhere better. Let me take you back to Frey's cottage, in the days after our time in the garden, when everything is golden and glorious.

There's a charge in the air, something that makes my skin tingle. It's there when I wake up to sunlight that feels clean and fresh, as if there's been rain. The feeling's so strong that I go outside and kneel down to touch the grass, feeling for signs of damp in the soil. The ground's dry and thirsty, the grass beginning to struggle, but I can't shake the sensation of change and newness. When we sit at the table and work on our colouring books, I take risks with my choices and the risks pay off, so that Josh smiles and passes my book to Frey for inspection. Frey's eyes slide sideways over the page, and after a minute he gives his slow, barely there smile. I sing as I make lunch, and catch Josh looking at me.

"You're really happy," he says at last. His voice is awkward, tentative, as if he's trying hard to make it sound like a question and not an accusation.

"I am."

"Is it the lovely company?"

Josh isn't flirting. There's nothing like that between us and never has been. Nonetheless, when our eyes meet, we both blush. There's a glitter and shine in the air, lighting up the room. I'm afraid to think too much about where it's coming from.

"I think the weather's changing," I lie. Josh looks doubtfully at the window. "You know when it's still hot, but you can suddenly feel that it's almost over and the rain's coming in? When I went outside this morning that's what it felt like."

"Most people get sad when the sun stops shining."

"I'm not most people." It sounds more provocative than I mean it to. Frey stands at the counter, spreading butter over a slice of bread, taking care to get it into every corner. His head is bowed, an artist focused on his work. When I pass him the chorizo slices, my fingertips reach out to touch his wrist.

What the hell am I doing? *Frey doesn't like to be touched.* Josh and I both know this. It's part of our basic understanding of how to take care of Frey.

But then Frey turns his head, slides his eyes towards me. Takes a deep breath. Raises his eyes to mine for a single, effortful moment. Then looks away. Music bubbles in my throat again, as urgent and undeniable as if I'm a bird. Frey drops the butter knife on the floor.

"Hey." Josh is instantly attentive. "You okay, mate? That's not like you."

Frey glances slantwise at the knife. To an outsider he might look mildly interested, or perhaps merely vacant. To Josh and me, his distress is like an air horn. The tiles have a yellow smear. Floss, well-trained, raises her head and licks her lips, but knows better than to take a chance.

"Don't worry, we'll clean it. Do you want a new knife? Or shall I wash this one?" Frey turns his head minutely towards

Josh. "This one washed. Okay. Why don't you watch so you know I've done it properly?" And Josh goes to the sink and Frey – unable to move until the floor is purged of butter – turns on the spot to watch him, and I get the floor cleaner and apply three long sprays of foam and wipe up the mess, swirling over and over with a damp cloth and then a dry one until the floor is utterly cleansed, immaculately dry.

Frey's close enough to touch. If I reached out my hand, I could close my fingers around the tender stretch of his ankle, trace the shape of the bones there. His skin would be soft and supple and vulnerable, pale velvet skin that never sees sunlight. Josh's ankles are sturdy and hairy. Frey is smoother, softer. Just a light, downy sprinkle, like fuzz on a peach.

If I were to hold my hand out to Josh, he'd want to reach back, to give as well as take, curious and eager. Touching Frey would be like running my hands over a sculpture in a museum. Blissful. Peaceful. Also, utterly wrong and against the rules. No, it would be even worse than that, because Frey is not a sculpture but a living human. I imagine it for a minute, his passive terror beneath the hunger of my touch. Frey is so gentle. No matter how much he hated it, he wouldn't fight back.

But he looked at me. He made eye contact. It's the same as when he took hold of my wrist, came with me into the garden. He's pushing himself to endure things he knows are important to me. He's trying to feel his way into my world. He wants to make a connection with me, because he…

Time flows past like honey. Josh and Floss go out, and Frey and I sit at the jigsaw table. We're working on a puzzle Frey doesn't choose often; a Japanese print of a wave about to break. Small, flat boats float in the wave's shadow. In another moment its weight will spill and shatter. Their future's already set. It just hasn't arrived yet. Is Frey trying to tell me he senses the weight in the air?

I could touch Frey now. I could let my fingertips meet his with each piece of the puzzle. I won't do it, but I can feel the rebellious urge building anyway. I hand over another piece, watch a fragile little boat take form beneath that impossible curl of water. For the first time in months, I'm conscious of the camera in the corner. Conscious that I might be being watched.

Where is she, in those times when she watches us? Our lives here are as exposed as anyone's can be, but Linnea remains mysterious. She could be at a lab bench in a glass-walled space with no external windows. In a sleek corner office looking out over black water. In a sunlit, empty classroom, wooden floors and an old-fashioned blackboard. Maybe she's working from home today, or taking time to recharge, thick black coffee and rich pastries consumed slowly, wrapped in a soft blanket. Perhaps Linnea has a permanent feed open on her computer so she can glance in at any time. Perhaps she's built an algorithm to feed her random check times. Perhaps she trusts us enough by now to never check at all.

'There'll be other cameras', Josh said once, casual and devastating, describing a natural law of the universe. But there are no cameras in the bedrooms. I know that because of the time Frey was ill. For night-time, Linnea puts her trust in the knowledge that there are always two of us there. Josh and I are each other's guardians and each other's spies. God, why am I thinking about Frey's bedroom? I pass him another piece, being extra careful to hold it by my fingers.

Frey takes it, as always. Pauses, as always. The pause stretches out. It feels like he's steeling himself for something. It feels like he's waiting for me to act.

Before I can stop it, my fingertips reach out to his. For a moment, there's contact. My breath quickens. A strange, sweet freeze trembles against my spine. I want to ask him, 'Is this all right?' I want to hear him reply, 'Yes, this is lovely, this is what I want'.

Is this what he wants? Or is he only doing it to please

me? And would that be such a bad thing? What if pleasing me is what he wants, because he...

That evening, Josh and Frey play *Minecraft*, and Floss and I watch. I never play because I've never got the hang of working the console, but I enjoy the slow music, the gradual accumulation of resources, the steady progression of whatever they're working on. Frey likes building vast, soaring structures of stone and wood, great empty spaces like cathedrals. On supermarket days, he often directs his avatar to the village, where strange little people make muffled greeting noises and offer him one thing in return for another. I hadn't made the connection until Josh asked, "Do you think he's recreating what we did this morning?" That was my way into their *Minecraft* world; realising that when he invited us to watch him build, Frey was sharing himself. I could watch it for far longer than the two hours we're allowed.

Tonight isn't a supermarket day, so there's no bartering. They're working on the underground railway, as they have been for many, many nights. I'm very conscious that I'm the only woman in a house with two grown men who are not related to me. When I take Floss outside so she can pee in a corner then snuffle about after a hedgehog, there's a little too much black sky over my head.

"Right," says Josh when Floss and I come back inside. "Bedtime." He inhales as I pass. "You smell of the outside."

"It's gorgeous out there," I say. "Frey, you should try it. Come out with me and Floss onto the lawn. We could look at the stars together."

"D'you fancy it, mate?" Josh never assumes, always checks, even when he knows the answer. "No? Not to worry, just checking. Right, it's time for a shower and then bed."

I haven't told Josh yet that Frey has been outside. I could say something. I should say something.

I don't say anything. The moment passes.

It's Josh's night to sit outside Frey's bathroom door. My night to do the last round of the house, tidying and adjusting the few small items displaced by our existence. One of the kitchen clocks has stopped at a quarter to ten. I slot in the new battery and reset the time. I should have noticed when I took Floss out, but my mind's elsewhere tonight. Normally I'd be ready for bed, looking forward to the respite, but tonight I'm restless. I open and close drawers, not sure what I'm looking for.

"Frey's sorted," Josh says, behind me. "Floss is with him. Are you all right?"

Slowly, I come back to myself. I'm standing in the middle of the kitchen, holding a wooden spoon like a baton, staring blindly at my own reflection in the window. I look a bit unhinged, a bit lost, a bit sexy. I look like a woman I don't like to think about. I don't want my mother in my head at any time, but especially not when I'm here.

"I'm fine."

"You're sure you're okay?" Josh's fingers rest for a moment on my arm, shy and tentative. "If you want to talk about anything… I'm a good listener."

"Thanks." The temptation to let a little bit of what's building inside me leak out is demanding and primal. "It's just the weather. Outside. It smells so good."

"Summer nights are lush. Even the sea smells different."

"Is it still cold?"

"It's always cold, but it gets warmer from about April. I thought maybe something had happened with Noah."

"With *Noah*?" I feel an electric jolt of guilt. My head and my heart are so entirely *here* that I've almost forgotten Noah exists. "No, he's fine. Why? Have you—" I stop myself before I can ask my ridiculous question.

"No, it's nothing like that, no weird premonitions or anything." Josh is scarily intuitive. He knows humans are, on average, far more superstitious than they want to admit. "But you seem… not quite in the room. Like you've got something on your mind."

"Sorry."

"Don't be daft." His hand's on my arm again, a soft, gentle touch like a question. "Take it as a compliment. You normally never let on you've got any life outside of here." His eyes flicker over mine. "You're so good at this. Way better than me."

"Don't be daft, you're brilliant. I'd never manage without you."

"Well, back atcha, mate, I'd never manage without you either." He's sounding blokey and jokey but he's not feeling that way at all, I can tell. He's feeling small and honest and vulnerable. "And Frey… he really likes you, you know."

"He likes both of us."

"Yes, but. I mean. It's different. Because he. Ah, you know what, I'm just going to say it. I think he's a little bit in love with you."

I can't help the blush that floods my cheeks.

"It's all right. I'm not laughing. I wouldn't laugh at that. Probably you already knew."

My heart thrums in my chest. I'm very conscious of my breathing, the rapid, awkward rhythm of it.

"Can't exactly blame him for it," Josh adds, then turns away hastily, refolding tea towels that are already immaculately neat.

Josh likes me. I can't believe I hadn't seen it before.

"Well, he likes us both better than the others anyway," I say. I drop the spoon into the open drawer. The rattle of its closing shakes loose the sweet tension between us. Josh, a good sport, a good person, makes himself laugh.

"You're so competitive," he says, which is what he always says when I talk about the others. "They've got names. You can say them. Go on. Let me hear you do it."

"I don't perform to order," I say primly, and go to my room.

If I were to describe for a stranger the slow, repeating rhythm of our work days, their first questions would be, 'How do you not go mad with boredom? Don't the walls close in on you at night?' The truth is that when ten forty-five rolls around and Frey folds himself into his bed, we're all exhausted. Our days are simple but draining. I can feel the insistent tug of sleep, drawing me down into the dark. I hear the small sounds of the house settling, the silence that follows.

I'm usually asleep by now. There's a clock on my phone, but I don't let myself look. Obsessing about time is the first step towards insomnia. My skin tingles. It's hard to lie still beneath the heavy cotton cover of the duvet. The bedding, like everything else here, is luxurious and expensive. When we wash the covers on the morning of changeover day, their weight drags the washing line down so that they almost brush against the earth. My bed smells of the garden. Of the day Frey and I sat beneath the honeysuckle and he held my wrist. Josh thinks Frey is a little bit in love with me. What if I was a little bit in love with him in return? What would happen then?

Josh will be asleep, his face pressed against the pillow. Floss will be curled into her basket. Frey will be asleep too. When we first came, he tapped on this wall every night, almost every hour, unable to let go of his terror of being alone. I'm right on the cusp of sleep, about to plunge downwards into the dark. The sound that pulls me back up could have come from the real world, or from my dreams. *Tap. Tap. Tap.*

I tap gently back on the wall. Wait. Wait some more.

Nothing. Frey must be asleep. Even if I didn't imagine his call, he might not need any more than this small reminder that I'm there. He'll be asleep, his body soft and relaxed, his mind at peace. But I'm fully awake now, restless and anxious. I want to make sure he's all right. I'm allowed to do this. I have permission to go into his room if it's to check that he's all right.

I pause at the door. My pulse throbs beneath my skin. I hear Floss sit up and shake her head, the rattle of her ears. I tap three times, as if Frey has summoned me. I wait, as if he's tapping back. Just in case Linnea's watching. I push the door open. Wait in the doorway. Go inside.

Floss is Frey's guardian, and she always knows if he's upset or distressed. When she sees me, she turns around in her bed and tucks her nose back under her tail. I take it as a sign that I'm welcome here, that I'm not upsetting Frey or causing him any distress. I just need to see him, to make sure he's all right.

He's curled onto his side, his breathing slow and even. He's so beautiful when he sleeps. He's so beautiful all of the time. His fair hair. His long shape. His soft skin.

He doesn't need anything from me, he's sealed away in the safe places of his own dreaming mind, but still I stay and watch. There's no harm in watching. No harm in letting my feet carry me a little closer, in letting my hand reach down to touch his cheek.

Asleep, Frey turns his face a little further into the pillow.

I'm kneeling beside the bed now, my hand and palm growing greedier. My face tilts towards the sweet tangle of hair at the base of his neck. He's the cleanest man I know but I can still smell the faintest tang of sweat. Frey makes a small murmur in his throat.

I can see the shape of him, his body a question mark, curled over at the top and straighter at the bottom. My hand creeps a little lower, petting at his shoulders, fingers dipping beneath the soft, clean cotton of his pyjama top. I wouldn't touch him like this while he's awake, but this is surely harmless. Maybe if I do this enough, he'll grow accustomed to it, build up a tolerance that will carry into his waking hours. He wanted to touch me this afternoon, while we were working on the jigsaw. He wants to be able to show me how he feels.

I slide one hand beneath the duvet. My fingers find the curve of Frey's hip bone.

I know straight away I've gone too far. Frey turns over, pushes himself up onto his elbows, looking around in confusion. I snatch my hand away, stand up, take a step back. Frey turns his head to look at me, his eyes sliding over my body.

"It's all right," I say. "It's Callie. Don't worry. It's Callie. It's night-time and Floss is here and everything's fine. I was just making sure you're all right."

Frey rubs at his eyes. Smooths out the surface of the pillow.

"It's all right," I say again. "I'll stay until you go back to sleep, if you like."

Frey lies back down. Closes his eyes. His breathing slows. Floss rests her cool nose against my ankle. I wonder if he was even awake just now, if my visit will come to him the next morning as the memory of a sweet and half-forgotten dream. I touch my lips to the edge of his jaw. I'd like to kiss his mouth, but I can't reach it without disturbing him, and he looks so peaceful.

I go back to my own bed, determined to sleep, but my body won't let me. There's a restlessness I can't ignore, an insistent feeling like an itch that demands my attention. I slide one hand beneath the waistband of my pyjamas. I won't feel ashamed of this, I won't be embarrassed. It's just my body, wanting what it wants. I'll be able to sleep afterwards.

Is Frey doing the same thing, on the other side of the wall? Perhaps he is. Frey isn't a child or an animal, he's a grown man, and he has an adult's needs. There's nothing dirty or wrong about it, nothing about Frey could ever be dirty or wrong…

The thought of him touching himself sends me over the edge, biting at my lip to stop myself calling out.

Perhaps one day, I'll be able to go into his room, slip beneath the covers and lie beside him, let my hands roam over his sleeping flesh. Perhaps one day, I'll be able to share this with him while he's awake. The man I love is very strange and very different, but lovers always find a way.

"I love you," I whisper, the movement of my lips so small that even an infrared camera would not detect it. So softly even Floss would never catch the sound.

Chapter Twenty-Two

Close

This one is for you, my love. (It feels so strange to call you that, but it's true; you are my love, just as I'm yours.) I'm telling your story now, but I think that's all right. You're not the only one who's needed an interpreter to stand between you and the world. I'm happy to be that for you.

So, this is the story of how you fall in love:

Your life is very different since the day your sister came and saved you. You still can't quite believe you're out of that other place. When others say 'I can't quite believe it', what they mean is 'I'm really, really glad'. For you, it means living with a deep, permanent mistrust in the nature of your world. The love your family have for you was not the bedrock you imagined; their permanence in your life is not guaranteed. Without that, you can't rely on anything else. Any change, any unexpected difference, could be the first sign that ends in you being abandoned once more. Going outside has become impossible, unbearable; you only feel safe in a place you know. For a few painful months, you can't let your loved ones out of your sight for a moment.

You're aware of how awful you're being, but you can't make it stop.

The restoration of your faith begins the day a dog comes to the house. She's sweet and attentive, soft-eyed with ears like silk. She watches you from the corners of her eyes, making her mind up slowly, thoughtfully. You like that about her. The man who brought her says her name is Floss. He gives you a packet of treats, invites you to feed her. Her nose is damp against your hand.

While your family and the man who brought the dog talk amongst themselves, you and Floss have a long conversation of your own. In small movements, soft touches, you promise to be kind, to be gentle, to feed her, to love her. In return, she promises to lend you her courage and her strength. When your mother asks, "What do you think? Shall we keep her?" you're confused by the question. In all the ways that matter, Floss is already yours.

You've never been responsible for someone else before. You wonder how you'll manage to give her all the things dogs need, but your sister tells you not to worry, you'll have help. You wonder how this is going to work. Right now, your mother, your father and your sister are taking it in turns to stay with you, but you can already see the cracks starting to show. You've all tried this before, and it worked for you, but not for them.

A few days after Floss comes, your sister brings her laptop to you and shows you a film. It's a slightly wobbly video-tour of a house you've never been to, shot by someone walking slowly and methodically through each room, turning the camera into every corner. The house is clean, still, and empty. Its walls are thick. Its floors are smooth. You're wondering who lives there when the film shows the back door opening, the camera flaring with light and then adjusting as whoever's holding it walks outside into the bright chaos of the garden, and you have to turn away and pet Floss because it's too much to look at, all that movement, all that noise. But when your sister puts her laptop down and picks up her book, you rewind the film to the beginning and watch the slow walk through the house again, then again, and then again. And then again.

After a while you realise she's watching you. You wonder if you've done something wrong, but she's smiling, she's happy. She asks you a strange and wondrous question. "Would you like to live there?"

They tell you over and over how this will work, slow and patient in the way you need, a conversation for many days. It's not comprehension you struggle with – you can hear perfectly, and make perfect sense of the words – but believability. Can you really trust what they say? What if this is somehow going to be the other place? What if this is simply another version of that?

The drive there is horrible, terrifying, you'd never have made it without Floss. But you and she endure it together, and when you get out of the car at the other end, there it is, the house you've walked through a million times in thought, exactly as it looked in the pictures. The clean gravel of the drive. The solid front door. The swoop of the wall like a bird's wing.

When you go inside, it already feels familiar. You feel held, enclosed, cocooned. You wonder how you'll ever leave it again. Maybe you won't have to. Maybe now you have your own house, you'll be allowed to live the way you want.

You'd love to keep your family with you for always, but you finally understand now this can't happen. The different ways you all need to live don't mesh together any more. Instead of your family, you'll have the others.

The others will come in twos, stay for two weeks each, then disappear for two more weeks and be replaced by their counterparts. You like the symmetry of all this twoness, all these repeated pairings. The days when they change over will be when the moon is waxing gibbous, and then a waning crescent. The others won't mind eating the same food on the same days, doing the same things at the same times, watching the same few television programmes, never going out. They'll be able to do all of that in their two weeks off. You don't have to try and live in their world any more; they'll be coming to live in yours. Each day will be exactly as you need it to be. They tell you this often, but you try not to hope too much. It seems too impossibly good to ever happen.

Your family promise you can help to choose the others, which seems strange and risky to you. How are you supposed to *choose* a person?

She's only one of four, at first. Thanks to your sister, you know more about her than she realises. You know she was a nurse, in her former life. You know she has a brother she has to care for. More symmetry here, more connections that make her being here seem like fate. She's only one of four, but she's kind and attentive. You like how she looks. She seems to like you.

Something else; something unexpected and wonderful. When she first comes to see you, she's filled with tension. Her movements are quick and nervous, her breathing shallow. By the time you've finished your first jigsaw together, she's calmer, softer, more peaceful. She was knotted up like tangled wire. Now you've smoothed her out. She's here to help you, but you've done something for her in return. You hold that thought in your heart like a pearl.

On her first supermarket day, everything seems a little easier, and part of what makes it better is her presence, her intuition. You have enough energy left to notice more about her. She's sensitive to the opinions of others, desperate to please and afraid of failing. When the checkout lady praises her, she doesn't know what to do with that praise. It's not the connection that hurts her, but the way it's being made. She turns away from the well-meant words the way you yourself turn from touch.

Impulsively, you slip a box of chocolates onto the conveyor. You choose the prettiest box you can see, hoping she'll understand the message: *these are for you both, I like you both, but they're also for* you, *singularly and in particular.* When the equinox comes, you mark it with a rose on her napkin. The crawling horror of reaching outside to pluck it is worth it when you see her expression.

The way you all live is laid down by your sister, who knows you to the bone. Routines keep you anchored to your spot in the universe, and this woman you're growing closer to, she knows that. All of the others know that. Still, she finds ways to adjust your way of living, in subtle ways that also feel like a rebellious yell.

For example: the others are supposed to change bedrooms each night, taking it in turns to be next to your room. You know why this is. You know how exhausting you can be, on the nights when the terror creeps in and you have to check and check and check that you're not alone. But by the time the solstice comes, the room next to yours is hers alone. The change makes you uneasy, but it also pleases you. You like knowing she's on the other side of the wall. You like knowing that if you need to see a friendly face, it will be hers.

She's made a change, and that's hard at first. But because she's special to you, because you want to make her happy, you've accepted it. You can do more than you thought you could. She's given you a strength you didn't know you had. What else might you do for her, if she asks?

The next thing is the bread. She makes it one afternoon when, despite all the cleaning, the outside world creeps in and turns the contents of the bread bin mouldy. You're so horrified, they have to throw away the bread bin and order a new one. Bread-making reminds you of the other place, the endless activities they tried to force on you, and at first you can hardly stand to stay in the room. But she has her back to you, which means you can look your fill and know there's no danger of her looking back. Before you know it, you're captivated. You linger so long that she invites you to join her.

Of course, you say no. You say this the first time, and the second, and the third. It's too reminiscent of the other place where you were asked that question, by voices that were too loud and cheerful, accompanied by invading hands on your shoulders and back. Her way of asking is kinder. Just once, quietly. Your answer accepted without question. At the same time, a recognition that 'no, thank you' this time doesn't have to mean 'no, thank you' forever.

And would it be different, with her? Could you find a way to stand beside her and join her in creating, let her instruct and direct? You're not sure, but you think it over for a while, and finally decide you might like that. A neat inversion of your time doing jigsaws, where you're the expert and she's only there to assist. A way to connect without physical contact. A way to be close without words.

The first touch of the dough is sickening, but you make yourself do it anyway. After a while, you find you can bear it, it's possible. More than that; it's worthwhile. Your shudders of disgust are drowned by the triumph of this new ritual, something only for you and her. It's your first taste of the exclusivity of longing.

She has a brother, who is both like and unlike you. You've known this since before you knew her, but now it comes to your mind more often. The thought of this brother torments you just a little. You're not jealous of him – you have exactly equal shares, everything divided perfectly. Still, he troubles you. She loves her brother, and you're fairly sure she loves you too. But is it the kind of love you crave? You don't want to be her second brother. You want to be special in your own way, to have a place in her heart that's separate and unique.

Josh likes her too, and he has ways to connect with her that aren't available to you. He makes her laugh, he touches her arm, he looks her in the eye. You like Josh, he's a good person, he helps you with Floss. You don't want to be jealous of him. It's the first time you've even had to consider such a thing.

Now she's talking about a plan she's made to get a tattoo. She wants a picture on her body. What a strange thing to want. When they're both occupied, you take a pencil and do something you've never let them see before. This is one thing you can do that Josh can't.

You don't know if she'll see it. Even when she looks at it, tears off the paper, you don't know if she's understood. The uncertainty is hard for you to live with. But when you next see her, the picture you drew for her is etched into her skin. Your heart sings.

She's done something for you. Now it's your turn to do something for her, that's how it works. Josh and Floss are gone, the two of you are alone. You're thinking about the things other couples do when they're alone, the things you've seen done sometimes on screens. You've watched it the way your sister watches horror movies, glancing from the corners of your eyes, appalled but unable to turn completely away. The thought of that much contact makes you shudder. You want to please her, you want to make her happy, but how can you ever do that when all of this is out of reach?

She's talking to you, telling you about the garden. You've grown used to its presence, you're willing to see it from the window. But going into it – letting the breeze touch your skin, enduring the sensory assault of the outdoors…

And yet. She wants it. She wants it desperately, not just for herself, but because she wants to share her joy with you. You're already asking so much, asking her to love you. There's so little you can do for her in return. There will be no restaurants for the two of you, no romantic walks by moonlight, no sun-soaked afternoons on soft white sand. No impassioned declarations. No kisses. No children.

You remember the time when you were ill, when the world came undone around you and you were taken somewhere bright and terrifying. In that moment of extremis, you did something you'd only done once before, the day your sister came to rescue you. You reached for her hand, and you didn't let go.

Your fingers close around the place on her wrist where she's marked herself with your drawing. She could have listened to anyone's ideas, could have let Josh choose, could have let her brother, but it's your drawing inked into her skin. Now wherever she goes in those weeks when she's not with you, a little part of you travels with her. You'll be connected to her until she dies. She did this for you. So, now you'll do something for her.

The garden is terrible. The garden is horrifying. The garden is also worth it, because after that, everything's different. You watch her as she realises this too, glancing sideways at the feeling that's grown between you. She looks at it the way you look at everything, in small, sipping glances. You can see her slowly adjusting, accommodating your feelings into her understanding of the universe. Another man might be impatient, wanting her to accept it in a single greedy gulp of knowledge, but you are yourself, and you're glad of the chance to savour it.

An understanding, then, but what comes after that? Are you lovers now, the two of you? What you have is enough for you, but you know what other people mean when they say 'lover'. It's not just a state of mind or an emotion. To love is a verb. It's making a connection. You've got this far with small gestures, proxies for the words you can't say and the kisses you can't give. Since the garden, the thought of something is taking shape for her.

Do you want what 'more' implies? Until now, your answer's always been an instant, effortless 'no'. There's a disconnect between your head and your body, taking the pleasure of someone else's touch and turning it into a blare of *danger, danger, pain.* Your own hands on your own flesh in your own private space with the door shut, safe and predictable, everything under your command; yes, of course, why not? Your skin pressed against someone else's; something you can only endure in extremis.

You do want it, though, because you want to please her. You want the closeness, the specialness. You want to find one more thing to share with her that's only for the two of you. You want all of this, but you know in your bones you can't have it. 'Frey doesn't like to be touched.' That's the first rule your sister always teaches, because it's one of the most fundamental truths about you, one of the differences that make you who you are. You want to like it, but you don't know how to shut off the sirens, how to make your body obey your will. It would be like putting your hand into a fire and then keeping it there until the skin crisped and the fat melted. At some point, no matter how hard you try to resist, the body takes over.

Sometimes you almost reach out to close the circuit between the two of you, almost let your fingers touch. Each time, you hope you'll have found the mechanism that shuts off the sirens under your skin. Each time, you feel that same shock of almost-contact. *Danger. Danger. Pain.*

You're still wrestling with this conundrum when, against the odds, she finds a way.

You half-wake in the night to a small sound against your

wall. *Tap. Tap. Tap.* The signal that you're not alone. It's comforting sound. She's there with you, you're together in this house. Beside your bed, Floss sighs and stirs, then settles down. You let your eyes fall closed again.

The triple tap at your door nudges against your consciousness. You're adrift in that border country between waking and sleeping, your mind half-aware, your body still and slack. It's all right, it's all right, it's just her, it's nothing to be afraid of. This is something that's allowed. She comes in on silent feet. Stands by your bed.

You don't know what to do, but that doesn't matter, you don't have to do anything. All you have to do is to stay where you are, in the place where you're not exactly waking, and not quite asleep.

Awake, her hand on your cheek would set off the sirens. Adrift, you feel her fingers on you and know you can survive. You don't like to be touched. It's the first, the most unbreakable rule. But she's found a way for you to endure it. Beneath your skin, the sirens whine, fall silent, whine, fall silent. Because you love her, because she's come to you when you're barely even here, you and she can slip together past the lines of your own defences.

She's kneeling beside you now, and her breath is warm on your neck. Her fingers explore, slowly, delicately. Is she enjoying this? Are you? It's the first time you've been able to get past *danger, danger, pain,* to feel the possibility of something else, something new. You don't like it, but you might do one day. You turn your face into the pillow, trying to feel only what she's doing to you. Trying to share her joy.

Your neck. Your shoulder. Your collarbone. Her touch lights tiny fires along them all. You keep yourself in that fire for as long as you possibly can.

Then, her hand on your hip is too much, and you come awake, sitting up and turning around. You couldn't stop it, couldn't help it, couldn't take any more. She murmurs reassurances to you, tells you not to worry, that you can go back to sleep, everything's fine. Another minute, a bare brush of her mouth on the edge of your jaw, and she's gone, you're alone again, the fires fading, the sirens quieting.

This is what love truly is, then. Not just the feelings you have about her. Not just the pleasure you take in her company or the gratitude you feel for her continued presence in your life. But what you're willing to endure to make her happy. The measure of your love is what you'll tolerate for the one you want to please.

And will it be enough? Will she be content with what you can give her? You lie awake in the darkness and wonder.

But it will be enough, Frey, it will. You are more than enough. She loves you too, she does. Because you are kind, and thoughtful, and perceptive, and talented, and sweet. Because you see her and understand her in ways no one else ever has. Because you've helped to heal her rotten wounds, so old she'd forgotten she even had them. Because one day not far from now, you'll help her create a new reality where her brother and her father are still alive. Because when she stands in the morgue and looks down at their bodies, the thought of seeing you the next day will sustain her. Because you know the terror of being left. Because you will never leave her.

Chapter Twenty-Three

Spell

My mother stands in her kitchen and waits for me to speak, looking at me as if what she's just said makes sense.

We're home from the morgue, somehow. I'm vague on the details. I'm not sure if we said goodbye and thank you like civilised people, or if we simply ran. I remember a hand wiping that glob of spit from Dad's face, but I'm not sure if it was mine, or hers, or maybe someone else's, or even if I simply wished someone would do it, make him clean and undefiled. I do remember, very clearly, looking at my mother's profile as she tore out of the car park and pulled onto the road without even looking, and thinking, *if I could kill you and bring them back, I'd do it.* It's a thought I've had a lot over the last two weeks, but never with such bright clarity, such absolute lack of guilt.

And now, here we are in her kitchen, again. Here she is, offering me a drink. From a bottle of brandy I didn't know she had. But she knows I'm leaving. She knows I can't stay after what she did. Doesn't she? Surely, I must have been clear about that.

"It'll help," she says.

"Help what?"

"We're going to talk. And it's going to be hard. So you might want a drink."

"No." That's the other thing I remember about getting home. My mother flashing past a red light as if it didn't exist, the terrified faces of the other drivers, too frightened even to swear at her; and a picture of myself, in my own car, in the lay-by where Josh and I meet. *Twenty-four hours more,* I think, and then, *no, I don't have to wait, I can leave whenever I want.* I don't have to be here, in this house that perches and stares like a bird ready for flight. There's nothing holding me back.

"I'm going," I say.

"You're not."

"You can't stop me." I sound petulant and fearful. When I'm with my mother, a part of me is always eight years old.

"We're going to talk, you need to understand. Stop being silly and sit down."

I can go upstairs and pack my things, and she'll have no power to stop me. I can get into my own car and drive away and she will not follow. Even if she does follow, I can go into the house I shared with Dad and Noah and shut the door, lock her out. This is all perfectly clear in my mind. It's my body that betrays me, insisting in a primal way that she is my mother, and I have to obey. I sit down at the table and think about banging my head against it.

My mother finds two glasses, slops brandy into each, and pushes one across the table.

"I don't want that."

"You'll need it. We both do."

"I have to drive."

"You don't need to drink it all."

"I don't drink, not ever, I don't like it."

She slaps the table hard enough to make the glasses jump. There's a terrifying violence about her tonight. I wish I had a pebble to hold. "For God's sake, Callie, will you let me take care of you?"

I could knuckle under, do as she says. I could take the brandy and sip it. I could even say thank you. Instead, I push the glass away and stare right into her bright, mad eyes.

"And that's looking after me, is it? Giving me something I don't want, so I can't leave?"

"You're always so stubborn," she mutters. "Always so stubborn. You're just like—"

"Like who?"

Her mouth is as tight as a trap. She won't even say his name.

"Like Dad," I say. "My lovely, lovely dad. Who loved me and took care of me. Even when you didn't. And he loved you too, for some bloody reason. I'm glad you left him. He didn't deserve to live his whole life with someone as horrible as you are."

The fury in her face makes me want to cower and hide. But I'm not eight years old any more, and I can summon a fury of my own.

"You might not have loved him," I say. "But I bloody did. He was wonderful. And he was a much better parent than you were."

"I did my best."

"Your best was piss-poor."

"You always preferred your dad."

"And you always preferred Noah. Let's face it, we'd both push each other over that cliff if it meant we could have our favourites back, wouldn't we?"

"Callie," she says.

"Don't bother. I know it's true. I've always known it. And now here we are. We both got stuck with our least favourite choice."

"I do love you," she whispers, as if it's a dirty secret, as if it's a curse.

"No, you don't, don't you dare say that, you never loved me, not ever." My chin's wobbling, and I take a sip of brandy so she won't notice. Its astringent taste dries the inside of my mouth and the fumes go up my nose, but infuriatingly, my mother is right: it does help. I have control of my face again.

"That's not true. It was just – difficult."

"To love your own daughter?"

"To love your father's daughter." She sips at her own brandy, grimacing just like I did. Two non-drinkers, sipping brandy from water glasses. What a pair we are. Maybe this would be easier if we were wearing our new red dresses. I think of phrases that would get myself out of this. *I've got to pack. I've got a long drive ahead of me. The traffic's supposed to be bad tonight.* Or I could keep it simple, no excuses. *I'm going now. We'll talk about the funeral. Bye.*

"Is that really what you think?" my mother asks. Of course she's the one who speaks first. Of course she's in control.

"It's what I know. You tried to pretend sometimes but I always knew the difference. Why worry about it now?"

"I did my best." My mother squinches her eyes shut, opens them again. "It was never your fault."

"So it's true, then."

"It wasn't you, I swear. It was – your father. The way he was." My mother stands up, takes the single stride needed to cross the kitchen, turns, strides back, sits down. "I can't talk about this in the daylight. Stay until sunset and I'll tell you in the dark."

"No. I have work tomorrow, I want to get a good night's sleep. If you want to talk, then do it now."

"Please." My mother holds out a hand to me. It's shaking a little. I clutch my glass of brandy.

"Please what?"

"Please don't make me do this in daylight. I don't think I can."

"Then don't," I say, and go to pack my bag.

It takes minutes only; I'm good at exits, and this one requires no thought or planning. I simply have to pack everything I own. I consider leaving the scarlet frock, but it folds into nothingness and I have room in my bag, and if I leave it my mother might think I'm coming back. Better to take it, throw it away when I get a chance. I wrap it tightly around the matching shoes, daring them to puncture the frail silk. Let it be ruined, let it be destroyed. I don't care.

I'd half-expected my mother to follow me up, to beg me to stay. A part of me wants this. I want her pounding on the door, ignoring my instruction to go away, bursting into the room, declaring she can't cope without me. It would be so satisfying to finally be the one pulling back, the one you glimpse from the corner of your eye but who can't ever be caught.

But of course she doesn't come. Her performances of need never last long. I pack my bag unmolested, while my mother sits in the kitchen and drinks her brandy and waits for me to leave so she can be alone with whatever's happening inside her head. The stairs feel steeper on the way down, a little too provisional under my feet. I shouldn't have had that brandy. I hope I'm still fit to drive.

"Right," I say, through the kitchen door.

"Fine." My mother looks at me bleakly. "You win."

"What?" I'm not trying to win anything, I'm done playing games. All that's left is the leaving.

"I'll tell you. Right now. Since you're insisting. Sit down."

I can leave. I am free. I have free will. But my mother has always been a witch, and her first and most powerful spell was to bind me to her, firm and tight. I've never been able to walk away when she calls.

My mother takes a deep swallow of brandy. I see it move in her throat. The sunlight falls on her face, exposing the signs of age. This is how I'll be when I'm older. There's enough of her in me to see the resemblance. One day, if I'm not careful, I will also be a lonely woman, sitting alone in a kitchen, unloved and unwanted. And if I am careful? If I am careful,

I'll get out of this room alive and make it home. You only need one person to make your home. Just one person who—

My mother says, "Your father raped me."

My mother says, "He did it again and again."

My mother says, "He used to wait until I was asleep and then he raped me."

I'm not here, not at all. I'm somewhere else, a place of scent and light and heat. I'm in Frey's garden. His fingers are around my wrist, touching my pulse beneath the bumblebee tattoo. When I'm home I will take Frey and we'll go out into that garden and never leave, never go back indoors. We'll sit together and he'll learn to love outside, its changes and its unpredictability. He'll learn this, because—

My mother says, "It started when Noah was small. I didn't want – you know. Sex. I mean, I was tired! I'd just had a baby. When Noah finally started sleeping through, all I wanted was rest…"

My mother says, "I thought he understood."

My mother reaches for her glass and takes another mouthful.

This is the last time I'll sit in this kitchen. I came here because my mother called me and because there was nowhere else feasible for me to go, but I don't need to come here ever again. I have choices, options, things that are possible now that weren't possible before. Noah and Dad have left me, but in a strange and terrible way, they've also set me free. From now on, I have only myself to please.

Other people would think, *I could travel!* Other people would think, *I could work in a coffee shop by the ocean.* These are the things we're taught to want, the things we're told to dream of. I have my own dream, my own longing: more time with the man I love.

My mother says, "I don't know exactly when it started. I used to dream sometimes that he – not always sex, but intimate, touching me, and he'd be moving – but I thought I was dreaming. You know. It's something people dream about, isn't it?"

My mother says, "Then I woke up one night and he was…"

My mother says, "It didn't hurt, he wasn't hurting me, he was very quiet, very gentle, but still he was – I think I screamed the place down. I know I woke Noah."

Josh and Frey and I could make it work, together. It would be a strange way to live, but I've already proved my credentials in the art of living strangely. We don't need the others. And if we were there all the time, we could make Frey's world bigger. I've already given him the garden. He wouldn't try with anyone else, but he'd try with me, because—

My mother says, "I need you to listen, Callie."

Her words are a spell, always a spell. She could stand on a mountaintop and call to me from across the world, and I would hear her cry and be forced to go to her. I can run as hard as I want, hide as deep as I dare, but I will never, ever be free.

My mother says, "I nearly left him that night. I was angry enough. It was the practicalities I couldn't get my head around. Where do you go with a toddler? Noah wasn't even two. That's the hard bit about leaving. Not deciding. Actually physically doing it. It's so bloody complicated."

My mother says, "I don't want to talk about this, don't

think this is easy for me. But I've got to tell you otherwise you won't…"

My mother says, "God, I wish I smoked so I could stop talking and have a cigarette."

Frey's cottage wasn't always home, not for any of us. It was just a place where I could be *not a nurse* and Josh could be *not a farmer* and Frey could be *not an outsider*. We all three started with a negative, but we've made it into something whole and real. I shouldn't be thinking about this here. I don't want to bring it into my mother's kitchen while she tells me this awful story.

My mother says, "Anyway. He swore that was the only time. He swore on Noah's life. I took that seriously. Even though I'd had those dreams…"

My mother says, "I remember thinking, *If you believe him, it'll be so much simpler. You can go back to sleep and pretend it never happened.*"

My mother says, "And the stupid thing is, I felt guilty! Because it's normal, isn't it, to want sex with your wife? He wasn't going out and sleeping with other women. He only wanted me."

My father, the lover. I know something about the exclusivity of wanting, the strange magic of it. It makes no sense that Frey, of all people, unlocks the yearning in my heart, but he does, he does. I love him. I can't explain it properly, but I love him.

My mother says, "I stopped being able to sleep. Just couldn't do it."

My mother says, "He was frantic. He said he'd broken me

and he'd never forgive himself. He offered to sleep downstairs. But I didn't want to kick him out of the bed. If I did, he'd know I didn't trust him. I didn't want to break his heart."

My mother says, "He said I should go to the doctor and get some pills."

Practicalities. I know what Frey wants, what he feels, but how could I ever tell Linnea? Frey's ways of expressing himself are hard to learn, harder still to explain to a sceptical outsider. But how we feel is real; that's the one thing I can hold on to. I only need to be patient. There will be a way across the abyss.

My mother says, "So, I did. I didn't get hooked on them, it was just for a few weeks, while I got back into the habit of sleeping. And then, only on the nights when I needed some help. And it worked. They worked. It was so lovely to rest again…"

My mother says, "I thought it was all okay. I thought *we* were okay. I was even thinking we might – start having sex again. It had been a long time. Two years, apart from that one time…"

My mother says, "If he'd just been a bit patient with me."

I don't recognise the man in this story. We don't want to think about our parents being sexual, having sex, needing and seeking and taking. But it's more than that. My mother is desecrating him. It's not enough that he's dead, it's not enough that she spat on his shattered remains. She still has to put on her red dress. She still has to dance on his grave.

My mother says, "I started feeling sick in the mornings, just like with Noah. I wanted to laugh about it, like *If I didn't know better…!* But I couldn't. I think I did know better. I did the test, but I knew anyway."

My mother says, "I didn't know how to tell him. I was scared he'd accuse me of cheating. I was even scared I might have cheated, and forgotten about it. Or got pregnant from a toilet seat. Do young girls still believe in that? Getting pregnant from a dirty toilet seat?"

My mother says, "I thought about leaving him then too, but, I mean, Jesus. If I couldn't do it with a toddler, I certainly couldn't with an almost pre-schooler and another baby coming."

I don't want to be here. I want to be with Frey, in the stillness of his house. Just cool enough in summer, just warm enough in winter. Thick walls and recessed windows, with ground pumps warming the floors and radiating comfort into the air. My mother's kitchen is both too hot and too cold, and her shape fills every inch of it. I'll never escape. I'll be trapped here until I die. I press my fingers against the bumblebee tattoo. If I press hard enough, I might break a bone.

My mother says, "He started crying as soon as he saw the test."

My mother says, "He said he couldn't help himself, he just loved me so much, he'd been so lonely and he wanted to feel close to me but he didn't want to upset me by asking, and I was fast asleep. He said it was just that one time. Again. And I wanted to believe him. Again."

My mother says, "I wanted to love you. I really did. And I did, part of me did. Your hands. Your little face. You were so sweet. Callie, I swear, part of me has always loved you."

Where do babies come from? I never asked my mother this, because even as a child I knew it was dangerous to ask her for anything. I asked Dad instead, and he told me, "Babies grow inside their mummy's tummy until they're ready to come out." So I asked, "How do they get in there?" and he told me, clearly and carefully and with only a touch of embarrassment. He described it as something that people do who love each other very much. So much that they want to make a new life.

And a few hours later, the thought arrived. *That's what's wrong with me. It's because Daddy loves Mummy, but Mummy doesn't love Daddy. I'm made wrong and that's why she doesn't love me.* I remember being proud of myself for reasoning it out so well.

My mother says, "Noah used to visit. He got your dad to drive him."

My mother says, "He'd get your father to drop him at the bottom of the street and he'd walk up. I'd get a sort of feeling when he was coming. I used to watch from the window so I could see."

My mother says, "That's why I bought this house. So your father could never catch me by surprise again. I wanted to live where I'd always, always see him coming."

Dad wasn't perfect. I knew this already. But I won't let my mother's words hurt me, and I won't let them destroy my memories. Dad wasn't perfect. I loved him anyway.

My mother says, "Noah asked me. He asked me. He said, 'I'm worried Dad's doing something to Callie. He gives her sleeping tablets. I've seen him do it. But they're always telling me at the hospital I don't know what's real and what's in my head, so it might not mean anything, but I think it means something…'" Her imitation is eerie, necromantic.

For a minute, she's conjured Noah. My mother has always been a witch.

My mother says, "I had to do it. No, Callie, don't put your hands over your ears, don't do that, you need to listen."

My mother says, "I told him. I told Noah. How you were conceived. I had to. He deserved the truth."

I want to leave but I can't. I have a home but I can't go to it. I have people who love me but I can't reach them. In all this world there is only this room, and my mother inside it. I can't leave until she sets me free.

"Mum," I say. "Please tell me. That time in the Lake District. When you left me in the cottage. *How long were you gone for?*"

But she's not listening. She doesn't hear me. She only hears herself. Maybe I didn't even ask the question aloud.

My mother says, "As soon as he said 'sleeping pills' I knew I had to tell him what…"

My mother says, "I wouldn't have left you with him if I thought – but – I was his wife, I was supposed to – but you, I didn't think he'd – not his daughter…"

My mother's eyes are burning coals. I can't look away. I can't stop listening.

My mother says, "Is that why Noah killed him, Callie? Did Noah kill him because he was doing it to you too?"

Chapter Twenty-Four

Roof

Oh, Noah. You tried to tell me, and I missed it. There was a moment when I could have stopped you, but I didn't see.

The Saturday afternoon before my shift, the last time I'll see Noah alive. If anyone could see us, my big brother and me, we'd look peculiar at best, suicidal at worst. We're sitting on the edge of a flat-roofed office building, legs dangling, sunshine warming our backs even as the sixth-storey breeze cools our faces. It's clearly dangerous, clearly forbidden. But once you've braved the *Do Not Enter – Dangerous Building* signs, there's only pigeons and graffiti, empty tablet packets and broken glass. We're high and free, which is why Noah likes it. I don't like heights, but Noah coming here on his own is far more terrifying.

"Shall we go out somewhere?" I turn cautiously, afraid I'll dislodge us, or perhaps break the precarious shell of concrete, sending us to our doom. "Where do you fancy?"

"We're already out." Noah's expression is a rare one of peace. There's been something different about him this last fortnight, and with Noah, *different* is always a concern.

But this afternoon he's happy, and his happiness fills my cup too.

"We could get some food. Are you hungry?"

"Always." Noah sighs. "Bastard meds."

"They keep you well."

"I thought being overweight was the single biggest cause of preventable illness after smoking."

"Noah, come on, you don't need to worry about—"

"I know, I know. I'm allowed to be fat because it's better than the alternative. Special dispensation for the mad. A mad bastard and a fat bastard. Ooh, and an actual bastard. Did you know that?"

A pigeon patrols the edge of the roof, its head tipped to one side. "Did I know what?" The pigeon won't knock me over. I don't need to be afraid.

"They were already having me when they got married."

"Really?" The pigeon will not flap its wings. It won't fly at my face. Any minute now it'll go away. Any minute now. It's more afraid of me than I am of it.

"They got married on the 7th of November. I was born on the 12th of January."

"Huh. It doesn't matter, though, does it?"

"Is that pigeon bothering you?" Noah, unafraid, waves his arms. The pigeon flies off. I will the wild thunder of my heart into steadiness, and scrub my palms against my jeans. "No, it doesn't matter. It's just I only realised three weeks ago."

"What happened three weeks ago?"

Noah doesn't answer. His fingers find a flat flake of concrete. When he flicks it into the air, it spirals downwards like a dead leaf. So that's why he's been strange. He's been to see her.

"I don't mind you going," I say. We both know this is a lie.

"That crow still visits," says Noah. "How long do crows live anyway?"

"Maybe it's not the same one."

"Maybe not. I think she'd know the difference, though."

I'm never sure if I believe in the crow, but it's possible Noah's got it right. Once he insisted our neighbours were smuggling and selling vast quantities of illegal cigarettes. I didn't even consider he was on to something until the police raided their garage. Noah scrabbles for something else to throw, some substitute for the leap I suspect always lurks in his bones.

"She asked about you," he says. A fat chunk of brick sails through the air and tumbles towards the deserted car park.

"What did she say?"

"She asked how you are."

"And what did you say?"

Noah sighs. "I didn't tell her anything."

"Good."

"She really does love—"

"Please don't," I beg. "I know she doesn't, she never has. I don't mind. I've got Dad, and I've got you. That's plenty. What? What?"

Noah's hand is on my shoulder, pressing me down. "You're wobbling about."

"I won't fall."

"Shall we go back down?"

"Not yet." I move his arm off my shoulder, carefully so neither of us is thrown off balance. "It's brilliant up here."

Noah smiles. "It is, isn't it?"

"Yep. The view's amazing."

Noah flicks a pea of gravel towards another pigeon, triggering a startled clatter of its wings. "And the wildlife's exceptional."

"And you can feel the breeze."

"We should go down now, though."

"Already?" I swallow the glad thump of relief. "Why?"

"Because," says Noah, "you hate it. But you won't say so, because you love me."

If I think about my terror, the singing in my ears and the sweaty drag in my ankles, I might never move again. To prove to Noah that he's wrong, I risk a single glance over the edge, and have to close my eyes. Freed from the repressive power of my gaze, the world swoops and tilts.

"Shit. It's all right. You're all right. No, God, don't struggle, it's all right, you're safe." Noah's hands ground me, pull me to safety. Concrete scrapes the backs of my knees, my calves, and then my head and back as he lays me down. After a minute, I open my eyes.

"You scared me," Noah says.

"Sorry."

"Don't be sorry, you dipstick, it's my fault for bringing you here when you can't fly, not like me. That's a joke," he adds. "Stop worrying about me and concentrate on yourself."

"I'm all right." I try to sit up.

"No, stay put. Get your breath back."

I want to show Noah I'm fine, but my body won't co-operate. I settle for an awkward faux-casual pose that looks a little less helpless, while still keeping me low to the ground. (*Not the ground, the roof,* I think, remembering the fallen ceilings and dark corridors beneath. *Dangerous Building.*)

"What's he like?" asks Noah, quick and sudden as a bee sting.

"Who?"

"That man you take care of. Frey, is that his name?"

"I didn't know I'd told you that."

"You didn't, I saw it on some paperwork you had from that mad person who gave you the job – Linnea, is she called? His mother?"

"His sister."

"Huh." Noah smiles to himself. "I thought it was his mother. I was picturing a terrifying Swedish woman with short grey hair and really well-cut trousers and a silk shirt, who's probably got a Nobel prize in a cupboard."

"No, it's definitely his sister. They've got a mother too, but Linnea's in charge of all his stuff."

"So no short grey hair? And no really nice trousers? And no Nobel prize? Another dream dies."

Actually, Noah's picture of Linnea is alarmingly accurate; he's just a little early. In another few decades, she could be everything he's described. It's an eerie act of deduction, tickling at a place in my brain I try not to visit too often. Noah sometimes thinks he can read the future. 'It's like looking down a straight road', he says. 'It's not completely fixed, by the time you get there other people might have come in ahead of you and changed things a bit, but the basic structure's set. It's just waiting for you to arrive.' And it does sometimes seem… I could almost believe…

"What are you thinking about?" Noah asks.

"Whether I could pull off a silk blouse and really well-cut trousers."

"You could if you wanted to, but you don't want to."

"I might want to."

"But you don't. Those clothes are for people who want to look like grown-ups. You're too young to dress like that."

"I'm nearly thirty."

"You're my little sister. That means you belong in party frocks and rainbow leggings. Are you sure that's what you were thinking about?"

"What? When?" I can't keep track of my own thoughts when Noah starts talking. He doesn't leave enough silence for you to remember.

"Or were you worrying about me?"

I can't meet his eye.

"I'm all right, you know," Noah says gently. "I'm fine. Everything's great."

"That's good." Is it good? Or is he too happy, happier than his circumstances would allow? What's an appropriate amount of happiness for the limited, medicated life Noah's forced to lead? One of the cruellest aspects of his condition is that even his happiness is suspect.

"So let's focus on you," Noah says.

It's the kind of statement that should come from a middle-aged man wearing a boring jumper and unfashionable slacks, or perhaps a woman with a long skirt and a non-threatening cardigan. The kind of person who sits in a room with Noah – dressed today in red moleskin trousers and a white jacket with gold-foil spots, topped with a purple fedora whose brim frames his pudgy face like a halo – and listens to the restless chatterings of his mind.

"I'm fine," I say.

"You never talk about your other life."

"I don't have *another life*, I have a job."

"But you do," Noah says, gentle and insistent. "You have another life with two blokes I've never met, and you never talk about them. Tell me about them now."

"He's…" I don't know where to begin. "I mean, he's…" Noah's right, I don't ever talk about Frey. And when I'm there, I never talk about Dad and Noah. I like keeping my life segmented. "Frey's nice."

"Nice." Noah's mouth twitches.

"Yes." Noah's right. 'Nice' is a terrible word. "And he's quiet. I mean, like, properly quiet. He doesn't – doesn't talk. Not out loud. But then, when you get to know him, you realise he's got loads of stuff to say. You just have to know how to listen."

"Is he young or old?"

"A bit younger than us." It seems funny to think about Frey's age, since that implies that he was once young, will one day be old, and will therefore be different. Frey is the most constant person I've ever known. "He's – well, he's great. Really special." I feel squirmy and awkward. Talking about Frey feels wrong, as if I'm violating someone's privacy.

"And what's the house like?"

"Oh, it's lovely. It's right in the country, hills all round, and the soil's red, properly red. It's a really new house, like on *Grand Designs*. You know, underfloor heating and a granite kitchen and curved walls and weird angles."

"Is it like that upstairs too?"

"No, there's no upstairs, it's all on one floor, a bungalow,

I suppose, but it doesn't look like a bungalow. It's not big, but it feels big. It has really high ceilings and lots of spotlights, when the bulbs blow we have this massive stepladder."

"Frey helps change the bulbs?"

"He gets the bulbs out for us sometimes." I'm telling the truth, but I'm also holding back. A blown light bulb, like any small destructive change to his environment, causes Frey a profound unease that glues him to the spot until Josh or I can fix it. When he goes to the maintenance cupboard and takes out a spare bulb, lays it out on the sideboard like a gift, it's always before the light has actually blown. Josh and I have wondered how he knows, if one of the many things Frey keeps track of is the average lifespan of a light bulb. Another small reminder that Frey walks in his own time and space, and we're only clumsy visitors.

"So it's the other one, the other carer, who helps with the ladders?"

"I can put up a ladder. It's the twenty-first century."

"What's his name again?"

"Josh."

Noah snaps his fingers. "That's the one. So he does the ladders?"

"Well, actually, yes. Mostly."

"Is he the one you got the tattoo for?"

"He's a *colleague*."

"You're allowed to fancy your colleagues," Noah says mildly. "I bet he fancies you."

"Don't. That's weird."

"It's not weird, it's normal. I'd love you to have a bit more *normal*. So it's you and two blokes? Just like at home?"

"And Floss."

"Who?"

"Frey's service dog."

"Do you remember," Noah says, "when we were about… ten and seven? And we really wanted a dog? All those trial runs we did? Hunting out dog shit around the neighbourhood?"

"God, that was so gross. I can't believe you talked me into it."

"I'm sorry it didn't work."

"That's okay, it wasn't your fault." I know whose fault it was, but I won't say her name. Mostly I forget she even exists. Only Noah ever reminds me she exists.

"Well, I'm glad you've got a dog now."

"She belongs to Frey."

"But she likes you too." Noah says this as if he's met Floss, had a chance to find out her preferences. "She thinks you're lovely."

"She prefers Josh," I say. "He takes her out for extra-long walks."

"And what do you do while that's happening?"

"Frey loves colouring, so we do that quite a lot. He has these gorgeous books, you know the posh ones you see in stationery shops. And nice pencils as well, loads of different colours."

"Not felt tips?"

"He doesn't like them." Josh once brought a felt-tipped pen in by accident, turning it out of his pocket along with the car key. Frey's shudder was the way I'd react if someone blew their nose on the palm of my hand.

"Tell me some more about Josh."

"What do you want to know?" It's a nothing kind of deflection, a feeble attempt to bat away Noah's gently relentless enquiries. "Anyway, why now? I've been there a year."

The question lands much harder than I'd thought it would. For a minute, Noah's face is bleak and lost. We're safe in the centre of the roof, well away from the edge, but still I have the sensation of falling. Then he smiles and looks me in the eye, and I wonder if I imagined it.

"It's because I'm mad," he tells me. "I'm allowed to be weird and mercurial and do new stuff out of the blue. And today I want to annoy my little sister into telling me everything about her job."

"You're not mad. And you're not annoying me."

"I am and I am, but tell me anyway. Then we can get some food. I know, it's nowhere close to teatime. So you have to save me from myself and distract me, so I won't get even fatter than I am and eat myself into an early grave."

Noah jokes about his weight because he hates it. I wish I could make him see how little it matters, how little I care that he's not the skinny, pretty boy he once was. I wish I could make him understand that I almost like the extra weight, which makes it harder for him to slip his moorings and leave me.

"All right. Well, we have a really strict routine."

"I know, I saw the paperwork."

I keep all my paperwork in my bedroom, where I can be sure it won't get tidied away by Dad, or absorbed into one of Noah's projects (the papier mâché elephant that consumed my notes from my nursing degree, plus our household's bank statements for the last five years, was a painful learning experience for us all). Noah must have been in there without me.

"You don't tell me," Noah says. "So I have to keep an eye on you in other ways."

"I don't mind," I insist. "But if you've seen the routine, you know everything. That's it." I lean back on my elbows, trying to look relaxed. "Nothing more to tell. What?"

"You look," says Noah, thoughtfully, "like Jeff Goldblum in *Jurassic Park*."

"That's what I was going for."

"I'm so sorry."

"Jeff Goldblum's a god, I'll take that."

"Not for that. For being mad and ruining your life."

"Noah." I scrabble onto my knees. "You haven't ruined my life, don't be stupid."

"I have, though."

"Shush, this is silly—"

"No, it's not silly. I need you to listen."

"I'm listening, but—"

"No, don't say *but*. Please just let me talk. I need to talk and then I need you to tell me what you think about it. I've – I've – oh, look, Callie, I don't want to do this but I've got to, that's why I brought you up here, I've got all this stuff in my head and I don't know if it's real or not. I need you to help me."

I'd thought we were having a nice day out. Our last afternoon before I go off to my other life. The sun's blazing hot, white and merciless, but still I feel a chill.

"Tell me," I say.

Now he has my attention, Noah doesn't seem to know what to do with it. He shuffles his feet restlessly against the gravelly surface, takes off his hat and resettles it on his head, then takes it off again, turning it slowly around in his hands.

"The thing is," he says slowly, "I never know, really, what's true and what isn't."

"I know."

"You don't, though," he says, not angry, just correcting a small but understandable error. "When you see something, you know you've seen it. When someone tells you something, you know they've said it. You don't have to question, I don't know, whether gravity's real or time works the way you think it does or… I mean, even the little things, you know? Like, right now I'm starving, but I know I don't need to eat. I can't even believe my own body. It's exhausting, suspecting every single thing that happens."

Noah never talks like this. I want to think it's a gift he's giving me, a rare moment of insight. Instead, I'm thinking, *what does this mean? Do I need to be worried?*

"I'm talking about myself again," Noah says. "But I want to talk about you. I mean, a thought I have about you. I keep having it and I don't know if it's real or if I made it up."

"Go on."

"Okay, so this is the thought. When we're all together, when you're not at work and Dad is, it's like he's your husband and I'm your child. No, please, don't talk, just listen. Seriously, Callie, that's what it's like."

279

"Okay, so I need you to listen to me now—"

"Me and Dad between us, we've ruined everything for you. I mean, I've known for ages *I've* ruined it, it's not like there's any doubt about that, none whatsoever," Noah says, and there it is, that manic gleam, that tumble of words that can be the first sign of trouble or that can be nothing at all. Sensitivity: the ability to correctly identify an illness. Specificity: the ability to correctly identify its absence. I'm good at the first, not always so good at the second. "God, that first time, you came to visit me and you looked terrified, worst thing I ever saw, it was bad enough Dad or Mum coming, but I didn't want to frighten you like that ever again…" His words stutter to a halt; his hands fidget with the brim of his hat. "But it's not just me. It's Dad too."

"Nobody's ruined anything. Stop being dramatic."

"He's never had a girlfriend since Mum left. Why do you think that is?"

"Because he doesn't want one, I suppose." One of many things I haven't forgiven our mother for. Dad loves her, still. He has her photograph by his bed. He told me once that he wanted to be buried with that photograph against his heart, that he'd written it into his will.

"I know he looked after us after Mum left. And he's still looking after me now. But you don't owe him for that, Callie. That's not how love works. He doesn't get to have whatever he wants from you, just because you love him."

My neck prickles. There's an echo in here of Noah's delusions, the stories he spins out of thin air and darkness. Dad's hurting me. Dad's keeping me prisoner. Noah has to rescue me.

"No," says Noah immediately. "No, it's not that, I'm not hiding my tablets, I know my brain's fucked and I need them. That's why I'm asking you. Because I can't trust myself."

"So ask me."

"What I think sometimes. What I *see* sometimes. I know it's not real. But just imagine if it was real. I know it isn't. But just... *if*. If he was – hurting you. Would you tell me? Would you tell anyone? Or would you just let him do it? Because you love him and you want to make him happy, so you'd find a way to stand it?"

Noah's eyes are bright and glittery. I can see the madness in him, lurking just below the surface. I'm very conscious of the breeze gusting around us, the height that divides us from the ground. I'm terrified; I'm only here because I love Noah. But is that really so wrong? How else can you measure love, if not by what you're willing to endure for the one you care about?

"But he isn't," I say, as gentle and as firm as I can manage. "He isn't hurting me. So it doesn't matter."

Noah's eyes don't leave my face. I hold his gaze and hope he's listening.

"If you had to choose," Noah says, "would you live with me and Dad all the time? Breaking into abandoned buildings and riding roller coasters? Or would you live with Josh and the other one, that Frey bloke?"

"But I don't have to choose."

"But if you did?"

"I'd choose you, of course," I say, and hope Noah won't see that I'm lying.

Was there something I could have said, that last bright afternoon, that would have convinced Noah he was wrong? I have to believe there wasn't. I have to believe I did the only thing I could, which was to climb down from the roof, scramble out through the ground-floor window, drive to KFC and buy a bucket of hot, greasy chicken for us to share, before I left for Frey's house.

Chapter Twenty-Five

Sleep

Our dreams mean nothing. Our brains, processing and filing the events of the day, fling up a handful of memories, tumble them into a new shape, and flash the results across our resting inner eye. It's as relevant as the scatter of thrown playing cards. You can draw whatever conclusion you like from the conjunction of the queen of diamonds and the seven of spades, but the only true meaning is *this is how the cards fell today.* An event can be both unique and unimportant.

Our dreams mean nothing. That's why, when I wake in the seat of my car, mouth dry, head throbbing, I don't need to dwell on the horror show I've seen. It's not a record of events. Not a recovered memory. It's only my brain, shaking up the pieces and letting them fall.

I lasted fifteen miles before I had to stop. I fled my mother's house as if she might come after me. I wasn't fit to drive but I got behind the wheel anyway, and made a clumsy, jerky, frightening journey in any direction that felt like *away.* I chose roads I didn't recognise, terrified I'd accidentally end up at Frey's house, all in case my mother might be following. She wasn't, but I felt as if she was. Then the shock and the grief and, yes, the brandy overcame me, and I pulled into a lay-by as a substitute for crashing into a wall. I cried for a while, then tipped the seat back, closed my eyes and let myself go under.

Our dreams mean nothing. I don't need to be disturbed by what I dreamed.

Here's what my brain conjured for me:

It's the night when Noah and Dad died, but it's a mistake, they're not dead, it's only some trick of my mother's. I leave Frey's house and head home.

The road is strange but familiar, time and distance stretching and contracting in the way of dreamscapes. Outside my house, Dad's car is there, intact, and Dad comes to greet me.

"Where's Noah?" I ask.

"He's not here, remember? He's in the hospital for a while."

And because this is a dream, I do remember. Noah was climbing on the roof again, so he's gone to the hospital to get well.

"It's just you and me," Dad says, and hugs me. He's wearing pyjamas, and I can feel warm skin through the worn cotton of his T-shirt, through the soft flannel of the bottoms. It feels slightly arousing, slightly wrong. I shouldn't be noticing him this way. I let go.

"It's bedtime," he tells me. "Are you tired?"

I'm in my favourite childhood nightie, green with pink flowers. My mother threw it away years ago. It's so good to see it again.

"Yes," I say.

"Off you go, then." He kisses me on the forehead, and I'm ashamed for the thoughts I had when he hugged me. This is Dad. There's nothing wrong happening.

I climb the stairs. It's lovely to be home, just me and Dad. I imagine my mother, knocking on the windows for admission; but the curtains are closed, and she can't see in. I'm dizzy with tiredness, as if I've been drugged.

There's someone coming into my room, but I'm too heavy with sleep to move. The footsteps move closer. It must be Dad, come to check on me. I'm supposed to be asleep, he gave me a tablet that's meant for him really and I shouldn't have taken it because I'm a nurse so I should know better, but nurses and doctors are the worst for breaking rules about medications, and Dad likes to share. He's always liked to share.

Now he's standing by the bed, but I don't need to be frightened. He only wants to know I'm safe. And I love him. I love him. I want him to be happy. He's watching me as I sleep, and I don't really like it but I let him do it anyway, pretending I don't know he's there because that's what he wants. He wants to watch me while I sleep. That's all.

His hands pet at my hair, in the way he likes and I don't. I keep still, keep breathing. It's all right. Nothing to worry about. He's wearing his pyjamas. I'm wearing my nightie. We've both got our clothes on so that's all right. We're just sharing space. Nothing more.

After a minute, he moves closer. My eyes are closed, but I'm dreaming, so I can see him kneeling. His face is very close to mine. One hand slips beneath the cover and strokes down my back, over the curve of my hip.

Oh God, I think, unsure if I'm horrified or thrilled.

His hand is slow and gentle, going no further than my hip. His breath is warm. I don't really want him here, petting my face and back while I pretend to sleep, but I'll let him, because it makes him happy.

"Shhh," he whispers against my neck. "It's all right. I've got you, you're safe, everything's fine. I love you. I love you so much."

I make myself keep still. I don't want to upset Dad, because I love him, and I want him to keep loving me. When you love someone, you accept the things they want and you don't, because it's a way you can make them happy. If I let him know I'm awake, he'll stop instantly, but I won't. He loves me and I love him, so I'll keep pretending to be asleep and wait for it to be over. My head is fucked but my heart sings with tenderness, and I don't know which part of me is betraying the other, which is true. This is something I'll accept, willingly and maybe even gladly, because the measure of your love is what you'll tolerate for the other person.

He sighs, deep, shuddering. When he lifts his head from my pillow, the mattress moves slightly. The weight on the floorboards shifts. He's leaving.

That's it; it's over. It was nothing really, it was fine, I'm fine, he got the reassurance he needed and I got through it. I feel a bit grimy, a bit unsettled, but I'm also happy, because when you love someone you want to please them. You'll even do things that frighten you, because you love them. And it was nothing. I got through it. It's finished now.

But what if he wants something else next time? What if this is a prelude? There are other things he might ask for, things lovers have a right to expect. What will I do then?

No, I think frantically. *None of this is happening. This is just a dream. Wake up now.*

I open my eyes to golden light filtering through the misted windscreen. I haven't slept long. Maybe half an hour, punctuating the shift from the nightmare of my mother's house to the sanity of Frey's. My body's trembling, my hands shivery. I haven't had a dream that vivid for years. The unconscious is such a weird thing. Why on earth did I dream *that,* about—

It doesn't matter. It's just my head, processing. Our dreams mean nothing. *I don't need to be upset,* I tell myself, even as my body tingles with disgust. It doesn't mean anything. It doesn't.

My mouth tastes repulsive. I have a bottle of water in the

driver's pocket. It's been in there for God knows how long but I swallow a few lukewarm mouthfuls, trying not to think about plastics leaching out from the walls, bacteria slowly multiplying from the last time I opened it. My stomach's a little uneasy, but it's all right, I've got a handle on it. I'm okay to drive. More okay than I was anyway.

It was just so vivid. So incredibly vivid. My dad, next to my bed, his hand on my hair. The warmth of him. The muzziness in my head, the feeling of being unable to move...

Our dreams mean nothing. I know this. But what if I'm wrong?

This is my mother, getting inside my skull. The awful things she said, creeping up on me, daring me to look. My mother told me that Dad... she said he...

She actually told me that. She actually used that word. My mother sat in her kitchen, a glass of brandy in her hand, she told me that's how I was conceived. That she only had me, I'm only on this planet at all, because Dad...

I ought to believe her. I'm a good person, a good feminist. When another woman shares something like this, the correct response is 'I believe you'. But this is my mother, talking about Dad. And he wouldn't do that. He wouldn't.

"Was he doing it to you too?" Her harsh voice, her eyes like liquid fire. She was talking nonsense, I don't need to think about it. If she'd stopped at telling me what she claimed he did to her, I might have believed her, maybe. But suggesting he'd done it to me too, as if these two potential acts belonged in the same category... no. No. I might have believed Dad wasn't brilliant at recognising sexual boundaries. That he wasn't as skilled in understanding consent as he should have been. But that's totally different from seeking out his own daughter.

Except...

That last afternoon with Noah on the rooftop. The questions he asked. 'I'm asking you because I can't trust myself.' Noah was mentally ill. His delusions had even less value than a dream. But what about memories? What if this is a memory?

No. This is my mother talking. I thought I'd left her in that kitchen but she's travelled with me. She's made herself small, nestled against my skin like a tick curled deep within fur, gorging on me, filling my bloodstream with poison. She's taken everything from me, everything. She doesn't want me to have a single scrap of love or kindness. She wants to spoil even the memory of Dad, she wants to drown me in the contents of her black, wicked heart. Dad didn't do that. Dad *wouldn't* do that. He didn't... do that... to my mother and I am not the child of that act and he certainly, absolutely, no question about it, he did *not* offer me sleeping pills so that he could creep into my bedroom and look at me and stroke my head and back while I slept, a prelude to God knows what. He didn't.

I really want a shower.

Dreams don't have any kind of moral value. People dream about taboo things all the time. It doesn't mean they want to do them. It doesn't mean they happened.

(Oh God, the way he felt. He smelled just like himself, that combination of deodorant and skin. That smell had always meant safety to me, before. His hand on my back, his breath on my neck. I can't leave the thought alone. So many times I've told patients off for peeking beneath bandages, slipping fingers beneath casts, tugging gently on stitches just to see what happens.)

It's getting late. Driving will steady me. Exercising muscle memory is a good way to fight back against intrusive thoughts, and that's all that's happening here. I'm besieged by intrusive thoughts. By my mother's face, looking at me across the kitchen table and saying...

By the thought of Dad, kneeling beside my bed and...

First gear. Indicator on. Check mirrors. Nobody coming. Pull out. Accelerate. Second gear. Here we go. I've spent almost two weeks with my wicked mother, but now I'm free. I'll go to that awful empty house, get through tonight, and then I can go home...

I can't cry. I'm driving. Slow down for the village. Sign for the main road.

It was just a dream. Our dreams mean nothing. I've only got to last one more night, and I'll be in the place where Dad and Noah are still alive.

Will I be able to fool Frey? He'll see the shape of the damage I've taken. He'll want to make it better. Maybe he'll come out into the garden again. Maybe the tender, innocent touching we've already done, in the border country at the edges of sleep, will make him ready for more. Maybe we might kiss.

Our dreams mean nothing. Maybe that's why it takes me so long to draw the lines between the dots of my mother, my father, myself, and Frey. I keep driving, keep concentrating on the road, steadfastly not seeing the connection, the warning.

The feeling of Dad's hand, stroking my hair and my back. Not the furtive brutality of my conception, but something gentle and tentative, something more like a beginning. What I dreamed was not what my mother described, not what she so ridiculously suggested Dad had done to me too, so why would I...

I can see what it means long before I'm ready to admit it. I drive on and on, queasy and tired and sweaty, not letting myself look at what squats in the seat beside me, gradually expanding until it fills the car, until there's nothing more I can do to avoid it and I have to stop on the hard shoulder so I can scrabble across the passenger seat, fling open the door and throw up.

Chapter Twenty-Six

Reconstruction (3)

And so, finally, I have all the pieces of the puzzle. With them, I'll make my final, truest picture of how it happened:

Noah's been unusually quiet. He's working things out, trying to decide what's real and what's real only to him. If I was there, I'd have noticed, but Dad isn't as good at seeing the signs. He's always optimistic, always happy to ignore what he doesn't want to see. He'll never quite give up on Noah becoming well.

So. Dad and Noah go about their day. Noah spends a lot of time in his room. I'd recognise this as the warning sign it is. Noah withdrawing from us, however subtly, is something we need to watch for. But Dad, the optimist, thinks only of an unexpected couple of hours off. I don't blame him for this, any more than I blame him for the way he'll fill those hours, which will be to sit on the sofa and watch undemanding television with his brain switched off. If you haven't lived a carer's life, it's hard to understand the allure of sitting still and doing nothing.

Dad rests and thinks of nothing, and Noah paces his room and thinks of everything. Sometimes he makes notes, half-finished sentences and lists of words that look meaningful from a distance but fall apart under inspection. To me the only thing these notes convey is *I'm starting to unravel*, but they have value to Noah. He's lived most of his life with the painful awareness that he can't be sure of anything. So he does the best he can with what he has, with his own self and his own observations.

Meanwhile, Dad, oblivious, slips into a little doze.

Noah joins him for lunch. We're supposed to restrict Noah's calories, but Dad can't bear either of us wanting something and not having it. Dad serves Noah more food than he's supposed to, eager for approval. Noah, who's clever even when he's spiralling, smiles conspiratorially and thanks him. To achieve his goal, he has to hold himself together.

(Were there signs, and Dad missed them? Or was Noah better at hiding things than we ever knew? How many battles did he fight in private? How often did he beat back demons we never even saw?)

After lunch, Dad asks Noah where he'd like to go. Noah does better when we take him somewhere each day, fill his eyes and his ears with reality. And Noah tells him.

He suggests a drive. A trip to the coast, he says; very on-brand for Noah. He mentions our mother's home town. He insists he just likes the coastline there, but there's an unspoken subtext of *if we did happen to see her you could always say it was my fault* that Dad will hear and appreciate. Dad, the optimist, has never given up on winning back his one true love.

He writes his note to me. I know now what was in Noah's head, what my mother told him, her madness intersecting perfectly with his own. What I don't know is if he wanted me to know what he was planning. I do know he wouldn't want me to worry, wouldn't want me to feel any guilt. It's possible he hadn't even fully committed by this point. I have all the pieces, but there are still so many things I'll never know. This must be how life was for Noah all the time, constantly second-guessing what he thought he knew.

Perhaps some of the neighbours watch their departure, mention it the way we all point out small events in the days of others. But it won't stick in their minds. My family's provided many memorable additions to their stores of *do-you-remember*, but not today.

At some point, Noah persuades Dad to let him take the wheel.

This might be something they do a lot, when I'm not around to police them. Noah adored those few short months when he was allowed to drive. His speed terrified me, but his reflexes were lightning-quick, switching the car around tight bends easily, effortlessly. After a while I relaxed and began laughing. We were stopped by the police, and Noah was given a speeding ticket and a stern talking-to. The officer told Noah, "You're risking your little sister's life, driving like that," and Noah looked honestly bewildered and replied, "I'd never do anything to hurt Callie." That was just before his third hospitalisation. After that he was told his licence was being taken away. He cried over that. My big brother, who always saw the silver lining, who so rarely cried over anything.

I'd like to believe the changeover was easy. I'd like to picture Dad handing over the keys without reluctance, without even much thought. I want to believe he didn't see the end until it was almost on him. Nonetheless, it's possible Noah had to persuade. To beg. Maybe even to—

No. Noah wouldn't have threatened Dad. It would have been in a public place, a crowded place. People would have been watching, and it would have taken just one magic word from Dad to bring down the angels of mercy. Noah needed Dad to be willing.

They pull back out onto the road.

Noah might have seemed different by now. There's a limit to how well he can hide his illness. But then, Dad might have put it down to Noah concentrating on the road. I want to picture Dad serene and unknowing, as peaceful as a dog on its last ride to the vet. Animals often sense when bad things are coming (I think of Floss, the way she always knows when we're going to put her flea treatment on). But humans are used to control. We've lost the knack of looking for danger. I let Dad's head fall against the glass of the passenger window as he watches the unspooling of the world.

I want to build in a diversion, give them a final walk on the beach. Maybe that's where the changeover happened, on the slow, fat road beside the sands. Noah was kind. He would have wanted Dad to have the best last day he could manage. Maybe they went over the cliff with salt in their hair and sand between their toes.

But I don't think this can be right. They would have been seen and noticed. People always remembered seeing Noah. The police would have been less puzzled by their presence if there'd been a walk on the beach. There was no last moment when they stood beside each other in the salt waves and watched their toes turn white.

They've left the main roads and entered the town; they're driving past parked cars and houses. They don't go near our mother's house. She would have seen them. From her house of windows, she sees everything.

And where am I? I'm in the kitchen with Josh and Frey. I'm thinking about the separation that's coming, feeling sad but also feeling happy, because I've recently come to understand that this place is my home. My wrist is branded with the bumblebee tattoo.

Noah presses hard against the accelerator. They begin their climb up the hill. Noah's face is determined. He's afraid, but he knows he's doing the right thing. He's not avenging a wrong, because he loves Dad and he understands, as I understand, that Dad has done his best. He's simply doing the kindest thing he can do, which is to keep me safe, irrevocably and for always. Maybe Noah is also ridding me of the burden of himself.

Or maybe he just wants to finally, finally, fly.

In her sterile kitchen, my mother sits at the dining table with her back to the street. For once, she's gazing out of the windows that look seaward. She isn't watching out for her ex-husband. She isn't watching for any kind of danger at all. She's simply sitting, and staring.

From the curve of the cliff, a burst of movement resolves into a burst of scarlet. Something emerges from the clutter of trees. Its fall is as inevitable as anything that's ever happened. But first, there's a moment when the world pauses. In that moment, it seems possible that the car might resist gravity, stretch out white wings, and take flight.

Chapter Twenty-Seven

Over

There was happiness in this house once. In the cool dawn light, I sit in my car and I remember golden afternoons when Noah and I played on the climbing frame or swung on the swing set, and our parents sat in the sunshine or worked in the flower beds. I remember the joyous mania of Christmas mornings, Noah dancing on the end of my bed in festive pyjamas and a Santa hat. (Noah and his hats! He always loved dressing up.) I remember quiet moments, special only because I was happy in them, tucked away behind the sofa or folded inside the curtains, finding an unfamiliar corner in an utterly familiar place. I look at the house that was once our home and think, *I'm right, I am. We were definitely happy some of the time.*

But then, I suppose even prisoners have occasional moments of joy.

There were other houses, for my mother and my dad. Noah lived the first few years of his life somewhere else. His first clear memory was the day they came to live here, his second was the day he came to meet me in hospital. I was the last to arrive, and the most poisonous.

It must have felt like a new start for my mother, coming here. Maybe there were times when she let him touch her willingly, wakefully. Maybe there were times when she reached out to him. No, that can't be right, or she wouldn't have been so sure that I was the product of… of…

Some words are too ugly to say out loud. That can't be where I came from. Dad and Noah couldn't have loved me as much as they did if that was where I came from. And I definitely couldn't have loved Dad as much as I did if he really was a… if he really did… if my mother was telling the truth and my conception was the result of—

I wince away from That Word.

I climb out of the car. My limbs are stiff from a night of driving, dozing in service-station car parks, buying coffee, driving some more. The front door looks unfamiliar, the way your own home can do when you've been away for a while. Imagine if there was another family living in there, an ordinary family whose ordinary happiness filled the room like smoke. What would they make of me?

I'm so close to what I want. In just a few hours I'll meet Josh in the lay-by, counting down the minutes so we can time our arrival just right. The routine's so embedded, my mental picture so vivid, that it feels like the journey's already happened, like there's a version of me doing exactly these things, right now. The day's forecast to be warm but not too warm, the evening will be delicious, so probably they're leaning on the wall and enjoying the sunshine, my doppelganger and Josh. They like each other a lot, these two. Even though they'll have almost every minute of the next two weeks together, they're still spending these few off-the-clock minutes together rather than apart. In a different world, they might become a couple.

In this world, I'm sick with longing for something I should never have thought about taking. I put my key in the lock, turn it, open the door. The scent of home, laced now with the stench of gently rotting rubbish, tumbles out. I wish I was in the lay-by, waiting for Josh. I wish I was anywhere but here.

There's someone coming up the path towards me. Mrs

Curtain-Twitcher, a thin veneer of concern concealing her very real glee.

"Callie," she says, and puts a hand on my arm.

I don't like her using my family diminutive. I don't like her touching me. I make myself keep still.

"Hello."

"Love, I'm so sorry. I heard about the accident. How absolutely dreadful."

How in God's name has this dreadful woman heard about Dad and Noah? It happened far from here, and surely wasn't interesting enough to be in the papers. But the neighbourhood grapevine has its roots in places none of us can see. Somehow, through channels of gossip and hidden connections, people always know what's going on.

"Thank you."

"Were you sitting outside the house in your car all night? I saw you there this morning—"

"No, just a few minutes." I fumble for an explanation. "You know. Working up the courage."

Her face makes a shape she probably imagines looks sympathetic. "Of course you were. Oh, you poor love. If there's anything I can do…"

"Thank you."

"Has anyone told your mother? I know you two aren't close but she'll want to know. If you need anyone to talk to her, I could—"

"I've just got back from her house," I manage through clenched teeth.

"Oh, that's good. That's good. It's important to cling to what you still – I mean, now there's only the – oh dear."

"Thank you," I say. What I mean is *fuck you*, and that's clearly what she hears, because she finally retreats. But she's completed her act of performative kindness. She's got her nugget of gossip for her friends. *That poor girl, all alone in her car, couldn't bring herself to go inside at first.* My rage carries me inside, through the musty hallway and into the kitchen. The mugs from the day the police came are still in the sink.

I put the bin outside the back door, not bothering to open it. Then I fill the washing-up bowl with water. The tap brims with heat – I didn't touch the thermostat when I walked out, didn't even think about the boiler heating water and radiators for people who would never come again. Just a few hours more, and I can go back home, see Josh's familiar smile as he spots me in the lay-by, pet Floss's silky ears as she pushes her nose into my hand. And Frey?

Oh, Frey.

There was happiness between us, there really was. I can't be imagining that. Frey loved me – Frey loves me – and the quality of that love was different, is different, from the affection he has for others. Those chocolates, chosen secretly in the supermarket. The elaborate cutwork on the paper, the dainty ribbon. They were chocolates you choose for a woman, his first gesture of interest. He listened to Josh's story of the young man he'd cared for, and drew the bumblebee that's inked into my skin. I was the one he turned to when he was ill, the one he clung to. He braved the garden, simply because he knew it would please me. And I didn't do anything wrong, I didn't do anything that would hurt him. That time I went into his bedroom, he was asleep. I didn't... would never...

But what if I would? When I go back to him, who knows what else I might do?

I scrub savagely at the mugs, trying to convince myself that if I get the house straight, my life will make sense too. But there's only so long you can spend cleaning things before you have to stop and face up to reality. I sit down at the dining table and make myself be still.

I went into Frey's room without permission. I touched his face, his neck, his back, his hip. When he woke up, I stopped. But I wanted more, I know I did. And if I'd insisted, Frey would have given in.

Frey never fights back, never argues. He only withdraws

and shuts down. And he wants to please me. He wants to please me, because he loves me. He hated the garden, but he came anyway, let the sun blaze and the insects buzz and the wind assault his skin. He'd do it again if I asked him, because he loves me.

Frey turned his face into the pillow. Acted as if he was asleep. Maybe that's what I'm drawn to. His utter stillness. His absolute compliance. His silence. Is that what Dad found so irresistible? Am I, like him, a—

(*No, I won't think that about myself, I can't*)

Maybe it's not my fault. I'm my parents' child, the product of my father and my mother. I can't help the genetic hand I was dealt, the nurture I was given or not given during those crucial early years. I wasn't beaten; apart from one memorable occasion, I wasn't starved. But still, but still, but still… I did end each day feeling sore and bruised by my mother's indifference. I did go to bed each night hungry for the love she never gave.

That dream I had. Dad – my dad! My own father! – beside my bed, touching me the way I touched Frey. It was only a dream, the raw materials for its construction instantly obvious. Just the memory of my mother's words, and my own well-buried guilt.

But what if it wasn't? We all know that what's done to us, we do to others. Doctors use this all the time to get children to co-operate. 'You put the stethoscope on my chest first, then I'll do it to you.' When they get home, they'll beg for a doctor's kit, practise on a younger sibling or the family dog, declare, 'When I grow up I'm going to work in a hospital.'

We're taught to watch out for the children who copy other, darker behaviours. The ones who kiss you on your lips or put their tongues in your mouth, cornering smaller children and taking their clothes off. The behaviours are grotesque, but the children aren't predators, they're only damaged. How badly damaged would I need to be, to be forgiven? I imagine saying the words out loud. *I think my dad may have—*

(No, I still can't say that word)
… and the memories have just started coming back.

If Noah was right. If my dream was more than a dream. If the answer to my mother's question was yes. This is a story with a monster in it, but the monster doesn't have to be me.

For a golden minute, I sit at the dining table and wonder if I might not need to despise myself.

Perhaps I'm a victim. A survivor. I could go to a therapist and lay my pain at their feet, have them raise me up and comfort me. *You're not responsible. You need help. You need caring for. You've been damaged.* I'd like to believe this is true. There's something very comforting about knowing you're not to blame.

But there's no evidence. They could strip me naked, examine me from head to foot; they wouldn't find anything. No marks, no scratches, no signs of penetration even, because in my dream there was no penetration. Nothing left on me or in me. If it ever happened, he was gentle and tender. I didn't fight back.

There's something on the seat of the chair where I'm sitting, something soft but with enough structure to press against my flesh. It's one of Noah's hats, a red knitted thing with flaps over the ears. He said he liked it because it made him look half-witted. The kind of joke only the very damaged get to make.

Noah asked our mother for help. Instead of telling him he was delusional, Dad would never do that to me, she told him her own story. And now Noah and Dad are both dead.

And then, my mother got to me, put the idea in my head. "Did he do it to you too?" Her entire story a plea for forgiveness. *Pity me,* she begged, as she talked and I had to listen. *I didn't kill Noah, it was your dad.* That was the point of her story; to make herself the victim. Nobody wants to be the villain. We'll say anything we can to shift the blame.

Dad's possessions are still on the sideboard – a neat pile of receipts, a bank statement, an access pass, a handful of coins.

He was kind. He loved me. He did his best to make up for all my mother's failures. He protected me from her darkness. He kept me safe. And there's a world of difference between wanting to have sex with your wife, and wanting to have sex with your daughter. He might have…

(*No, still can't say it*)

… my mother, but he definitely wouldn't… do anything… to me. I know this with sudden, unshakeable clarity, the way you can suddenly know God is real. My dad loved me and would never hurt me, never. My dad, who loved me throughout my childhood, who kept me from the darkness and always, always cherished me. My dad, who stepped into the gap left by my mother and did his best to make sure I never felt her absence. My dad, who was not and is not perfect. But who is still, and has always been, my hero.

Noah, I think. *I love you, but you were wrong. You have to have been wrong. Dad wouldn't have done that to me.*

Which means that I, myself, have no excuse.

And I, myself, am a—

I walk around the house, saying my farewells. In each room, I make one small improvement that makes it feel less abandoned. In the living room, I neaten the cushions on the sofa. In the dining room, I throw away the half-dead flowers. In the bathroom, I bleach the toilet. In each bedroom, I change the sheets.

The hours crawl by as they always do when you're clock-watching. It's too early to leave, but I go anyway. I can't stand it here a minute longer. I carry the dirty bed sheets to the car and cram them into the boot. Then I go back to the front door and lock it behind me, checking three times to be sure. I don't want the neighbours going in without my permission. Mrs Curtain-Twitcher is watching from behind her voiles, trying to guess what's going on. I wonder if there's any chance she'll guess right.

I get to the lay-by with over an hour to spare. Now I have to wait, and as I wait, I have to think. To separate what I know from what I don't; the impossible task that's haunted my family for all of our lives. How can we ever really know what's true, when all we have to go on is the contents of our heads?

I exist because of what my parents did together, that's one thing that's knowable and true. But whether it was as my mother said, or the way we all hope and assume we've been made, I'll never know. I'll never know if Noah was right, if my dad came to stand by my bed sometimes the way I came to Frey's. I'll never know if he stopped where I did, or if he took it further, sought comfort in the flesh of his own child as she slept.

Maybe Noah was haunted by thoughts like these, by all his doubts and contradictions, by the fear of getting it wrong. Maybe this was how he filled in the moments just before he pressed his foot against the accelerator and turned the wheel to the left, over the cliff. I hope he didn't think he was a failure, though. I hope he knew that, in the end, he was the best and bravest of all of us.

Noah was brave. Now it's my turn. I'm the monster in this story, there's no getting away from that, but if I can only find the courage, I can be the slayer too. Noah has my back, as he always has. His death has given me the excuse I need to walk away from Frey and our life together. I can walk away from what I'm on the cusp of doing. I can do the right thing.

But here's the terrible truth: I don't actually have to do that at all. I can walk right back into my life and keep on living it. I can wait for Josh to arrive, and instead of telling him what's happened to my family, he and I can go home together. I can keep Noah and Dad alive, keep my two weeks here the way they've always been. I can live inside the same routine that brings us all such peace. I can keep on loving Frey.

The one true thing, the only important thing, the one part I absolutely know: I do truly love Frey. I love Frey in the same way Dad loved my mother. I love him endlessly, utterly, in spite of his strangeness. I love him selfishly, cruelly, in defiance of what he needs. If I'm given the chance, I will love Frey to death. I come from a family of monsters, and I'm their true and natural child. If I go home, I won't stop. I'll go into Frey's bedroom again, do more and worse than what I've already done.

And he'll hate it. And he'll let me. Because Frey loves me, and the measure of love is what you'll endure. I have a choice to make, and the moment to make it is almost here.

A curious thing about time: sometimes it stretches out and out, letting you experience a million possibilities, until you think you might stay here for always as the endless stream of *now* becomes *forever*. But humans aren't made for infinity. Eventually you have to step into the next moment, begin the painful transition into the future.

I sit still and quiet behind the wheel of the car, waiting for the next moment to come.

Acknowledgements

Thank you, as always, to my amazing editors Lauren Parsons and Cari Rosen, to Tom Chalmers, and to the rest of the fabulous Legend team. Working with you is such a joy, and your faith in my work means the world to me.

Thank you to the Sisterly of Hull, Lynda Harrison, Michelle Dee and Louise Beech. Sometimes we sneak off to the woods at the crack of dawn to write, sometimes we escape to the seaside to perform poetry in bookshops, sometimes we drink champagne in secret gardens, and sometimes we can only meet via Zoom because we've all been locked in our houses. Whatever the circumstances, your presence in my life is always an inspiration. I'm so lucky to know you all.

Thank you to my wonderful family and friends for your support, your belief, your love and your strength, for coming with me on insane tours of landmarks that aren't even there any more, for saying things in passing that take root in my head and one day grow into a hundred thousand words of prose, for buying me Motivational Chocolate Raisins, for reading the manuscripts that are for no-one's eyes but yours, and for generally putting up with all sorts of nonsense on a daily basis. An extra big thank you to our dearest H, who this book is dedicated to.

Thank you to the First Story students of Headlands School, whose determination to keep writing during Lockdown, in spite of every obstacle, showed me what commitment really looks like. You genuinely transformed my own writing practice, and it was a privilege to work with you all.

Most of all, thank you to my wonderful husband Tony – you make everything possible. Even after months of Lockdown, you're still my favourite person in the whole world to spend time with.